DEAD
TITANS,
WAKEN!

DEAD TITANS, WAKEN!

DONALD WANDREI

Nampa, Idaho
2017

ISBN-10:1-878252-87-9
ISBN-13:978-1-878252-87-6

Book Design by Michaela Waltz

CONTENTS

A Note on the Texts

The texts of both novels presented in this edition are derived from surviving typescripts at the John Hay Library of Brown University. The typescript of Dead Titans, Waken! is evidently the one circulated by Wandrei to his colleagues and submitted to at least one publisher in 1932. It was heavily revised in pencil in the 1940s when Wandrei was rewriting it as The Web of Easter Island; I have removed all these revisions to recover the text of 1932. A few marks in pen appear to date from the time of the novel's first composition, and are usually corrections of minor typographical or other errors; these have been incorporated in the present text. The typescript is missing pages 97–100, but these pages have been supplied through the generosity of George Locke.

The John Hay Library also owns a revised typescript, now titled The Web of Easter Island, in which Wandrei has made still further revisions beyond the pencil revisions written on the typescript of Dead Titans, Waken!

Both the autograph manuscript and the typescript of Invisible Sun survive, and the latter has served as the basis of the text.

I have made a few small corrections of apparent typographical errors and some other minor emendations, but on the whole I have presented both texts as they appear in the existing typescripts. My afterword treats the genesis of the works and offers some critical evaluation; since this afterword must necessarily discuss the plots (including the denouements) of both novels, I have placed it at the end of the volume rather than at the beginning, so that readers can enjoy the texts without having their endings given away. I have also appended some notes to the novels, elucidating names, titles, and other features cited in the texts. Since the insertion of footnotes is not conducive to the reading of the novels, no footnote numbers appear in the text.

I am grateful to Steve Behrends, Philip J. Rahman, and David E. Schultz for their assistance in the preparation of this edition. Particular thanks are due to Dwayne H. Olson, who provided valuable biographical data on Wandrei that have helped to elucidate several features of Invisible Sun.

— S. T. J.

DEAD TITANS, WAKEN!

DONALD WANDREI

I. MYSTERY AT ISLING

The Vadia is an old, stone road that rambles past the village of Isling. It skirts Isling toward the west until it reaches the graveyard. There it comes to an abrupt end, and a dirt track branches around the graveyard to a point opposite, where the Vadia continues.

Legend has it that the Vadia was used by Legionaires in the days of Roman occupation, and that it had been built long even before the imperial army came. Archaeologists place no credit in the legend; according to them, the Picts and Gaels who roamed the wild hills and lowlands then were incapable of such an engineering feat. But many a legend holds truth that archaeology overlooks, and folklore has a way of basing itself on forgotten facts.

Isling is full of such legends, mostly centering around the Vadia. According to one tradition, its very name is a corruption of the Latin, Via Dei, and those who believe the tradition point to the graveyard which dates back no man knows how far. Others assert that the name derives from Via Diaboli, and support their conviction by how the road halts abruptly at the graveyard. Still others say it is just a name with no special significance.

Until that day when horror stalked out of the timeless crypts, the legends were old maids' tales told by a crackling fire. To be sure, Roman coins had occasionally been found, together with bits of pottery; and once, when a new grave was being dug, certain objects had been cast up which caused the vicar to place his stamp against the whole graveyard and order new ground to be used. That was in the reign of Elizabeth. A hundred years later when the Great Plague was raging at its height, the old burial ground was hastily pressed into service, but for some uncertain reason, no body was interred in it.

Ever since, the old ground had remained as a sort of melancholy reminder of the ancient past, and the few sixteenth century headstones, worn and fallen away, yet seemed strangely new compared with the two-thousand-year-old vaults said to lie deep under the surface, covered now with the refuse and matter of twenty centuries and more.

Rumor said that blasphemous rites had been carried on, that wild orgies took place during the Roman occupation, that Druid rituals were performed even earlier, that the devil had laid claim to the ground before that even. There was an entry in musty records, made by one John Clelonde, in the year of our Lord, 1665: "This day, nineteen more poor mortals buried, nor are the women and children spared. The wrath of God continues unabated. I did command them all not yet stricken to give their souls to the keeping of our Lord, and to pray that his vengeance be lifted. The shops all be closed. Scarce does any man dare venture abroad, lest he be smitten of this pestilence. We are hard pressed to bury the dead. The ground new broke is already filled, and we durst not use the Devil's graveyard for the accursed image found there this day week."

The image does not exist now, if it ever did. But the legends persisted, passing down from generation to generation as oral tradition has preserved folklore from the days when images fixed on tablets of the mind were the only records that the people possessed.

These legends were again to take on an appalling significance when, in the late afternoon of a muggy July day, eleven-year-old Willy Grant returned to his cottage and proudly showed a little object he had found.

"What is it?" asked his mother, whose sight was none too good.

"I dunno. Me an' Bill an' Jack found it, but I got it first, so it's mine."

"Where did you find it?"

The boy hesitated a minute. "Well, we all went into the old graveyard when Bill dared us an' I saw it stickin' in the ground so I pulled it out an' brought it along."

Superstitious Mrs. Grant had already heard more than she wanted to hear. "Give it to me," she commanded in that final tone of voice with which there is no arguing. Willy handed it over to her. She took it and immediately hurled it toward the roadway. "Tomorrow," she continued in the same tone, "you take it back where it came from and leave it there. Now get in the house, and if you ever go near that graveyard again, you'll get the strapping of your life."

Willy whined but his mother would not listen to a word, and repeated that if he ever went near the graveyard again or had anything more to do with the object, he would be whipped blue.

Near nightfall, John Grant came home from the day's toil, and Mrs. Grant scurried around preparing the evening meal. She said nothing to her husband about Willy's discovery. Perhaps she had forgotten about it already, nor did she notice that the boy had slipped away for a minute and returned to his room furtively carrying something with him.

After the repast, the rest of the evening was passed with the small talk that had concluded their every day for a dozen years and more. At nine-thirty sharp, Willy was sent to bed, and at ten Mr. and Mrs. Grant followed, in the unvarying routine of their existence. The night was still, but hot and damp. Mr. Grant, weary from hard work, neverthe-less quickly dropped off to sleep. Mrs. Grant was restless, and for a long time lay awake, but she too finally sank into a troubled slumber.

For the first time in many months, she dreamed a dream; and her dream was of an extraordinary and terrifying kind such as she had never before had. She thought that she was walking by a graveyard with hundreds of old, white tombstones rising eerie everywhere. She wanted to run away, but the mesmeric power of dreamland held her rigid. While she watched, a curious small gray thing with the face of her son scuttled across the burial ground and pulled a carven image out of the earth. As it did so, the white tombstones suddenly turned into carven images and soared skyward until an army of colossal, implacable monsters stood before her. And beneath their feet, the tombs opened up and discovered vast corridors leading down into the bowels of earth, and from their immeasurable depths rose the stench of ancient corruption. The thing with the face of Willy scampered away with its prize, she tried to cry out and warn it to drop its burden, but no sound came from her throat, and the little beast scurried away the moment it saw her. And now the titans moved in great strides, until they stood in a circle around the gray creature. Slowly, slowly, the giant limbs closed inward on the captive, the ring became smaller, impassive Gargoyle faces stared on the animal that whimpered wildly around trying to escape. She saw it being forced toward one of those bottomless corridors, nearer, nearer —

From the realms of rest, John Grant and Madge Grant awoke at the same instant, their ears ringing with a shriek of terror. John Grant leaped from his bed and raced to Willy's room while old Madge lighted a lamp with trembling hands and followed. She heard her husband call, "What is it, son?" but she heard no answer. She brought him the lamp, and together they looked in.

John Grant cried out, but his wife made no sound as she slumped to the floor. The lamp crashed, and a little tongue of flame ran out, and at that he chose the living from the dead and carried his wife to safety. The hideous form on the bed, green and rotten, pitted with corruption as if some foul enormous worm had gnawed out bits all over, was an obscene travesty of the Willy who had been theirs; and the black eyes that looked blindly at them were never those of their son. And John Grant in spite of his grief gave silent prayer as the cottage burned to the ground.

Old Madge was mad Madge when she became conscious. She mumbled of a "…green little big stone that ate Willy", and the neighbors shook their heads. She took to wandering along the Vadia, and prowling around the graveyard, with her hair matted and her eyes glary. If asked what she was looking for, she would answer that she was hunting the green stone that ate Willy. Had she not been insane, her reply might have raised embarrassing questions from the curious; but they considered her words to be the raving of a demented woman, and the lips of John Grant were sealed. He was content to let the villagers think that his son had died in an unfortunate but accidental fire.

The days slipped by, one torpid afternoon following another as July drew to a close. It was a fortnight after the tragedy when some of the villagers saw mad Madge running down the Vadia in the early twilight. She carried an object wrapped with her shawl, and gasped as if she had run far. No one was near her when she turned from the roadway and stumbled toward a vacant cottage which she and her husband were temporarily occupying. There was little curiosity about what she carried, for any peculiar action of hers was ascribed to her madness.

She entered her new home, to find her husband already within. He looked at her with surprise and pity on noticing her dishevelled appearance and the bundle she hugged tightly.

"What is it, Madge? What is it you have there?" he asked kindly.

She sucked the air and raved incoherently that she had found Willy. A weird light of madness and joy glittered in her eyes, she clutched the shawl closelier to her breast, she crooned meaningless phrases over it. John tried to see what it was that she carried, but she backed away snarling and hugged the object still more tightly. The shawl became loosened momentarily when she sat down in a chair, but all he could see of what she held was that it seemed gray, or possibly greenish. She rocked back and forth, back and forth incessantly, talking and muttering to herself. John heard a phrase that was getting on his nerves, "The little green stone that ate

Willy," repeated over and over, together with mumbled pleas that something would "Please give me back Willy, he didn't mean anything by it."

Throughout the evening, heat lightning flickered in the sky, the air hung sultry and heavy. Clouds were piling up overhead, and it seemed as if a dry spell of weeks was at last to be broken. Just after nightfall, the first big drops fell. There was a minute's hush, then the wind arose, gusts of rain whipped against the windows.

At bedtime, mad Madge let herself be led away, but she carried with her the object still wrapped in its shawl. John made another half-hearted attempt to find out what it was or take it away, but decided it would be better to humor her, when she drew her lips back like a wild beast at any advance he made.

She held the bundle even in bed, like a child with its doll. John heard her talking for a long time, but her voice finally died away. He lay awake a while after, thinking back on the mysterious death of his son, and what to do with Madge. He wondered if it might not be that both of them were mad, and that the whole adventure was merely a dream of delirium. What power could have caused so malignant and monstrous a change in their son? Perhaps it was some horrible disease that he had not known of. Well, he would never know, now; and it might have been for the best that death came quickly. The way of the Lord was inscrutable.

Outside, the wind prowled around the house and whooped through the trees. Squalls of rain from time to time swirled against the window-panes. In spite of these elemental sounds, John was dozing off when he heard his wife begin to mumble again. He looked at her during a brief lightning flare, but her eyes were closed, though her lips moved.

"N'ga n'ga rhthl'g clretl — "

What fantastic gibberish was this that came from the lips of his wife? It was meaningless, he could not recognize a single familiar word in that harsh jargon of consonants and breathings, but the low voice went on in a kind of rhythmic chant, " — ust s g'lgggar septhulchu nyrcg — "

John Gaunt dropped asleep while trying to catch the unintelligible syllables; as consciousness left him, he had a queer delusion that across the moors a great rustling voice was booming "N'ga n'ga rhthl'g clretl ust s g'lgggar septhulchu nyrcg — "

Some time around midnight, giant bolts of lightning split the sky wide open. Disturbed by the noise, a Mrs. Sayres whose house was the nearest one to the temporary quarters of the Grants awakened just in time to see a dazzling flare envelop their cottage, with a crash as of bursting worlds. She thought she saw a vast green smudge sprawl off the roof and waddle away. Stunned for a moment, she believed that a bolt had struck that house by the Vadia. But when she finally ran to her window, the sky's reflected glare showed the house still standing, at least till a furious downpour completely obscured the view. Thinking that no harm had been done, and deterred by the wild night if any had been, she returned to bed.

Mad Madge was not seen the following day. John Grant did not appear at work. In any small town or village the world over, the neighbor's affairs are a vital part of your own existence; and when no sign of life became evident in the Grants' home, the idle curiosity of the villagers rapidly became more immediate concern. Superstition and speculation ran riot.

Several gossips remembered having seen mad Madge run down the Vadia clutching tightly some object.

"And you know," said garrulous Mrs. Dakin, "Jack said he and Willy Grant and another boy went into the graveyard, let me see now, it must've been a fortnight ago, or maybe three weeks; well, and they found something, that is Willy did and took it home with him, and Jack says it wasn't like anything he ever saw, a funny little stone man only it wasn't a man at all, and I always *did* say no good ever came out of the old graveyard, and now here it's proved before our eyes, the Lord's got his curse against it. Why you know that very night their cottage burned to the ground and poor Willy with it and John had a great to-do to get Madge out in time and now there's no telling what's happened to the both of them, poor souls."

"Maybe they're dead," added Mrs. Sayres helpfully. "When I saw that big bolt strike, I says to myself, says I, 'It's a good thing it wasn't *you* that it hit,' meaning me of course. Like as not both got killed or hurt, and they're up there now waiting for somebody to come after them.

"Of course," she tacked on apologetically, "I couldn't go out in that terrible storm, there's no telling what might have happened to me, it was that bad."

"It's just possible," put in one of the more intelligent townsmen, "that mad Madge got to poking around until she dug up another one of those funny things that Willy found."

"Well, *I* don't like the looks of it," went on Mrs. Dakin, "and if *I* had my way I'd've been out of Isling all these years just to get away from that Devil's graveyard. Why the storm woke me up last night and made such a racket you never heard and I thought somebody was shouting outside but I couldn't understand a word of it; I never did like these foreigners, anyway, English is good enough for me and it's good enough for anybody, *I* think." And on she went.

By mid-afternoon, interest and curiosity had been worked to their peak. It was decided that an investigation ought to be made. "Especially," as one of the gossips wisely remarked, "since it won't be long till night comes." After some hesitation, three men were selected to find out if anything was wrong.

They walked up to the house and pounded on the door, but only the echo of their knocking answered them. They shouted to John and Madge, inquiring if there was anything the matter, but no voice came back to them in response. In the pause that followed, they held a short consultation and agreed that it was now their duty to enter.

They opened the door, only to be met by so vile and nauseating stench that they were forced to retreat until the foul air had partly cleared away. When they finally reëntered, the sickening stink compelled them to breathe through their handkerchiefs and sleeves.

A hurried search of the ground floor discovered nothing. They halted again at the door for breaths of fresh air, then climbed to the first-story bedroom. Its door was also shut, and apparently unlocked. They tried it, but it did not give. A weight had been placed against it from the inside. With growing suspicions of what they might find, the townsmen put their shoulders against it and heaved it open far enough to enter. They could hear the weight dragging as they shoved it backward.

Inside they found a body half-fallen from its bed, and another that seemed to have been clawing at the door that led to escape. Mad Madge and John Grant were dead, if indeed those forms had been theirs. In that mass of greenish corruption, gouged and pitted, there was left no resemblance of either. Before their horrified eyes, the bodies went through a transformation worse than any optical trick, melting and changing from flesh to slime, from man to beast to stone, a shocking and hideous illusion that sent the three searchers running downstairs with a fetid smell as of a thousand graves poisoning their lungs and seeping into their souls.

An inquest was held under an atmosphere electric with mystery and fear; the verdict returned, "Death by lightning." Unanswerable questions were evaded. How could lightning have brought about so unheard-of a change? Why were not the bodies charred or burned? What was it that mad Madge had held as she ran down the Vadia? Whose voice had rumbled guttural syllables while the storm raged? And if death had not been caused by lightning, what malevolent agency was responsible? No human power could have brought about so sudden and profound a difference in the very organic structure of the two corpses. Against his will to believe, the village doctor denied that Madge and John might have fallen victims of disease, for nothing in his practice, nothing in his experience, and nothing he had ever encountered in medical books bore the slightest relation to the baffling condition of the bodies. The absence of any known motive or any possible motive only made the riddle more inexplicable. There were absolutely no marks of violence. Murder and suicide were disposed of for lack of supporting evidence. Madge's shawl was empty; whatever she wrapped it around had vanished. Death by lightning was the sole explanation left, and it was no explanation at all;

but on this makeshift theory, Isling was content to rest. No one was henceforth to be seen on the streets after nightfall. Over every household hung the terror that walks in darkness. Who? what? why? and how? were questions to which the answers were missing.

Through the medium of great dailies, Isling acquired unsavory publicity overnight, for the story was one such as newspapers love; and in their columns appeared accounts of the double death, of the strange tales told at the inquest, and of the legends with which the village was filled. Thus, deviously, the incidents came to the attention of Carter E. Graham, professor of archaeology and anthropology at the Ludbury College of Historical Sciences.

II. THE DEVIL'S GRAVEYARD

G reat God!" Graham murmured to himself. "The time must be near!" His coffee cooled on the table, and his toast was already cold, but he had forgotten them. After his cryptic utterance, he went back to reread the half-column story of the mystery at Isling in his morning paper. For some reason, the narrative possessed extraordinary interest for him and held him absorbed.

Graham was in his early forties. A fairly tall man, his height was emphasized by his slender build. Most noticeable of his physical characteristics were his thick, black hair, dark, clean-shaven face, and deep eyes. He moved with an ease that indicated reserves of strength. His quiet, confident method of taking any action suggested the careful thought with which he had previously prepared his way.

Now, having read the newspaper account through a second time, he sat for several minutes with a far-away look in his eyes, as if he were reflecting on memories newly aroused. The images that fleeted through his mind in those few minutes hardly seemed relevant to what he had just read: he was thinking of the explorations he had made in Egypt, in Tibet, at Stonehenge, among the Mayan remains, and on Easter Island. Perhaps he would one day publish the results of his work, but he had never believed it likely. For some time he had neglected his early achievements, in order to study the Roman remains in England; but all in an instant, a newspaper story had started him off again on the burning fever of his life: a cosmic riddle connected with certain ancient remains found in different parts of the world.

Passing reference to a small image, said to have been found by several boys and to have disappeared since, was the sole point in the Isling affair to which his thoughts kept returning again and again; for if that image was what he believed it to be, providing the newspaper report was correct, he might yet be able to take a long step further on his quest of twenty years.

"Can it be possible?" he asked himself. "At Isling — less than a hundred miles away. And I have travelled to the ends of earth! Still, the reporter may have been wrong — you never can separate truth from imagination in news stories. Well, there's only one way to find out."

Snapping from his lethargy, he crossed quickly to the telephone, raised the receiver, and called the train station. His connection was made in a few seconds.

"Hello! At what time does the next train leave for Isling, Wiltshire?" There was a moment's pause. "At 11:25? And it arrives — at 1:40? Thank you."

He looked at his watch as he hung the receiver up. It was now a quarter before ten. His decision was made instantly, and he swiftly set to work packing a bag with what necessities would be required for a short trip. If longer time were needed, he could easily return for other necessities.

Before departing, he examined a map of England. His memory had not failed him — Isling was roughly eight or ten miles west of Stonehenge. He made a mental note to revisit Stonehenge after he had completed his present trip.

The journey was tedious to his eager mind; he passed the hours reflecting on those of his past excavations which might be connected with the incident at Isling. Promptly at one-forty, the train reached Westmor, the stopping place for Isling which lay approximately twelve miles due north. After inquiring when return trains could be caught, he scouted around until he had obtained a hack for his last lap. His plans were made before he arrived at Isling. They largely concerned going about his business quietly and avoiding curiosity-seekers on this preliminary survey, unless he found it desirable to make excavations.

It was more than half after two when he alighted at his destination, a hamlet of only two or three hundred inhabitants. He could tell instantly that his arrival would be old news within the hour: Isling looked like that kind of a town. But it made no especial difference to him, except that his beloved privacy would not exist.

An extra one-pound note persuaded the hack-driver to wait until eight o'clock for his return. He expected to be back well before then, and if desirable could still dismiss the hack and obtain lodging for a night or so in Isling.

There was no need to ask for directions in so small a place. Taking the bag he had brought with him, Graham walked first to the Vadia, which his account had told him skirted Isling on its west side, and proceeded northward along its course.

The Devil's Graveyard he found to be about three-quarters of a mile from the point where he had first stepped on the old stone road. He noted with interest how the Vadia came to a dead end a few yards from the cemetery gate. Either the burial ground was actually of greater antiquity than the road, or part of the road had been torn up to make room for it. The alternatives were equally implausible.

"Here is another point which may be worth future investigation," he mused, but for the present he must let it pass. There remained to him less than four hours in which to make his survey, for his watch indicated that it was already past three when he entered the cemetery.

Setting his bag down, he opened it and removed a small collapsible spade, a similar pick, and a geologist's hammer, but left them by the bag ready for quick use while he examined his field. The site was unevenly circular and about two hundred yards in diameter, he estimated. It covered the top of a low hill which sloped away gently in all directions. Years had obviously passed since the graveyard had been taken care of; weeds and brambles overran it, discolored headstones were sinking sidewise or had fallen entirely, and several faint indentations marked where wooden caskets had finally been reclaimed by earth. Graham walked completely around the burial ground, getting its lay and idly reading inscriptions as he walked along; many of them were illegible, but among those which he was able to decipher none were later than Elizabeth's time.

Satisfied with his tour of inspection which ended where he had begun, he lifted up his spade and shovel with a directness of purpose as if he had found what he wanted and made his way toward the slightly higher central ground. He again looked carefully around him after he had arrived at his goal. A disappointed frown came into his face.

"This is odd," he murmured; "something must be wrong. Unless I've been on a wild-goose chase all my life, I ought to have found an altar or possibly a monument here. But there's nothing, absolutely nothing." He stood perplexed, for he could find no indications that a monument of any kind had ever occupied the spot. But as he continued to walk forward, his keen eyes caught signs indicating that the weeds and even earth had been recently disturbed. With hope beating high once more, he promptly turned aside and knelt down before his discovery. Trampled weeds in an area scarcely a foot or two in breadth, and freshly loosened earth in their center, were all he saw, but they were sufficient. He scraped away the weeds, and with his spade began patiently removing dirt, a little at a time. He had been digging only a few minutes when he struck something that gave out a dull, semi-metallic sound. He dropped the spade in a fever of excitement and used his hands for scooping dirt out. A greenish-gray stone surface came into view, his hands moved faster, the sweat ran down his face and dripped from his brow. Another minute's furious work was enough. Nitroglycerine was never handled more gently than the object which he lifted out.

For a fleeting second while Graham examined it with a mixture of surprise, long unsatisfied pleasure, and loathing alternately or together assuming expression on his face, a shadow seemed to obscure the sun, day darkened around him and time opened its ancient womb. Graham held in his hands an image about eighteen inches high, carven from some substance unknown to him, but apparently neither of metal nor of stone. Its entire surface was pitted in a singularly repellent fashion. Greasy green in color, it had the disgusting hue of corruption and decay. But its most abnormal aspect was the hideous illusion it gave: in his very hands the image underwent a change from being a creature to stone and then to some ultimate, yet more ancient evil at which his heart turned sick. His hands grasped the obscene thing firmly: his eyes saw its outline waver back and forth incessantly in a series of strange mutations; and each beginning or end when it shifted backward through cosmic and forgotten eons of time to a horror old before ever the races of man peopled earth, old even when a molten world flamed out of terrific nebulary fires, he thought that it mushroomed out above him and absorbed him as it soared skyward like a titan of the stars.

Carter Graham had seen many curious or terrifying scenes during the course of his travels; but his steel nerves had never known panicky fear until that minute when he held in his hands a loathsome image out of oblivion, an image that suggested in no single way and yet in all ways age beyond comprehension. His head was aswirl with racing thoughts, he almost hurled the thing back to bury it again in clean earth, his mind changed anew as its spell-binding fascination gripped him and he felt an impulse to seize it and run.

With a slow and profound effort that brought beads of sweat to his face and forehead, he succeeded in throwing off the depression that festered on his soul like a sexless succubus. His hands trembled but he deliberately placed the image beside him and turned his attention once more to the hole he had been digging. Experienced archaeologist that he was, instinct told him to go a little deeper, that great finds were seldom made on the surface. He lifted his spade and resumed work.

Fifteen minutes, a half-hour, an hour passed all too swiftly. Progress was slow with his under-size spade; he now employed the pick also, to break through for easier shovelling.

Six o'clock came, and six-thirty; not more than a half-hour remained if he intended to find his hack at Isling and catch a return train. He had given up hope of making further discoveries and had nearly decided to end his efforts when a blow of his pick was answered by the same dull, semi-metallic sound which had greeted him once before.

Whatever Graham anticipated, he had had not expected to encounter a second image; surprise showed plainly on his face. As rapidly as possible but working with care, he shovelled the soil out. He could not have excavated much longer in any case, he reflected grimly. He would just be able to draw himself out of the hole he had dug, perhaps eight or nine feet deep; the sun was fast westering and he labored in a half-gloom.

Beneath his feet there gradually appeared a flat surface of the slimy green substance which composed the image; he had not uncovered a second statuette after all. A hasty glance at his watch indicated a quarter before seven. He removed several more loads of dirt, then dropped on his knees to examine the yard-square patch which lay exposed.

Graham was frankly puzzled: he seemed merely to have added another archaeological mystery to those that the world already knew. Characters unlike any picture, sign, or alphabet writing with which he was familiar were cut deeply into the slab on two opposite sides; these inscriptions, if indeed they possessed significance, were divided by a group of symbols whose chief design was a circle inclosing an oblong.

The more he scrutinized his find, the less it meant to him. He felt as philologists must have felt in the presence of hieroglyphs before the Rosetta stone was discovered. He regretted that he had no time to make a transcription, but his rewards for the afternoon's labor had been rich, and there were future days for additional investigation. He took a last glance, and ran his fingers lightly over the symbols: blind fear of death swept upon him, he clawed wildly at the inscriptions, nausea sickened his inner being.

In the flash of an instant while his fingers fumbled about, earth grated, an incredible metamorphosis transformed the slab; it tilted without moving; its plane became an angle, an arc, an oval, it collapsed and dissolved in a manner that defied all rules of geometry. Graham got one appalling glimpse of blackness below him, of a gigantic corridor that plunged into the bowels of earth through stupendous depths, he heard a hiss of rushing air, and to his nostrils came a wave of unutterably vile rottenness. In that same instant as he clutched frantically the retransformation occurred, he saw the geometrical enigma reverse itself, where he had expected a drop into a pit of hell he found himself reesting on solid stuff...

Had it all been a dream? There was nothing to show that any chance had taken place.

White and dazed, trembling like an aspen shaken by wind, Graham pulled himself out of the hole and rested for a minute to recover his nerves. He stood upright with an effort and began replacing as much soil as he could. Fading sunlight and fresh air, hard work and the touch of steel in his hands helped restore him to normal. He ceased his toil at seven-fifteen, leaving it uncompleted, for he could delay no longer. Then wearily, with his implements under one arm and the icon under the other, he strode downhill. When he arrived at his bag, he halted momentarily to replace his tools and to wrap a piece of cloth around the statuette. With a little difficulty, he squeezed it also in, after he had taken out some unessential odds and ends. He next strode off again toward Isling, bag in hand, while he employed his free arm in a none too successful attempt to brush the dirt from his clothing.

It was hard for him to think clearly. He had taken no food since breakfast, his physical labor had been considerable, and he was tightly keyed up from the afternoon's excitement. One thing was certain: he would require trained assistance to continue his explorations in the Devil's Graveyard, but such assistance would be impossible to obtain at Isling. He decided in favor of an immediate return to London and gave silent thanks that he had paid the hack-driver to wait. There was small likelihood that the scene of his activities would be examined by other eyes; local superstition was probably sufficient to keep trespassers away, and he expected to be back on the morrow.

There was no flaw in his timing. He reached Isling shortly before eight o'clock, slung his bag in the hack, and took a seat. From the speed with which they raced south toward Westmor, he guessed that the driver during his absence had not missed a single superstition or bloodthirsty tale. Graham smiled grimly. This was not the first time that he had seen how well the power of legend acted as a safeguard for secrets.

Darkness had almost fallen and the stars were brightening when they drew up at the Westmor station. Graham paid and dismissed the hackman with a fairish tip. After a moment's reflection, he decided to allow himself the luxury of a compartment in order that he might while away an hour or two studying his prize safe from curious onlookers. His train was not due until nine-twenty, and with his ticket purchased he made the best use of intervening time by cleansing himself and temporarily staying his hunger with a hasty snatch.

Refreshened and feeling better, he boarded the train and relaxed with a sigh of relief. He had been under a greater strain than he realized.

The wheels moved and began to click faster and faster while the train gathered momentum until they made a steady, rhythmic beat, unexpectedly soothing; as the train pulled out, Graham stared absently through the window, his thoughts far away on the mystery that obsessed his life. He remembered the disastrous love affair that had originally driven him to the remote corners of the world; and how his successive explorations among remains of antiquity had furnished him a new passion to claim his devotion. Atlantis, Lemuria, the Sphinx, Stonehenge, Easter Island — they were magic names that brought a quicker beat to his heart. Colossal monuments, giant statues! What was their origin? Did they have any connection with the ogres of popular fairy-tale? And why had their builders vanished into oblivion, so that no trace of them existed? Riddles — inexplicable riddles, all of them! They had baffled him from the day that he first adopted archaeology as his hobby and his profession; and they had continued to baffle him in spite of his subsequent researches into folk-lore, anthropol-

ogy, and geology. Sometimes he had deemed himself near a
solution, as he believed he now was. But granting his possible
discovery of an answer, would he have advanced much further
than before? Each step backward into the past necessitated
another step, until one became lost in a labyrinth of origins and
prime causes, or ran aground on the greatest secret of all, the
beginning of life itself.

"Snap out of it!" he suddenly commanded himself, breaking
a futile chain of thought; and added moodily, "Or you are likely
to end your days in a place where someone else will do all your
thinking for you. Well, my ugly little beauty, it's high time that
we have another look at you."

Rousing himself from the torpor into which he had sunk,
Graham unlocked his bag and took out the image. As he
unwrapped it, he vividly recollected the afternoon's events:
saw himself digging around his first find, felt again that later
frightful sensation of hanging above empty space. And undiminished his former loathing returned when he held the icon
in his bare hands and watched its outline waver incessantly
through change after eerie change. There was no accounting
for them. Did it possess a hypnotic power which resulted in
optical illusions? Or was he a victim of hallucinations from
strain and overwork? He doubted whether this last guess had
any truth, for his nerves had always been strong; as to the former, there might be something in it. The image compelled
attention, and he knew that auto-hypnotism could frequently
be induced by intently focussing one's eyes on a certain object.
But this was merely a possible, not a positive, explanation. He
remembered the paradoxical postulates of Einsteinian mathematics, nor could he forget the visible testimony of his own
gaze when he had witnessed geometry go askew and a solid
body become a plane or — he hesitated over the thought — vanish momentarily from time and space. Graham sighed. There
was a possible key but he did not understand its use: if the slab
was not subject to the accepted rules, why could not the statuette also be an exception, since both were composed of the
same material?

Graham muttered in perplexity.

"H'mm, it doesn't look like metal, and it doesn't act like stone. What on earth can it be made of? It might be mica or soapstone or quartz or quicksilver to judge by its feel. And yet it's none of them. Specific gravity — much less than water, but it's hard as steel. Why, my pick hasn't even nicked it!"

He finally gave up his attempt at identification. The substance was totally unknown to him.

"Now that we've disposed of its nature and properties," he murmured drily, "we can decide what it is." And as he continued his speculative examination, it dawned on him with growing irritation that he really did not know *what* it was! Sometimes it appeared to be a pudgy, toad-like monster, then it resembled a gargoyle, or suggested abysmal evil; and in its final phase, it passed beyond anything he knew but somehow seemed a titan towering to the stars. Queer, this impression of giantism, and queerer still, the precise way in which the little beast gave a semblance of bloating out to enormous size. If only it would stop that infernal shimmering so that he could see it at rest for even one second! But incessantly its outline swam until Graham, becoming giddy from his effort to keep pace with each transformation, tore his eyes away. He was possessed by a sudden blind instinct to choke it until it squealed, to trample it beneath his feet or hurl it anywhere again and again until it had smashed into a million bits. He resisted the impulse by looking through a window at objects outside until his sight was rested, then returned to his scrutiny with unshaken purpose.

"Devil-God, I shall conquer you yet!" he calmly remarked, though he had once more become tense inside and was not at all certain that he could master its secret.

Graham's next point of attack was the image's base, but nothing rewarded his pains. The misty veil was as impenetrable as before. Despairing of success, he was tempted to call it a day and put the thing back; he might have done so if thoroughness had not been one of his major virtues. There remained a lone, minute section of its surface which he had not viewed, and with hope at low tide, he turned the idol over.

A cry broke from his lips — only here was the outline steady; and there on the bottom, in clear, tiny incisions, were the same inscriptions and symbols which he had seen on a slab at Isling that very afternoon!

He would have given his earthly fortune for the ability to read them and understand their significance; as it was, their baffling aspect only added another meaningless enigma to the mystery into which he was steadily being drawn deeper. Graham did not claim to be an expert student of languages, but he was broadly familiar with the history of speech and writing; furthermore, his own experience had acquainted him with the appearance at any rate of many ancient alphabets. And no clue was forthcoming to his aid. More than this he could not say: that a combination of sign and character writing covered the figurine's base. The characters, with their whorls and curves and serpentine twists, meant absolutely nothing to him. Were they the language of Atlantis? Or did they antedate all the tongues of earth? Whose hand or what race carved them?

Though these questions were unanswerable, he was rather less mystified by the picture-symbols — or was he? A closed circle played a prominent part in them all, a circle that surrounded an oblong or a pyramid or concentric rings of smaller circles. Each of the outer two spheres was filled with infinitesimal dogs. Graham after long close study was convinced that one circle contained a map of the stars according to their present position; apparently the other sphere was also an astronomical chart, but if it was, it presented the heavens in such an unfamiliar light that he could not make a single identification.

Bewildered at every turn, he concluded that he had had enough for one day and would let the matter slide until tomorrow when a good night's rest ought to refreshen him for a new start. With another sigh, he wrapped and repackaged the image.

"Devil-God, you have beaten me — tonight; but we shall see what the future offers," he said as he put it away.

His watch indicated twenty minutes before eleven. London was still an hour way. Graham settled himself comfortably in his seat and brooded on the events of a crowded day.

Click-click, click-click, click-click.

He shifted himself into an easier position and with a deter-mined effort turned his thoughts aside from the whole affair. He was confusing himself without advancing a step.

Click-click, click-click, click-click.

The rhythmic clack of wheels and the swaying motion of the train were quieting to his nerves. His tired brain and fatigued body demanded rest. He welcomed the approaching pleasure of a soft bed.

Click-click, click-click, click-click.

His eyes closed, his head nodded, and he drifted toward the borderlands of sleep...

With an abrupt start, he sat bolt upright wide awake. He glanced at his watch and found that it was a minute or two past eleven. His nap had evidently been short — fifteen minutes per-haps. Something had awakened him. What was it? He looked around him, but saw nothing unusual. His instinctive feeling that all was *not* well persisted.

"A bad sign," he thought, shrugging his shoulders in annoy-ance. "I've gotten to the point where my imagination is running loose."

And even as his lips moved, he knew that his intuition was right. Above the noise of the speeding train, from infinitely far away, came a weird sound. Graham strained his ears to catch it: was it distant thunder or the harsh rumble of some animal? He strove to concentrate his attention. Faint and scarcely audi-ble at first, the sound was growing louder. Could it be a voice crying across the moors in darkness, rasping inhuman and for-eign syllables? Steadily the utterance became clearer and more distinct.

"N'ga n'ga rhthl'g clretl ust s g'lgggar septhulchu nyrcg s thar-goth k'tuhl s brogg meargoth s bh'rw'lutl ubwcthughu dägoth — "

Not a word or syllable of that husky jargon held any mean-ing for Graham — surely he must be dreaming! In mockery of his hope, the gurgle became louder, it grated his already grayed nerves, it excited and exalted and depressed him in a way he could not define. The windows rattled, the air vibrated with great beating waves of sound, his ears were deafened by hideous phrases that spewed and ruttled from some foul colossal throat. He closed the door and window to his compartment and the roar swelled heavier. He covered his ears and the booming syllables crashed through deeper still. Was he going mad? From everywhere poured oceans of unbearable sound that nothing could stem, the clamor and babel of giants crushed him, he was overwhelmed in the furious bursting of thunders.

"Stop it! Stop it!" he shrieked. "Great God, stop it!"

Outside his window flapped a hellish thing pitted with holes of corruption and decay, a titanic hulk towered in rottenness to the stars, horror from the utmost abysms of time and space leaped upon him, the loathly stench of putridity surged through his nostrils. In mad terror he seized the handbag and hurled it, smashing the window, toward that slobbering unspeakable monster outside. Even as he did so, he caught the cry of panic-stricken voices from the cars ahead. A woman's shrill scream pierced the night air. A grinding screech of brakes tore his eardrums, the floor buckled and collapsed beneath his feet and jumped toward the ceiling. He grabbed wildly at anything for support but his hands clutched emptiness. A dull, terrific explosion drowned the lesser crashes, Graham's car telescoped, tilted, spun crazily sidewise, and toppled over. There was a blinding blackness as something cracked his skull. He slumped down with a low sigh rattling in his throat, blood welled up, the entire fearful scene was blotted out.

III. THE DREAM-TERROR

All day long, under the dusky glare of a green sun that flamed across the sombre sky, he had been traversing a burnt and blackened waste in his search. All day he had been crossing a dead and utterly lifeless land, and when the green sun set he had not yet emerged from it. But even as the sun set, with its dying emerald glow it had lit darkly for a moment a forest of some sort far ahead. Toward it he went.

Night deepened around him as the sun sank from a strange twilight to a darkness and from the darkness to an ebony blackness that crouched upon the land, but he did not pause. Onward he travelled toward the forest, guided by faint and unfamiliar constellations of stars that burned coldly and whitely in the sky above.

For a long time he kept on through thick darkness, ever pressing toward that forest ahead, and it was only when he had gone more than half-way that the darkness lightened dimly when a huge blood-red moon swept up from the eastern sky and cast a livid, leprous glow on the land. In tremendous bounds it fled across the sky, surrounded by a many-colored rout of streaming satellites. The air hung heavy and listless, and in the unearthly light of the red sun seemed to be oozing with a myriad globules of blood. The land, burnt before, took on a desolation and an aspect of solitude as if a red rot were creeping through its rocks and sand.

He continued onward, and had almost reached the forest when the rushing red sun sank with all its satellites. But from every side, from each of the distant horizons, a horde of twisting comets rocketed up, and the suffering vault became alive with jagged streaks of light hurtling erratic and aimless from horizon to horizon.

Dank and dark loomed the forest; right and left it stretched in never-ending line until it faded and vanished in distant glooms. The wanderer plunged forward. In a moment he was threading his way through gigantic trees that towered up and up. The darkness deepened steadily as the branches of trees interlocked more and more closely, until the entire sky was hidden from his sight and the sullen branches formed a solid roof high overhead. He picked his way in and out through gaunt white trunks, strangely like tombstones and bearing fantastic inscriptions, that rose around him, and all the while that he moved forward they became thicker and thicker. Creepers began to make their appearance. From every side of the black forest he heard things chuckling in the darkness; ever and again faint whisperings reached him, and sometimes he saw shadows peering from behind the tree-boles. The still air was pregnant with a thousand sounds of sibilant whispers moaning through the forest.

But he pressed onward, always before his eyes a vision of the lithe and slender loveliness of his lost Myrna. The creepers thickened and thickened until he had to claw his way past them, until, finally, he drew forth the great green-bladed sword with curiously carven hilt that hung at his side and hacked his way through. And every creeper that he slashed shrieked aloud, and from the severed ends dripped a soft, warm substance...The forest became suddenly malignant and malefic. The baleful creepers twined insidiously about his legs, and all along his path the wounded ones howled in swelling ululations that made the forest echo with waves of fiendish sound. Thick vines clutched at him like the trailing talons of some huge and hairy arm. And when he cut them, they wailed like flayed children... He lunged ahead faster, and the branches whipped at him. His face grew scratched and bloody from the flailing of branches that ripped his shirt and flesh and that twined around him. He beat them off and staggered onward.

Suddenly the ground underfoot grew damp. He halted — just in time. For in front of him, stretching away until it vanished in the night ahead and on either side, lay a vast, slimy slough. The forest came down to its very edge, and even throughout it, here and there, stood gaunt, dead trees, and in places half-submerged logs rotted. As far as he could look to his right and left, the swamp spread its interminable length. He debated for a moment; he looked again at the logs, the stumps, and the occasional unfallen trees that rose at intervals. Then he decided to risk it, and ran forward.

The going was easy for a time. He walked across great tree trunks lying in ooze, or jumped from stump to stump, or swam through patches of stagnant water covered by a luminous green slime. Sometimes he dragged himself through mud that made a husky, sucking sound when he pulled out his legs: like the sound of some enormous witch that smacked her lips. On one or two occasions, it seemed to him that a shadow passed overhead, a sweeping shadow as of a huge nocturnal thing... He shuddered as he stumbled onward.

He came to an open space, brown-covered. Unthinking, he plunged in and swam. The entire surface instantaneously lived with a million million wriggling shapes that swarmed in hellish motion. Hissing snakes moved from his path and piled up on each side; cold vipers slithered across his back and neck, squirming like fat worms in a carcass. He dived under the surface and swam as long as he could. When he rose, the water was moving with mounting waves of serpents, and great bunches of snakes threshed on every side. The affrighted air trembled in one mighty hiss that ascended from the hordes.

When at last the water ended in mud and he pulled himself up on a rotting log, he lay for a long while regaining his strength. The seething mass of reptiles gradually subsided, and when he resumed his way was quiescent. Above, the comets had fled from the sky, and the heavens were void and absolutely empty in a terrible blackness.

Hour after hour he ploughed through foul swamps and slimy water. The noisome odors of the place made him dizzy after a time, but he fought onward. He occasionally thought of casting away the sword which hung heavy and cumbersome at his side, but he kept it. He knew not what he might encounter.

He must have travelled for leagues before he staggered from the slough unexpectedly. He was on firm ground, but the forest had ceased. He lay down on the earth for a while to rest his weary body, and carelessly looked back across the slough. From far behind came a shuddering heave; as he watched, something gigantic and horrible rose out of the depths and mounted upward. At the top of the soaring bulk he saw a head swaying from side to side with one huge central eye gleaming blindly.

In a trice he had leaped to his feet and was trotting forward until the slough and the monster were entombed in the deepening gloom behind.

The ground was level and covered with a tall grass or reed that rustled gently. And a soft nightwind began to arise in fitful moans and whisper with the grass in a reedy rustling. The melancholy music came dim from the sounding darkness, infinitely somber and plaintive, in strange, minor harmonies and lonely chanting as if sorrow embodied drooped and floated through the reeds. From every side as he passed came, low and elusive, the rhythmic cadences, a sad litany from the susurrous grass. All the plain seemed weeping at his passing, and he became filled with the desire to rush through the trackless extent and soothe the crying of the grass. But his eyes envisioned the shadowy, haunting beauty of Myrna: in one fearful second the sounds melted together and streamed in speeding waves to the utmost darkness. And the plain was as a thing that, having lived, had died.

Winding and tortuous his way became shortly afterward when the plain abruptly ended near a range of hills. As he entered them, the darkness again began to lighten. By the time he had crossed the hills, a wan, immense moon was spreading across the sky like a decaying thing that fled, shunned by the aloof, ebon depths of the heavens. It cast a pallor, sick and deathly, on the ground; it limned the gaunt trees pallidly against the sky; it laid a soft and fat wave of white rottenness on everything it touched. Under its ghastly paleness the wanderer's features took on the appearance of a walking corpse. A nameless fear commenced creeping through him, and he went on faster toward the mountains towering beyond the hills. An utter solitude and silence had settled over the dreary waste. The aspects of the country which he had crossed crouched faintly luminous far behind, but he did not turn. Once he scanned the vault above, but the entire concameration was completely and desolately empty of all save blackness and that westward-waning moon. Only the steady, low fall of his steps broke the appalling silence; all things that lay on every side as far as he could see conspired to give him a sense of minuteness in an infinitude that bounded, ceaseless, upward and outward through the vacua overhead.

And as he mounted the trail that was now winding through the base of the mountains, the rocks and trees in some indescribable way began to absorb the light that fell upon them, until they moved stealthily in slow corruption. It seemed to him that they changed their positions at his approach...as if to block his path. He accidentally brushed a stone in passing. A shiver of fear ran over him, for the stone was *living*...panting like some monstrous toad. In a sudden anger, he grasped his sword and smote the rock. It was cleft so that the halves fell apart. And even as the sword touched it, the rock shrieked. From its core poured forth a horde of worms... And the rocks began to converge toward him, in crawling heaps of liquescence, and the trees began to walk. Gasping, he slashed about him. He could do nothing. Wet, cold things were gathering around his legs and creeping up them... Dead loathsomeness caressed his flesh... In his despair, he thought of Myrna: there came to his mind the picture of her slim, willowy figure, and half-shut dreaming eyes...

With a start, he came to himself. The rocks and trees were still and lifeless. The moon had sunk with all its pale deathliness.

He resumed his progress, and discovered that he was ascending an easy grade to the last of the foothills. He emerged upon its top to find before him a gently rounded plateau in the midst of which stood a city of sepulture. There was no way of encircling it, for the unaccountably paved road that he walked on ran straight through its heart, nor could he see any other path which he might take. Without pausing, he continued to walk forward, his steps falling mechanically regular.

It was a city of overwhelming strangeness. Its fantastic spires fretted a raven-colored sky, and all the thousands of buildings beneath, even as they, were monoliths and cenotaphs and obelisks, devoid of windows or doors. He went unchallenged. The inhabitants, if the city was ever occupied, had mysteriously perished, leaving behind them only their sepulchral architecture gradually to crumble and dissolve. There were giants in the earth in those olden days, for these were the monuments of cyclops, and their peaks assaulted the citadels of heaven and the infinities of space. It somehow seemed natural that vanished hands had engraved upon them a counterpart of the cryptic legend scrolled on the hilt of his sword.

He wished for a face he had known, or a familiar sound out of the lost years: he saw a ruinous city of death, heard his steps echo hollowly away among deserted aisles and corridors. The inertness of stone maddened him, he unsheathed his sword, cursed imprecations against the diabolic gods who had entrapped him. Meaningless syllables burst from his lips in a language as uncouth as the structures that dwarfed him. Had the monoliths trembled in defeat? They were become monsters of measureless size, earth opened beneath them, they were claimed by gulfs more irrevocable than time. He traversed a bleak and barren plateau.

For hours he wandered on. The path steadily rose and wound upward through topless mountains that loomed on every side. Darkness reigned, but the path lay distinct.

It was only when he had toiled nearly to the midst of the central range of mountains that the gloom again lightened. Ahead of him loomed a cup-shaped circle of monarchs over which hung a faint and almost impalpable phosphorescence that illuminated slightly the grandeur of stupendous and colossal peaks which reared skyward. He did not pause to survey the scene, but followed the path where it led through a rift in the cup to the hollow itself.

Phosphorescence shimmered everywhere, and as he passed it seemed to be thickening. The air suddenly and indescribably became fraught with expectation. It was as if his arrival were awaited.

When he reached the center of the cup, he stopped on the margin of a pit that blocked his way; and when he stopped, there came a change. The slow-drifting phosphorescence leaped into life and rushed toward the mountainous walls in one cataclysmic surge. There the sweeping luminosity collected and condensed, and around him in a great circle sprang up a low, running line of flame. In a moment the circle was completed and the light rose upon itself. He could not have moved had he tried, a solid wall of cold radiance burned about him, mounting in immense waves. All the light was flame, and all the flame was waxen.

And now there began to come a sound, a faint sound as of the moan of distant waters, while higher, higher, higher mounted liquid waves of light around the cup. All the light was flame, and all the flame was red.

The distant moaning came louder and louder, rising in an ever-growing roar of mighty, warring seas. The light began to converge in a funnel-shaped roof above his head, drawing after it the thicker waves. All the light was flame, and all the flame was green.

A titanic wash filled the air, alive in quickening motion, and thunder as of all the billion billion waters of all the worlds boomed with a space-annihilating crash of sundering stars toward the funnel. The sheeted flame above commenced a spinning gyration until it whirled furiously and dizzily in a twisted wrack of shifting radiance. All the light was flame, and all the flame was black.

Abysmal storms howled and boomed toward the funnel in roar on deafening roar. The funnel widened and lengthened suddenly and swept apart to form a maelstrom around an immense vacancy that led to outer space. Far overhead, the blackness of the sky moved and streamed in ebony oceans that serpentined madly toward the funnel.

He stood dazed and deafened by the fearful thunder of space-leaping winds and the uncontrollable forces lashing themselves to savage fury all around. Instinctively he tried to cry out, but no word issued from his lips.

The flame flung itself together in a coalescing bound. It soared zenithward, one huge, solid pillar of fire. He followed its lengthening already league-long height far above. It seemed to him that a greater glare gathered at its peak, and that something had formed there.

Again he strove in vain to cry out.

All the howling winds poured downward and fled in hurtling rout around the pillar of flame, walling it with a speeding blackness. He tried to move but was powerless. There was the briefest tension, the pillar became motionless in subdued gales, as if expectant, and *they* were waiting — waiting —

But he remained helplessly immobile.

The tower of flame which had hung still for a moment leaped outward toward the eternal blackness. Thundering, screaming winds swept vengefully down and about him. He was torn by a million waters fighting, smashing, and the noise of all enormous seas burst through his ears. He stumbled forward toward the pit, battered by angry, pounding tempests. His arms waved wildly, he clutched for support, slipped, and now at last found his voice and cried aloud, too late, bitterly too late: his sole answer was mounting winds that raced away after the flying pillar of flame. Incredibly distant already he saw the living stream of fire that rocketed mockingly into space. He was whirled and twisted in the after-suction of the blasts, all around was a jetty infinitude of shouting darkness that hurtled in the flame's wake.

His futile cries were drowned, there answered him only the sardonic, gusty mirth of vanishing hurricanes, the hiss of a measureless sea that washed farther and farther distant, the dying echo of a cosmic whisper that faded into nothingness.

Down — down — he plunged through the pit, points of light flashed by him like stars, worlds and universes swam from sable below and were erased in blackness above. Each second was an eon, eternity was an instant, time and space had swallowed him, down — down —

He abruptly wakened from his dreaming reverie, and found himself in the midst of desert wasteland. A green sun was crawling over the horizon and bathing him in its necrophilic glare. Wearily he resumed his quest.

The gods had cheated him, he thought, with pain and despair in his heart; and all the hideous way was yet to be travelled.

IV. MISSING: A GOD

Graham slowly opened his eyes. His head ached ter-
rifically, sledge-hammers throbbed in his brain. When
he saw the white cot on which he lay and smelled the
disagreeable odor of antiseptics, he guessed that he occupied
a hospital ward.

He had difficulty thinking. How did he come to be here? He
remembered vividly the nightmare that returning consciousness had broken off, and before that — ah yes, the train wreck
and the blow on his skull. And before them — he wondered if
the phantasmagoria had actually occurred, or whether it was
not just another evil dream like the one he had come out of a
few minutes ago. He almost hoped that it was; and yet, when
he recalled his life's work, the fever of challenge and excitement and mystery burned in his veins again.

He tried to sit up. The effort sent a wave of nausea over him
and he fell back, his face contorted. The sledge-hammers beat
louder. He raised an arm feebly and found that bandages
swathed his head.

For what seemed a long time he lay very quiet and motionless until his headache became more bearable.

Here, under the influence of sunlight and prosaic surroundings, the adventure seemed unreal, remote; but it must have
been only too real, he reflected grimly, or he would not have
awakened with head bandaged in a hospital. Perhaps it was
fortunate for him that he regained consciousness at all. As for

the image, well, he had lost the first battle but was not defeated yet. As soon as he was able to get up, he would immediately open the bag —

It struck him with a sudden shock that the bag when last seen had been crashing through a compartment window. If it were lost... No, that could not be, the bag must have been found near him in the wreckage. It was impossible that he should be checked when he had made his most important discovery and advanced a great step further toward his goal.

To make certain, he cautiously turned on his side and surveyed the small room, even peering under his cot at the expense of another agonizing headache. There was no trace of the bag. He sank back, plunged into gloom, wondering whether his trouble had been wasted, or worse still, whether he might not have been a victim of mind mirage.

But was it necessary that the bag be in the room with him? He sought for some loophole to explain its absence. Possibly it had been picked up by guards and was being held for a claimant. Or it might be awaiting him now in the hospital's receiving ward. Graham brightened visibly. Of course, there was the likelihood that the missing bag had been crushed by debris, a catastrophe which he decided against: the chance was small that anything short of irresistible force could damage an idol with such peculiar properties and so impregnable to the blow of a steel pick. At any rate, it was useless to worry over the whereabouts of the bag until someone in authority entered his ward.

His thoughts next pivoted around their original starting point, the nightmare he had just emerged from on his return to life. It was an unusually persistent dream and kept intruding itself into the main stream of consciousness. Interesting in its own right, with the bizarrerie and convincing paradoxes of the dream-world, the vision possessed an additional fascination for it blended and symbolized the happenings of the previous day. The sequence had certain elements that bothered him, there were parts whose meaning eluded his grasp. Perhaps he was over-emphasizing its importance but he felt instinctively that it contained significant warnings or hints — if he could find them.

The sledge-hammers were beginning to pound louder once more. This at least was a warning that he could not miss. Graham sighed. It was sometimes an effort to think, but how much greater the effort not to think!

Why did not a doctor or nurse come? Not that he needed attention, but that he was eager for the answers to several questions. He estimated he had been conscious for fifteen minutes or a half-hour, since it seemed like two or three hours. He now raised himself cautiously again to find out if there was a service-bell. There was. He cursed himself and punched it. Scarcely had he relaxed when his ring was answered by quick, soft steps. Condensed sunlight entered his ward in the form of a tawny-blonde nurse.

"Did you ring?"

"No, the bell did," he responded irritably. He hated superfluous questions, especially those of feminine origin.

The nurse smiled like a tooth-paste ad at his unexpected reply and retorted, "If I were to answer in kind, I'd say that Sir Warren left a piece of his own wit in you."

"Sir Warren?"

"Yes, Sir Warren Gifford. You were operated on yesterday for skull fracture and concussion of the brain."

Graham digested this bit of information slowly. Recalling his nightmare, he knew without asking that he had been on the brink of the great precipice. He gave silent thanks for skilled care. Sir Warren, a noted brain specialist, was an acquaintance of some years' standing; otherwise he might not have had such excellent aid, and in that case —

He left the morbid thought incomplete and asked, "Where am I?"

The answer was a model of efficiency: "Private ward L, Middleton Hospital, London."

"How long have I been here?"

"Since early yesterday. You were rushed here shortly after the wreck and operated on immediately."

Mention of the wreck reminded him of his missing valise. "Was there a brown, medium-sized handbag among my possessions?" Anxiously he awaited the answer.

"I don't know, but I can find out."

"Will you, now? It is of great importance to me."

The nurse vanished. Suspense and doubt had set the sledge-hammers beating anew by the time she returned. Graham looked at her face, and guessed the answer.

"No, your valise isn't here. I was told that nothing of yours had been checked in."

Hope died in his face, giving way to a dogged resolution to ransack England if necessary for some trace of the elusive image. Time was precious. "How long will I be here?" he inquired.

"At least a week, maybe longer."

He remained silent after this new blow to his hopes. A week! By that time, whatever slight chance he now had of regaining his valise would have completely vanished. He mentally determined to close the hospital door from the outside, with or without permission, long before a week had passed.

The nurse looked at her watch, then busied herself a few seconds with bottles and glasses.

"Drink this," she commanded, handing him the results of her work.

He obeyed without question and swallowed the mixture. The sledge-hammers faded away, quiet soothed his aching head. He heard the light steps of his nurse glide off as he fell into a deep and dreamless rest.

He awakened in late afternoon to find Sir Warren at his bedside. Graham promptly gave a series of urgent and wonderful reasons why he simply could not remain where he was for another week. By dint of fast talking, persistence, sufficient cause, and the promise that he would indulge in no physical or mental labor for the next month, he won reluctant permission to leave in three days, providing he did not suffer a relapse and his condition steadily improved; the risk of hemorrhages was a responsibility which he took into his own hands.

With this promise he had to be content. He solaced himslf with the reflection that a dead Graham could solve no problem, whereas returning life would at least give him opportunity to try his wits.

The intervening time dragged slowly. Graham made use of it chiefly in planning what was to be done, and in ransacking his memory for some explanation of the phenomena he had witnessed. Forgotten data were exhumed from the accumulated knowledge of years, yet he was halted at every point by blind alleys and dead ends. Recovering the lost statuette became a mania, an obsession; he felt that he must find it at the sacrifice of all other duties. Here was mystery that dwarfed the archaeological riddles he had already encountered, and mystery it was likely to remain unless the icon came to light. And that cyclopean thing that had bulked at his compartment window — did it bear any relation to the image?

For once in his life, he regretted a lack of intimate friends whom he could confide in. As it was, he had always run free of the pack, and if he talked to outsiders about his adventure he knew only too well the certain result — "Graham's case was sad, wasn't it? And he *did* seem to be doing such good work. But that's what usually happens, overwork and then a breakdown."

He made a wry face. There was no help for it, he must go ahead alone.

During part of his forced leisure, Graham tried to recall the uncouth syllables he had heard just before the wreck and to transcribe them on paper. *"N'ga n'ga... clretl ust s g'lgggar septhulchu... thargoth..."* What did they mean? They neither sounded nor looked like any language with which he was familiar. Well, here was another riddle to investigate.

Maze upon maze since the idol had first emerged from earth! Of only one matter was he sure: he had been dropped into a labyrinth, he would explore all avenues for the way out.

Modern surgery performed in three days the miracle that a preceding geneation could not have accomplished in a month. Graham, head bandaged, but well on the way to recovery, left the hospital eager to resume his quest. Three priceless days wasted! He would have to work fast if he expected to make them up. And he would work fast, for he had laid his plans thoroughly during those days of recuperation.

He first walked to a newsstand and purchased every issue of every paper printed since the wreck. He spent the better part of two hours reading all the accounts in detail, scanning also the lost-and-found ads and the agony columns.

A paragraph appearing in one of the early reports puzzled him. It ran: "The cause of the disaster which late last night killed nineteen and injured thirty-seven is as yet unknown. Investigators rushed ot the scene reported that the track was clear, no rails being loose or bolts pulled. The engineer, who died shortly after the wreck, could offer no clue. He said he was speeding on a straightaway at approximately fifty miles per hour when a terrific tug from behind broke the train into two sections. The front half jumped the rails, ploughed along the roadbed for a hundred yards, then crashed into the ditch. The second half piled up on top of it. The fourth car of the nine-car train was flattened by some freakish accident, as if a great weight had been dropped upon it. Eleven bodies were removed from the fourth car, all of its occupants having been instantly killed." Graham with a sudden faintness remembered that colossal thing which he had seen outside his compartment window.

The later accounts had nothing further to add. They were already crowded from the front page by fresher news — a trans-Atlantic passenger plane had fallen in New York harbor with heavy loss of life. Graham had had enough of disaster and skipped the story. But nowhere could he find mention of the missing handbag.

Finally discarding all but three of the papers, he hailed a taxi and drove immediately to his quarters. From there he telephoned all the dailies and ordered the following notice inserted in both the personal and lost columns the ensuing week. "Fifty pounds reward offered for the return intact of a brown handbag or for its contents; lost in Friday's train wreck at Nottington. No questions asked."

He next called a car-renting agency and requested that an automobile be driven to his address. Promptly on its arrival fifteen minutes later, he paid the security price, settled himself in the seat with a package beside him, and drove directly toward the scene of the wreck. He stopped only once on the way to replace his lost implements.

Threading his path at what seemed a turtle's gait through streets and suburbs of western London, he stepped on the gas and drove furiously as soon as he reached the open roads. In little more than an hour he had reached his destination. He parked his car on the roadside and walked across some two hundred yards of meadows to the railroad tracks.

The rails were already repaired and the wreckage had been removed. Graham had small hope of finding his handbag but he was checking up every detail in his efforts to regain it.

He first walked along the tracks for a half-mile, looking around him and scanning the ditches and meadows. He then beat up the grass and weeds thoroughly until not an inch of ground or single clump of possible hiding place remained anywhere to be explored. Exactly nothing rewarded his search.

Somewhat disappointed even though he had not counted on success, he returned to his automobile and continued on his way, heading now for Isling. He remembered the news story that had originally sent him to Isling, and the legends it had mentioned. His last hope was that the elusive statuette might have been somehow restored to its reputed resting place of centuries.

He stopped briefly once more for lunch, then sped onward again. He arrived at Isling in mid-afternoon and headed straight for the Vadia and the Devil's Graveyard. At almost the precise spot where he had entered several days earlier, he parked the automobile. The package and the newly purchased tools he carried with him. In a few minutes he stood beside the small mound of dirt that marked his previous excavation. There were no signs that it had been tampered with during his absence.

Working carefully with frequent pauses for rest, he commenced digging. Since the soil was still loosely packed as he had left it, his progress was as rapid as before and he steadily went deeper. He waited for the sound of steel striking stone, and each pebble he hit made his heart beat faster momentarily.

Hours passed. When he finally heard the sound he expected, his last hope died in him. Not a trace of the image had he found, though he had reached bottom where the great green block lay.

Graham took his failure with resignation, largely because his secondary purpose at any rate could be accomplished. With infinite pains, in constant readiness for a leap to safety at the first sign of danger, he shovelled soil out until the surface with its inscription was laid bare. Opening the package he had brought with him, he lifted from it a bottle of white powder which he dusted over the surface. Loose flecks he blew away until the inscription stood out boldly.

From the package he next removed a camera and took several flashes of the inscription. When his task was done, he gingerly climbed back to earth, expecting at any moment that the gulf might open up beneath him. He uttered a sigh of nervous relief when his feet were back on reliable ground. Later on, he planned to explore whatever lay beneath the green block, but at present there were other matters to attend to.

It was dark by the time he had arrived in London, but not too late to leave his films at a specializing shop and have their development promised for nine a.m. the following morning.

Though weary from the strain of his trip, Graham was not yet through for the day. After an American quick-dive dinner, he returned to his rooms and until late in the night sat at his desk poring over data, notes, diaries, memoranda, and miscellaneous records of his past work. Not until his overtaxed brain became confused and muddled did he give in to sleep.

As he examined his films early in the morrow, he found some consolation in their perfect clearness. Not a detail was lost even in the enlargements. Since nothing had so far developed from his ads, he was convinced that his only chance of progress lay in deciphering the symbols.

A slender assignment! How could those queer whorls and unfamiliar loops be read by anyone except their author, let alone be pronounced?

And the thought had scarcely entered his head when he shouted from the glee of a brilliant guess. "The voice! I'll wager a fortune that it spoke in the language of these symbols!"

He made a dash for the telephone and excitedly gave his number.

"Hello — hello — Professor Alton? This is Graham speaking. Will you have leisure for an appointment today? Yes — rather important, something that I am sure will deeply interest you. Concerns an ancient language — no, I don't know what it is. I — eleven-fifteen? Yes, splendid! Good-bye."

Graham rang off with a chuckle. Alton would have invited a cityfull of tramps in at two o'clock in the morning in case their jargon was new to him. If anyone could help Graham, Alton was the man. A leading philologist and foremost student of languages, he had made himself an international authority with his elaborate work on the Polynesian tongues and his pathfinding commentary on the translation of Mayan pictograph. Graham knew him well since they both held chairs at the same college. Alton was at present laboring on a comparative study of African dialects.

At the appointed hour, Graham was ushered in to Alton's library. He wasted no time as he whipped out the photographs and the sheet containing what few words he had been able to remember of the colossal thing's utterance. Alton peered intently at the inscription for a space of mintes.

"Hmmmm. Where is the original?"

"At Isling, twelve miles from Stonehenge."

"At Isling! Here in England?" Alton burst out incredulously.

"Yes, I took the photographs myself. Here is what I think may be an approximate pronunciation of some of the symbols."

Alton looked at Graham's handwriting with a frown of concentration and doubt and surprise mingling on his face.

"Can it be?" Graham heard him mutter. "The hitherto unknown precursor of Sanskrit — and a modification of the Ulonga chant — and yet the two together — here — in England of all places — "

He suddenly broke off. "Will you leave these with me for a day or so? I think I may be able to do something with them, but I will need to examine my notes. I confess myself profoundly interested, though it would be a bit premature to assert that I can decipher and translate the characters. As a matter of fact, the possibility is small, but we shall see, we shall see."

Graham, wisely refraining from a complete narration of his adventure, left him already buried away in piles of books and papers. For the first time he felt that he had begun to make progress. If Alton failed him, he would be deadlocked, and if the missing image were not found, he might pass the rest of his life in ignorance and darkness unless the green slab opened a way to solution or concealed something that would throw light on the phenomenon. But Alton's achievement had been so remarkable that Graham for all his anxiety was not yet ready to admit himself defeated.

On returning to his rooms, he telephoned the newspapers. No information about the valise was forthcoming. He decided to make the best of circumstances and resumed his examination of notes. In order to bring them up to date, clippings on the wreck ought to be added, he thought, and withdrew the three newspapers he had preserved from the cubbyhole where he had placed them.

The first yielded a complete story with graphic descriptions of the accident. The second contained a résumé, further small details, and theories advanced as to the cause. The back of this clipping was a front page play-up of the airplane crash in New York Harbor. He skimmed it in passing to make sure that he overlooked nothing.

A paragraph lead several sticks down caught his eye. His heart leaped with excitement. He devoured the paragraph, went back and read the entire article. When he had finished he sat still for a long period with his head awhirl in bewildered amazement.

V. FOUND: A DEMON

Dan Farrell staggered to his feet and dazedly looked around him. What had happened? Ah yes, the train crash. There was a dull cackle from ahead, the hiss of escaping steam, the red glare of fire, and above all moans and screams of agony from trapped passengers. Night was hideous with the sounds of disaster and suffering. A man lay at his feet with blood creeping from his ears and nostrils and mouth. His head was crushed. A few feet beyond him, a girl's arm hung limply from a mass of crumpled steel. Under the edge of a derailed car was a gruesome, pulpy head whose humanity could hardly be recognized. Dan did not know if it was man or woman. He heard the grinding of brakes, the roar of automobile motors, shouts and commands mingling with the shrieks of those dying. He saw headlights on the road a couple of hundred yards away, figures with small kits running toward the wreck, stretchers being hastily borne up, groups of men laboring like insane demons to extricate bodies before the flames won victory.

It was a scene out of hell, but Dan barely had eyes for it. He was cursing his fate and racking his brain for a way of escape. It would now be morning before he reached London. The trans-Atlantic cabin 'plane took off promptly at seven a.m. for New York City. His life and freedom depended on getting that 'plane. His passport had been o.k.'d, everything was ready, escape had been within reach – and now the wreck had spoiled his plans.

His need was desperate. Only a few short hours before, the scheming of months had been climaxed by his murder and robbery of a wealthy old recluse at Arvyle. He had at the latest not longer than the following morning until the crime was discovered. His greatest safety lay in flight to America. And with several thousand pounds in a thin flat package he carried, he was ready to risk anything for freedom. Capture meant swift death. His plans had worked so smoothly thus far — he must get away!

He had no idea what hour it was. By the number of people collecting at the scene, the physicians and ambulances, he judged that some time, perhaps an hour, had elapsed since he was stunned in the smash-up. He savagely cursed misfortune again as he walked along the ditch, thinking hard and fast in an effort to evolve a substitute procedure of escape. His actions were mechanical. He scarcely paid attention at the moment to where he was going and was all unprepared when he stumbled and fell over something in his way. He burst into more profanity as he rose, then stooped to pick up the object that had tripped him.

A flash of inspiration came as he examined his find. It was a medium-sized valise that might easily be mistaken in the darkness and excitement for a doctor's kit.

Dan struck across the fields to the road at a hurried gait. He passed several running men who bawled questions at him but he mumbled indistinct replies. Stretchers were being carried by him, some empty, some full. A man with his head bandaged sat dully near the roadside. A young doctor worked like mad over the bloody form of a child. Two nurses were giving first aid to passengers with minor injuries. No one paid attention to Dan except the man with the bandaged head who feebly called to him for some kind of aid. Dan turned away as if he hadn't heard.

Ambulances and automobiles were parked along the road. He raced to the line and examined each as he passed. In one that he came to, a powerful roadster which might have been a doctor's private car, the ignition was turned on. It had either

just been driven up or was about to leave. Dan slung the handbag on the floor, jumped in, pulled out, and tore down the road.
He heard a shout from behind, saw a figure dash to the middle
of the road and cry angrily after him. He stepped on the gas for
answer and roared around a curve on the direct road to
London.

He now ran a new risk. If the license number of the stolen
car were flashed to headquarters rapidly enough, he might still
be caught and the game would be up. It was a necessary
chance to take if he expected to escape.

When he arrived at the outskirts of London, he branched
north, then swung east again, coming in on a less frequented
road. So far he had not been challenged. He continued until he
caught sight of a hack stand. Turning a corner, he parked the
car, and with the handbag under his arm strolled casually back
to the road and hailed a taxi.

Several times during the next hour or two, he changed cars
until he felt that any possible pursuit was side-tracked. He
could have gone into hiding, but there was the danger of falling
asleep and missing his connection. Once soon after he entered
the great metropolis and again near the time of departure, he
stopped for breakfast and coffee that was either strong enough
or vile enough to keep him awake. He was relieved to find that
early editions of the paper carried no mention of his crime.

Fifteen minutes before the scheduled departure, he alighted
at the civic airport and five minutes later occupied a comfortable seat on the middle, passenger deck of the huge, twelve-
motored seaplane. Eighteen or twenty passenges were already
aboard. Most of them looked like business men taking the
twenty-four hour air run for speed. The only women embark-
ing were the wives of three of the men, and two young
American girls evidently seeking the last thrill of a holiday in
Europe.

When the fueling had been completed and the crew shipped,
the pilot entered to take his seat. The doors closed, the motors
droned, the hangar raced away behind them. Dan who had
never before travelled by air felt an exhilarating sensation of

lightness as the man-made bird soared, circled for altitude, and straightened out on its westward course. London dwindled in their rear. The countryside became a patchwork quilt overhung by blue summer morning haze. Fields and meadows and hills sloped horizonwards until they faded into mist. Villages drifted toward them, crept by like toy-towns, and were lost in the rising sun. Occasionally the 'plane dipped in an air-pocket or swayed pleasantly. Except for these indications of flight, the steady roar of the motors, and the drift of fields below, Dan might have thought he was suspended over revolving earth.

The vast sweep of the Atlantic emerged out of haze. The quilt of fields beneath ended in cliffs, and these in turn receded behind them until the English coast became shadowy, and finally was veiled by the Eastern horizon. A ruffled surface and tiny tips of white betokened the breaking of waves; but from their height, it was not easy to tell how heavy a sea was running.

Dan was too hard and practical a person to look for poetry in the scene; and though not entirely oblivious to its grandeur, much of its spaciousness and mystery and beauty were lost on him. His dominant emotion was glad relief when England had faded behind them. In the neighborhood of one hundred and twenty-five miles per hour, they were speeding toward the harbor three thousand miles away that meant refuge and safety.

Dan leaned back with a sigh of relief. He had scarcely realized how tired he was. It must be all of thirty hours since he had last slept. After a furtive glance at the other occupants, most of whom were absorbed in peering out windows, and a reassuring pat of the pocket that held his automatic, he hunched down into a more comfortable position. After all, it would be better to make up for lost sleep during the day, for he needed to be wide awake and on guard when his goal approached.

He dropped off into a heavy slumber.

Around noon, he was roused by the steward's call and wakened long enough to take a hearty lunch that made him as sluggish as before. He slept the sleep of strain and exhaustion for another five hours. At dinner time, he awoke greatly refreshened. With a generous sampling of the kitchen's fine cuisine under his belt, he returned to his seat and speculated on the pleasant uses of thirty-five thousand dollars that his bank-notes would become in the United States. He looked out of his window from time to time at a dusking world.

All the passengers craned their necks once when a miniature liner dawdled along far below them. The atmosphere was clear of the haze that had attended their start but fleecy clouds hung high in the sky. The dark bed of ocean deepened in tone as twilight approached. The liner disappeared over the rim of the eastern sea. No living thing remained in sight save the white seaplane winging on its way through the immensity of sky and water.

A fiery ball marked the setting sun. Across gray-black waters crept a crimson path. The clouds became molten-edged, pearly centers shading to rose-coral and to smoky red. There was ominous splendour in sunset; a sphere of flame smouldering like a bloodshot eye withdrew itself slowly down the western horizon. Its brilliance of noon was lost; and now, dull, ruddy, its dying ember was fast extinguished.

Something of awe came over the passengers. Sunset from the sky in the midst of infinite dark meadows had supernatural sublimity. Where there were rifts in the clouds, myriads of stars emerged in brightness and splendor unknown to dwellers of cities, a magnificent, spectacular blaze of such snowdiamonds as were never found on earth.

How brief a step from majesty to trifle! A porter began changing the convertible seats into berths, and when his seat was approached, Dan retired to the smoking room and inhaled a couple of cigarettes. It was probably after ten when he parted the curtains to his berth.

A valise was resting on its foot.

Dan looked at it in momentary surprise. Then he remembered. It was the bag he had picked up after the wreck, and which he had automatically carried with him, dropping it under his seat, there to be forgotten until the porter uncovered it. Sturdy, well-worn, unpretentious, it had nevertheless saved him from the ignomity of emplaning without any luggage whatsoever.

Curious as to what it contained, he set about opening it. Wearing apparel he would have thought the handbag's most likely contents except for its weight.

The bag was locked. Dan without hesitation drew a bunch of master-keys from his pocket and promptly unlocked it. A look of disgust came into his face as a pick, spade, and hammer flanking a cloth-wrapped bundle were exposed. Dan lifted a flap of the covering and peered within.

"Well I'll be God-damned!" he whistled to himself, astounded at what met his gaze. Every evil instinct in him leaped forth in response to the thing, he was sickened by its hideous appearance yet at the same time a kind of mad rapture boiled in his veins. He would have liked to send it hurtling into the sea, he felt as if it compelled adoration, he did not know what he felt, an abominable hypnotic influence drugged his faculties with a mixture of loathing and love.

Dan did not understand. He was as scared as a child in the presence of frightful dreams. Why he was apprehensive, and of what, he did not know. But in that eternal second when he stared at the green thing, he was claimed by the power of a corruption ancient, monstrous, he wanted to smash and fondle it, curse and worship it. With a half-hysterical laugh, "Christ! What a rum thing!" he mechanically let the wrapping fall back like one who has received a profound shock.

A blind impulse possessed him. He grabbed the valise and crawled to a window. Again and again he strove to drop it plunging into the sea. His forehead grew damp. Strength died out of him at each effort. He could no more get rid of the image than he could have halted the moon in its course. He wanted desperately to fling it forth; an insidious force deterred him, crushed him so that he was impotent. Exhausted as if he had struggled to push over a mountain, he fell back on his berth defeated.

After a few minutes rest, he slid out and walked to the smoking room. His fingers trembled as he lighted a cigarette.

The incident was uncanny; and that which is even slightly out of the ordinary disturbs the man living on a harsh material basis far more deeply than it does one who makes the extranatural his bread of life. Dan was a realist. He lived in the fierce present. And now he was up against something he could not comprehend. His immediate distaste of the image was already become fear.

The first instincts of anyone confronted by the unknown are to run; to rationalize the situation; or to fight back in the last extremity. But Dan had nowhere to flee; the occurrence was utterly beyond his power to explain; and how could he fight back when he had no knowledge of his antagonist? Concepts, emotions, essences can not be assaulted by physical means. The only action he could take was to get rid of the valise; and again he ended in a quandary — how was he going to free himself from it if it could so strangely sap his strength? What a boomerang the valise had turned out to be! That lucky find which had helped him escape seemed an unfortunate discovery in the light of later developments, doubly unfortunate in that he had nothing to go on. His response to the detestable statuette was as unthinking as the image itself was incredible.

He nervously paced the floor wondering what to do. It took him a long time to decide that he might as well remain where he was. He had no special reason for occupying his berth since he had slept a good part of the day. Let the valise stay in its place, and when the 'plane landed he would see to it that it was left behind.

He settled himself for his long vigil, smoking innumerable cigarettes. Occasionally his mouth opened with a yawn. Current magazines in a rack did not interest him though he idly scanned them. That the ordeal would soon be over was small consolation. The minutes dragged wearily. Dan wished that another passenger would drop back for a smoke and while away some of the miles in conversation. But they evidently had all retired, the crew's quarters were on a different deck, and the pilot room was forbidden territory.

He had reached this point in his thoughts when he was aware that the door behind him had gently opened and closed. He turned around with a hopeful smile that froze on his face.

One of the American girls, barefooted, in scarlet-fringed black pyjamas, was stepping across the room. But he had no eyes for the esthetic side of the picture. He was dumbfounded to see his valise in her arms.

As she passed by without paying any attention to Dan, he broke from his bewilderment and leaped toward her.

"What are you doing?" he rasped, clutching her arm. The valise dropped.

She halted. Her eyes opened and closed and opened again, her expression changed, dawning consciousness and surprise mingled on her face.

"What are you doing?" Dan repeated.

She looked at him with eyes still half adaze. "I — I — how did I get here?"

"You just walked in through that door."

Terror suddenly seized her, she sank into a seat with a catch in her throat. "I must have been walking in my sleep — oh it was awful!"

"What was?"

"The — the dream. It was horrible! And then I thought — I thought that I was told to go somewhere, and get something, and carry it to — to — "

"Never mind," Dan interrupted bruskly. The girl's nerves were badly shaken. "Forget it. You've just had a nightmare and picked up my valise by mistake. Better go back to your berth and rest yourself. Come, I'll go with you."

"I — I guess so," she murmured vaguely.

Dan escorted her to her berth, then continued onward to his own. He had no intention of reclaiming the valise. It could remain in the smoking room till doomsday for all of him. Perturbed by its unpleasnat way of coming back to him, he flopped on the bed and wished that the 'plane would speed faster, the sun rise sooner. In spite of himself, he felt irritated and oddly disquieted by the girl's random words. He was beginning to be haunted by the infernal valise. He had not been able to throw it away, and when he had abandoned it, the satchel had followed him by the indirect assistance of a sleep-walker.

Relaxed on his berth, he gradually grew calmer. A glance at his watch disclosed that it was well after one o'clock, Eastern Standard Time. He yawned again. The United States and refuge were only a few hundred miles distant. He caught himself napping a couple of times and forced himself into wakefulness. He really ought not to be sleepy even if he could afford to be. Regardless of his daytime slumber, his eyes closed. Funny thing, this dopy feeling. Almost as if he had been mesmerised...

His breathing came slowly, regularly...

After an uncertain period, his eyes opened. There was a weight on his chest. He bolted upright in panic. For the briefest second he had the hopeless despair of a man in the death-house when the electric switch is about to be thrown, for the hideous image nestled in his arms, glowing weirdly with a phantasmal light such as he had never seen the like of. His berth was darkened, and no illumination shone into it, and every other object was invisible, but the image with a cold radiance of its own that seemed to come from nowhere and yet to be a part of it wavered and bloated and shimmered in its hellish cycle of mutation. Dan struggled wildly from his berth and raced back to the smoking room.

His valise lay on the floor, opened.

With his heart beating erratically and unreasoning fear that burdened his mind, he collapsed. It was bad enough to be running away from retribution for his crime without the additional nerve-tormenting torture of trying in vain to escape from unknown danger. Had the girl obediently walked in her sleep once more in answer to the hypnotic command of someone or something and deposited the image in his berth? Or had he victimized himself, he who in all his life had slept dreamlessly, soundly, and to whom no suspicion of somnambulism had ever been attached?

For ten minutes Dan fought a battle with himself. There was a tocsin within warning him to dump the image overboard, telling him to make haste before it was too late. Side by side with it was another unheard voice that told him he was powerless, that he had no control whatever in the affair. Dan hesitated. He would rather handle snakes than the thing in his berth. And yet, anything would be better than this deadly waiting. So long as the idol was aboard, the terrifying might happen at any instant. He hated to go through a second struggle on a nasty job, but once the object was heaved out, he could rest content. His mind was made up. Grimly, with one hand caressing the butt of his automatic to restore his confidence, he rose and crossed to the door.

He swung it open and stopped dead on the threshold. The girl, not five feet away from him in the dimly lighted corridor, with a ghastly look of evil and cruelty and lust and abysmal horror distorting her features, was sleepwalking again, and she held the atrocious icon in her arms closely, and her lips moved to form animal-like sounds, and there was an ecstasy of triumph in the way the icon was gyrating dizzily from change to change. Dan's heart turned sick, but he steeled himself and took the arm of the girl, intending to lead her to the bed. Her eyelids fluttered when his fingers encircled her arm, her features writhed to more normal appearance, she looked straight into his eyes, and then at the thing she carried. The blood drained from her face as she crumpled in his arms. Her burden dropped and lay there in the aisle, glowing wickedly with the ineffable suggestion of obscenity out of the stars of uttermost space and vileness from the most abysmal gulfs of time.

A sigh crept from the lips of the girl, she mumbled incoherent phrases. Dan picked up her limp body and staggered to her berth. He thrust her in. He was tempted to waken one of the other passengers, but there was no time for explanations and no certainty that he could give any satisfactory ones. Getting rid of the image and getting rid of it immediately had become an obsession. He did not know why or stop to think. There was neither logic nor reason in his action, but only instinctive fear.

With a shudder of violent distaste he bent over and lifted the eldritch object. It seemed to palpitate in his hands like a stone heart and its narcotic power drugged his will with the poisonous strength of opium. A surge of forces as deific as they were unholy swept through his veins, he could hear the pounding of his own heart there in the deserted aisle, a singular dull pain creeping into his head. A spasm of horrible nausea seized him, he staggered crazily. The image slipped, he fumbled to keep his grasp and felt as if he were battling a sentient opponent. He lurched down the aisle. His dizziness increased, loops and spirals of light flickered before his eyes, vague, vast sounds grated out above the drone of motors. Dan, terror-stricken, endeavored to hasten faster. An insistent agonizing ache had somehow gotten into his brain, the image swam and absorbed him, he fought through a waking nightmare. The pain seared in waves of white fire tormenting his head more than any headache, and he had never in his life had a headache. The aisle was endless, his desperate efforts advanced him only one labored step after another as though he struggled at the bottom of a viscid sea. His muscles strained and bulged, it was all he could do to make any progress. With infuriating slowness he drew nearer the door at the aisle's end, reached it, paused to open it, then changed his mind as he felt the image sliding from his grasp. He kicked it open and stumbled toward a window.

For one horrified second he halted in the paralysis of fright as he glimpsed a colossal green pudginess bloating from sea to stars outside his window. The idol slipped from his hands, he whipped out his automatic and fired at it as it fell but the bullets caromed away. The spat of his gun was answered by spurts of flame and the crash of glass. A putrid stench suddenly assailed his nostrils, the pain in his head skyrocketed to the agony of torture, he shrieked as if the life was being sucked out of his brain and body by that shapeless titanic horror. His eyes glazed while the seaplane halted in midair, screaming bodies and pitted corpses catapulted into the sea while a thousand fragments of wreckage dropped hissing through sky and water.

VI. IN THE EARTH BENEATH

"Everything ready?" Graham called.

"Everything set!" the answer came back.

"Let her go!" he sang out.

There was a creak of winches unwinding. Graham and his co-worker Bjort Liska slowly dropped into that mysterious aperture in the Devil's Graveyard, whether toward journey's end, or discovery, or blankness, they did not know.

The last two days had been crowded with preparations and bustle of activity for Graham; once his course of action was decided, he set forth to work following it out.

Unexplained circumstances surrounding the destruction of a trans-Atlantic cabin 'plane off the Atlantic seaboard near New York city had already made it as deep a mystery of the air as the Marie Celeste was of the sea. No passenger had survived; and the corpses which were recovered told nothing, not even those in an unbelievable, unnatural state of pitted decomposition. Newspaper mention of that strange decay caught Graham's eye, and he instantly guessed somehow his lost image had been aboard the seaplane. How it got there he could only imagine. He supposed that after the train smashup his handbag had been confused with the luggage of someone else and accidentally carried aboard. To be sure, there was the possibility that his handbag had not been aboard, but in the absence of other clues to its location, and in view of those peculiar deaths which so closely resembled earlier deaths at Isling, he believed his conjecture to be correct.

He debated with himself on which of two courses to take. Should he immediately cease his work in England and book passage for America in trail of the image? That would be a blind chase at best, for if the green idol had been aboard, it had probably perished. Or had it? As he resurrected in memory its imperviousness to steel and its amazing properties, he became convinced that while it brought doom in its wake, the idol itself remained unscathed. Where was it now? At the bottom of the Atlantic? Somewhere along the coast? Or spirited away to unguessed-of places? Unless further news came to light, it would hardly be sensible to go aimlessly wandering for several thousand miles on the slim chance of recovering his lost figurine.

On the other hand, should he try to piece more loose ends together before resuming his hunt, and risk wasting valuable time? There were the symbols that Alton might have a report on in a day or two; and in case he successfully translated them, the puzzle would very likely be a little closer to solution. Miscellaneous information stored away in his diaries and notes had not yet been fully tapped. In the heart of the Devil's Graveyard was buried a slab whose secret required investigation. There were books to be gleaned — tomes on Stonehenge, Angkok, Easter Island, on folklore and ancient remains; on tribal rites and religious ceremonies; on philosophy, archaeology, and a dozen othe subjects. His logical action would be to pursue his investigations from the point where they had been interrupted, unless the disappearing image bobbed up again. While Alton was trying to decipher the inscription, he himself need not be idle; he decided that his immediate step would be a thorough examination of the green slab at Isling and whatever it concealed.

It was too late to go ahead that evening when he found his first clue to the missing idol's possible whereabouts, but he spent the succeeding day in a bustle of preparation for which he drew largely on the resources of Ludbury College. From stores of equipment which had been used on expeditions often headed by himself, he selected only materials that were essential, including winches, quantities of rope, flashlights, photographic apparatus, oxygen tanks, masks, and various implements.

He hesitated a long time over the question of aid. He would undoubtedly require assistance, but the danger involved, the risk of death even, deterred him from asking for it. Abandon his project he would not, obtain help by deception he could not; and going it alone was physically impossible. In the end, he approached Bjort Liska, a brilliant young assistant who had frequently accompanied him, and whose ability was equalled by his courage.

"Could you spare time for a two or three days trip, if necessary?" Graham inquired.

Liska looked at him in curiosity. "Yes — where to?"

"My destination is Isling, a village in Wiltshire. I recently uncovered there a hitherto unknown relic of antiquity — a block of stone covered with unique symbols. There is reason for believing that a vault of uncertain depth lies beneath it. The discovery seems to me sufficiently important to warrant close investigation. I am about to explore the vault and may get under way tomorrow. The job is too big for one man to handle, otherwise I would see it through alone. There will be grave danger connected with the expedition, and I warn you that it may be a toss up with death."

The assistant smiled in answer. "It sounds exciting — and mysterious. I'll go. I've shaken dice with his majesty the white worm before; and I'm still able to toddle."

Graham told him as much as he deemed advisable about the Isling affair and a few details of his own adventure. Liska's readiness to go was undiminished; if anything, his eagerness increased.

One more man was needed for surface work while the other two went down. Graham secured him without much difficulty; another staff member who had performed on previous parties the mechanical but important duty of remaining behind to see that everything progressed according to schedule.

With its hastily assembled equipment, the trio led by Graham descended on Isling a day later. Several curious villagers gathered around the graveyard but did not enter. They contented themselves with watching the foolhardy strangers prepare for what they felt was certain death. Not for the wealth of Indies would they have dug beneath this or any other graveyard, an action from which only evil was sure to follow.

While Thomas, the third man, unpacked, Graham and Liska took turns excavating. With no delays and with each giving his full strength, their goal was rapidly won. Graham made arrangements in order that it would be himself who cleared away the last foot of dirt; but before proceeding, he waited until the windlass was adjusted and a rope safely tied around him. Then only did he scramble into his miniature well and lay bare that enigmatic stone. Without drawing Liska's attention, he fumbled across its surface.

Nothing happened.

He felt a pang of disappointment and wondered momentarily if he had been obsessed by a hallucination. He strove to recall exactly what he had previously done. Had he not run his fingertips over the top rows of characters and then across a group of those middle symbols? Yes, that was it. As identically as possible, he repeated the action, a faster beat coming to his heart. He traced out lines of characters, continued through circles, pyramids, cubes, planes —

And instantaneously the transformation occurred, unexplainable, ghostly, as though stone had dissolved into shadow before his eyes. There were no hinges, no signs of leverage, and absolutely no trace of the block he had been standing on a moment before. Below him, blackness, a vast corridor dropping toward what subterranean regions and what unsuspected end? One second — he stood on firm rock; another — he dangled over emptiness.

What had become of the green slab? And how would he recover or restore it later? Disappearing stone — planes that were arcs and cubes that seemed like tiny spheres — charnel miasma that rolled upward almost like a wave: Graham shivered in a sudden nervous reflex as he signalled to be hauled out.

He untied himself when he was safely back on earth, but all he said to Liska was, "I moved the keystone. It works on a secret spring. We can go ahead now." He added, "I advise you to remain here while I go down. There's no telling what lies below."

"Not me — this looks too promising. Phooey! What a stink!"

Graham made no further efforts to dissuade his companion. He had given sufficient warning; and in any case, the very nature of the work militated against success if his efforts were unaided. Moreover, his head was still bandaged, though mending well despite his constant activity.

Both men donned gas-masks and oxygen tanks after making sure that Thomas understood their signal system. A large canvas bucket was fastened to the rope. Graham and Liska took their stance on opposite sides of the bucket while Thomas dropped several implements that might prove useful into it. All three were armed.

The lowering-hoisting apparatus was of such a type that a child could have managed a weight many times his own. Thomas resumed his position at its crank. Then had come their query and his answer, followed by creaking and motion as they began to descend. They had commenced their exploration.

Standing upright, each held firmly to the rope. Now they were headed for whatever lay beneath. Walls of greenish gray slipped by, smooth, unbroken. Graham could not tell whether they were of the same unknown substance he had already encountered, or whether they were ordinary rock with a coating of slime and moisture. In either case, who or what agency had constructed this vertical corridor, when and for what purpose?

The patch of light above them dwindled, contracted to a point. As blackness overtook them, they switched lights on, Liska watching below for bottom, Graham examining the sides as well as he could. And the more he pondered, the less he understood. What possible reason must there have been for building and sealing a perpendicular well out of which nothing could emerge? For that matter, why had it ever been made? And above all, and this was what perplexed him most, whence came the engineering skill to conquer so vast a problem offering such insuperable difficulties in those olden centuries when savages or primitive tribes at best roamed through Wiltshire? For obviously and beyond dispute, this corridor antedated the Vadia, the Devil's Graveyard, Isling itself, and the regional records. The Devil's Graveyard — how unexpectedly appropriate its name had turned out to be!

His reflections were interrupted by an exclamation from Liska, his voice muffled and almost inaudible through the mask.

"I say, Graham, this is a most extraordinary thing to find!"

"What is?"

"I mean this well. Why, we've dropped several hundred feet already and there's no sign of bottom yet. How do you account for it?"

"That's just it, I don't," Graham answered grimly. "I thought at first that this must be a burial vault of some sort, but heaven knows what it is. We may have made a discovery of considerable importance from either a historical or archaeological point of view."

"Have you any estimate of its age?"

"Nothing definite. I've never been down here before, as I told you. Judging from the guardblock, it must be, well, much older than Stonehenge, for example."

"Stonehenge — 1800 B.C., more or less. Phew! I don't see how that's possible, unless our knowledge of the period is all wrong. Whoever sunk this hole was far more advanced in civilization than the tribes we know of."

Graham made no answer to the last comment of his alert companion, partly because speaking was difficult through the mask, and partly because there was no reply that he could make. The evidence was before his eyes, but he had no more explanation than Liska had.

He watched the steady upward drift of walls with growing surprise. It was uncanny there in blackness pierced only by the stabs of their two lights. How much deeper to go? And now he was assailed by a new doubt — suppose that even their great lengths of rope were too short? Minute after minute passed and their regular descent continued. Surely they could not go much farther before the rope gave out!

The air was chill and damp, an unhealthy clamminess far below ground level that contrasted with the hot August sunshine they had left. A profound silence held sway. And in the strangeness of it all, Graham yet found time to speculate on a technical puzzle — by what miracle had this passageway without buttress or support been preserved through centuries, when terrible pressures and stresses of earth should have forced the sides together under normal conditions?

There came without warning a cry from Liska, and Graham felt his arm grasped in sudden excitement. His companion was gesticulating and pointing downward. Graham deflected his light alongside Liska's and looked at what the dual beam discovered a hundred or more feet beneath them.

They saw whiteness and grayness in little balls and oddly shamped lumps and thin, short sticks. A cry burst from his own lips — skulls!

And by some subconsicous awareness, he realized at the same instant that the corridor sides had swiftly receded. Their improvised elevator was approaching bottom in the midst of a giant cavern between a thousand feet and a mile below ground level. The skulls became larger and clearer, rushed up to meet them. With a perceptible crunch, the canvas bucket came to rest.

For a long, long minute, Graham and Liska surveyed their landing-spot, gripped by its lethal eeriness. Everywhere lay skeletal remains, white, gray, brownish, some in plain view, others crumbling to powder or half-buried in dust and sediment. Blind eyesockets focused on the intruders, fleshless jaws froze in an unchanging ghastly grin, limbs and hands naked of all covering and stripped of the house of life gave them silent welcome. A city's dead could hardly have equalled the profusion of these relics of mortality. Male and female, adult and infant, by hundreds, by thousands and thousands their bones rotted here, slowly dissolving until they should finally have returned unto the great mother that gave them birth and that would reclaim them in the end.

Despite their scientific training and familiarity with death, both men were spell-bound. That awe which most onlookers feel in the presence of human decay was not theirs to repulse. It seemed as if the mystery overhanging their trip from its very beginning had here come to its climax. For Graham, the stench that had met his nostrils when he stood on ground above was explained, but new problems of conjecture were raised. Whence came these remains and why were they deposited in such a fashion and in such a place?

Every mystery led to another, and every explanation raised a host of other questions increasingly difficult to answer!

At length shaking off their trance, and when they had emerged from their first shock of amazed wonder, the two stepped out and began to survey their surroundings more closely. They themselves looked curiously unhuman, with their oxygen tanks and masks.

The skulls were those of modern man and ordinary human beings. Graham casually examined a couple, then moved on to investigate the chamber proper. He had taken perhaps a dozen paces while flashing his light before him when he was arrested by a shout from Liska.

He wheeled around. His associate was running toward him and waving something in his hand. He could hardly talk intelligibly from excitement. "Graham! Look at this and tell me what you think it is! And there are dozens and dozens of them everywhere — lying on the surface and God knows how far underneath — it's the find of the century — "

Graham took the object while his assistant rattled on. It was a skull, brown from age and disintegration. The lower jaw was completely gone, the left cheek bone and most of the facial structure had badly deteriorated, but the cranium was in a good state of preservation. He instantly recognized it — an unmistakable skull of Neanderthal man! Yet his astounded eyes could hardly credit the reality of what he saw and fingered. Neanderthal man — here — where no previous trace or smallest fossil had ever been found — and at the bottom of an artificial well beneath the Devil's Graveyard!

"Where did you find this?" he suddenly asked.

"Half-buried over by the wall and the place is filled with them! Why, anything may lie beneath these surface remains of modern man! Come, I'll show you!" Liska chattered for answer.

They strode over the great white mound, their feet slipping occasionally on a skull and crunching in debris. Sometimes a sharp crack indicated that a bone had snapped, very likely a rib or a humerus or an ulna. In spite of himself, Graham shivered. He could not remember having entered a more creepy burial chamber of the dead, if indeed this was a burial chamber.

Liska dropped onto his knees with nonchalant indifference to his surroundings, and the fervor of a Magellan or Galileo, at a spot where he had made his find. Graham noticed in passing that accumulations completely obscured the original floor. Where the layer of recent skeletons thinned away along the pit's edges, a broken, loosely packed surface was exposed, a conglomeration of ossuary remains whose depth he could not estimate. He had an unpleasant suspicion that this entire mass did not contain enough native earth to fill the bucket in which he had descended.

His aide was not in the least fazed. He scooped off dust, mould, and bones, all those musty deposits of flesh and clothing, with a cool disregard of their nature. A few inches down, he worked more slowly until he had exposed another skull which he handed over to Graham. It was a duplicate of the first, another semi-fossilized, semi-decayed relic of Neanderthal man.

Graham himself caught the fervor of discovery. He joined Liska in a preliminary examination of the heap. Side by side they sunk a small shaft, laying apart such larger pieces and better preserved fragments as they found. The same thought was behind the efforts of each. If the funerary debris was thick enough, why not fossils of earlier man still deeper? They worked madly, dug almost carelessly because their material was so rich. At every new find, there was an excited brief conference before they resumed labor. And their wonder increased until the most remarkable discovery, from sheer excess of marvel on marvel and surprise after surprise, would have seemed commonplace.

Here were fragments and bones and teeth and complete skeletons in different states of preservation or decay. Here were greenish stains of oxidized copper; and occasionally a stone weapon or ornament; but all near the surface, for farther down the stains did not occur, nor the ornaments, and only flints and eoliths and stone weapons came to light. To each of them, as to any anthropologist, the stains betokened the bronze age, and their absence the stone age, of man. But it was not these that made them toil with such concentrated attention and reckless energy. It was the skeletons themselves. For as they sunk their shaft, a parade of man's life on earth passed before their eyes, amd what they found in one hour would for ever have made their reputations. Here was Cro-Magnon man in an untold number of perfectly preserved complete skeletons. Here were Neanderthal man with his lesser cranial content, the Predmost race and the Grimaldi race; and behind them Heidelberg man and Eoanthropus or Piltdown man, and in a variety of types, of which some had never previously been known. Centuries rolled into tens of centuries, and thousands of years mounted to hundreds of thousands as they sifted through this great wastechamber of all the races and all the ages of man. Rhodesian man, Pithecanthropus Erectus, Peking man, Sivapithecus were here, and the offshoots between, the side-races and branches and transition types that had died out after brief existences. Dawn man and the missing members of the genealogical tree turned up one after another. And the skulls became thicker-boned, the brain capacity smaller, the head more beetling and apelike as they dug yet farther down. And then came the sub-men, Propliopithecus and Notharctus, the line from Miocene times backwards, until they finally reached strata of bones and skulls which had so mouldered that only guesswork would suggest any clue to their age or nature. Five hundred thousand years had they burrowed into the past, a full half-million, and more, how much more they had no way of telling. Perhaps a million years from the life of man was represented in the successive layers and deposits which they had pierced. And when they at length ceased their furious labor to indulge in a needed breathing spell, the incredulous awe in Graham's eyes was reflected by the amazement in Liska's.

How had so complete a fossil history of man accumulated here? What protecting hands had entombed and preserved these remnants of all the dead through abysses of time? What unheard-of power had built this monument and guarded it while continents emerged or disappeared, while glaciers crept out of the north, while earth buckled, and mountains were upheaved, and the sea reclaimed portions of land, and the hills wore away in constant transfigurations and mutations which had altered the globe? That the chamber with its ancient bones, or the deep corridor with its verdigris-colored walls, had been recently made was unthinkable; yet it was no more preposterous than to believe that such a subterranean vault could have withstood unchanged the enormous pressures and stresses and strains of earth during ages that defied comprehension, during gulfs of time that had watched the world formed and re-formed and refashioned through incessantly shifting designs.

Graham felt suddenly tired. The maelstrom of mystery in which he was caught, instead of narrowing, swung wider and wider. The utter lack of answers or explanations, the futility of conjecture, and the piling of phenomenon on phenomenon, question on question, were transforming his prime headlong enthusiasm into weary plodding. But no riddle could fully or permanently halt his tenacity, however much he might blunder in darkness. Persistence was the invariable factor in his researches.

He rose to his feet and selected a few of the finest specimens which had been unearthed.

"We had better be going," he remarked. "Our oxygen is running low. We can take some of the skulls with us and look them over above. Perhaps the foul air will clear out enough by then so that we won't be encumbered on our next descent."

"Right," Liska replied briefly. "But why don't we stay here and look around a while longer? For that matter, we could have a couple of new tanks let down and we wouldn't need to return yet. Why, this is one of the greatest finds of the century, and frankly I'd like to make the best of the opportunity while we're here."

"Well, it might be worth glancing around or cursory exploration, but we'll need considerable assistance even to sift through the burial heap alone. Supposing I go up with these specimens, get the oxygen tanks, and bring a camera back with me. The whole chamber should have been photographed before we touched it. I won't be long and you can look around in the meantime if you wish."

"Splendid!" Liska answered succinctly. He was about to say something further when a listening, intent look came into his face. Graham himself involuntarily stiffened. What had his friend heard? The question had barely sprung to his lips before it was answered.

A gentle swishing came from the center of the cavern. There was a faint rasping, and a steady, dull thud on the skeletons, and a crack as a bone snapped.

Both flashed their lights toward the bucket.

"Look out, Graham!" Liska suddenly yelled and with a sidewise lean sent him crashing against the wall. Some object whipped viciously by them and lashed the bones with a thud that was immediately answered by several sharp cracks.

The two men struggled to their feet and turned circles of bright light on the object almost simultaneously.

It was the rope that had lowered them. Cut off from the surface, they were marooned far below the Devil's Graveyard with absolutely no way of getting out.

VII. THE DEAD SHALL ASCEND

For one long, heartbreaking minute, Graham and Liska stared blankly at the rope, with dismay in their hearts. Not a sound could be heard. The dismal silence was like an ominous warning. Skulls and bones which had lately seemed mere implicit of decay acquired all at once an aspect of malice. There was evil in their fleshless grins and gaping smiles and hollow eyesockets. The cavern of death had somehow and eerily become symbolic. Were their own skeletons to be added on these immemorial reliquiæ?

To Graham a disturbing new thought unpleasantly sprung — supposing they were entrapped in the lair of the monster he had encountered on the train? Theirs would be a hideous fate if they were. It was a reflection that he promptly put out of mind. He felt instinctively how truthful it could easily be, but at the same time it was too ready and too gruesome an explanation, besides raising queries that he was in no position to offer the solution of.

The spell snapped. Mobility returned. As they strode toward the fallen coils, hope artificially buoyed them.

"The rope may have frayed against a rough edge," Liska said.

"It's possible," Graham answered nomcommittally. But there had been no rough edges. "More likely there was a weak spot which gave way." But the manila was comparatively new and had been tested before their departure. "Let's look at it."

"We might as well, but Thomas will probably send another rope down."

"It may take him some time to get one," Graham replied. "I don't think there was enough left to reach this far again."

They bent over the end and examined it. Puzzled frowns came into their faces.

"What do you make of it?" asked Liska.

"I don't know. It evidently didn't slip off the winch. It seems to have been severed, and yet — "

And yet! The more they scrutinized it, the more mystified they became. The rope had not abraded or rubbed against an obstruction, for if it had, the break would have been ragged and uneven. But neither had it been cut, apparently, for there were no marks of steel. If it had been deliberately slashed with a sharp instrument, half the strands or more would have been smoothly levelled, and the rest frayed from the point where it broke and fell of its own weight. The end presented an appearance that was uncommon to say the least. It was evenly severed, and fuzzy. But if it had not slipped from the winch, or broken because of an unnoticed flaw, or been intentionally cut, what on earth had caused it to fall?

"It looks as if somebody had broken each fiber separately," Graham said hesitantly. "But I don't quite see how that explains it."

Liska was silent while he peered at it closely. "H'mmm," he finally mused, "I've never seen a break that looked exactly like this one. But it might be just a freak. The fact that ropes ordinarily don't separate like this doesn't necessarily mean that they couldn't."

"It's hard to say," Graham replied cautiously, "though I confess I don't like the looks of it."

After a short pause, he gave up speculating. "We're wasting time," he said abruptly. "There's no telling when we'll get aid and our oxygen won't last much longer. I don't fancy breathing this vile air even if it isn't poisonous. The first thing we ought to do is to go over the whole chamber carefully and see if there's any other way out."

The younger man obediently followed his directions. "We'll start from the spot where we were digging. Now you go along the wall to your left and I'll take the opposite way until we meet. There may be an opening somewhere — you know the signs to look for."

Liska set out, minutely examining the walls, the ground, and even the arch of the ceiling fifty feet above his head. Graham strode off in the opposite direction. They almost immediately lost sight of each other, since the walls were curved and a direct cross view was prevented by the ossuary mound.

Graham kept a close watch for inscriptions or drawings, but the greenish surface was devoid of markings. He frequently tapped the walls as he progressed. They invariably sounded solid. No crack, opening, or aperture of any kind was visible.

This was a grim business, he thought while he continued circling. He felt a double responsibility in that he had persuaded Liska to accompany him. If anything serious should happen, he would have only himself to blame. He hoped that the falling of their liferope would turn out to be merely an accident, but some inner warning that he could not fully disregard made him apprehensive. The tomb's atmosphere was conducive to depression if not despair; this enormous mass of earthly remains; the solitude that blighted every thought; and the idiot grin of lipless mouths and the stare of sockets whose eyes were gone and the taloned clutching of thin white fingers all preyed on his nerves.

His hunt was still unrewarded when he had probably halfway or even further circumpaced the vault and come once more in sight of his assistant. The younger man had halted and was kneeling, busily at work.

"Have you found anything?" Graham inquired as he approached.

"I'm not sure. There was a depression here. My feet sank a little and the debris seemed looser, so I thought I'd dig down a ways. What success did you have?"

"None. There was no sign of an exit."

"That's odd. It would certainly be unusual in my experience if there's no exit or entrance except the one we came down. We'll be up against it if this proves to be a false lead that I'm working on."

"Not necessarily," Graham replied. "Thomas will make connections with us sooner or later." In his heart he was not so positive. Some fate might have overtaken him already for all he knew. And in any case, it might be hours before Thomas noticed that the rope had broken, and succeeded in obtaining more.

He dropped beside Liska and helped him exhume. The material was loose, he noted. He scooped for a few minutes, then too impatient to wait, struck a match and held it next the wall as far down as they had advanced. They watched it with bated breath. It burned with an unsteady flame, flickering slightly away from the wall.

"There *is* a draught!" Liska exclaimed excitedly.

"Yes, and do you notice the fitful flame? It would seem to indicate a deficiency of oxygen here, and the brighter glow must come from the faint seepage of fresher air!"

They worked harder, ignoring the priceless remains that they tossed out. The hole fast grew larger. They burrowed feverishly for several minutes more. Graham's hand slipped without warning into a recession in the wall.

"Here it is!" he cried with exultation and glad relief.

They redoubled their efforts and furiously cleared away the stoppage. They could hear bones and loose stuff occasionally sliding down. When the opening was of sufficient bigness for a man's body to pass, they together squeezed as close to it as they could and sent their lights flashing ahead.

A long incline running sharply downward for perhaps twenty yards or so met their eyes. It was strewn with skulls and skeletal fragments and protruding deathsticks. It ended on the floor of a corridor that extended indefinitely beyond range of their lights. The passageway was at least five yards wide and ten high. Its roof was on a level with their eyes.

"Good heavens!" muttered Liska. "This mound we're standing on is all of thirty feet deep!"

"Yes," said Graham, overwhelmed by a turbulent rush of thoughts. "And the chamber — what would you estimate its diameter to be? A hundred and fifty or two hundred yards? God! There must be tens of thousands of skeletons here altogether!"

He was staggered by the picture. What appalling destiny had created this most gigantic of all mausoleums? And whither led this corridor which swept away like an imposing cathedral arch? And what hands had carved it out in what forgotten vistas of time?

"Are you ready to slide down?" Liska broke in on his meditation.

"No, not yet — wait a few moments." Graham thought rapidly. He did not intend to let his companion run any more risks than necessary. The corridor was an unknown quantity. It might lead to freedom, or it might lead to peril. The vault wherein they stood was undoubtedly the safest place, especially now that the putrid air would have an opportunity to clear. Furthermore, aid from Thomas was likely to arrive at any time. One of them ought to remain behind while the other explored.

"You stay here and watch for a message or new rope from Thomas while I go ahead," he commanded. "We can't afford to overlook any bet while escape is still uncertain."

"It would be fairest to both of us if we tossed a coin to see who stays," Liska promptly rejoined, and Graham silently cursed his idiomatic use of "bet."

He could not argue Liska into remaining behind, and he could not prevent him from exploring the chamber if the impulse possessed him. After all, with life itself at stake, they were on equal footing. Rather than cause friction, he acquiesced. The second man fished a shilling from his pocket and flipped it.

"What is it?" he asked.

"Heads."

Liska uncovered. Heads it was. "You win. What's your choice?"

"I'll go," Graham responded, glad that chance had favored him. From the canvas bucket he took an extra battery for his flashlight, a loaded automatic, and a belt of cartridges. Before departing, he peered upward through the tube but could make out nothing. No star or patch of light could be seen. He was disappointed, though he had not expected that his vision would reach to so great a height.

"I'll leave my oxygen tank here — you may need it," he said, and waved away Liska's protest. "The air will be cleaner in the passageway than it is here. If I find an exit near by, I'll return. If it's very far, I'll come back by way of the surface. And if Thomas reaches you first, keep a lookout for me. Should I fail to appear in a reasonable time, it may be advisable to send out a searching party. Use your own discretion. And keep a gun handy."

After these final brief words, he walked over to their excavation. He halted long enough to whip off his oxygen tank including the mask and tie a handkerchief around his head for breathing. During the second between adjustments, he got a whiff of nauseating corruption. He handed the apparatus to Liska, wriggled through the narrow opening, and went sliding down. His last glance backward showed Liska vaguely outlined, the bright patch of his flashlight, and behind him darkness deepening into a dense, pitch-black obscurity. It was an uncanny, Dantesque scene, or like a Doré picture: the man dimly shadowed and ghostly, faint against the sable, with mouldering bones and vestiges of earthly ruin strewn thickly around him. And then the picture faded as he struggled to his feet and strode onward.

Minutes crept by and crawled into hours as he continued through the spacious corridor on as strange a journey as he had ever made. The gentle thud of his shoes died away in mysterious reaches beyond the beam thrown by his flashlight. There was a rhythmic flowing of blackness from ahead into blackness behind. And the silence was sepulchral, with something of the age and imposing grandeur of an illimitable cathedral aisle. There was never a division in his single way, for a side passage, nor any deviation from the straight. The air was close, and musty, but not intolerable. It appeared to be imperceptibly in motion, but he was not positive. It might be stagnant, and the faint breaths he detected only the stir of his passing. A monotonous cadence came from his even steps; and the light echoes lost themselves eerily in recesses all around. There were bones on the floor from time to time; there were ornaments of ancient years and implements of prehistoric ages. He chanced upon a gold coin of Caracalla, and some Greek girl's tiny perfume jar; and there were occasional eoliths or flints, but never a mark upon the verdigris-hued walls.

At what point of his progress, or at what distance from the burial chamber whence he had emerged, or even at what hour there came a change, he could not say. But a transformation had occurred. He had been aware for some while that the obscurity was becoming less intense, that the walls and murk and every object were increasingly distinct. His first thought was, I am approaching daylight; it will be good to see the sun again. He turned off the current of his handlamp. For a briefest interval, he faltered in his stride, and his second thought was, am I dreaming? For this can not be sunshine.

As far ahead as he could see, and the corridor plunged onward for miles until sight failed him, and as far behind, the walls, floor, ceiling, every particle of greenish surface, even the air itself, were shining with a phosphorescent glow that emanated from no visible source. It was a sinister and awful radiance. Like a pygmy dwarfed in wide reaches and spacious lengths of a stupendous tunnel he peered around him. All things shone with cold, flowing flame, and luminous waves poured from the roof arched high above him. It seemed as if the walls contracted and enlarged, as if their dimensions underwent a geometrical realignment. The corridor swept onward, and somewhere indefinitely ahead he saw it dwindle to a point; yet all around him it gave a semblance of swaying and collapsing and expanding, an illusion that made him giddy to watch. Absolute silence prevailed; and the close atmosphere remained undisturbed by motion; but the paradoxical unrest of solid matter continued incessantly.

There may be experiences so contradictory to the tenets of reason, or so in counter-opposition with laws of nature, that they assume in memory an aspect of uneality. Such a situation was Graham's during the rest of his pilgrimage, until the witnessed phantasmagoria became inseparable from figments of imagination. There were times when he walked straight ahead with as terrific difficulty as though he climbed a precipice; and there were times when he catapulted frantically forward as if he had fallen from a great height; but all the while the corridor plunged onward on its even course, neither ascending nor dipping. Had Euclidean mathematics permitted a horizontal plane to become vertical at infinity, and without deviating from the horizontal, this unique circumstance might have been more easily comprehended, but bruised and tossed about as he was, Graham needed his dazed senses to save himself from serious injury, and found no leisure for speculation. How long or for what distance the untranatural buffeting continued was beyond his knowledge. He came to have the dull, automatic persistence of a drowning man who struggles blindly against forces that owe no subservience to human wishes. He doggedly advanced through the interminable nightmare toward any goal or anything that lay beyond. Minutes were as hours, and time prolonged itself upon itself until Graham felt that he must go under. Loss of physical strength mattered little, but the drain on his mental powers was far more disheartening. Impalpable flame, cold fire of a color which bore no relation to any color of earth, reeling miles down a sunken gallery of godlike or gargantuan dimensions, floors that swam free in space, stone mockery of repellent green surfaces and everlasting necrophilic silences crushed his spirit as he grimly fought his unhuman antagonist.

Somewhere, sometime, the end came at last. Graham, through sweat and blood that blinded him and the vertigo of swimming proportions, realized slowly and in the half-con-

scious awareness of utter defeat that the corridor terminated
flatly with a dead wall. No escape, no exit, nothing beyond. The
long bitter struggle wasted. The longer, harder struggle in
returning yet to undergo. And still the drunken dance of walls
and floor continued through oceans of frozen fire in expanding
rings and contracting spirals and distorted ratios as though it
were a Clavilux phantasy magnified and conceived by the elements of earth. In that maelstrom of foreign forces he noticed
a patch of symbols as foreign as they; and their cryptic lines
retreated and advanced in unison with the telescoping corridor. Slipping, staggering, thrown fiercely from side to side,
Graham found himself unintentionally lurched against them,
and flung away again while he strove to maintain his balance.

It was an incredible thing that happened then. As though he
stood on the floor of a house that spun around him, bottom and
walls and ceiling revolved and his feet clung weakly for support
on the ceiling with the floor above him. Spaces and curves and
distances and accepted geometry ran wild. The vertical became
the horizontal, duration and extent and being merged in another
dimension that interlocked them all. The luminous energy
bathing the corridor with elfin radiance poured out wickedly in
a dazzling fury. The play of cosmic power surged around him.
Dynamic vortices whirled where the walls had been, solid surfaces dissolved into opaque mist and radioactive cascades, the
ceiling disintegrated under his feet. Clawing for support at stone
that became as cloud and fog to his touch, he dropped through
a magnetic funnel. Thunder of his own blood deafened him and
blackness from within blotted out the shimmering cascades.

After eons of darkness came the sound of a cricket chirping
and the elixir of warm, fresh air. Graham opened his eyes.
Remote specks of light resolved themselves into stars of the
early night sky. His cheek rested on grass, and he breathed in
that cleanest of odors, the scent of earth.

His body seemed a mass of bruises and throbbing pain as he
stiffly arose and tried to remember what had happened. The
corridor — its cul-de-sac — phosphoric irresistible activity —
and now, involuntary escape.

Great shapes loomed around him, huge sentinels of stone ringed him in, fallen monarchs rested everywhere, masses of hewn boulders covered the ground. There was something familiar about these giants of earth, and Graham realized with a shock of dismay and perplexity that he stood in Stonehenge. At his very feet lay the altar-stone, and farther away stood the lordly trilithons, and outside them the inner ring of blue stones, and outermost of all, the circle of sarsens. He felt that sanity must have left him. Impressive remains of forgotten hands that had builded mysteriously for purposes beyond certain surmise, their inscrutable enigma and the testimony of their broken ranks had been during the centuries a challenge for conjecture. But it was not the enduring riddle of Stonehenge, though that Hyreynian Wood was as unfathomable as the Sphinx or the smile of Mona Lisa, which bewildered Graham. What gave him incredulous doubt of his reason was the puzzle how he had arrived in the midst of Stonehenge, a full ten miles from Isling. Try as he might, he could not bridge the gap in consciousness between his subterranean Odyssey and his awakening above ground.

But as full recollection came, he gave up idle speculation for the time being. In the neighborhood of a dozen miles away he had left his fellow archaeologist entombed, and Liska might still be imprisoned under the Devil's Graveyard far below the surface for all he knew. It was his immediate duty to return and aid in the rescue if it had not yet been effected.

Exhausted as he was, he picked his way through the Gargantuan ruins and set out across the Salisbury plain. He would have walked the entire distance had it been necessary, or until strength failed him. But it was not so late that all cottagers had retired, and after trudging the first couple of miles, he won though rather dearly his transportation for the rest of the way. Fatigued and aching in body, nevertheless he would not permit himself even a short nap before he had made certain that Liska was safe. The miles were hardly slower or less interminable than they had been underground. He impatiently fidgeted. He knew he was depending on mental determination and nervous reserves to carry him through, but the price was worth it if he could rid himself of worry.

When still some distance from Isling, he heard the echo of a dull boom, and wondered what its cause. As he reached the outskirts of the village, he heard another, louder detonation and saw a flash of light across town toward the Devil's Graveyard. He urged the driver to greater speed. They swung through Isling and along the Vadia and so at long last came to a halt in front of the tumbledown cemetery.

A small crowd was gathered around it. Graham leaped out. Flinging back his debt of gratitude to the Samaritan, he pressed through the group. A man stopped him as he was on the point of entering the cemetery.

"Sorry, sir, but no one is allowed to pass." The stranger was polite and firm. He spoke with authority.

"But I'm Graham — Carter E. Graham! I must get through!" Graham protested.

Some of the nearest men wheeled when they heard his name. The stranger gave him a hard, queer look and said, "Graham and another man are trapped underground. We're trying to get to them. Can you identify yourself?"

Graham fumed. "I escaped through a tunnel. Call Burton Thomas, the third member of my party, if he's here. He will recognize me. Who are you?"

"Inspector Frank Leighton of Scotland Yard." Leighton summoned another guard, whispered a quick command; he faded away into darkness, and after a few moments returned with a man of haggard appearance who Graham realized was Thomas.

"Thomas! What happened?" Graham shouted.

Thomas turned a dead white when he recognized the missing archaeologist. Then he rushed forward with a cry of relief. "Graham! God, I'm glad to see you safe! Is Liska with you?"

"No, I left him in the chamber," he answered, and as Inspector Leighton waved them ahead, they raced over the cemetery trying to piece their stories together. There were several figures grouped around the excavation. Lights had been hastily set up. An acrid odor of explosives hung in the air.

"I don't understand it," Thomas was saying. "There's a green stone blocking the way and we can't budge it. We tried digging around the edges. Picks don't even nick it. We've just been blasting but couldn't get a single chip off. What on earth is it? Everything was clear when you went down and then a while later I looked over and there was the stone and the rope running right through it. *Through it,* I tell you!" His voice rose to a half-hysterical cry.

"I turned the crank to haul up and the rope broke off. You can still see fibers sticking out of the stone. Where did it come from and how did it get there?"

"I don't know," Graham answered evasively. "What happened next?"

"I ran back to Isling to get help. We couldn't make any progress, so I wired to London for more rope, and dynamite. Some of the people in Isling said mysterious things had been happening there lately. They asked Scotland Yard for help. We've been trying to break through since early this afternoon."

They had now arrived at the edge of the hole.

"Is the winch ready?" Graham asked abruptly.

"Yes — why?"

"I'm going down. I've had experiences similar to this and may be able to move the stone. They often work on secret levers, you know."

"It's no use. We looked all over for a spring. It hasn't anything except a lot of odd markings."

"Well, Liska and I got through once. Maybe I can do it again," was his noncommital answer. "It won't do any harm to try. Here, help me fasten this rope."

The second Scotland Yard man cleared the way for him. A charge that was already being tamped in was ordered removed. When everything was ready, Graham swung himself into the hole. The green stone like a sinister enemy blocked his way. There were the unsolved characters and the geometric designs. And there too, almost in its exact center, was a round spot with fuzzy threads protruding. But not a scratch marred any part of it. The stone was impregnable except by means of the key-inscription.

He wasted no time before tracing the pattern, and again the miraculous metamorphosis occurred. And as the stone dissolved beneath him, he suddenly thought of a solution. Perhaps the barrier re-integrated automatically after a certain interval. If this was true, the perplexing manner in which the rope had been swallowed would be explained. It was a wild guess, but he could think of no other postulate that would agree with circumstances.

"Lower away!" he shouted up. This was no occasion for tarrying. He saw Thomas's startled eyes peer over, heard the winch unwind, and then the walls arose as he descended. An unspeakably putrid miasma of decomposition greeted his nostrils. He hastily tied his last handkerchief around his head and prayed that he would survive the foul stench. Anxiety to save Liska had made him forget half a dozen precautions. He carried with him only his automatic and somebody's flashlight which he had snatched when he dropped into the hole. He might have put on a gas-mask; he might have shown Thomas how to displace the stone in case it blocked his exit before he returned, but he somehow felt that any delay was too long. Liska had been trapped for eight or nine hours.

With exasperating slowness, the walls crept upward. Noise and tumult died away, lights and stars focussed smaller until even they were gone. He thought how convenient it would be if an elevator would drop him swiftly through the shaft. It was a futile daydream. He had an uncomfortable feeling once. If the green stone resumed its position while he was in midair, and his rope broke again — he put the thought from him with a shudder. Steadily the walls flowed past. And what of Liska? How had he fared these many hours? Was he still awaiting escape? What had happened after their separation? He might also have taken to the corridor after dreary watching for aid that did not come. Or had he succumbed finally to mephitic gases and baneful influences? Graham felt more apprehensive than ever. His efforts to favor Liska with a better opportunity for escape had only proved a boomerang. So much would have been saved had they two investigated the corridor together, and now the end was not yet. Almost hypnotizing in their monotony, the walls crept by. Minutes dragged with as little haste as the ascending shaft. The rope began to hurt his side. He eased himself temporarily by grasping it a length above and shifting weight into his arms, but the strain was too much and he soon released his hold. Still the walls mounted out of darkness below and narrowed high above.

At last this regularity was interrupted. The sides curved away, his flashlight beam grew longer, a feeling of spaciousness came upon him in place of his previous more cramped sensations. The great mound of dead appeared, floated toward him. Even before he dropped upon it, he shouted, "Liska! Liska!" His cry reverberated, echoes were flung back, but no voice answered his.

The moment he landed, he slipped from the noose and stood for a few seconds looking around, sweeping the chamber with his light.

"Liska!" he called again. "Liska! It's Graham — where are you?"

Liska was thrown from side to side in decrescendo and whispered back and forth through inkiness, but not even a feeblest response could he detect.

He illuminated the ground at his feet. The bucket and coils of fallen rope rested near him. Something gleamed shinily among dirty white and grayish brown reliquiæ. He picked up the tiny object.

It was an exploded cartridge.

A sudden faintness weakened him. He steadied himself with a none too convincing reflection that possibly Liska had fired in order to attract attention.

He stumbled over death's-heads and crackling bones to
their excavation. He crawled into it and shot his beam through
the corridor, but no sign of Liska was visible down its malignant, stately aisle.

"Liska!" he yelled. "Liska!"

There was no reply as his voice hollowly died out in its farthest recesses.

With increasing alarm, he scrambled once more to his feet
and began a systematic search of the chamber. For a start, he
decided he would encircle it, following the wall. He set forth;
sweeping arcs of his light illuminated his path and the sloping
huge tumulus of rotting remains.

He had gone at least a third of the way before he sighted
another trace of his assistant. Some yards ahead, Liska lay face
down, inert, crumpled. Graham hurried on. His first perception was paradoxical: he thought how badly Liska's clothing fitted him. It was much looser and more baggy than need be. Not
even his posture could have been completely responsible for
the shapeless garments. As Graham hastened forward, he also
noticed his automatic lying a few feet away from his body, and
several exploded cartridges. Liska was quite motionless.
Graham, uneasy and fearing that he had arrived far too late,
sped over the last few feet and turned the body around.

A horrified cry involuntarily issued from his throat. Its echo
eerily skirled away and became lost, and the darkness was
filled with a phantom presence, and a stone stillness prevailed.
He swayed, but whether from dizziness or shock or foul air he
could not make sure. He thought the mound of ancient dead
were mocking him. It must have been an illusion born of light
and shadows and darkness. There were hideous things in the
gloom, but they were no more frightful than the object before
him.

For when he turned the heap over, there was a fleshless, dry
rattle, and a skeleton grinned up at him, its vacant eyesockets
not a foot from his own eyes. The chamber swam, time became
a confused nightmare in which he was barely conscious of any
action. He vaguely remembered struggling with the grisly

thing, and huskily muttering that Liska would never be added to this dead mausoleum. Somehow he got the bucket readjusted, and then came a wild, giddy ride skyward, with his macabre companion flopping grotesquely, and thin white fingers that scraped across his own, and empty eyes and a leering jaw, and the caress of bones that had lately been robed in warm raiment. There was a constriction in his throat, and a ripple of hair stood out on his arms, and a cool breeze blew upon his heated face. The thing he held was like ice, and yet the blood boiled through his veins, and the pounding of his heart came so rapidly that it seemed one unbroken beat. And then the dark retreat was ended, and friendly hands helped him out. He heard cries and a babble of noise, but he left Liska for those who would give him his last home. He slipped away to find Thomas, and when he found him, asked unsteadily, "Is there any dynamite remaining?"

"Yes — and some nitroglycerine too."

"Where is it? Get it! There's no time to lose!"

He remembered walking very carefully, very slowly toward the pit, and dropping dark cylindrical sticks and tubes of fluid into it; the frantic scattering of people; an ominous quiet; a tremble and distant boom; and then a black pillar of dust and smoke and fumes that roared from the hole as earth buckled and its walls crashed for ever on the chamber that had lost its challenge to eternity.

VIII. WHAT WAS IT THAT I SAW?

Back in his London suite, Graham awakened late the
following afternoon. He still was weak from his harrow-
ing experience, and the events of yesterday were like
an evil dream, already amorphous and unreal. The Scotland
Yard man after questioning him about Liska had returned with
him to London. An investigation and inquest would be held
when he was in better shape. For the time being, in the face of
evident physiological phenomena for which he could not readily be considered accountable, he was released on his own
recognition.

Long, heavy slumber had done much to refresh him, and
now, as he sat down for belated breakfast, papers and mail
were laid before him. The papers he put aside for subsequent
reading, and the letters except for one thick envelope that
looked important. This he reflectively turned over. It was postmarked nine-thirty that morning. The superscription was in a
hand which he did not recognize. He tore an end off and drew
out a single written sheet and a second envelope. The single
sheet contained a terse note:

"6, Hammervil Ct.,
   London, W.C., 1,
7th Aug.
"Professor Carter E. Graham, etc.
   "My Dear Professor Graham:

"The inclosed envelope was left in his desk by the late Professor Charles Alton. The unfortunate accident that overtook him has necessarily caused some confusion in his affairs. His communication to you would appear to have been the last matter on which he was engaged. However, Professor Alton frequently forgot his intentions, and the letter may be several days old. I trust that this will explain sufficiently, and that its contents, whatever they may be, have not lost in importance by any delay.

"Should you desire further particulars, you may communicate with me at the above address. I remain, etc.,

James Marten, Sec'y."

The second envelope was addressed in a shaky, ill-formed scrawl that had none of the beauty, neatness, and legibility which were characteristic of Alton's handwriting.

"Evidently written in haste," was Graham's mental comment. He slit open the envelope and eagerly removed its contents. They consisted of a dozen or so sheets. The early script was loose, while the lines became steadily larger and more poorly shaped as the letter drew to a close.

After his quick superficial scrutiny, Graham began to read it carefully through. It was dated the preceding night. "My dear Graham," it commenced, and went on:

"A dead man writes to you. When you receive this letter, I shall have joined that vast throng the recorded symbols of whose existence I have devoted my life in translating. These are my own final characters, for which there is no more fitting reader than you, in whom this result had its cause. My heart informs me truly that my time is ended, even though my physician encourages me with words of dubious promise. I am content, for one must be content with fate, but I could have wished for a few days more and a better understanding of this to me inexplicable occurrence. I have had you telephoned this evening, but your absence has made it, I fear, impossible to speak with you again as I had planned. My hours are not many. I am thus compelled to write. I rely in whatever god there may be that I shall have sufficient time to write fully.

"In all modesty and candor, I believe that no other man alive could have successfully coped with the inscription which you requested me to decipher, for I do not know of another scholar with similar appropriate training and special background. As much for fear, then, that my labors on this final problem may be lost as for hope that you can shed light on the fatal accident attending my work, I am sending you these results, imperfect perhaps, surely uncertain. Since I feel instinctively that you are engaged on an enterprise of the utmost danger, if my injury is to be regarded as indicative, I am all the more anxious that you receive the information you requested.

"But before I take up the inscription proper, it may be well to mention one or two preliminary matters of some pertinence.

"As you know, I have spent a large part of my life in other parts of the world. My interest in languages, both living and extinct, has carried me on many a wild goose chase, and on a few ventures from which, not unlike Jason, I returned bringing golden fleece of a different kind. These researches into the origins and growth of languages have included for subject matter all peoples, all countries, all centuries. I can not claim absolute knowledge of the totality of man's infinitely varied symbols, oh rare dream that I should like to have achieved, but I have attained a familiarity with every known spoken or written language, and a mastery of many of them. I have also in that part of my work which I prize most highly rescued from oblivion a hitherto unrecorded tongue and a forgotten language. It is these two that now assume a new importance.

"About fifteen years ago, I accompanied the Richter-Angley expedition. Assembling at Hyderabad, we went north toward Chitral, our real starting point. From there we took a difficult route over the Hindu Kush Mountains, across the Pamir Plateau, onward to the Altai Mountains, and then eastward through the Desert of Gobi to Peking. Our purpose was to search for traces of early man in the region often referred to as 'the cradle of mankind'.

"We had extraordinary fortune almost at the outset. Approximately one hundred and fifty miles north of Chitral in wild country we stumbled on the ruins of a lost sanctuary or temple. There we made our first major discovery: a few mouldy parchment leaves which were all that remained of a once bulky manuscript. These leaves were covered with characters rather like Sanskrit, but of considerably earlier date. Their resemblance to Sanskrit was analogous to that of Anglo-Saxon to contemporary English.

"I named this forgotten language *Kanja* after the site in which it was found. Working backwards from Sanskrit, identifying roots and stems, guessing when analysis and synthesis failed me, I evolved a translation, an attempt at reconstructing its grammatical basis, and a hypothetical pronunciation. You may have seen my published monograph, *The Kanja Fragments, Edited, Translated, and with Notes on Their Relation to Sanskrit.* The pieces themselves were of a religious nature and comprised fragments of a ritual; but I shall omit a detailed explanation of their content since it has no particular bearing here.

"Years later, I was a member of another party which went into the Dark Continent; and from Africa came the second of my discoveries, the unrecorded Ulonga dialect. I was then collecting material for my still incomplete comparative study of native tongues. In that region where Abyssinia, Uganda, and the Sudan are adjacent, I made my find and took down copious notes entirely from oral observation. I shall never finish the study begun then, or publish the results of my work; yet it was not wasted effort, for those records gave me the first key toward solving your inscription.

"Without your aid I might have got nowhere, or at least have been delayed for months. As it is I have been able to accomplish in two days what ordinarily requires years of industry. But understanding had provided a new perplexity, and now my life draws to its close before I can ever contend with a fascinating and remarkable maze in linguistics.

"These were my materials: the Kanja fragments; the Ulonga dialect; the Isling inscription; the phrases you had written as a possible pronunciation. I should like to know where you heard the phrases, and how you found the inscription, and what is the meaning of these widely separated in locale and in age links to one chain. I can not know. The moving finger writes.

"But I am wasting time in useless regrets and the time for guessing is ended so far as my life is concerned.

"The materials mentioned offered me a choice from two plans of procedure. I could work backward from the Kanja fragments to the Isling inscription as I had worked backward from Sanskrit to the Kanja fragments, identifying stems, roots, and so on, until I should have a translation of the message. This was a logical and systematic method. It was also one of slow results. Or I could begin with your phrases, compare them with Ulonga, and compare these in turn with the Isling fragment. This was a much faster method. It was also liable to greater error. I chose it because of your urgent request. For the sake of accuracy, I intended to use the alternative method later at my own leisure.

"My task was immeasurably simplified by your key-words. *'N'ga n'ga clretl ust s glgggar'* bore a striking resemblance to the Ulonga chant which begins *"Nya 'nya ke re telus tse gul ge ge gar',* and so on. The numerous but minor differences in pronunciation were easily accounted for as a natural modification of the original during centuries of oral transmission. It was more surprising that the variations were not greater, since the Ulonga territory is thousands of miles from here, and from India; and since both the Kanja fragments and the Isling inscription must belong to a much earlier period in the history of man.

"But to continue. Your half-dozen words were a clear indication that what you heard was the Ulonga chant or rather a modification of it. My next step was a bold one, dependent entirely on the accuracy of your observation. If your words truly indicated how to pronounce the Isling inscription, then the Ulonga chant might conceivably be the spoken counterpart of the entire inscription. Now, since I already knew what the Ulonga chant signified, I would then have both the approximate oral sound and the translation of the Isling inscription.

"Having progressed thus far, it would be a simple matter to recover the exact pronunciation of the entire inscription. I could accomplish this in two ways: by modifying the Ulonga chant along the lines that your key-words indicated; or by assigning the key-words to their corresponding written symbols on the inscription, substituting oral sound wherever these characters recurred, and filling in the gaps by reference to the Ulonga chant. I made use of both methods before I was through.

"I suppose all this may sound very confusing and muddled but it was really a systematic and basic procedure. I began with your key words, 'N'ga n'ga clretl ust' and so on. These resembled the Ulonga chant, "Nya 'nya ke re telus' and so on. Your key-words were the oral equivalent of the Isling inscription. Therefore the Ulonga chant was a complete but modified pronunciation of the entire inscription. I recovered the original sound more accurately by revising the chant along the lines shown by your key-words. And since I already knew the meaning of the Ulonga chant, I knew also the meaning of the Isling inscription.

"That is to say, I knew its English equivalent, for I am not at all sure of its meaning. Tribal memory has here preserved a ritual through generation after generation from remote ages though its origin and purpose have been utterly lost. There may be significance in the fact that the Ulonga bucks, no matter at what time of day or night they chanted the ritual, invariably faced eastward, *and upward.*

"I am failing fast. My minutes are fewer. You will find my reconstructed pronunciation of the glyphics, and their English equivalent, appended together with your photographs. The fatal malady which I wrote of earlier is rapidly overcoming me. I mention it only because it is related in some occult way to your problem.

"About two hours ago, I completed the preliminary drafts of my work. I read the Isling inscription aloud in an effort to voice its uncouth and almost unpronounceable phrases. As the last syllable fell from my lips, the sound was succeeded by dead silence. The atmosphere became electric. My nerves were taut, but I thought my tenseness was a result of long concentration. And next I thought I was on the verge of a nervous breakdown, for it must have been a delusion that I seemed to hear as from infinite distances a repetition of those very sounds that I had just spoken. Or was it a delusion? I do not know, Graham, I shall never know. There was a guttural voice rumbling the unknown language, an approach of hideous noise, a roaring cacophony as if monsters of the abyss were snarling for prey. The walls of my library became as mist. I saw a vast greenish Cyclops gibber to the stars, a thing of such colossal size and utterly frightful appearance that I shrank back in horror. I hit my head on the mantel corner and must have fainted from agony and pain. When my senses returned, I felt nauseated and extremely weak. A pool of blood enveloped me. The shock and the loss of blood from the gash in my head have done for me.

"A profound depression dominates me. Vague blurs of places I know not and things of which I have no comprehension drift through my thoughts. Perhaps it is madness. Perhaps it is the prophecy of death. And perhaps it is the telepathic imagery implanted by a thinking entity different from life as we know it.

"My thoughts wander. I am finding it harder to concentrate. But now I begin to understand how you knew the pronunciation of some of the Isling glyphics. Fate be with you on whatever mystery you are trying to solve, and may your destiny be more fortunate than mine.

"Great God, what was it that I saw?"

Here the letter came to an abrupt end. Graham could not have made out the signature if he had not known the handwriting. Depressed and shaken by this latest catastrophe, he slowly folded the pages and turned to examine Alton's translation.

The philologist as always had done scholarly work even though his time had been short. What Graham found was analogous to the Rosetta Stone. Alton had first copied a line of the inscription. Under each line appeared the corresponding line from the Ulonga chant, then his reconstructed pronunciation, and finally the English equivalent.

After a quick, cursory glance, Graham read the four lines consecutively and thus obtained an uninterrupted translation. Querulous wrinkles formed on his forehead as his efforts produced the following result.

"Awaken! dead titans of time and of space and of being, lords of life, lords of death, lords of spirit. On the night of resurrection fall through the stars from your great world beyond to your little world within. Claim your own and return to your great world beyond. Oh Keeper of the Seal, take from us that which the titans have given and that which is theirs, even as they shall take in fury on the night of resurrection. We are yours as we are theirs, awaiting them, we summon you. Dead titans, awaken!"

Dead titans? What dead titans? Who was the "Keeper of the Seal"? And where was the "great world"? A hundred questions came to Graham, and not one could he answer. For that matter, was the ritual anything more than a senseless jumble?

Graham sighed wearily. And his despair increased, a more leaden weight settled on him as he noticed that, though Alton had translated the inscription down to the middle geometric designs, he had not carried them through the lower half of the ritual. There stood the rest of the glyphics, unsolved, perhaps unsolvable, challenging him with their whorls and spirals that meant nothing, or that might mean all the difference between success and failure.

IX. PESTILENCE WALKS IN DARKNESS

The lines on Graham's face were harder and he looked more tired when he had finished reading Alton's letter. Whatever he did brought a train of disaster. Every attempt at struggling out of the labyrinth in which he was lost led him into deeper entanglements and fresh morasses. He had asked for assistance from two colleagues, and Liska had suffered a ghastly death that no one had any explanation for the circumstances of, while Alton had been a victim of the titanic thing which had almost caused his own death. The sacrifice had been great, but the rewards were nearly as great, if solving one puzzle while bringing to light others could be considered a reward. Graham believed that they were, just as he believed that success in his life's work would be worth any cost, human or material.

For a long time, he stared moodily through his window. A fiery sun was setting in a coppery sky. The roofs of buildings and the tops of trees glowed with a dull flame. Murky shadows lengthened on the ground. It had been a sweltering day. The sky was like a furnace. The sun burned with the glare of a mad, bloodshot eye, and the buildings wavered through heat-waves. The myriad noise of a metropolis drifted up, and the ants of the city crawled their way with hearts in the stone about them and eyes on the pavement. He hardly noticed them, for he looked far away, and beyond the city, and beyond the world about him. Today's crumpled newspapers lay unheeded now on the table behind him, but he could not forget their flaring headlines, and the late news flashes, and the crimson theme that had been a dominant motif or a sinister undercurrent of virtually every article in them.

What frenzy was this that had come upon the world, a blight over all humanity as an eclipse darkened the globe or as parasitic fungi sapped the life of a tree? London became less present among his thoughts. In his mind's eye, he saw the nations and peoples and races of earth, and his heart despaired. There were thousands of voices crying in the wilderness, but he had no manna to give. Pestilence that walketh in darkness was come again, but he had no power to aid the helpless. Sickness of soul and agony of the spirit were abroad, infinitely more dreadful than any disease of the flesh, but his years of striving were still barren of fruit. And now had come dozens of recent events as though to heap coals of fire upon his head.

Wearily Graham at length turned his gaze from the flame-tipped buildings and crimson horizon to the papers lying at his elbow. He knew what he would find, for he had already skimmed the pile. But more carefully now he went through them, reading each item word for word as he clipped it out. The papers were late editions of London, New York, Paris, and Berlin periodicals. Every one yielded a harvest of curious happenings.

The first clipping was a despatch from Cape Town, headed:

NATIVE UNREST SPREADS

The outbreak of unrest among black tribes of the interior is rapidly spreading. First reported last week from Rhodesia and the Transvaal, the uprisings have now extended to Tanganyika, the Congo, and other areas as far north as the Sudan.

Authorities have as yet taken no action. It is felt in official circles that the natives are merely indulging in one of their periodic magic ceremonies. However, it is understood that troops are ready to enter the danger sections from a dozen camps in case the need arises.

There is some doubt as to the exact cause and nature of the unrest. Travelers and boat passengers report that tom-toms are beating incessantly day and night throughout all Africa.

Lieutenant Colonel James Mulreavy, returning from Tanganyika, states that the savages there are in the wildest pitch of excitement he has ever seen. He believes that the witch doctors are responsible. Every sort of black magic is being practised. Human sacrifices have been offered in large numbers. Flagellation, torture, and primitive rites of the most debasing sort are an hourly occurrence. He adds that the tribal leaders claim they are preparing for the return of a god. When questioned, the tribesmen only shook their heads and pointed to the skies.

According to another observer, Mr. T. H. Wilson-Grant, licensed trader at Mepli, the negro tribes have developed a kind of mob madness. He says that obscene images and objects have suddenly appeared in great quantity, that the natives are in a dangerous state of revolt, and that the witch-men are using fear and religious fervor as levers to inflame the tribes. He reports also that the savages are proclaiming the visitation of some monstrous deity from the skies.

A Paris despatch narrated a bloody rebellion in India.

PRANJHIPOK QUIET
UNDER MARTIAL LAW

The sudden rioting that swept Pranjhipok yesteday evening has been suppressed by native and English troops. More than two thousand Moslems, Hindus, Sikhs, and whites were killed during the native attack that came without warning shortly after sunset. An unknown number are wounded.

Armed with knives, daggers, pistols, rifles, and smuggled machine-guns, the natives attacked each other and jointly assaulted the foreigners in the European quarter. In addition to the casualties, serious fires are being brought under control.

Widespread looting and crime continue, but martial law is again establishing order. The property damage it is estimated will reach a million or more rupees.

The cause of the attack has not yet been ascertained. Religious mania evidently swept the natives under some unknown impetus. Shrines, temples, and holy men are literally besieged by mobs of the faithful. The daily calls to prayer are drowned out by the continual bedlam of praying fanatics. There is some obscure rumor current to the effect that ancient gods are about to revisit earth.

The Moslems claim that Mohammed is making his second visit. The Buddhists, Brahmans, Tsaoists, and members of other sects assert that their particular god is returning. In the general confusion, racial hatreds and religious antagonisms have flared up to violent heat.

Additional troops are already being rushed to Pranjhipok from Calcutta and Bombay. It is expected that the leaders of the revolt will be punished by the end of the week.

Of far different nature was a clipping from the *New York Courier.* It seemed to have no connection with the other items that he saved, but Graham clipped it anyway.

KALEN TAKES OWN LIFE
Noted Artist Leaps From
Park Avenue Studio

The body of Glen Kalen, internationally famous painter and sculptor, was found yesterday at 4:15 p.m. on the courtyard of the Wilmyn Arms, where he had resided for the last three years.

He left two short notes in his studio. One to his wife read, "Good-bye, dear, join me as soon as you can. The time is near. I would rather commit suicide than be taken by *them*."

The second note was addressed to a mysterious Mr. "Septhulchu". It merely said, "When you come, I at least will be gone. Even the gods can not prevent me from choosing death."

In Mr. Kalen's studio was found a number of extraordinary paintings, of so decadent a nature that they were destroyed by his family. A gruesome sculpture was also discovered, depicting a hideous monster in the act of consuming a mass of tiny human figures. Despite its interest as a sculpture, and its daring use of planes, angles, cubes, and spheres in a non-Euclidean fashion, the work was so hideous that it was likewise destroyed.

Mr. Kalen's wife stated that he had been acting in such an abnormal manner of late that he was about to be committed to a sanitarium.

She could give no motive for his act. He had won the highest honors of European and American galleries. He had no financial difficulties. There were no personal misfortunes in his life. He enjoyed excellent health.

About a week ago, however, he became depressed and complained of having remarkable dreams. These nightmares persisted so vividly that he attempted to capture them in his work. He also made strange remarks to his friends of some great calamity that was to overwhelm mankind.

It is believed that in a fit of depression or temporary insanity he leaped from his studio window.

Efforts to identify the Mr. "Septhulchu" addressed in one of his notes have this far proved fruitless. Police are working on the theory that he may have been the victim of a blackmailer or madman.

To his growing pile of clippings Graham added the story of some unusually brutal murders which had occurred near San Francisco:

FIEND-SLAYER ESCAPES
AFTER NINTH ATROCITY

19-year-old girl is
latest victim

The body of pretty Jane Dorel was washed ashore early this morning. She had been attacked and murdered in hideous fashion. Miss Dorel is the ninth victim of the maniac who has spread a reign of terror in this vicinity. Three children, two men, and four girls have now been murdered in the past ten days.

Mr. J. S. Schilton, investigating coroner, reported that the girl had been dead at least three days. After being criminally assaulted and slain, her body was horribly mutilated. The slayer with some sharp instrument gouged out pieces of flesh from upwards of a hundred places on her head, limbs, and torso. The corpse was then tossed into the ocean.

Police have found no clues to the slayer. In each case, the victim met his doom in a lonely spot, and all the bodies were mutilated in the same ghastly manner.

Investigators believe that a degenerate or homicidal maniac is responsible for the crimes. "We are at a loss to explain why the murderer should have pitted the body in so hideous a way," Mr. Schilton said. "A degenerate will often dismember the corpse, or slash it viciously, but these are the first cases in our experience where a fiend has literally dug out gouts of flesh from all over the bodies."

Another strange item, in the London poetry journal *Helicon,* caught Graham's eye next. He promptly clipped it and added it to the others. The cutting was an obituary, stating that the gifted young poet Aubrey Lellith had died by his own hand, leaving behind him no explanation for his act, except a mystical, prophetic poem which was posthumously printed in the same issue. It ran:

THE MONSTER GODS

The monster gods wait in the heart of the mountains,
The monster gods dream an apocalyptic dream;
The monster gods sleep by Faëry's phantom fountains,
The monster gods hid where the fen-fires gleam.

The elder gods have promised a day of returning
When post-historic revels will unfetter them,
When skies turn to flame in a universe burning,
And ashes consume what the elder gods condemn.

The monster gods then will tremble and waken
And rub out the granules of sleep in their eyes,
When death has been captured and time overtaken,
The monster gods will answer the Ancient Ones and rise.

The monster gods will walk then from hills and from high-
lands,
When four-dimensioned vaults revolve and open wide;
They will spew from the sea and climb from sunken islands,
From time-gulfs and planes of space they will glide.
The monster gods wait in the heart of the mountains,
The monster gods dream an apocalyptic dream,
They sleep a long sleep by Faëry's phantom fountains,
And they hide in eerie lands where the fen-fires gleam.

But among all the articles that he saved, the one which
impressed Graham as being most frightful was an account of a
tragedy at the Teuffelskopf Insane Asylum. He read the poorly
printed German text twice through to be sure he translated it
correctly.

TWENTY MANIACS STILL AT LARGE

Inhabitants of the entire district of Saxony are warned to
protect thesmelves and to report any suspicious character to
the police. More than twenty of the insane who escaped yesterday are still at liberty.

A full story of the disaster has now been put together. Herr
Dr. Bräuning states that, beginning about sundown, a fearful
uproar swept the whole asylum where approximately three
hundred dangerously insane are confined. Inmates shrieked of

hellish nightmares, of vast, bloated entities that were hovering over them, of wingy terrors that soared to great heights and that came down from above.

All guards were immediately placed on extra duty. The uproar increased hourly. Somehow, a little after midnight, five inmates of the left wing broke from their cells and rushed at the two guards. Both opened fire, and three of the maniacs fell. The remaining two, however, with astounding strength cracked the neck of one of the guards, instantly killing him before the second guard could intervene.

In the meantime, it was discovered that the rear wing had been fired while the fray took place. The fire spread beyond control almost immediately. It was necessary to unlock the cells and lead out the criminally insane. Hardly was this done when, as if at a signal, they made a furious attack on the guards and keepers. The fire continued to spread amidst the rioting, shooting, and incessant screaming of inmates.

Thirty-eight insane were burned to death or slain, twenty-one were injured, two guards were killed and nine others wounded. About thirty-five more inmates escaped of whom only a dozen have as yet been recaptured.

Herr Dr. Bräuning says that he can not account for the tragedy. The asylum was a model institution conducted on the most modern principles, except that it was an antiquated, semi-wooden building.

On the walls of the charred cells were found traces of the most extra-mundane and frightful pictures that diseased minds could invent, in which a filthy and wholly unnatural linking of human caricatures was made with foul, fantastic abnormalities. Besides these drawings, Dr. Bräuning avers that in all his previous experience he had seen no such similarity and unity among the actions of the insane. It was as though an identical madness, the same horrifying dream, had suddenly obsessed every inmate.

When Graham had finally gone through the heap of papers, he was amazed by the quantity of clippings. Almost every part of the globe was represented in them. He had compiled a feast of disasters, horrors, tragedies. Sacrifice to age-old ceremonial gods in China; vodu in Haiti; savagely persistent drumming of tom-toms across Africa; unparalleled frenzy among the insane in the sanitariums of every civilized country; vast, troublous dreams that came to the poet, visions of Cyclopean cities and enormous pitted things that perverted the work of artists; the whimper of a child in the dark of night at Petrograd, whose cry brought alarmed parents to find an idiot where fright had come; the fanatical warnings of prophets on a thousand street-corners and bazaars; a wave of suicides among people of sensitive temperament; brutal murders by the mentally subnormal; a baffling unease that settled even upon the common people — all these and many another happening were recorded in Graham's newspaper selections.

What did they mean? Was it mere coincidence that like events had occurred in places the world apart on the same day or within the space of a few days? Not unless some malady or contagious madness was sweeping the world. And everywhere, allusions to titanic things, Gargantuan monsters, equivocal gods that came from the skies. A blight seemed to be overwhelming the kingdom of man, a disease all the more deadly because its nature was uncertain, its origin unknown, its purpose and end unpredictable.

Graham raised his glance to a huge map of the globe that decorated one wall of the room. Idly he located the scene of each news item. The points were scattered indiscriminately. Perhaps it was accident that made him recall the hideously pitted image he had found, and its disappearance with his black handbag. Perhaps it was chance that his eyes crossed from London to New York where the trans-Atlantic air liner had fallen. It could only have been intuition that made him extend the general direction of that course to —

Easter Island.

On the next air liner to New York, Mr. Carter E. Graham was a passenger. His luggage was small. It consisted partly of notes, clippings, memoranda, reports, and so on.

At New York he immediately transferred to a cross-continental transport plane. At San Francisco he chartered a trans-Pacific seaplane and instructed the pilot to fly directly to Easter Island in the South Pacific.

And on that long, tedious trip from England to Easter Island, half-way around the world, he spent much of his time piecing together a connected account of his work, and of that life-ambition which now seemed to be so near realization.

X. GRAHAM'S DIARY: THE SEARCH BEGINS

The spaces between the stars or the dark side of the moon may contain mystery deeper and more profound than that which I have met on earth; and in the abysses outside the known universe it is not impossible that stranger horror than I have found may even now be awaiting to engulf whatever traveller spans first the immensity between. These things may be, yet I know not how they can be, or what; for my own eyes have witnessed ultimate evil beyond which I hardly believe it possible to go. Earth has yielded up her greatest enigmas, out of time and space have come such cosmic riddles that the mind bows before them and is overwhelmed, life itself trembles on a pit which there is no comprehending, yet I am uncertain whether I have penetrated or will penetrate to the heart of all secrets. There are many explanations, too many; and how may I know the one that alone holds truth? The very essentials of law and order that life on faith assumes to be unchangeable have been broken while I watched, and that acceptance and unthinking trust which are part of us from birth can never more be my lot. Out of infinite physical weariness and spiritual decay I write, attempting to solve the unsolvable; and what though I succeed? Beyond each puzzle lies another, every explanation raises further questions, and the circle becomes wider and wider until the mind confesses defeat. I feel that I have challenged the titans in my own little fashion, but have I won? Or do they still stand afar and mock my efforts? I can not say.

"Let me begin at the origin of all things for me, and try to bring at least a seeming order out of what I fear to be and for ever chaos. Of my parents I know little for they died during my childhood, leaving me, their single child, a modest but sufficient income. I chiefly remember my father as something of an impractical dreamer, and my mother as a woman worldly wise yet gifted with intuition approaching mysticism. I suppose that I inherited from them my innate love for peering beneath the surface of things, a love which I have nurtured and given free rein.

"The earliest clear memory I have is of my father's death. I remember looking at the quiet, white face and asking mother, 'Why doesn't dad speak to me?'

"And her grave, gray eyes peering darkly into mine as she answered, 'He is dead — he can not speak.'

"'Why? What's death?'

"'Because — because — well, because. Everyone dies.' And the sound of sobbing.

"Everyone dies! I never forgot the words. Even at that early age, I wondered what mother meant. She followed father not long after, and then I realized that this enemy death had taken away those closest to me, those whose understanding was so true that not a single unhappiness had I known.

"What was death? And what was life that it must give way and be conquered?

"I was now alone in the world, so far as intimate companions were concerned. Private tutors instructed me. During my leisure hours I usually read. I early tried my hand at composition, and decided to prepare for a career in letters. By the time I was twenty, I had taken my degree at Oxford. I was familiar with English literature, cherished a fondness for Greek lyric poetry and tragedy, took pleasure in Latin works of the decadence. And the great undercurrent in all these literatures which fascinated me was their fierce passion for life, their piercing regret for olden days and unreturning years. I had delved into philosophy and rejected its innumerable vague answers to the riddle of life and death. I had explored the arcana of religions in an effort to obtain some certainty. Mystic orders and brotherhoods, pagany and christianity, were sifted for what they could offer. Histories of witchcraft and sorcery, spiritualism and black magic were devoured in my insatiable thirst. I read cursorily in different sciences. And for years I met with failure, so I thought; but all the while I was storing away for future use information from many branches of human thought, knowledge, and experience. And the more I knew, the more I came to realize how little I knew, how utterly insignificant was the sum of man's knowledge considering the several thousand years he had had to accumulate it.

"Was there, indeed, a single thing which I did know and did understand completely? The ripple of wind in trees outside my window was no more supernal than the lovelight in the eyes of the beloved, and the annual budding of verdure, the flush of color in a pearl, the pounding of waves on a beach, the pavement beneath my feet were for ever as elusive to understanding as the wonder of birth or the tyranny of death. Each grain of sand no less than the skies above me was possessed of a mystery all its own; and I surveyed with equal awe and delight and curiosity the cities that man had built and the universe that domed them in. Somewhere I felt there must lie an explanation, but always could I go only so far and no further because I became lost in trying to bridge the ages. My attempt to discover the meaning, the why, the cause, the source, call it what you will, had advanced from a hobby to a fever of pursuit. I frequently had the impression that I was, as it were, a detective of time and spirit, engaged in ferreting out the key to a labyrinth that baffled me whichever way I turned. Confusion invariably rewarded me. The problem trailed off into obscurity, vanished before the dawn of history to the mist of unrecorded beginnings.

"I know not where my speculations might have led me if at this time an event had not occurred which changed the course of my life and sent me off on different roads.

"There is so little likelihood these memoirs will be seen by others and read that I will save myself the pain of re-describing a personal tragedy by appending here a short narration of it which I wrote at the time. It seems, as I peruse it again for the first time in many years, curiously unreal and remote; and yet the disaster left an indelible mark, and the sketch that crystallized it came to my aid two decades later.

Myrna

'In the twentieth year of my life, I met Myrna. For the first time in the dark record of my existence, I fell in love, with a maiden whose talents were as unusual as her youthful beauty, and my days were happy. My life till then had been solitary and concerned only with matters of the spirit. I had lived in the realms of my mind, and my mind explored the inner places before it knew the visible world. For years I had walked alone, and lonely, even though I wandered in regions of beauty touched with strangeness where the gods dealt in millions of years instead of twenties.

'But one day, I met Myrna. I had never before come down to earth. When I saw her, I first realized the existence of a visible world about me. I came out of the shadows of my inner realm and in my return to the world I saw objects as physical rather than phantasmal units. And I saw things because I saw Myrna, and seeing Myrna, my thoughts and their regions were a closed book.

'I loved her. I loved her as I never desired anything in the world or out of the world. I loved her with a passion that ran the entire course of human emotion from the physical to the spiritual. I saw her as a material but lyrically lovely girl of soft and exquisite face. I saw her as the perfect embodiment of the beauty that was my ideal. I saw her as the glory that woman may be when her face was transfused with the rapture of returned passion. I saw her as a woman and more than a woman, as the incarnation of earthly beauty and the expression of unearthly beauty that transcends human grasp, the strange and mysterious beauty that comes to us in dreams. She might have been Christabel and Lesbia in one, if so rare a union may be imagined.

'I was idolatrous, I worshipped her, she was godlike and sacrosanct in my blind devotion. I emerged from my isolation and the old worlds crumbled before this fulfillment of sudden, supreme desire. In the delirium and burning rapture of finding tangible expression of intangible fancy, I forgot even the vestige of my former solitary life. I had Myrna. And Myrna was all that I now desired.

'I was happy in those days that I knew her, happy and almost content. The spring and summer passed. I whiled the days away with Myrna in long walks through the woods, or in drowsy indolence on the river bank during hot days; and in the evenings I made love to her, and stroked her crown of gold thick hair, and held her lovely and feverish face in my hands, and caressed her soft cheeks and the lids of her dreamy gray-green eyes. And we were happy. I sometimes whispered of the quest that had drawn me on and of a riddle I sought beyond the stars and of a path I trod from nowhere into nothingness, but I whispered of these things only till I realized that the night was waning and that we had each other. And then we would cease our imaging in the joy of the other, she with rapture in her face and I with that first madness of love in the possession of her who made me of the world, her whose charm and whose beauty were unearthly and perfect enough to draw me from the realm of the unreal to the material world. But there was a paradox and anomaly, I forgot even the world when I was with Myrna, and time did not exist. There was splendor in my dreams for the first time. The problem that had occupied my waking and sleeping hours gradually faded, giving way to beauty and an earthly paradise.

'I loved Myrna, and all through spring, all through summer, we were happy.

'On a dull and melancholy day of early autumn, when flower and leaf again fell before the seasonal processes of decay, she died. She died of a malady that gave no warning and left no trace. She died, in all her beauty and in all the glory of her youth. She died, with a smile on her lovely face, and ecstasy still in her mysterious eyes for me. She whispered sweet and dear phrases of regret even as her eyes were closing. And when they closed for ever, I was standing by her side, and the world dissolved around me.

'What time was it? The cold moonlight streamed in through the casement over the figure of one sleeping. A deathly pallor lay on all the white and silent room. And I was mumbling in my desolation and groping for something that was no longer mine. What was that strange white face on the bed? The hair streamed out in long dark waves over the pillow. What was that white pallor over all the room? But there was a whiter face on the bed, and the eyes were closed. What was that dead thing in the sky? Was it the moon, the blind eye of night? There were dead eyes on the bed, and darker night though all the room was ghastly in the pale moonlight. What was the cold silence outside? There was colder silence in the room, and a cold, still face on the bed. And far away, something was beating on the chambers of my brain and torturing my mind. What had happened? But there was a black pall that covered the cold moonlight, and I could not find my way. Over and over, the tolling of a terrible bell, over and over, the dreadful and regular tolling of doom, over and over, a horrible knell that drove me to frenzy. What was this throttling night, and the monotonous and fearful tolling, tolling, tolling of a bell? But there was a white face on the bed, and dark hair streamed over the pillow. And it was quiet. God! How quiet it was! And the moon made cold patterns of light and shadow on the floor and the walls and the bed. And there was a stranger pattern on the pillow.

'What time was it? Days had passed, for the figure on the bed was gone. But there was a white moon in the sky, and I walked in a solemn place where many people sleep. Where was Myrna? She was mine, and I had lost her. And I had sunk by a bed with moonrays whitening the room and the still form of Myrna who slept the sleep of lilies, with her pure, white face set in the dark hair that streamed over the pillow. But they had taken her away, and she was mine no longer. What had they done with her? They had taken her to a narrower room, where she must lie for ever lonely.

'There was no time. The black years of my life stretched out interminably behind me in their long and endless array. And the black years of the future whirled out into infinitude in measureless eons. And the black years of the present stretched on and on, laboring and slow and incessant, with the seconds dreadful centuries, and the minutes whole cycles, and the hours appalling records of eternity whose end never approached. And I lived on and on, aged and yet enduring longer and more insufferable epochs of my terrible existence. But the moon rode high, and I walked in a place where the people sleep and know not that they sleep. Was Myrna sleeping here? There was a name I found, and there was never another name of those syllables on the tongue of mortal. And I had my Myrna, whom they had placed in a smaller room that stifled her.

'What time was it? The moon, the blind eye of night, hung low in the west like a tired dead thing. The stars were pale. And then I leaned against a stone, and crossed my arms over my face, trembling, and shuddering, and babbling to the night, sick with horror as I remembered the tomb that I had violated and the body I had defiled. And I shook with innermost racking pains and stumbled through the night, crazed and sobbing and vainly attempting to forget the shocking rites I had performed in the sepulchre of Myrna, performed on the body of her whom I had passionately loved in life, and whose love I carried to the grave and beyond the limits of any grave.

'I tossed all day trying to sleep, but my head and eyes were feverish and I got no rest. Toward night, I dozed, but my sleep was a fearful delirium whose images of blasphemous and sacrilegious rites raised their obscene heads, a sleep where nightmare after nightmare stormed the chambers of my brain. I saw graveyards and graves and crypts and sepulchres opening up all around me and stretching away to illimitable horizons, I saw tombstones mounting like gigantic monoliths to the sky, and everywhere I saw the lovely face of Myrna lovely in death as she was in life, and I saw other things that brought me wide awake with my breath coming uneven and heavy while I vainly attempted to shut out the terrific evil images that streamed through my brain like a running corruption.

'I stood by the tomb of Myrna, and the tomb was open. I looked at my hands, and my hands were soiled. And then the horror of the thing swept over me and I turned faint and sick under the dead moon as I realized what I had done. I shook as though my body were trembling in dissolution, I clawed at my face and eyes, I cursed from agony of spirit the world that gave me birth, I thought of the clay of Myrna lying in a violated sepulchre, and my face set in a frozen hideous mask but the bitter tears of anguish burned down my cheeks. Twice had I defiled the little stone house of Myrna as she lay in death.

'What time is it? The graves open up all around me in long and endless array, there is a leer on the face of the worm-king, the tombstones rear their vast white marble to the sky, the dead moon fills the entire heavens in one great blind white eye staring on a chaos of yawning graves and tottering tombstones, and everywhere rises the white face of Myrna drifting in the air and through the sky and on the ground and in the graves, with her dark hair streaming out around her and her figure before me wherever I turn. Is it all a hellish nightmare, a frenzy of grief and a craze of the house of life riven asunder?

'There is blood on the body of Myrna.'

"Across the years comes this cry like an echo of the despair that possessed me. Nearly mad with morbid melancholy and writing such material as would very likely have cost me my liberty had it been read by other people, I yet realized that my only hope of preserving sanity was to forget, to occupy my mind fully so that I could not brood because I had no time to brood.

"I purchased passage to Cairo. Two weeks later, I was treading Egyptian soil. During my journey, I had again worn myself out on the old riddle and tragedy fresh in memory. The white conqueror had obtained the lives of those who had been dearest to me: mother, father, beloved. I vowed that I would devote my years to investigating the nature of spirit and being. I vowed that I henceforth would neither love nor marry, that I would not, could not take it on myself to give to anyone so futile and meaningless and wretched a life as this. I felt like a chessman moved against my will by huge antagonists in a game where neither victory nor defeat mattered, and where the play itself had no sport.

I was crushed. I had little hope that the change of climate and scenery would benefit me, but God knows I would have succumbed to insanity had I remained in that country where every object reminded me of lost happiness and present grief.

"And then one day I stood before the Sphinx."

X. GRAHAM'S DIARY: IN THE HEAVENS ABOVE

That great, enigmatic structure drew me across a gulf of centuries, I was enthralled and quickened by its inhuman stoniness, I puzzled on its meaning and origin and purpose. The lure of Africa and the spell of ancient worlds had fallen upon me. I read with avid interest accounts of the remains of antiquity. I visited them, I delved into archaeology, investigated, explored, excavated. Imagination could offer wonders no greater than those I experienced and saw. I became a student, an expert, forged my way to the front as an authority. But my interest was not in monuments for their own sake, it was for 'the thing behind the thing'. Whence came they and why?

"I studied the pyramids. I went into Tibet and Mongolia. I examined the stone circles scattered in various parts of England, Stonehenge whetted my curiosity still more. I was with Alton-Richey's expedition to Easter Island and spent six months studying its colossal stone platforms and enormous statues. I penetrated the jungles of Yucatan and scrutinized the remnants of Mayan civilization. I ransacked ancient literatures for their meager references to Atlantis and Lemuria. Deserted Angkor-Wat rang to my footsteps.

"Each of these sites and a dozen others that I examined offered questions I could not answer. Why did their builders employ so largely the circle and the pyramid? Easter Island alone was ringed in concentric circles with its inexplicable remains. And whence came a certain singular uniformity in the conception of the builders? Above all, whence came this giantism which was everywhere apparent, this striving to suggest or embody vast size? I thought that there must be a better explanation than those commonly given. And what series of cataclysms or holocausts had utterly wiped out so many of the races that had built them?

"And now I come to the first definite clue I discovered.

"In Paru-Sai in the heart of Tibet, on a great mountain facing, curiously, southeastward, I encountered during my travels a shrivelled old Sekhite, member of a vanishing cult, and found with him lodging for the night. That element which the world would call mysticism in me broke down the barriers that are raised against all outsiders. We talked. In the course of our conversation, I told him frankly of my journeying, of my excavation, of my quest. And when I mentioned my speculation about the origin of these remains, and their vast size, he looked at me with fanatic eyes and in the language of his forefathers called me 'blood-brother'. He disappeared into the chaplet of his cliffside temple abode. He emerged bearing a book with ivory covers lettered in gold, and inside were a score of parchment leaves. Their age was incomputable, their language unknown to me. It looked like a more ancient tongue related to Sanskrit as Sanskrit is to English. The symbols of that language were faintly suggestive of Sanskrit, but rounder, spiralled, more graceful. The wizened Sekhite opened that record out of anterior time and read me a passage, translating as he went. This was what he read.

"*When the stars are set and come to the positions prophesied, then will the dead titans awaken and return again. Earth shall open up. Out of tombs deeper than the clouds are high shall the seven images issue forth at the bidding of the titans. They shall become even as the titans and take their places on Crltul Thr. The waters shall boil, the earth shall split, the lightnings, the rains, the storms shall burst. From their homes in the stars shall the titans descend. All life shall perish, even unto them, from whom it was. These things shall come to pass when the dead titans awaken when the stars are set, lest there come one who pierceth the veil and knoweth their secrets and the secret of secrets even as they. If he challenge them, and if he succeed, then shall the seven images return to stone until their masters summon them again. But woe unto him who faileth; he shall die sundered, his soul and his body shall be claimed of the titans. And the kingdoms of earth shall perish.'*

"This cryptic ritual was almost meaningless to me. It sounded like that vague jargon in which pseudo-mystics have always endeavored to conceal their lack of sincere thought. Yet I was impressed; to such an extent that I made a copy of the passage and a translation of its meaning.

"For several years thereafter, I continued my investigations in familiar and remote corners of the globe. The oldest remains of antiquity, the most primitive monuments of man, were my special study. Originally, I had become interested in archaeology and my morbid desire to know, what is death? But now the thought of my researches became, what is life, and whence came it?

"I sought, I discovered, and I got nowhere. Always there were blind alleys, clues that trailed away into the mists of time, remains from prehistoric ages that told nothing of their builders. Finally, in despair, I shelved my work and accepted a position in the Ludbury College of Historical Sciences.

"While I lectured, I continued my wide reading. I acquainted myself with the electrogenetic theory of life: the theory in other words that what we call life exists only while a positive-negative interchange of electrical impulses occurs in the body. I familiarized myself with the new mathematics, the Einstein theories, and four-dimensional geometry. I sifted the various hypotheses about the origin of the world — the theologic, the nebular, the planetary, and so on. I made a particular study of myths and legends and folklore of all races.

"But all my thoughts and activities produced only the alternative: either human life originated in some spontaneous fashion upon earth; or it was brought to earth from elsewhere. If it originated on earth, I probably would never know how or why; but if it was brought from outside, another alternative arose:

either it came accidentally, on a comet or meteor, or it came as the result of deliberate intelligence. If it came accidentally, again I would probably never know why or how; but if it came as the result of a purposing will or rational intelligence, then there might be hope of progress.

"Here my reflections came to a halt until that fateful day when I read an account of the weird stone image discovered at Isling. The reference to it made the sculpture seem like a duplicate of an extra-terrestrial figurine I had once seen long ago on Easter Island; and so extraordinary was the coincidence that I immediately went to Isling. I not only found that cosmic thing; I discovered a bottomless well that plunged deep beneath earth; and nearly lost my life on my return to London, for when I ran my fingers across a series of fantastic symbols carved in the base of the image, it seemed to me that a monstrous voice grolped thunderously and a terrifying titan mounted hugely and frightfully outside the train window.

"There could only be two possible explanations of that eldritch adventure. I might have suffered a hallucination. That was unlikely; impossible, I should say, in view of the train wreck and the unexplained mystery surrounding it. Or I might have actually witnessed what I thought I had, in which case forces and powers beyond any with which we are familiar had come to devastate the peace of the world.

"Incredible as it seemed, I believed this guess to be correct. And careful recollection convinced me that my manusensus of the cryptic signs carved in the idol's base had summoned the enormous horror.

"But how? I did not believe in spiritualism, and I was positive I had not suffered a mental delusion. Then I recalled one of the simplest of our scientific principles: our wave-theories. The telegraph, telephone, radio, tuning-fork, television, and similar devices are too common to need explanation. But here was the key; my manipulation of the strange characters had acted as a signal; and in response had come the gigantic nightmare.

"What was the image? By what means had the warning been communicated and the colossal entity brought?

"The solution lay in the statuette itself. I had already ascertained that it bore no resemblance to any element or metal or mineral or rock of earth. The answer then must be that it was of some hitherto unknown element of earth, which was impossible; or that it was of non-terrestrial origin, and as such, perhaps not subject to the laws of earth; indeed, it must obey laws that were totally alien to those governing matter and earth as we know them. If this were true, the image must have been brought to the world, planted, as it were, by beings from elsewhere, for some definite reason; a specific purpose of such importance that any tampering with it immediately called forth some sort of guardian. Furthermore, the very nature of the statuette, its freakish properties and sinister vitality, its artistic success, implied craftsmanship deriving from a civilization of the very highest degree.

"The monster that I saw, I reasoned, must be either a guardian, raised by unfamiliar means of cosmic-ray communication of a kind as yet unknown to our scientists, or perhaps the entity itself which had at some time placed the sculpture near Isling. Why had it done so? When had the teleportation been accomplished? For what purpose? And who or what was the demoniacal vision?

"I felt that age-old gods were stirring in oblivious crypts; I felt that the mists of time were lifting to reveal secrets that ought never be known; I walked in an atmosphere of ineffable suspense, with the psychic impression that some unguessable catastrophe was about to overwhelm earth. But what? One can not make facts out of feelings, and my vague theorizing brought only equivocal results.

"Then I recalled that strange, vivid hallucination which I had imagined while I lay unconscious. Some parts of it I could easily explain — the long quest and the defeat were reminiscent of my death-defeated love for Myrna. The tombstones with fantastic carvings were symbolic of the greenish-gray pitted image. But the conclusion of the dream — that appalling vortex to empty space, and the dream-horror of waiting endlessly for the intangible and the unknown — what did these signify? Perhaps, I thought, they interrupted my latent impression that beings from outside were about to return to earth. But why?

"Here again I struck a blind alley. One among a thousand hopeless quests that I had been pursuing all my life. But I continued. I went to the scene of the train-wreck, learned nothing. Later I heard of the fate that had befallen my handbag containing the idol from the Devil's Graveyard.

"I returned to Isling and explored the subterranean well and chamber and corridor which lay underneath the graveyard. Why had the mysterious protecting slab or seal been placed in the passage? I did not know. Perhaps one of the seven images — the one I found — had been preserved in the chamber. But whence came the mammoth heap of bones? They may have been sacrifices, I reasoned, made over a vast continuum of time to some deity, for they comprised modern man and his predecessors back to earlier human remains than any that had ever been previously discovered. The sacrificial cult theory seemed improbable; then it must be that the bones were those of victims captured and brought there. To feed the monster? That was also improbable, unless life itself were some kind of sustenance — to what? The green image? How could the life-flame feed living organic matter, to say nothing of inorganic? Or could stone be organic in a different universe? My head began to spin as if I were going mad. Yet I instinctively knew that I was becoming warmer in my wild, remote detective hunt through time and space, ambiguities were beginning to assume a clear form and a potential substance.

"However, I was so unnerved by the death of my assistant Liska that I voluntarily destroyed all entrance to the underground cavern. How had he met his fate? And what incredible terror had consumed every vestige of his flesh in less than a day? I do not know. But nothing familiar to science could have been accomplished and so eerily that phenomenon. My cosmic antagonist had scored again. For already I sensed that I was, as it were, playing a game of chess, against overwhelming odds and against a supersensible opponent, with all life at stake.

"I thought long over my escape from the corridor — my exit into Stonehenge — the remarkable properties of the slab protecting the well itself. In all these there was definite suggestion of ultra-Euclidean geometry; of the laws, in other words, of a universe or existence differing from ours. More and more strongly, the conviction grew upon me that man's little earth was being invaded by a superior power.

"Stonehenge itself might be a primitive structure erected to the service of monstrous gods whose works were known or suspected to lie underneath. It might even be that the possessors of those innumerous bones, when the clothing of mortality still enveloped them in far-off gulfs of time forgotten, had entered the subterranean necropolis by way of the four-dimensional exit, there to sacrifice themselves or to be slain, having come of their own deliberate will to die, or by compulsion, and their flesh or their inessential being to nourish an unknown corporeal matter or incorporeal presence.

"I next turned my attention to the photographs which I had taken of the markings on the greenish portal to the subterranean necrotomb. I was especially interested in the two sets of astronomical charts. One of these I easily recognized as a plan of the heavens as they are. The other baffled me and caused me a disturbing unease that I could not wholly account for. There must have been a purpose, deliberate, exact, prophetic, behind the two sets; they must have been indicative of some future event of major importance. But my knowledge of astronomy was small, and I could make nothing of them. I simply guessed that since they very likely were related to, or connected with, each other, and since the second diagram marked the stars as they now are, the first might indicate the heavens as they once had been.

"I finally sent them to a colleague of mine, Professor Alex Hrvask, FRS, FRAS, etc. His reply was puzzling. 'The two charts are extraordinary,' he commented. 'One of course exhibits the first magnitude stars in their present positions. The other presents the heavens as they would have appeared half-a-million years ago. I might add that the viewpoint is odd;

as if the stars had been charted by *someone beyond the universe, instead of on the earth.*' The italics are my own. I was so impressed by the phrase that I deeply underlined it.

"One chart of the heavens... As they are... A second chart of the stars... As they would have appeared half-a-million years ago...To someone outside our universe...

"And again inexorable truth forced itself upon me. The first map indicated the period when these unknown titans had first come to earth... And the second map showed when they would return. And the time has come.

"For the stars are in their courses, and already I have seen, if not one of the titans, at least a servant of them. And a hundred newspapers gave out strange bits of information concerning dream-horror that had gripped men and women and children the world over. Prescience — forecast — warning — dreams of titanic entities bloating foully to the stars themselves — visions of megalithic cities whose bulking spires proudly challenged infinity...

"Why have these bodiless lichs come to earth? Why are the dead titans wakening?

"Perhaps I will never know, but I remembered and pieced together bits of scientific information that I had been accumulating for years, and made a hypothesis that is taking me now to Easter Island.

"I conceive of my antagonist as the Old Ones who originally brought life to earth. I conceive of them as having deliberately created human existence. And at the end of five hundred thousand years they are returning — perhaps to survey the result of their experiment, perhaps to destroy it and begin another.

"Five hundred thousand years? Why not? The whole universe as we know it may be but a complex microscopic atom in some part of some super-universe, just as an atom itself may be part of a pebble which is on earth which is part of the solar system — and so on endlessly, beyond the reach of imagination.

"And the full five hundred thousand years of murder and love and hatred and death and birth and invention and slow progress toward civilization might be only a second or a minute in the time-scale of those monsters from the ultra-macrocosmos. A little fly that we know, the ephemeris, lives its full life in a day, and is gone. But to the ephemeris itself, that day must seem as long as man's life of a hundred years does to him. So, to the beings of the greater universe of which ours is only the tiniest particle, our concept of five hundred thousand years may be but an hour or a moment.

"And the pitted stone images are the guides to the experiment of life. Half-a-million years they have lain on earth. It is as if the chemists, those enigmatic giants in a gigantic universe above time and beyond space, to which our universe compares only like a mote to the solar system, had performed an experiment on a speck underneath a microscope in an ultracosmic laboratory; and that experiment resulted in a germ multiplying to millions on millions all in a short hour or day, from the viewpoint of the titans; and now that human life has flourished, the experiment is to be completed — by oblivion? By transmutation? By variation? How can anyone guess? Perhaps that whole atom, our universe, is to be annihilated. Or it may be that they will withdraw the gift of rational existence to organic matter and leave the universal atom lifeless, as preparation for some new and better experiment.

"Herein may lie the key to Liska's death. Were not the corpses of Mr. and Mrs. Grant at Isling found pitted with holes in a shocking state of decomposition? And so also the victims of the trans-Atlantic cabin transport disaster? It is possible that my assistant's body would have presented the same abominable appearance had I found him a few hours earlier. It is my belief that all the grim events taking place throughout central England pivot on the Devil's Graveyard and its buried secret. What more natural, then, than a heightening of tragedy at its very source: so that hideous decay, which required a period of a day or so nearby and elsewhere would need only a few hours for complete disappearance of the flesh at the very heart of the cause — the chamber of the dead, the home of the pitted image?

"But how and why was that dissolution effected? I think that Liska must have discovered some valuable secret, perhaps an essential manifestation of the image or of the titans. Perhaps he was merely claimed as a sacrifice like the vast throng that preceded him. I have wondered... There are mystics who can pass needles through their flesh yet feel no pain because of their nerve-control. There are recorded cases of people who could make livid spots appear or vanish on their bodies at will; others who were able to bleed when and where they wished. I think the titans, through the medium of their abysmal images, may be cannibals of the soul; sucking the life-stream from their victims; and implanting in the nerve-system just before the end so frightful and fiendishly vivid a picture that the body in death realized it, pitting and melting and wasting away in abnormal putrefaction until it consumed itself to the bones, to the very skeletal core.

"Vague, tremendous dreams! Imagination gone mad in an endeavor to think the unthinkable, to encompass more than the universe, more than life, more than thought, within the limits of one finite but yet how infinite mind! What occult and elliptical meaning can there lie behind these abstruse, these abstract symbols and intangible wonders?

"I do not know. But all this eerie play of forces in which I have been swept up now centers around Easter Island. Thither I go, to a spot a thousand miles from other land, and where the ancient titans may have had their prehistoric coming embodied in the huge burial blocks and the lordly statues that strew the entire island.

"What shall I find? Will my lost little ugly beauty turn up there, as I think it might? And shall I see the titans again? Who knows? But the stars are set in the position prophesied long ago by a Sekhite in Tibet, and by the two astronomical charts on the green slab. The time must be very near. For I have known terror, and all the world dreams an evil dream. The dead titans are wakening; a phantasmagoria of the vast unknown frightens man in his days and nights, the more frightening because the origin is so obscure. The gods of legend return. Will their coming bring disaster? A sense of impending horror possesses me. My thoughts are troublous.

"For what shall I do if the beings from a greater universe descend? What can I do? The Sekhite prophet said, Unless one comes who shall challenge the titans and succeed.

"Am I that one? How can I challenge them? — I who am little acquainted with them and comprehend them less. But there ought to be a way, if only because the prophecy has thus far proved true. Obviously, I can not challenge them — if the act be possible on the level of humanity or the world as I know it, for they are beyond earth and follow laws — if they follow any at all — of a different universe, another dimension, a higher complexity, a more baffling structure, than ours.

"Then I must meet them on their own ground. But how? Is there a key or clue among all the weird items I have assembled? I must examine my records carefully.

"And what though I meet the titans and challenge them? To lose were to lose eternity. To win were only to add bewilderment to conjecture. For who are the titans? What is the nature of their universe? How did they come into being and what is the extent of their civilization?

"These questions, I fear, I can not hope to know the answers to. Even if I were to find out all I desire to learn, I would scarce be a bit farther advanced in my cosmic detective hunt. Once I wanted to discover what death and life are, whence we originated and toward what end. Neither earth nor thought offered a valid answer. And if these godlike creatures explain our life, what explains them? A still more gigantic universe in a still more unfathomable plane of multidimensional existence, with dimmer and more recessive reasons to account for the entity of substance completely beyond the deepest and wildest scope of our comprehension?

"What are the titans? Organic matter like human beings, of solid stuff, eating and breathing and living a crazed life till some invisible snuff extinguishes them? Inorganic matter, some doubtful anomaly of mineral compounds imbued miraculously with thinking energy? Or some substance of which we know nothing, some ulterior product of universes, partaking of matter that is beyond our grasp? May they not be wholly insubstantial? Pure energy, pure concept, pure force, intangible, beyond analysis, without definite form or resolvable constituents? If a gas could think, or lightning deliberate, I would understand the titans better...

"But I wear myself out on speculation of a frenzied nature. The irrational has become my substitute for the real. Let the philosophers enter, for I have done with misty enormities. I must make my preparations, if there are any to make; and scrutinize my data for a guide to possible victory when certain defeat is all that anyone could expect.

"Already I seem to see Easter Island looming remotely in the wilderness of waters beeath us. How great the prospect! — Everywhere below a rolling infinity of dark seas, the Pacific in its bleak immensitude, no birds in the skies, and only the sinister cirro-cumulus clouds that change suddenly for gales and storms; it is a wild scene, peaceful at the moment, but peaceful with the treacherous deception of nature that obeys no thought and is beyond good or evil...

"I was right. Easter Island has been approaching for the last fifteen minutes. It is a lonely and isolated spot in the Pacific. I see no other land in this waste of sky and water. The sun sets with a murky splendor; glowing dully, yellowly, in the hazy distances of the orient, even broodingly. There is a great burden of destiny and fate overhanging the world. I know that nature is implacable in its crushingly impersonal existence, but I feel the gloom of all history and the tragedy of all life in these deserted regions where I arrive on a hopeless journey to solve the unsolvable...

"Easter Island..."

XII. EASTER ISLAND: DEAD TITANS WAKEN

The realization that he was alone on Easter Island came as a disconcerting shock to Graham. There had always been natives, and usually a few white men running the Chilean governmental concession.

He had too easily echoed his pilot's "goodbye" when he was finally landed in late afternoon. He found no wood for a fire, but an alcohol cooker sufficed for his meal. Of greater concern was the extraordinary silence of the island: he heard the everlasting wash of the sea, and the dull roar of breakers, but aside from those and the whispering wind — nothing. A sprinkling of stars shone dully far away: the damp atmosphere made visibility poor. He saw no trace of fires anywhere within eyesight; nor heard the sound of a single voice. All this was odd, for inquisitive natives usually were waiting for any arrival, so rare were newcomers to the island.

But no one greeted Graham. He passed a solitary night, troubled with dreams.

When morning came, he began a systematic exploration of the island. He remembered its topography clearly from his previous sojourn. Rano Raraku — there was no mistaking the volcanic king of the island. He got his bearings from it and set out.

At noon, he admitted failure. There was not a single other human being on Easter Island. What had occurred? Had the natives died off since his last visit? Had the white masters then gone back to Chile? Or had disease swept them away? Might some great fear have driven them away? There had been a report in the papers that the island had sunk; a vessel, driven far south of its course in a wild January gale, reported no land where Easter Island should have been. Had the island been engulfed, then spewed forth again by the great waters? Graham doubted it, for patches of grass grew in open spaces, and a few dwarfed pandanus and coconut trees fought for a starved existence.

There never was another so desolate island. It was the barrenest land on all the seas, volcanic, basaltic, black, with porous, infertile soil. Jagged rocks lined its shores, boulders lay thick everywhere, sharp masses sprawled to cliffs that rose precipitous. And from Akahanga along the shore to Toatoa enormous fallen statutes loomed irregularly, titans bowled over, while in the sculptors' workshop on the slopes of Rano Raraku far away hewn and half-hewn colossi looked stonily out to sea. And the eternal ocean beat a solemn requiem on the rocks, a swelling and falling dirge incessantly, day and night, through irrecoverable years, a perpetual chant to the monsters carved out of rock.

Inhuman giants! Immutable mockery of imperious faces that even the ravaging storms and winds could only erode, never annihilate! Who had gouged these titanic blocks of the memorial *anus* from the cliffs? What vanished race had left a heritage of thousands of vast, forbidding sculptures that watched the sea as if waiting — waiting for what? Over all Easter Island had hung an atmosphere of mystery ever since the Dutch navigator Roggewein chanced upon it early in the eighteenth century. Every man who had ever visited that lonely spot in the turbulent south seas of the mid-Pacific felt the pull of its unfathomed riddle, a riddle beside which that of the Sphinx became minor. An army of men working for generations could hardly have accomplished the feat of hewing and erecting these thousands upon thousands of carved basalt and conglomerate statues and memorial cairns. Surely the island could never have supported more than a tenth of the people whose labor would have been required with the primitive tools available. Had less or more than human hands helped in the shaping of those great ones? For that matter, why had the rings of burial piles, the *anus,* been raised and the megalithic statues set up? And why had all this tremendous task been abruptly deserted at its very height so that unfinished titans and roughly cut monoliths sprawled where they had been when work stopped? Half-a-dozen scientific expeditions had gone to the island at various times; but never a one returned with anything more than guesswork and conjecture at who the sculptors had been, and when they had toiled, and for what inscrutable purpose.

And now there was something even more frightening in the aspect of Easter Island, for always before, the few hundred human beings upon it had softened the mental weight of the haughty colossi; but now there was no one else, not a voice or a footfall to be heard, not even the dead body of a single inhabitant to be seen, and the puzzle of their disappearance added another bit to the veiled history of the spot. The wind blew gustily, had been blowing stiffly since noon; whitecaps rose and broke and rose again, and the long surging waves began to boom upon the jagged beach-cliffs and boulders; a strange, shuddering disturbance gave an alien chill to the air. And Graham felt that fear of man in the presence of an unknown and antagonistic universe descend upon him.

He spent the entire afternoon exploring the south coast from Akahangi along the beach toward Rano Raraku. Many a minute he stared at the imperturbable monsters that stood proudly, or lay toppled, yet lordly and conquering even in their fall. The thin curve of lips, the strong nose, the brooding eyes and high cheek-bones were the sculptured record of a race of masters. The sun began to sink westward, and shadows crept along the ground, every hollow held a handful of dusk, a deeper frown seemed to settle upon the faces of the sleeping titans, and ever the wind whispered eerily and the sea thunderously chanted a funeral dirge against those other rocks. Then it was that Graham's heart gave a nervous leap and almost died in his breast, nausea claimed him and he felt the hairs crisp upon his scalp. He had rounded a great boulder near Toatoa, and there in the rubble before him was a deep, recently made rut extending to the shore. But what gave Graham a feeling of supernatural yet terribly physical fear was the unaccountable way in which that deep rut suddenly ended; yet not wholly unaccountable, for the print of a gigantic foot marked a great hole in the iron-hard ground, and a hundred yards inland sank another huge impression that had sheared off and pulverized tons of basalt from one of the largest of the *anus,* and like a tremendous warning those tremendous pits at hundred-yard intervals and more progressed toward Rano Raraku rising sinister in the distance and darkness of twilight. These were fresh made tracks within the day or two; but God in heaven, what hellish entity from nether space and ultimate abysses of macrocosmic infinitudes had spewed from its lair to descend upon Easter Island? And even in that first, trembling moment of shock, Graham sensed the answer, that something had slid ashore out of the seas, and that some nameless lich had met it and borne it to the workshop of the gods on Rano Raraku. He gave one long, apprehensive look at the somber volcanic cone; then, very carefully, he began retracing his steps to his camp. The wind prowled curiously; shadows fast gathered, and his imagination created a dream-horror out of each boulder and every sculpture; but was it imagination that from infinite distance the rocky cacophony of inhuman laughter poured toward him to grate his ears? Surely it must be fancy. The wind had blown suddenly stronger and stronger, or a rock had fallen or the sea had crashed harshly against cliffs that crumbled. Graham gave a quick glance back and upwards toward Rano Raraku, and turned no more. There are some sights that one can bear in daytime, but which at dusk or night, when one is alone in crushing great spaces, point the way to madness. Graham may, or may not, have seen a wild, phantasmal light flowing and glowing and gathering mistily on the peak of Rano Raraku, a light the more terrifying because it was of a color utterly unknown to earth, a hideous, ambiguous color, fluid, vital, corrupt with all decay and everything obscene, a malignant exhalation that had found its way from its home in the stars. It flickered and pulsed evilly in the center of the cone; and to Graham's eyes seemed to extend limitlessly and foully zenithward toward the most labyrinthine regions of ultrastellar space. But of this, or any part of this, he could not be completely sure; for after that one instant of frozen stupefaction, he turned and continued his way back. And the wind whooped dismally, and the restless sea boiled against the bases of black rock-masses, and the stony titans were sentient with shadowy prophecy as he passed them.

The meal he prepared was the most disheartening he ever had, the most joyless; and afterwards, by the light of an electric flash, he pored over certain of his notes, and in the dark hours did a strange thing, moving his lips bizarrely as though forming a series of singular words. It was very late, when he retired; later still before he slept; since, throughout the evening and night that atmosphere of potential forces that hung over Easter Island increased gradually in power and strength so that it seemed as if the air thickened. It was a dead weight, an oppressive burden of fear and suspense, that increased hourly; and miles away, an evil flowing unearthly color played around Rano Raraku and shot toward the remote abysses of empty space, threatening, ambiguous, and malignant with an incorruptible evil more ancient than the peoples of earth or the stars of heaven.

It was a fitful sleep into which Graham finally dozed, a sleep broken by nervous awakenings; and always he heard the rising skirl of winds, and the dull pounding of the sea; and once he sensed the echo of that unknown devilish laughter, mirthless as death, inhuman as oblivion, as stony as the primal rocks; and once he heard the decrescendo of a faint cry; but it was his own voice breaking out in the throes of torturing dream. And far overhead, the vague stars shone hazily, with an unwonted dimness and preternatural weakness, like candles burning low before they flickered quietly out. The loneliness of sea and land and sky was such as he had not believed possible; a complete and unrelieved isolation at which his heart deadened and his spirit sank and the flame of life lessened.

The wind rustled in the pandanus trees, and swished the short grasses; it moaned around the rocks and whined shrilly by the cliffs; and out at sea it blew in great sweeping gusts like the open-stops of an organ in abysmal spaces; and the Pacific roared its eternal answer.

And so at last Graham fell asleep again, and dreamed a dream. He was falling like a comet through the gulfs beyond the solar system; but falling faster than any comet, faster than light itself; hurtling onward at such a terrific velocity that stars streamed by him like the sparks of a pinwheel, while the multiple-ciphered vastnesses of astronomical distances sped past as so many leages. There was a curious illusion: the stars appeared to converge toward him from ahead and expand away from him behind; so that gradually he felt that space had become bent in some abstract manner, curved in a dual way, and curved in a four-dimensioned continuum; and the trillions upon trillions of miles collapsed to the briefest of inter-related arcs; and he was sliding along planes of space, exteriors of time, centuries of light-years in distance, and cycles of geologic aeons in time, all in fleeting seconds and flying miles. And then suddenly the stars had swept behind him; and there were no more; and he plumbed sickeningly a horrible blackness that yet had no existence; a mid-region beyond all known laws or hypotheses of speculative science; and after a formless chaos, there came a sudden, weird pallor; and his dream-self came to rest after the cosmic journey, came to rest on some material substance; and his dream-self saw that it stood on an atom under observation in a laboratory of many infinities; and beyond it was the super-universe; and all the universe it had left, Graham's dream-self realized, was that atom on which it now stood, having emerged through the shell; and that tremendous atom with all its worlds and stars and life and human beings was merely a speck, invisible, ultramicroscopic, in the macrocosmos; and Graham's dream-self trembled in fear; where did the progression end? The expanding universes within greater universes? And his dream-self went sick with a loathly horror at the half-glimpsed vision of the titans, soulless,

inhuman, of a different nature of things and frightful in the
hideous completeness of their wholly alien, wholly abnormal
aspect, for by no human sense could they be comprehended,
they who were outside the range of senses. And Graham's
dream-self, crushed by the enormity of these other-dimensional colossi, trembled; trembled at the heavy flux of forces and
energies and powers that weighted the ether; trembled at the
malefic strength that emanated from those unphysical giants;
trembled at the shifting interchange of circles and pyramids
and points; trembled at the cosmos-assaulting citadels of an
architecture ineffably unstable, unthinkably old, that must
have outlasted the years of oblivion on many earths; trembled
at the deific yet satanic fusion of all things that should not and
could not be, but were, in the burden of nocturnal dreamlands;
and trembled most of all at the purposes beyond this super-universe, the dimly-felt intent of the titans, the appalling madness
of irrational reason and exvoluted civilization which had antedated time and would be post-historic to oblivion, which had
created the dimensions on which their existence depended
and would perdure when the foundations and the strange
spaces themselves had reverted to the negations of rest.

With the fantastic illogic of dreams, Graham's trip and its
happenings had been compressed into an instant; and all that
passed through his head was hardly a ripple on the subcon-
scious mind; and now, with the same paradoxical slowness of
eternity combined with lightning-like speed, the titans became
aware of him; and in the dream he saw their immense statures
bloating to nether skies and abstruser dimensions, shifting for
ever through formless mutations of size and being so that he
could never know exactly what they were; imperceptible to
mortal senses, godlike in their unapproachable nature, wavering through cycles of suggestive outline and whirling in
immensitudes of superior existence, they were above apprehension. But they knew of his presence, and he knew that they
knew; and a wave of hate and black triumph surged from them
as some invisible miasma, and they moved, these mountainous
things, with the instantaneous rapidity of thought; and in the

dream Graham felt a terrible fear grip him, and all the horror of dream-immobility lay upon him as he tried to fly but could not; and then again the illogical blank, the transference of events; and the sensation of falling from heights above to abysses below.

Graham awakened with a dry, burning skin, and gasped in the weakness of the aftermath; and heard the dreary swoosh of the growing winds, and the sullen crash of waters; and slept anew.

He dreamed a dream. He walked in the dark places, and from afar came low, ironic laughter; he walked for hours, and sometimes ran, sometimes halted, listening intently; but whether he walked or ran or halted, the brutal laughter echoed in his ears; nor could he discern a single object in the wilderness of gloom; yet he walked on. And the dark places grew darker, and the gusty laughter accompanied him, voiced but voiceless, without meaning. And then by his side walked Myrna; and he was uncomforted, for the antagonists chuckled mirthlessly as ever before. Side by side they walked, and the darker places grew darkest, and torment assailed him. But there was quiet in Myrna; so quiet. He was comforted. Had he lost her? It was long ago — an old dream that was false. This was now; and Myrna walked beside. His hunger deepened in him; this was now, all else, all past, all dead, but the dream of a dream. In the darkest places his heart cried out; and the haunting, remembered, forgotten face uplifted, with the shadowy eyes darkening into his; and in the ecstasy of the quiet he bent over and kissed the bloodless lips; and his mouth felt the cold bone, and his eyes peered into empty sockets, and his face brushed the fleshless skull, and his arms held the crumbling frame. And distant laughter sounded in his ears...

And from the skiey fastnesses a pillar of weird radiance pulsed into the heart of Rano Raraku, and deepened hourly in its baleful strength.

And in the gray dawn, Graham wakened, with the terrors of darkness and dream changed only for those of light. He arose as exhausted and high-strung as if he had passed the sleepless vigil of insomnia. Instead of feeling refreshed, he was weary, his mind perplexed with the equivocal shapes and the prophetic recollections that had obsessed his inner consciousness. In the dim mist of morning, the bulking masses of rocks and stone titans loomed mysterious, impressive, with a threat of superhuman reality.

The wind had grown to a steady blow, fine spray dampened the atmosphere, a spume of foam and dull waters broke on the black cliffs, ocean roared farther out, and the white-caps crashed from higher. As Graham stood up, a giddiness came over him, as if the island had shaken beneath his feet. There was a wild and tumultuous note abroad; the wind whipped his face, and with it came a foreign element, an uncertain quivering, a restrained turmoil, like a fitful breath of autumn underlying a wintry gale. A cirro-cumulus bank domed the firmament far above, but low overhead a wrack of smoke-dun clouds raced madly northward, driven by what might have been a forty-mile wind; and in the contrast of the high, serene, cloud-arch with the nearer flying wedges, Graham saw another portent of struggle to come; for the placidness of cirro-cumulus clouds in the Pacific is a deception of nature, forecasting storms and violent changes of weather.

To the resounding background of sea and wind that beat upon barren Easter Island, Graham started out in early morning and walked along the giants' memorial graveyard. The Cyclopean monuments and statues seemed inordinately oppressive; and their very presence was a load that overcast his thoughts. For two days he had not seen a human being, or heard a human voice. His sole company was this profusion of stony monsters and huge burial piles that repelled him oddly; imperious faces, all, gazing blindly and impassively into what eternities, what infinities, what unreturning oblivions? Had there been means of escape, Graham might have left instantly; but a seaplane was not to come for him until the following evening; and since he must remain here, he was grimly determined to face whatever happened.

Where treads of Juggernauts gouged deep into earth, he paused for a while; speculating dubiously as to what should be his course; and the Pacific surged defiance and the southwest wind whooped harshly; and in the irregular transitions from amber to gloom as clouds obscured the sun, Graham watched the shadows shorten; and finally he decided. Having nothing to lose but life, he set off toward Rano Raraku, following the huge holes that pitted the basalt at long intervals of a hundred yards — colossal strides of colossal limbs! In the light of morning they had lost none of that ominous aspect which had invested them the night before. If anything, they became pregnant with diabolic implications. There is an inevitability about terror and darkness; but the anomalies of day, the fearful unrealities that intrude upon the normal world are more fatal by far to mental security. Himself the only man upon the island, and his carefullest scrutiny having shown him no single other living creature of land or sky, Graham already had experienced the depression of lonely solitudes; a loneliness emphasized by turbulent waters and the stiffening wind; and now doubly lonely in the presence of a new menace — the thing responsible for these pits. Into his mind flashed a memory of the devil-god he had discovered at Isling; and he remembered again the gruesome suggestion it gave of being pitted all over. He wondered idly if there were any connection between the statue and these treads. It seemed preposterous — but could anything be really preposterous after what he had gone through, and when the universe itself consisted of the inexplicable added to the incredible?

He strode on, shaking his head as if to rid himself of fruitless thoughts. The ground rose more steeply. The sea surged its distant and sullen requiem. Graham's face began to smart from the sting of particles of sand that the wind blew against it. The patches of sunlight became fewer and more infrequent, giving way to an autumn grayness. There was the strangest sky he had ever seen, far down on the western horizon a sinister black edge, and in the farthest east a rim of woolly white, but directly overhead a fury of storm clouds driving wildly northward as though in pursuit or flight.

Graham strode on, over rocks and boulders, scrambling up steep ledges and crossing grass-plots. Here the titans were fewer, but the holes occurred with mathematical precision, here sinking deep into basalt, there pulverizing a mammoth boulder, next obliterating half of a rock ledge. Surely the limbs or the force that had gouged these pits must have been tremendous!

The gashes continued straight toward Rano Raraku, and up its slopes to the cone. Graham followed them, looking sharply around him as he traversed the sculptors' workshop. The outer slope of the volcano was covered with finished and partly finished titans, perhaps the oddest display on all earth. Most of the statues had fallen, and lay helpless, yet suggesting at the same time reserves of dormant power. A few had settled waist-deep; they looked if they were emerging from the womb of earth in stony resurrection. Their eyes stared expressionless toward the Pacific, facing land where land there was none for fifteen hundred miles. On what sunken continents had their gaze been fixed centuries ago? Or did they watch invisible worlds, awaiting the summons to life? Graham thought of the poet's mystical song; monster gods, that was what these were, primal gods that the unknown Ancient Ones had left in prophecy of their return. The haughty countenances were those of a superior race, an alien race, a race of conquerors: the imperious brows, the downward-curving thin lips, the firm nose, these were superhuman characteristcs, never those of mortals. Domination inhered in the gigantic stature of the figures, their bulking hugeness. A grotesque touch was added by the flat-backed heads which gave them a slanting angularity that definitely removed them from the sphere of human things. Majestically looming erect, or lying where they had toppled, or partly buried in rubble, or tipping at a tangent, whatever their individual postures, singly and in mass they presented an aspect of alien and insensate superiority. This was more than the sculptors' workshop: it was a graveyard of gods, a memorial mausoleum of dead titans for all the ages.

The wind blew with still increasing force, eddies whirled against Graham, he heard the eternal dirge of seas that pounded afar. But even though he surveyed with quickened interest this riddle that he had not seen for a dozen years, there was no slackening of his stride. The great holes continued beyond the great statues, and parallel to their course he followed, past the giant figures and up the last slope to the rim of Rano Raraku where the pits disappeared beyond.

Perhaps Graham had speculated on what he might or might not find; perhaps he had anticipated more or less than he discovered. He could not say, for his attention was completely drawn by the unreal reality before him.

The crater of Rano Raraku spread below him much as he remembered it, but with a difference. His heart seemed to leap in his breast, then subside and throb heavily, slowly. For his lost image of the greenish-gray material and the repellent appearance stood in the very center of the crater upon an enormous block of similar material, and the great holes he had been following ended before this altar. But it was not merely the re-discovery of his devil-god that brought him to a halt. The statuette squatted evilly on its base, and it whirled through the malefic cycle of its transformations, a blur of energy and shifting outlines, from beast to man to stone to nightmare, from pygmy to giant to space run wild, curving and collapsing and surging through angles, solids, and spheres in the difficult geometry of a universe beyond ours. It glowed with radiance of a color that did not appear in the spectrum. A baleful fire rippled into it and from it, a fire painful because of its intensity, appalling in its nameless uniqueness. The idol emanated a spectral glow, the block underneath pulsed with the same indeterminate flux, and from both or toward both leaped a gigantic pillar of unearthly sheen upward and outward beyond the infinities of space. Graham's eyes ached as he peered overhead at this phenomenon, and saw how it pierced the clouds; and something tugged at his heart as he noticed that the driving wrack could not close that gap. A force greater than nature was at work. He knew intuitively

that the idol was sucking vigor and guidance across the abysses of space in that stream of baffling phosphorescence. Even as he looked, he thought he detected a gradual thickening of the pillar, an intensifying of the unknown color, a wider range in the metamorphoses of the idol.

He lurched drunkenly ahead. He struggled to regain his composure. What had happened? The sea thudded viciously, the wind whipped stronglier, but it was not these. The whole island shuddered, a sickness swept him, and a gagging fear. Would Easter Island sink? Other lands had gone down in the Pacific; and twice already he had experienced the heave of shaking earth. Yet there came never a waver in the glimmering pillar, nor the faintest sign of effect on the devil-god; save that slowly and visibly their mutations broadened.

With that, Graham plunged forward. There is a kind of terror that draws its victim as a candle attracts moths: unwilling, yet fascinated by the shining death that awaits. He had formulated no definite plan, but he had to destroy that sinister thing somehow before its potentialities became actual. He slid down the inner slope, stumbled to his feet on the ancient lava bed. The detritus of centuries had accumulated, but jagged scarps and sharp rocks protruding at intervals made walking difficult. He was hardly aware of these things as he advanced toward the altar, the idol, and luminous misty pillar. The unearthly fire completely circled the greenish block on which the idol rested, extending a dozen yards beyond it in all directions.

Graham halted at its fringe. Little more than a pace in front of him, the color out of space beyond emerged from the abysses above and ended on the dark, hard ground, terrifying in its magnitude, flowing from nowhere and ceasing at the strange little statue. His eyes burned from the effect of this impossible sight: a new color behaving in an unpredictable manner, as far beyond radio-active rays as they are beyond ordinary fire. He saw the idol rush through its cycle of transformations, so that he became almost hypnotized in trying to follow it. There was mockery in the thing — he sensed mirth where there was no life, imagined a smile on its ugly features.

Hatred and rage possessed him. He lost his coolness and sprang forward. It was like hurling against a wall of rubbery glue. He could no more force his way into the circle of that radiance than he could have pushed over the Dover cliffs. At the end of ten minutes, perspiring and numb with the nightmarish incongruity of it all, he gave up. And still the aching glow increased, the idol whirled incessantly, ever the wind skirled and the south seas pounded.

And so Graham turned at last and hurried back to his camp. From his supplies he made a hasty selection, then retraced his steps. He had lost his conception of time. Hours or cycles or minutes might have passed before he again crossed the rim of Rano Raraku. The preternatural strength of fever impelled him. He cursed the monotonous roaring of the sea, the maddening push of the wind, the everlasting gloomy skies, the loneliness and wildness. He would go insane if this struggle continued much longer. Every move he made was blocked by the antagonists. He began to feel himself a pawn in a chess-game of gods. And the frenzy of the elements conspired to lash in him a greater turmoil.

During his absence, the phantasmal luminence had swelled, the idol pulsated with more vital energy. Deliberately, yet swiftly, like one in a dream, he set down his burdens. With a determination to conquer the idol at any cost which had become a mania that monopolized his actions, he inserted a clip of dum-dum cartridges in his sub-machine gun and raised it to his shoulders. The vicious rat-a-spat-tat cracked forth sharply. He swung the gun slowly in a five degree arc till the clip was exhausted, raking the region around the idol.

He could see no change whatever in the gyrating blur of the idol, no diminution in the color out of space. He walked toward the scene of devilish manifestation and halted at the edge of the fluid circle. His spent cartridges lay scattered along the ground for a dozen yards or more. Their noses were not flattened, nor even dented. They simply had been stopped by an insubstantial solid.

Without giving himself time to think on what this phenomenon might signify, he returned to his firing place, and gingerly carried the burden that he had left there to the edge of the ghastly color, lowered it carefully, and hastened away after lighting a fuse. The stuff he tamped in was Erthorum, an explosive of such power that one pound would blast out a cubic acre of rock. He had just time enough to reach the volcanic cone when a terrific detonation deafened his ears. He flung himself down. A great wind roared by him. Gouts of earth and masses of rock shot through the air. He smelled the pungent odor of gases as a yellowish cloud billowed toward him. Screaming pebbles pelted him, he felt blood where a splinter raked his face. For one instant there was utter silence after the blast: then the winds whooped louder than ever, the island swayed convulsively again. As soon as debris ceased to rain down, he raised himself to see what damage he had done.

The Erthorum had blown a large crater; and that was all. Not the change of an inch in the pillar of eerie radiance, not a mark on the evil idol, not even a newly-blasted rock lay within the circle.

Complete despair overcame him. What could mortal do against the magic circle?

A gyrating reverberation rumbled around him – like the echo of an exploding volcano, or the slide of riven mountains, or the laughter of stony-hearted stone-faced megalithic gods.

As if that deafening sound was a signal, the column of radiant energy began to expand its radius with a slow and inexorable widening of the circle. The shining ineffable evil light crept outward inch by inch, foot after foot, and as it flowed outward while the circle expanded, step by step Graham retreated before it. The flight of the storm-clouds became a rout, the wind howled shrilly, the seas assaulted with fiercer insistence the citadels of cliffs. The skies were arched with cyclonic black, ominous with a wakening fury. One heavy shadow darkened the ground, a thickness of murk obscured all Easter Island. But the endless tower of light palpitated with unholy ardor, encroached upon the barren spaces around. And in the heart of the baleful glare, the green idol flickered madly through hateful new vicissitudes of fluctuant being, a paean of diabolism, a savage fury of power running wild.

The living circle widened with a motion as continuous as time, and densened even as its dimensions increased. A luminous mist clouded the idol within, its outlines became vast, shadowy, an implacable smile of triumph formed upon the pitted features. To Graham it was as terrifying a spectacle as a specter of death made visible, with the greenness of corruption, and the rotting pockmarks of decay, and the cold inhumanity of the grave. But this was death in life, or life in death, and from a world beyond; he felt like the merest grain of sand, in the presence of this corrupt thing that bloated through its recurrent series of transmutations, and the pillar of indefinable fire whose immense girth was as nothing compared with the topless bolt that pierced the clouds and shot toward infinities of the cosmos.

And ever the sentient circle expanded, and drove Graham back to the rim of the crater, and over its edge, and down the slopes of Rano Raraku, past the ancient sculptures. One by one, they were swallowed within the circle; foot by foot the consuming cold fire followed after the fugitive. Never turning to find his way, Graham stared almost hypnotized at the monstrous prodigy; and always he backed toward the sea, for nothing human could withstand the deadly methodic march of the energized radiance. As the stone giants came within the circle, a sinister and significant change occurred; they seemed to absorb the strange force like a sponge water; and the color and the light rippled cloudily around the fallen ones, and they became electric with portent, and a dun pallor came upon the great faces, and the light pouring upon them was as the breath of creation upon rock and dust, or the animating force upon chaos. Was it illusion that the rough-hewn limbs filled out and a nervous disturbance shuddered across the titans? But the surging fire crept beyond them, and they brooded mysteriously and deeper within, and the swirling mists made them as foggy and vague as that Medusa that writhed in the heart of the flame.

The outer world perished for Graham's senses. Nothing existed but this enigma of time and space and spirit and matter. The strain on his eyes grew intolerable, his head ached, a sick dizziness gripped him, he thought that myriads of incandescent specks shot through the mist and the radiant color. And ever the vast wall forced him back, ever the endless pillar advanced, drawing unguessable stores of power from a reservoir that no one knew. At long last, the thrill an excitement of his cosmic detective-search were changing to defeat and fear; for the antagonists had moved, and in a way that baffled him, and he felt that this was the end.

Back, ever back, as in a mad delirium, neither knowing nor caring whether he hurt himself on obstacles, down the last slopes of Rano Raraku, and across the sparsely-covered flat places, Graham was steadily compelled to retreat. And the color out of space followed irresistibly. Once his nerves gave way and he hurled himself against the supernormal essence, and clawed at the fluid light; but he might as well have battered the strongholds of eternity, for the stuff was neither solid nor gas nor anything within the range of human experience; an unknown element soft as decay, impenetrable as oblivion; and so cohesive that he could not make the slightest impression on it. And it was as cold as a dead rat's belly; and the horrible substance chilled him curiously, at the same time sending a million particles of frozen fire to bubble in his blood; and even as he strove against it, he was pushed back and back.

Thus he returned to the beach cliffs with a lambent wall following him; and in his heart fell a bitterness that he would be defeated without having an opportunity to challenge the gods in answer, be pushed step by step into the dark waters of the Pacific while Easter Island was reclaimed by its creators. The now colossal tower of shining phosphorescence had a diameter of miles; and Graham found time to wonder and to marvel as he was pressed beyond the jagged rocks, beyond the rings of burial *anus* to the beach. The last statues were swallowed, the memorial piles passed into the devouring circle; and Easter Island to its very edges was centered by a limitless monopyre that traversed the skies above and the stars beyond. In this his moment of despair, when the column had extended its sinister glare to the final fallen giant and the outermost necrolith, as the sea was roaring at his heels, and when he was ready to abandon his weary struggle, there came to him an illusion that the color out of space was receding.

He halted, and saw that he was wrong, but neither was the element advancing farther. Had the hideous light expanded consciously, deliberately, to encompass the relics of antiquity which lay all around? And having done so, was its purpose finished? What would happen next?

In the unexpected relief and renewed apprehension of the moment, he suddenly became conscious again of the external world. He was soaked in spray, the breakers crashed higher than he had ever seen them, a dull, incessant roar issued from the Pacific. The waters farther out boiled and heaved, the ugliest sea in a decade was raging higher and harder every minute. His skin smarted from the sting of the wind: it howled steadily, lashed the waves to greater fury, whipped sand and foam against him, a gale the fiercer because it was deflected around the shining pillar. Overhead, the skies hung solid black, between blinding flashes of lightning that mazed the clouds at intervals. Graham had never before witnessed such a hell of elements, a madness of nature that he had scarcely believed possible. His loneliness depressed him, and in the presence of this savagery he felt that his mind must succumb. The scream of the gale, the booming of the seas, the exploding staccato reverberations of thunder deafened his ears so that they buzzed dully.

But above all this hurricane rose a sound that sent shivers racing across his flesh, a sound infinitely distant and faint, but one that neither sea nor atmosphere could drown out. Where had he heard it before?

"N'ga n'ga rhthl'g clretl ust s g'lgggar — " He had ridden toward London with a little greenish devil-god — and a throaty animal voice had ruttled acrss the moors, spewing a gibberish of senseless syllables —

"Septhulchu nyrcg s thargoth k'tuhl s brogg – " From infinitely far away, yet increasing in crescendo, the same jargon of consonants inhumanly uttered from the throaty depths of some foul, enormous lich.

Graham's eyes glazed from the rigidity of his stare, his face set in a catacleptic immobility that was as hard as the statues themselves. He saw the mammoth pillar brighten until its baffling and blinding nameless color burned with the incandescence of universes aflame, and in its very heart the abominable image hurtled into its supreme transformation and became frightfulness incarnate, beyond the most bestial distortion imagination could invent, a living, laughing eldritch nightmare whose mirth was born of madness and gigantism of other star-systems in super-universes. Incredibly the space-annihilating pillar contracted, involuted to a vortex of multiple dimensions, arced through immensities of space and bridged eternities. The remote voice rorked louder, from the other end of the flaming flux beyond the range of senses shot a colossal amorphous obscurity. Lightning fretted the black tapestry of heaven, every statue on Easter Island dazzled with molten-white bolts that streaked and flashed around it. Had they moved? Did the stony features emerge from the sleep of centuries and milliards? Did the breath of supersubstantial life animate the dead forms that had outlasted living mortality and transcended the diuturnity of time? The dead titans wakened, and the vast figures arose, and the rigid faces relaxed in the implacable impersonal stare of soulless gods. They wakened, and even as they waked the spell of the pitted monster was upon them, and they bloated to the immeasurable horror of that age-old corruption. The gigantic pillar of fire swelled to a destroying evil, and from the universe outside the titans entered through the door they had opened at the birth of a planet, and closed, and now were opening again. Graham witnessed the appalling loathliness of the thing that had swollen to the heavens when he peered through the window of his train, saw it and all the sick frightfulness of the titans that wakened and the titans that returned.

" — meargoth s bh'rw'lutl ubcwthughu dägoth — " This was the prophecy of their coming and the husky voice defiled the atmosphere once again. This was the awful fulfillment of the prophecy, and the monster-gods emerged from the hidden places. Universe was linked to universe, worlds within and worlds without, and the master chemists from their alembic of galaxies and their laboratory in the ultracosmos returned to analyze the results of their experiment. In ways beyond comprehension they had managed to bridge trillions of light-years in the briefest of moments, to break down the secret of the atom under their microscopes, and to send their own contracted forms into the complex heart of that atom which was Graham's universe. But if these colossal nightmares were in size only a minute fraction of the real titans, what unimaginable excesses of giantism were they in their true and undiscoverable form?

And now every stone sculpture was a living demon, and the massy monuments of Easter Island ponderously rose erect, and hundreds upon hundreds they ringed the symbol-statue that had given them being. The circle of titans was only less than the circle of mystical flame, and the flame was only less than the monstrosities that descended from the stars with the speed of cubed light, and ring upon ring the Great Ones returned and the carved ones arose for whatever purpose of theirs, beyond conjecture, inconceivable, defying logic, transcending the limits of thought. Implacable eyes stared beyond Graham and fixed on invisible worlds across the wilderness of waters, frozen faces set in the imperturbability of conquest, thin lips curved with the cynical brutality of gods come down from the high places to trample dust into oblivion. The thunderous voice rumbled a chant, a ritual, a command, opening the way for invaders, summoning dead clay to hideous resurrection, tolling the doom of planets and foreshadowing the extinction of life, a cacophony of sound that wrought miracles with pitch and inflection as light-rays bring a black paper into pictorial existence.

The pillar was a leaping maelstrom of corrupt color, fogs of somber splendor irradiated its length, it burned like an amorphous vortex where all the strangeness in the known world united with all the unknown outside. And the stony giants stood with the weird pallor of their new life hazing their faces, and a glimmering misty illuminence drifting around them; and the masters, the Great Chemists, titanic and terrible, loomed in the flame, expanding even as the devil-god had expanded to the stars, and vacillating through cycles of unnatural change, greenish and repellent, pitted with the gouges of dissolution and travestying normality with a subtle commingling of all that was highest and lowest in man, beast, spirit, stone, and gaseous protoplasm.

A last harsh jargon of syllables broke forth, the subhuman voice rorgled a crarking heterogeneity of consonants. Scarcely had the mighty sounds crashed out when the titans gathered as though at a signal to spew from the lurid pillar, or to accomplish whatever inscrutable purpose had brought them. The circle slowly, but with an acceleration that promised no limits, commenced to widen. Graham shrank as he saw it leap toward him; and in that interminable instant he visioned the circle rippling like a putrid wave across the cities and countries of earth, with the invaders, the attackers, the antagonists, the dead titans, reclaiming their own in one holocaustic orgy of cataclysm and Armageddon.

Automatically his mouth opened — but not for any despairing cry: a gibberish of unfamiliar phrases answered the monsters, their own unintelligible symbols were flung back to them, but with a difference; whatever difference existed between the characters on the upper half of the slab at Isling and the glyphics on its lower section. For Graham had reasoned that the auditory counterparts of the first group controlled and set in motion through some superior manipulation and control of obscure laws such forces as those he witnessed; and that the second sequence might logically be the key that would prevent those forces from becoming wholly realized. Until late at night he had sat up, memorizing the symbols and

Professor Alton's reconstruction of their sound. He knew that there was nothing else within human knowledge or experience to employ against these superphysical entities: only their own discoveries could combat them, only the extranormal could resist the extranormal. But would the trick work? Had he read the inscriptions correctly? Could his faint counter-attack and almost hopeless ruse achicvc anything against creatures of such god-like omnipotence? Desperately he shouted the symbols that controlled immeasurable energies; with agonized tenseness he watched for results.

As the consonants and throaty words of the incantation issued, he thought that he saw a suggestion of grim irony twist the features of the titans, then heaven and hell met on earth. The circle of fire surged over him and he found himself within. A cold and congealing ichor froze him in terrific flames of no heat, sparks like galaxies of falling stars danced whirling dizzily around him. At the same moment, the entire sky-vaults blazed with sheeted lightning, thunder crackled incessantly, the wind stormed to a shrill, prolonged scream. A strange and shuddering disturbance rocked Easter Island — the waters of the South Pacific boiled with a black and sinister fury — the island swayed and rocked again — in that terrifying moment before Easter Island was swallowed he saw the ocean mount gigantically far overhead — a quivering wall of toppling waters hung all around him — hurricanes and tornadoes and cyclones howled into wld destruction — a profound and collapsing blackness overwhelmed him — the world was a sound and a frenzy and an evil dream that the titans and the raging elements obliterated as Easter Island sundered and sank to its grave while the echo of mirthless mad gigantic laughter died in Graham's unhearing ears.

XIII. GRAHAM'S DIARY: WORLD WITHOUT END

From **too great a tragedy,** from too deep a fear, from too frightful a shock, it is difficult for the mind to recover. I wonder if this explains the utterly shattering experience that I now seem to be going through? Or is it still a dream from which I shall happily awaken? I have seen the impossible become the real, and the real become only the expression of a madder incredibility. Where will it end? This delirium of fantasia extends upon itself, lengthens beyond time. The nightmare grows with that steady, persistent, cumulative horror that the most terrifying dreams impart, so baffling are the events in which I am now involved, so far from comprehension. And I, like the victim in the nightmare, am spellbound, unable to flee, compelled like a pawn to move by another volition than mine. Only, for me there is no waking.

"That last, eternal hour on Easter Island — how can I forget it? Or how can I know the entirety of what happened? The coming of the titans, the surge of cosmic forces that overwhelmed me — and that gradual, quivering, sickening lurching motion of the island as it began to sink — indeed I can remember those. But afterwards —

"The strangest sense of suspended animation came upon me. The world wavered and turned to mist. A shadowy vast gulf enfolded me. Time ceased. I had no consciousness of space or being. I simply was, for the briefest yet inexplicably unending of seconds. The titans had vanished, weirdly, as they came. I had challenged them, and I had won. Yet I bore no feeling of triumph. A pregnant unease, a great doubt, possessed me. And that wild phantom mid-region of inertia in which I was cloudily trapped — was it the vortex of the flame and the color out of space? The flux where time and space united with multiple dimensions and darker powers in the laws of a greater universe, or at least a universe whose properties are wholly different from ours? I do not know. I was in a state of conscious death, unable to move, feeling the drift of tremendous alien energies, but powerless; my very life and being seemed to have been caged in an intangible prison — almost stolen from my body. I swayed like a weed in the grip of green ocean-currents, drifting slowly through long years and over wide expanses.

"For what length of time, I repeat, or in precisely what manner this feverish condition persisted, I do not know: though always there was a drone in my ears, and a curtain of haze before my eyes, and particles of fire like stars, but cold, whirling in confusion through me. And then these all died away, and there was blankness. And then I had a sensation of falling from a great height, and for a long time as in a vision. And then cold water soaked me, and I opened my eyes after the icy shock, and found myself floating on the sea, with the blessed golden light of day around me. A speck in the heavens grew larger, dropped toward me, and I rejoiced that I was saved.

"The speck came to rest not far off and I remember thinking what an odd looking craft it was — I had never seen so odd an airplane. There were no motors that I could discover, yet it was as big as a trans-Atlantic amphibian. It was long and narrow, too, with a stream-lined hull after the fashion of some futuristic designs I once examined.

"A door opened in its side, and a man stepped out and walked toward me. And so astounded was I that I gasped — I swallowed inadvertently a quantity of salt water — and choked violently: *for the man walked through the air toward me!* It was an uncanny sight that almost destroyed my belief in my sanity. Moreover, he was as grotesque a man as I ever knew, with an oversize head, and a shrivelled, gnarled body, and spidery limbs, and big, deep eyes. He looked deformed. But I thought my eyes had played me a trick about his walking on air, and the relief of my being saved after so nerve-crushing an experience made me overlook his defects. And then he stood *above* me, and I could only stare, stupefied. And then he spoke to me, in soft, liquid words that I did not comprehend. I shook my head as best as I was able, lying on my back in the water. He looked astonished. I asked him a question in English — Spanish — German — French — Italian — even   Latin   and Swedish and a little imperfect Arabic and Chinese that I had picked up — but he only looked more puzzled. Finally he floated toward me and offered me his hand. It was time this silly fantasy ended, I decided, and grasped the hand. I was amazed to find it real. I was more bewildered than ever when this frail creature lifted me and walked through air back to his curious craft. I laughed hysterically at the absurdity of it, the pent-up strain of my experience was relieved in a burst of frenzied mirth. My rescuer looked at me gravely, curiously, with a query in his deep eyes.

"So I was taken aboard, and met several others of these peculiar persons. And not a word could I understand of their speech, and they in turn seemed unable to make sense of anything I said. By now I was both mystified and a bit apprehensive: the whole incident was exceptional, as if I were a visitor from Mars, but the same old sun shone in the skies and the breezes blew fresh as ever of old, and salt with the tang of the sea. In the end, we were reduced to the most elementary of communication methods: he would point to an object and name it, and so, arduously, we built up a small vocabulary of nouns, writing them out as we pronounced. It was much harder to get the verbs, but we succeeded in solving the common ones, like 'to walk', ' to eat', 'to write', 'to speak', and so on. The written symbols I saw were as unfamiliar as the words I heard. They looked more like a highly developed phonetic script than anything else.

"In the meantime, he had closed the cabin door and pressed a series of simple dials; apparently without further attention, the ship rose and winged its way toward its destination which, I was glad to see, lay somewhere northeast. The other occupants surveyed me as curiously as I them; and I found even their garb exotic, with its Grecian tunic effect. I judged them to be intelligent, because of their uniformly large heads and their fluently articulate conversation. I can not convey the uneasiness that the scene conveyed me: the spindly men, their new language, the bizarre craft, the meaningless objects that adorned it, and everything so vividly real that I knew I was not dreaming; and yet so different from earth as I knew it that I began to believe the titans and the vortex has transferred me to another planet. To satisfy my curiosity, I managed with extreme difficulty to ask my rescuer what planet we were on; and I was certain that he thought me demented or perhaps actually a visitor from other worlds, but he told me this was earth, and I was more baffled than ever. Then I asked him another question, with I know not what hesitation and equivocal fears, what year it was, and he answered — I could see that it was with considerable surprise — the year 501,950.

"The year five hundred and one thousand, nine hundred and fifty! Surely he must be jesting, or had I misunderstood. I questioned him frantically — there was no mistake. A wave of the worst loneliness I ever had plunged me into an abyss of melancholy.

"If he was right — and good God how I prayed that he was wrong, or that I dreamed a dream, or that madness afflicted one of us! — I had somehow been projected a full half-million years into the future. That leap into time would explain the unfamiliarity of my surroundings, but it left me an avatar, a freak, an outcast in a world I did not know. The worst of it was that I could not tell my predicament to him; and even if we had been able to converse easily, I doubt whether I would have spoken. A man from half-a-million years back? Preposterous! I could see the pitying glances as I was sent to an asylum. Who would credit my story? What explanation could I possibly give when I was unable to gloss matters to my own satisfaction? Better to let them draw their own conclusions, or treat me as a victim of amnesia.

"Then I thought again of my rescue — how had that so providentially been effected? Perhaps I might find a little light there. Eagerly I quizzed Moia Tohn — which I had elicited to be his name — asking him how he had chanced upon me. His halting answer was not easy to grasp, but I managed to discover the gist of it. He had been piloting the seaplane when suddenly on his telephoto plate flashed a picture of a falling man. Most remarkable of all, he had been looking at this plate, and the falling object did not cross it from top to bottom, as the body would have done if it had dropped from higher levels. I simply materialized out of thin air, he said, and began to fall! He could give me no more information than this. So startled had he been that he halted the transport and brought it down to find out whether the man lived. There was no trace of any conveyance from which I might have come, no sign of any other aircraft in the sky at that moment. He was deeply inquisitive to learn by what mysterious manner I had suddenly appeared in mid-air, out of nothingness, and in bright daylight, but I took advantage of our difficulties in language to avoid giving him an answer.

"And so the adventure remained as cryptic as before, and to this day I continue to wonder exactly what took place between the instant that Easter Island sank under such strange circumstances, and the time when I was found struggling in the seas where it had been lost for hundreds of thousands of years, for Moia told me that not within living memory had there been land or island in the vicinity, and the name itself was one that he had never encountered.

"During a long period, then, I fell into a gloomy fit of abstraction, staring moodily through a cabin window. I was mentally fatigued to the point of exhaustion, if not collapse. The strain of my dreadful experience had aged me by years, and this fantastic aftermath, this bridging of five hundred thousand years, five thousand full centuries, in a single night of oblivion, had stunned me into a kind of crushing apathy. But I started to think about what great changes must have occurred in the world during my absence. How far had civilization advanced? To what peak had man arrived in his climb up the symbolic ladder from dust to social organization? By degrees my depression departed under the interest of this fascinating speculation. I imagined marvels of science, profundities of thought, miracles of intellectual achievement and developments toward the increased comfort, happiness, and knowledge of mankind. Maybe the Golden Age had returned. What if the secrets of the atom, the cosmic ray, and the galactic universe, problems upon which the scientists of my time had been working, were at last solved? It was not inconceivable that interplanetary communication, travel even, had become matters of fact. Supposing the riddle of death had been explained? Might not the children of this later day now learn the nature and origin of life as elementary principles of knowledge in their education?

"Thus I pondered, giving free loose to my fancy. And meanwhile the plane headed northeast, and finally paused in mid-air when we came to land where a large city stood; and we hung motionless while passengers stepped out and floated to the ground, as others who seemed to have been standing in emptiness entered. I asked Moia if he was going as far as London. He shook his head in token that he did not understand my meaning. I asked for a map of the world. He produced one and I studied it anxiously to see what physical changes had evenatuated.

"There was no London. The England I knew had sunk beneath the encroaching ocean. Only Ireland, Scotland, and a part of Wales remained as three small islands. It was a tragic and heart-breaking discovery. I thought of my friends; all gone and dead for oblivious years beyond memory; and all my customary haunts vanished, all my possessions and the places I knew lost without hope of recovery; and my native land only an ancient legend. With listless attention I scanned the map, and saw that the Japanese Isles too were no more, that a new sea had formed where the Sahara desert once was, that a new continent half the size of Australia now existed in the equatorial Atlantic, that everywhere old landmarks had been obliterated or new ones had risen from the depths of the ocean. And I realized that I could never again visit the land of my birth, or find a single scene that I had lived in. I had nowhere to go. I was a Crusoe who could not return to his people, a Rip Van Winkle whose coming would arouse no interest in even the oldest and wisest of living men, an Odysseus reappearing from an absence fifty thousand times as long as the wanderings of Ulysses, yet an absence as brief as a hiatus of only a page in a manuscript.

"I turned my eyes futilely away from the map. Already I was beginning to feel again that this was the irrational vividness of a dream. In answer to a question from Moia, I said my destination was Nuaya, the name of what seemed to me the New York of my time. I stared out the window once more. I now noticed that we must have been flying at great speeds, for the country swept beneath us at a furious rate. What I could make out of the cities was all strange and new; but I had not the heart to ask further questions then. I paid little attention to the curious foods that were served at meal-time, though they looked like concentrates and extracts. I have never known how the people walked on air; I suppose the secert of gravity was unlocked, and with the principle discovered it was not impossible to create a counter-force that would nullify its attraction. Nor am I certain how the airplanes — and of these I saw increasing numbers in the sky, and of many bizarre torpedo, disc, and cone types — were propelled, though I think the energy of the atom may have been released, or the power of sub- and super-cosmic rays harnessed.

"But why go on? A lifetime would hardly suffice to record every sensation and reaction I had toward a world that had left me behind. Everything is still surrounded with an alien and foreign atmosphere.

"When we reached Nuaya in late afternoon — having made a journey of more than five thousand miles in about six hours — I was turned over to an official who led me to a governmental building of some sort. With my head still awhirl, it is easy to see why the rest of that day remains a confused blur. As nearly as I have been able to understand, the world had advanced to a point a scientific record was kept of every person from the second of birth. My arrival created a minor sensation, for there was not the slightest indication that I had ever existed. I was plied with questions, examined exhaustively. I suppose they finally decided that I had actually come from some other planet, and that, confused by a new world, and hindered by the barriers of language, I could not make my wants known. At any rate, I was assigned luxurious quarters and evidently placed under the care of the state temporarily.

"The deepest and most far-ranging changes have transformed the world. Nuaya, instead of the massed canyons of skyscrapers that New York used to be, is a city of splendid, moderate buildings and spacious streets. Congestion has gone for ever. The luxury in which all people live is that of sybarites and billionaires; for birth control has been practised by the state for thousands upon thousands of years, and only as many people are permitted to be born as the world can generously provide for. Disease is a thing of the past, life has been prolonged by degrees until now five hundred years is a common age. There are said to be living men who are a thousand years old and more. The landscape has eroded and worn away, the animal kingdom has changed greatly, even the vegetation that I have so far noticed is widely different from that which I knew.

"I went one day to the public library, after I had mastered the universal language, and read through histories of the ages I had missed. What a tremendous panorama I saw, and the pageantry of man! Wars, conquests, famines, and pestilence through the thirtieth century; the age of interplanetary exploration and cosmic voyaging to the seventieth century; then the return of the ancient ice age, and a dangerous decrease in the numbers of man as the glaciation spread, attended by bitter struggles to control the livable regions; and afterwards, decadence, degeneration, barbarism, strife, until the ice-fields retreated and the rebirth of civilization occurred; and then, toward the close of the second hundredth century, the invasion of ferocious insects from a passing world which came heaven knows whence; and the rule of the insect until the coming of the cosmic cloud in 29,750 A.D., a gaseous cloud that placed a cataleptic sleep upon all humanity and wiped out all lesser organisms in the insect and parasite kingdoms; and so again the toiling and swinking upward towards a richer life; and always new inventions, new discoveries, new miracles becoming common property; and then the approach of an unknown comet whose mass created havoc and destruction on earth, transfiguring its surfaces; and though peace had been established between nation and nation for ever, for ever there was the battle of man against nature, man against the gods, man against an irresistible, impersonal, unconquerable universe, such a struggle as I went through against the titans; and the record of civilization is the story of man's conquest of himself, and the universe's supremacy and hostility to man. I will not attempt to state the impact that this bulky accumulation of historical data made upon me. I read with the naive inexperience of a child, the avidity of a victim of amnesia who craves to know what happened while his mind was a blank; I read as a mystic would read prophecies of glory and recollections of ecstasy; I read as the scientist, gathering datum upon datum; yet I read most of all as a traveller marooned in time, desolate in the midst of plenty, and with gravely wise companions wherever I turned, lonely in the heart of the highest civilization humanity had ever achieved, and aching with the burden of old griefs and irrecoverable years, of vanished cycles and an oblivion that had plundered me of my rightful life in the days when the world was young.

"August 18. I visited the Nuaya suicide chamber. In every community there has long been a goverment edifice, of classical beauty, dignity, and simplicity, where those who are weary of living, or overcome with the weight of intolerable grief, may enter unchallenged and painlessly snuff out their lives. I came purely by accident, attracted by the esthetics of the structure. I was politely informed that no visitors or curiosity-seekers were allowed to enter. My apology was instantly accepted, since I have acquired dubious fame as the man of whom there is no record, the only such individual in the twenty thousand years since the records have been kept. The caretaker said that suicides are rare; perhaps half-a-dozen a week in the Nuaya district. I had a fleeting intention to add my name to the list, and end once for all the nightmarish terror of my existence; but I suppressed the impulse and walked away.

"August 20. I wonder whether there was any connection between my being drawn within the circle of the pallid flame and my sleep of five hundred thousand years? My last clear recognition was of the color from space sweeping over me before the vacuousness of suspension paralyzed my faculties. Can it be that I was snatched from this world into the four- or many-dimensional space-time continuum of the titans, and that the moment which I lived in their dominion was an eternity in ours? I wish I could grasp the abstract principles of mathematics that are now current, and which are as far beyond Einstein as he was beyond Euclid. An understanding of them might go a long way toward a clarification of the farrago. According to this system, the geometry of solids is based upon three tangibles: length, breadth, and thickness; and two intangibles: time, and omega; the omega representing a fourth dimension which is the totality of the universe, obtained by the triunarization of infinite space, this hypothesis being that all matter is both infinite and eternal because its line of direction is so curved that it reverses upon itself and can be conceived as elliptical. Thus comets follow ellipses, planets have ovoidal orbits, straight lines become reversibles at omega, and an expanding universe such as Jeans and Eddington postulated in my period would ultimately be a contracting universe. Furthermore, relativity is integral to this mathematics. There is no specific, ultimate, fixed absolute in any of the tangibles or intangibles. Each bears a fluctuable relation to the four other elements of the mathematics, and to any observer at any point in the universe, observer, point, and universe themselves being fluctuant.

"Among the corollaries of this mathematics is the assertion that the three tangibles expand to a lesser organism than man, but the two intangibles contract; and that, to a higher organism than man, the three tangibles contract, while the two tangibles expand. Thus, to a little ephemeris fly, length, breadth, and thickness are enormities; but time and omega are brevities, for its entire existence is consummated in fulness in a single day; but to a hypothetical super-organism, length, breadth, and thickness would be trifles, while time and omega would be concepts of mind-surprassing magnitude.

"Another corollary is that, if any consciousness could be transferred to the condition of a lesser or greater organism, its perspective and relationships likewise would violently change. Therefore, if the titans succeeded in transferring me from my world and my relationships to theirs, a hundred thousand years on earth would be but the tick of a clock to me there, and the multiplied magnitude of the omega would conversely minimize the omega of my habitual world. All this is so absturse and recondite that I can barely follow it; yet it seems to explain, as much as anything can, my frightening experience. What made me pursue the subject was the terrible dream I had last night: a dream of the dead titans wakening, as they wakened on Easter Island that evening five hundred milliards ago. That terrific picture will never be effaced form my thoughts. I am reconciled to the probability that I will often re-live the adventure in my dreams. I ought to feel a glow of triumph in having defeated the titans with their own weapons, but I do not. I am unable to decide why. Possibly so much was taken out of me in that mystical conflict that I am incapable of returning to normal. At any rate, I dreamed of the loathsome idol, and the corrupt flame, and the pitted monsters, and the insufferable color, and all the horror, the disgust, the madness of the scene as Easter Island thundered to its grave.

"One other incident of note caught my attention today. On my way to the library to examine various mathematical treatises, I passed the suicide chamber and was surprised to see four visitors enter in quick succession. As I retraced my way later, I saw several others enter. I was rather interested in the coincidence, these victims representing more suicides in one day than there ordinarily are in a week. For some reason, the sight bothered me. I feel that only abnormal circumstances could cause so many of these gravely wise, long-lived people to extinguish their existence, as if a contagious and unhealthy longing for death had suddenly obsessed a group of them. But it is probably my sensitive imagination becoming excited over any little happening.

"August 21. I rose with a feeling of profound depression, and emerged to a heavy, windless August day of breathless heat. But it was not primarily the heat that discommoded me. I had another horrible vision last night. Mercifully, I can not recall all of it, but it was dimly connected with a search, and suggestive of laborious climbing *downward,* miles upon miles, as though I were trying to force my way through saturated sea water that buoyed me up and forced me back; only, it was not ocean depths that I plumbed, but stifling gloom thick as earth, retarding, yet wanly lit by an evil fluorescence as of stale phosphorus, and fires of no source that played shimmeringly about me; and after weary hours and interminable miles of this subterranean delving, the corpses rose about me, tattered and torn, dead but moving, all corruption and nauseous in decay, and animate with a foul purposiveness that inhabited them from strange, high, awful things that could make and did make these rotten frames move, and bright, living ones fall pallidly down where the green change of the grave awaited them; and in their firm flesh appeared a myriad heads, and the white consumers poured out and left little pitted places where they had been; and the stale light formed whirls and whorls and glowing cryptoglyphics of prophecy; and eternity was as a flame, and infinity as a devouring shadow, and my little life, my vagrant dreamself, trembled in the hidden places and the closed spaces.

"I went outside for relief from my dream, but the heat rose in waves from the pavement, a glare of sun burned heavily back from the walks, and an ominous torpor lay leaden over Nuaya. A feeling of dreadful secrets weighs me, I have a prescience of vast, invisible presences nearby; in brilliant daylight, and in the center of a city, I walked accompanied by fears worse than those of darkness; and without intending, I found myself passing the suicide chamber; and the causeless load pressed heavilier on my spirits and sank me into a deeper dejection when, during the few minutes that the temple was in sight, I remarked upwards of a dozen Nuayans enter the house of death; and on such faces as I saw at close range was a look, compound of great wisdom, restrained horror, troubled conviction of disaster, and renunciation of all that life, love, knowledge, and achievement could offer, that I felt, physically, whatever appalled these Solomons must be of shattering nature to an earlier intelligence like mine. Their faces were those of ascetics goaded by Succubi. But they went to their graves with despair, sanity, and strength. This attitude, so deliberate and so rational, unnerved me more than any show of emotion could have done, for surely, to choose death in so logical a fashion must be to flee from an evil surpassing conjecture.

"I hurried back to my quarters, prey to insidious thoughts. It would be easy to end the phantasmagoria of my life, to blanken for ever the brooding increment of incompehensibles that baffles me. As I stood before the death temple, temptation was strong upon me to escape the necessity of circumstance, to enter the classical portals and seek a nepenthe in oblivion. I resisted for a second time. There was, however, no consolation in my turning away, and I almost wish I had yielded. For the premonition has come.

"When I returned to my quarters, I sought to take my thoughts off their morbid course by utilizing the unitel. I had scarcely touched it before the official morning transmission was made. Something tugged at my heart, and I felt a chill, even in that sultry heat.

"All over the country, in every community, the suicide chambers are being used to capacity. Nuaya already has had more than fifty suicides since midnight. This sudden enormous increase had made emergency measures necessary. It was found from those who would volunteer their reasons that they had experienced dreams of such appalling and dreadful nature that life had been made ashes for them, for these highly organized people are eminently rational, without psychoses, and never dream; yet there has suddenly appeared a plague of dreams more vivid than reality, *dreams of titanic eldritch monsters, and vast corridors that plunge into the bowels of earth, and abnormal colors that do not exist in the solar spectrum, and hideous, pitted, formless shapes that bloat rottenly, towering into vacua of space.*

"The voice droned on... An investigation of the phenomenon was being made...The suicide wave had no justification... For the sake of civilization, those tempted were cautioned to delay and reconsider... If the increase did not stop, stringent measures would be taken...

"The voice came to me from far away, fitfully audible, only a background to my thoughts. I must have received a violent nervous shock, for I suddenly started from my recollections of my old adventure and the dead titans wakening to find that it was past noon. I dare not permit myself to develop the potentialities of the statements I heard.

"August 22. I am not certain that I could say whether I wake or sleep, for there no longer is any dividing line between reality and fantasy. In early afternoon I visited the Nuaya Museum of Antiquities. I may have expected to make a discovery, but my nerves are in so shaken a state that half the time I myself do not know whether I act on the laws of probability, or on the dictates of reason, or on unreliable memories of a giant combat that occurred aeons ago, or on intuitive impulses. At any rate, I went, and asked particuarly for material on Stonehenge; but there was none; and on Easter Island; but the museum contained nothing; and on the primitive tribes of Africa; but there were only a few common articles, and I was relieved. I asked if there were any interesting pieces from Polynesia or Melanesia, and was told there were some, including an acquisition that had been discovered washed ashore on the coast of Chile and put on exhibit only the previous day. So I asked to see them and was shown a room of curios, carvings, ornaments, and the usual selections. Then I was led to an alcove containing the late acquisitions; and the attendant cried out in amaze but I knew it was coming and only a deathly sickness shook me as I stumbled out to the clean light of day.

"There in the alcove, upon a pedestal, squatted a duplicate of the hateful image which I had excavated at Isling. Squatted? Yes; but the lifeless idol that the attendant had set up was now a fury of mutability; shaping and reshaping and changing before our eyes from pygmy to titan to demon of another universe; racing frantically from dust to stone to vegetable, animal, mineral, human life, and then to gaseous malformation and unstable solids of an existence defying every earthly law; gruesome in its parody of all that was mortal; a mockery, a ghoulish nightmare, summing and consummating ecstasy, frenzy, bestiality, and frightfulness; and loathsome with doubled horror because of the insane leer, the chuckle and mad laughter that writhed across its pudgy green lips and lidless eyes, so that a mirthless shudder racked the visage where pocks wavered in the cycles of hellish instability. God help me! The sorcery that I thought I had outrun when I was snatched from my rightful life is still upon me!

"August 23. The govermental transmissions today were pregnant with annihilations that these superior men do not even dream of. And I am helpless; to tell my story would be to invite disaster, precarious as my position already is. All day there have been announcements of uncanny happenings: the mysterious suicide of an attendant at the Nuaya Museum of Antiquities, whose body was found weirdly decomposed; the disappearance of an important image from the alcove where it had been on exhibit for only a day in the same museum; an outburst of manic-depressive aberrations throughout the south Atlantic continent Atalan; a steadily increasing number of suicides in the various country-wide mortaria; the glowing of supernal lights in the midst of an uninhabited expanse toward the South Pole; the discovery of a stupendous well that plunged below the sands of Egypt only a few rods from where the Sphinx of antiquity had crouched; and so through a series of extraordinary happenings that have turned the world crazy. From everywhere came reports of psychic phenomena, disturbances, visions, physical marvels, as if the whole normal course of events had gone askew. I listened and watched for a lengthy interval because I could not tear myself away from the fascination of the inevitable.

"There is a blank in my consciousness then. The next thing I remember is my walking along heat-white pavements, with a muggy atmosphere saturating my clothing and baking me in its intensity; and then I lowered my eyes from invisible worlds and saw that I was approaching the lethal temple. A procession of figures entered it while I watched; patriarchs, wise men, scientists, artists, I judged them to be, of all interests of life; and all fleeing from irresistible destruction that they sensed but did not comprehend; or did they? Theirs were the faces of dreamers, of materialists, of philosophers; idealist and realist alike, they entered one after one, to exchange the intolerable delirium of an hour for the serenity of world without end.

"My steps faltered, and I paused, and half-turned with a longing look toward the beauty of the temple, and felt myself succumbing to the quiet promise of its facades, and the peaceful fulfillment of its inner court. I may have taken a step toward it; almost I relinquished the world to those who wanted it; yet I turned away, not because I desired to, but because a power beyond mine, an instinct from the deeper subconcious, compelled me.

"August 24. This is the last entry that I shall ever make in my diary. I write as I live, because I can not help it; but it seems unlikely that existence will ravage me much longer, and perforce my entries will also cease.

"A madness sweeps the world. Life is a game played in darkness, against unknown opponents, with man for ever the loser. I realize, just before the end, though it comforts me not, what happened when Easter Island sank, the titans came in the old years when the world was young, and those ancient ones created our existence for reasons that are not ours to know; and they set the time of their return, to investigate the results of their experiment, for what may have been a minute, or an hour, or a day later, under their laws; but which was a half-million years or more according to our time; they may have returned, for that matter, and my seeing them at Easter Island may have marked the second occasion or the tenth, it matters little; but I challenged them, and won half a victory; and only half, for I was encompassed by strange flame and the evil color out of space; and I was whirled into their other-dimensional world, and subject to their laws; and one brief night was twenty-five thousand generations of man; but because I was on the fringe of the flame, and the border of their sphere, I was the sooner released from their laws and returned to the rule of ours than I would have been had I stood in the heart of that passage to realms beyond stars, universe, and imagination.

"The sun sinks in bloody skies, brooding, sinister, malignant, like an enormous wounded eye. The air is stifling. A hush has fallen. Fitful currents of heat from the pavements waver crazily, so that even solid buildings vibrate with a slow, frantic motion. Long shadows creep across the ground, and all the trees and spires are bathed in fantastic crimson, but dark masses grow larger upon earth.

"The kingdom of man totters. The game was worth it only because of the struggle, since causes were never found, and the end will never be known. The triumph and the failure, the past and whatever is to be of the future, even this uncertain and perishing present, the whole of the destiny of earth is but a dream of dust."For the dead titans waken again; and all the weary road that I travelled is yet to come."

INVISIBLE SUN

BY
CARROL AMWORTH

Dedication

*To the suns of our being
and a woman like the sun,
here lies love*

I BIRTH

Because of his thinness, the man who walked quietly into the room seemed taller than he was. He might have been twenty-five or forty. He belonged to that ageless type who look for ever the same during the mature years of their life. Reticent of manner, he had cool gray eyes, the mouth of an ascetic, an intellectual forehead ridged with moundlets, and a light complexion. He wore a moustache of almost silky black but his hair was the indeterminate color of Indiana limestone. It would not have been difficult for him to become a consumptive. His bearing suggested a life of study rather than labor, and his hands had nervous long fingers. He walked with a springy step but the wrinkles at the corners of his eyes were habitually tired.

He carried a huge bouquet of roses, chrysanthemums, and gardenias. Their fragrance disguised the odor of antiseptics, and their pastel colors softened the hospital whiteness of the room.

"How are you today, Mary? I brought you your favorites," he said. He bent over and kissed the lovely face of a woman whose cheeks bore the flush of subsiding fever.

Her eyes lighted and she looked at the flowers wistfully. "Oh, I'm all right. You shouldn't have spent more money on flowers, but they're gorgeous."

A faint cry came from beside her.

"How is the son today?"

She smiled as she looked at the raw and not very attractive baby.

"Our son," she murmured. "April son."

"The first-born, and a boy," he said. "Are you sorry that it was not a girl?"

"Well, yes, in a way, but maybe we'll have a daughter some time. He's a funny little mite. I think he's going to be awfully bright."

"Hush, you mustn't talk so much. I hope you are right but I do not see how anyone can tell from a week-old baby what he will be when he grows up."

"Women can. And I learned a lot when I was nurse at the maternity hospital. He's an unusual child," she insisted.

Through an open window flooded the cheery sunlight of spring. Lush green already carpeted the ground, and buds opened to young leaves on oak and elm. There was a damp wind from the south, a wind that dried out the sodden soil and told of warmth to come, a wind that brought the peculiar, compound scent of weakening nature; the smell of decaying lives, of wet ground, of green things growing, of tulip shoots that talled by day and branches that dipped by night. There was the cry of robins abroad, jays shrieked northward with the sun, larks already sang, and an early oriole flashed in the trees outside.

"Shakespeare's month," whispered Daniel.

"You know so much. I wish I could have had your education."

"Nonsense, angel," he replied, kissing her cheeks again. "There are many things that matter in this world — love, life, beauty, experience. You possess things that I haven't. And some day you may be able to finish up, correspondence work at the high school, you know. Don't worry, silly. I love you as you are and for what you are."

A smile of pleasure touched with regret illuminated her features.

"Have you thought of a name yet?" he asked.

"Oh, lots of them. I think my maiden name would be nice. Drew. Drew Gordon," she smiled down at the puckery face.

"Drew Daniel Gordon," he rounded out the name.

"Yes. Drew after me, and Daniel after you," she echoed.

The tiny countenance contracted to emit a squall.

Daniel laughed. "It sounds as if he already had a mind of his own," he said. "He seems to be objecting to his name."

"You shouldn't make fun of him," she reproached.

He stooped over in quick contrition and kissed her again. "I'm not, dear, don't mind me. Perhaps I am a little too happy to be quite sure of what I am saying. But I must hurry back to the office or the bills will never be paid."

She smiled at him briefly as he turned away. Before he had crossed the threshold she was absorbed in the man-child.

II PRECOCIOUS

I told you he was a bright child!" said Mary proudly, handing the certificate to her husband. "He's only six, just when other children are starting kindergarten, and now he's already passed to the second grade."

"It might be a lucky accident," Daniel answered with his usual caution.

"Don't be blind. He is unusual even if he isn't very well. I hope his health gets better."

"Yes, it would be too bad if he were again held back by sickness. He isn't very strong, is he?"

"I don't know what's the matter. He's been sick so much of the time. Just think, he's had measles, mumps, whooping cough, pneumonia, scarlet fever, and what was the other, oh yes, the flu, already and he's still such a child. I'm worried to death about him. I don't know whether he would live through it if he catches anything else on top of all those."

"Don't alarm yourself, Mary. He may be sickly but he has pulled through every time, which is more than most children do."

"Well, yes, I suppose we ought to be thankful but I can't help worrying."

"Nonsense. He'll be all right. We come of long-lived families, you know. There's granddad, now eighty-six, and grandma, eighty-two, and your folks — how old are they? Your grandfather's over ninety, and both your parents are still living. Why, nothing short of an earthquake can kill us off, or Drew either," he joked.

"I hope you're right, but I'm worried just the same. He's been sick so much that he hasn't got to know any other boys and he never plays outside."

"What is he doing now?"

"Reading up in his room. It seems to be about all he does. I've scolded and threatened but it don't do any good. And he's reading such queer things for his age, The King of the Golden River, and Poe's Tales, and let me see, what was it, I can't remember its name but it's a big book about stars with a lot of pictures of the moon and such in it. I don't see what he gets out of books like that. He's not old enough. I took them away one day and he was simply wild until I let him have them back. I don't know what to do with him."

"Don't do anything for awhile. Perhaps we don't understand him. Or he may be one of those clever children who get along well enough if left alone."

"You know I can't do that, Dan. He means so much to me that I couldn't bear it if anything happened to him. Remember that day he was so quiet and I thought I'd just leave him be for once and he didn't answer when I called him for dinner and we went up and there he was all a-fever. Now I always think maybe he's catching pneumonia again and I just can't help keeping an eye on him even if it does make him cross."

"You ought not to do that. It may cause him to develop the wrong traits if you keep it up. Let him alone for awhile."

"What can I do? If I leave him something may happen to him and anyway he'll just drift farther and farther away from us and if I don't you say he'll get cross for good or something else."

"Tosh. Don't fret so, Mary. By all means, keep an eye on him occasionally. The wise thing to do would be not to leave him too much by himself or be near him so often that he gets an idea he is being tied down. Moderation is best in the long run."

"Oh, yes, you've said that before, but he is our only child and I know it would kill me if anything happened to him."

"I am afraid that you exaggerate, Mary. I know you worry about him but worrying does no good. Let's save the rest till after dinner. I have had a rather hard day at the office and we'll have plenty of time to talk then. With one of your fine meals inside, and a glass of beer at hand, and a pipe, I know I'll feel better and be able — "

"Oh dear, I smell the potatoes burning — I hope they aren't spoiled — call Drew while I go fix them — "

III FEAR

Always dreamin', city kid!" said Jake with a mixture of disgust and anger mottling his brick-red face. "Now get up that road and get in before Maw's asleep. Scared of the dark, are ye? Well, it's time ye got over it."

The city kid almost pleaded, but he didn't quite weaken. He feared the dark woods, and the empty road, and the pallid moon that hung, evil, in the sky; but he feared also the voice of authority and the reproaches of men. So he took heart and started bravely off without a word in reply.

Jake could have accompanied him, but he wouldn't. Jake was his uncle. Drew's family had let him go for the summer to his uncle's farm at Rolling Prairie; and on this evening, he and Jake had gone over to a cider-party at the Wellens' place a mile down the road. Drew was supposed to be in at nine-thirty. Jake had let him stay till ten. Drew was afraid of the creatures of darkness. Jake feared nothing. The only cure he knew was the rod or harsh discipline. Drew wanted company. Jake knew it, but he'd be damned if he'd let any kid grow up to be afraid of his own shadow.

So Drew started off down the path, and reached the road, while the noise and lights of the party faded behind him.

A few hundred yards away, the woods began. They were sinister woods. They lined the road on both sides clear up to Jake's farmhouse. They were full of muttering things, and demons, and wicked monsters. Every tree was an enchanted man, every shadow a devil, every breath of wind the moan of a captive in torture. The moonlight lay wan upon the dirt road, and the echo of Drew's steps became as following thunder of giants in his ears.

He went on, as white-faced as the moonlight, with a dread and fear in his heart. His eyes took on a peculiar, shining tinge. He walked faster, then he hurried, then he broke into a dead run.

The trees crept by, eerily, strangely. The moon was a blind eye peering at him, its light a film of eldritch and ancient corruption lying across the forest. The trees grew taller and wilder, the shadows thicker and blacker, the forest longer, yet longer.

Drew ran, ran between aisles of trees soaring giantlike to the skies, ran with his hair crisping and his eyes shining like all those other eyes behind the trees. His breathing became hard, but not loud enough to drown the curious muttering and rustling that stirred the woods around.

He dared not look, he could not halt, he would not turn back. So he ran, with a great fear in his heart, and the woods all gloomy, and the moonlight ghostly upon the ground.

There was a pond by the roadside in the deep of the woods. Its surface was covered with scum that glittered phosphorescent in the moonlight. The eyes of dragons flamed out and winked again. A muskrat dove and the splash was a drowning sound. The dragon's eyes swam nearer.

And Drew ran — ran through endless miles of trees that loomed gigantic to the dead sky, where the moon drifted, low, and huge, and blind.

The wind made black sorceries among the trees. Each leaf had a tale of its own.

IV STORM

"Aunt Jane! Aunt Jane!"

"Hush, child, here I am, what is it?"

"What's that awful noise?"

"Only the old maple blown down on the corncrib."

"I'm afraid, Aunt Jane."

"There ain't nothin' to be afeared of. It's just the storm and the rain. The wind sounds like that. Ain't the lightnin' bright?"

"Don't go 'way, Aunt Jane."

"You're not afeared, are you? Why, you're seven already, a great big boy. You'll never be a man if you let the weather get you. It's often like this."

"What's that?"

"Must be the hail breakin' windows. It won't hurt you. I got to go and help Jake see that everythin's right."

"Don't go, Aunt Jane. It's awful dark here."

"We don't dast keep the lamps goin' in a storm bad as this."

"And I want to go downstairs."

"Hush, go to sleep. You'll be in the way. Stay here. I'll come back later. I got to help Jake fix that back window that blew in. Ain't the storm somethin' fierce? G'night."

"Aunt Jane! Aunt Jane!"

V FIRE

There was a shrill wind that October afternoon. The skies were lead gray. The air was filled with dust and blown leaves and bits of paper. Pungent smoke from grass fires crept into houses even.

Since it was Saturday, Drew did not need to attend school. He read all morning — *Grimm's Fairy Tales, The Treasure Seekers of the Andes, Tales from Shakespeare*. He read rapidly, devoting about an hour to each book. He had just begun a story with the promising title, *From the Earth to the Moon,* when his mother called.

After lunch, an ache still in his eyes from reading, he wandered out. The day reminded him of that other day when, toward evening, a storm had howled up and frightened him in a farmhouse. He did not want to be inside and alone if another gale broke while his mother was away for her weekly shopping.

A group of the neighborhood children were playing mumbly-peg and run-sheep-run in a vacant lot. Drew knew them by sight and stood apart for awhile watching them. Tomboy Ellis was with them. They called her Tomboy because she did not know any girls, or at least did not go with them. Her mother was a widow who did housework and took in washing for a living, and to put her daughter through school. As a result, Tomboy had many an afternoon to herself. She usually went with the boys for she was as good as they at boys' games. She had a kind of lonesome-looking face but with eyes that were already hard and wise, and she wore her hair cut short under a tam.

The dry, withered grass made an excellent field for mumbly-peg. The earth was just the right hardness too. Tomboy and a couple of boys sat in a circle. They yelled to Drew to join them. Half-a-dozen other kids were playing some game in the rear of the lot. Drew looked around and, since no one else was near, decided that they must be calling to him. He sat down with them.

He watched the flips intently until the jack-knife was passed for his turn. Right palm, left palm, back of right hand, back of left hand, right knee, left knee — missed. Drew chanced it and missed again. He would have to start all over when his next turn came. Disgusted, he passed the knife to Tomboy.

Right palm, left palm, back of right hand, back of left hand — missed.

"Chance it," said Tomboy.

Back of left hand — good — right knee, left —

"Jiggers! Tomboy's afire!"

Drew and the others looked up at that fearful cry. It was true. The boys in the rear had begun burning the dry grass. The strong wind had fanned their start to a blaze that raced across the field. Intent on their game, the four players had not noticed it nor even been warned, and now a ripple of fire swirled hungrily up the back of Tomboy's cotton dress.

"Beat it! Beat it!" the cry came from nowhere and all scattered like mice. Drew himself turned automatically in response to the command, then a horrible shriek pierced the air. Despite his fear, he whirled around. Tomboy stood still, a living torch, the insensate wind whipping long flames all around her while she screamed.

Drew tore off his coat as he ran toward the girl. He did not want to but he had to, he did not know why. Perhaps blind instinct, or the frantic appeal in the girl's scream of agony, motivated him. Perhaps he turned because he could not bear to see anyone suffer without trying to help. Perhaps he sped solely because there was no one else who would help. And all the while, the girl screamed, a dreadful, piteous, continuous sound without words. He ripped away handfuls of flaming fabric. He wrapped his coat around Tomboy and flung her to the ground, rolling her over and over in an attempt to smother the fire but she jumped up wildly. He tried to beat out the flames with his bare hands. Dimly he was aware that a passing truck ground to a halt, that two men leaped from it and hurried to help, that the screams grew fainter, that all the other children had vanished, that a sickening odor eddied on the whooping wind.

The cries diminished to a moan that finally ceased. A man stooped and lifted the slender, blackened form.

"Where does she live? You see, sonny, this is what comes of playing with fire."

Drew was too stunned to answer the accusation.

The man's face whitened, his voice broke. Bowed and shaking, he stumbled across the lot, a seared arm clinging around his neck.

Drew stared and stared and stared. He saw tattered strips of cloth burnt together with the girl's flesh. He caught a child's face, writhing no longer, but crisped and heart-breaking in the quiet of torture that had exceeded the limits of pain or the power of nerves to express. He saw a limp hand whose fingers twitched and curled and fluttered aimlessly. He saw a head, bald and splotched, that lolled upon a shoulder. He saw the back of a man who swayed as he walked.

Drew went home in a dream of horror. There was no one home. He sat on the porch outside, and the chill wind shrilled around him but he did not know it. He sat in a shuddering stupor, and the cold crept into him.

VI FIRST WITCH

"Hello, Mrs. Warren."

"How do you do, Drew? Did you see that girl wave a burning newspaper round her head this afternoon? She shouldn't have done it. She'll get hurt some day playing like that."

"It wasn't a newspaper. Her dress caught afire. I think she's going to die."

"Do you mean her dress burned off?"

"Yes."

"And she didn't have anything on then?"

"Yes."

"Why, that's shocking. Little boys should never see a girl naked."

Drew did not answer. A kind of redness boiled up in him. He turned and ran home. A girl burned, and all that old Mrs. Warren could think of was that she didn't have any clothes on. He heard only the beginning of an exclamation, "Well, I declare, I have never been so rudely treated by a — "

VII SECOND WITCH

Later the same evening, Mrs. Fitzhugh dropped in to call on Drew's mother.

"That was a terrible tragedy that happened across from our house this afternoon, Mary. Did you notice it?"

"No, Drew told me. I guess it shocked him pretty bad. He was awfully white when I came home and didn't seem to hear me. I thought for a minute he was coming down with pneumonia until he told me what happened. Drew's an awfully sensitive boy for his age. I almost wish it had been pneumonia instead of that terrible thing if it would save her life."

"How old is he?"

"Nine."

"Well, he does act older. You know, Mary, I can't tell you how sorry I feel about it but what could I do? I would have been able to help the poor girl if it wasn't for Johnnie. Johnnie's only three months old, you know. I'd just finished nursing him and put him to sleep when I looked out of the window and saw the boys lighting the grass. I wanted to open a window and shout a warning when I saw it going towards Mrs. Ellis's girl except that baby was asleep and he might catch cold if I opened the window and I didn't want to wake him up because I knew he just wouldn't get to sleep again if I did and I couldn't run away outside because he might wake up and fall out of his crib while I was gone and besides I thought that one of those children would surely shout a warning — why, Drew, what's the matter? You look so queer."

The ferocity on Drew's face was primitive in its savagery. He seemed to be groping for words that were not in his vocabulary. He mouthed an inarticulate cry, his face dead white. Then he was gone. Mrs. Gordon did not ask him to come back and apologize.

That night, Tomboy died. Mrs. Ellis did not have enough saved to pay for the funeral. The neighbors helped her. A little, frail woman, she went around doing her laundry and housework with a sort of far-away look in her eyes until they found her hanging from a rafter one morning weeks later.

Drew read the account in a paper. His thoughts flashed back to the tragedy, to the scruples of old Mrs. Warren and the selfish inhumanity of Mrs. Fitzhugh.

"God damn all women," he whispered in the quiet of his room. His first profanity scorched his first and deepest hate upon his brain. It lasted for ten years.

VIII POST OFFICE

Drew went to the party because his mother insisted. He could not bring himself to go to Mrs. Fitzhugh's house, even though most of the neighborhood children would be there at her oldest son's birtday party. He did not want to face Mrs. Fitzhugh. He did not want to have anything to do with girls. He wanted to be by himself and finish a wonderful book called *Sea and Land* which was filled with pictures of cannibals feasting, monsters from the sea, and sharks biting men in half. It had all sorts of gruesome illustrations, many in colors. It told about queer animals, and things in countries whose names he had never before even heard of. But his mother cajoled and threatened and pleaded, until he finally accepted the invitation.

He managed to enjoy himself while the peanut hunt continued. Some one played a piano. The children marched around. As soon as the music stopped, there was a scramble for chairs, rugs, window sills, radiators, victrola, and any other spot where peanuts might be hidden. When the piano began playing again, the line was hastily re-formed and the march resumed until silence feel once more. Drew was sorry that he did not win the boys' first prize, a fine, ten-bladed jack-knife. He thought he ought to have won if Carl had not cheated.

However, he forgot his disappointment after he had eaten largely of the vanilla ice-cream, cakes, cookies, sandwiches, and lemonade which were served. Then Mrs. Fitzhugh and the maid retired to do dishes.

Drew was dismayed when Billy announced that they were going to play wink. Most of the children ranged from twelve to fifteen. Drew, only ten, was youngest, but far older than they in knowledge. Yet he shied at the game, and raised objections which were over-ruled.

All the girls sat in a circle. Behind each chair stood a boy. Billy began by winking at the prettiest girl in the circle. She started to rise but her watchful companion put his arm around her in time to hold her. Billy tried again on a bright young redhead. She bounced up before her escort could prevent her and crossed to Billy. He kissed her while his girl rose and occupied the chair just vacated. The boy who had lost was now "it". He looked around stupidly and winked at the girl in Drew's chair. Drew made no effort to hold her until she was well off.

"Hey, wake up!" shouted his neighbor. "Whatcha doin', sleepin'?"

Drew mumbled a reply. He had let the girl go in some vague belief that he would be better off and released from having to put his arms around her. His heart sank when Billy yelled, "Your turn, Drew, hurry up!" and he realized that he must wink at one of the girls.

He winked at the first one he saw, the pretty one that Billy had wanted. She jumped up and came over. She had soft, brown-gold curls. She was cute with a saucy face but she might as well have been a papoose for all Drew cared. He became panicky. He couldn't kiss her. Not before all these kids. Or even alone. He didn't want her. He didn't want anything to do with her or the rest of the girls. What could he do? He stood miserably undecided, wondering whether to bolt.

She solved his worry by suddenly leaning over and kissing him before he was aware of her intention. A wave of sickness passed across him. Maybe he shouldn't have eaten so much ice-cream and cake.

Thereafter, she did not leave his chair. He hated to put his arms around her to restrain her, but he disliked more the thought of kissing or of being kissed again by a girl.

"I'm tired of this. Let's play post-office!" shouted Billy.

Cries and shrieks of delight greeted him.

"I don't feel well. I guess I better go home," said Drew to Billy.

"Whatcha tryin' to do, bust up the party? Yer awright. Are ya 'fraid?"

"No, I just don't feel good."

"Aw, gwan home then to yer ma. Yella. 'Fraid of girls." Arrogant from the success of his party, he taunted Drew.

"I'll stick." The sting of ridicule was worse than the game.

A strange tightness, a kind of nightmarish stiffness, settled over Drew. Without quite remembering why or how, he found himself in a closet with the pretty girl.

"What are we supposed to do now?" he asked dully.

"What's the matter? You got my number. If you're as dumb as that, go on out. You're a back number."

Unhappy, Drew fumbled for her in the dark.

"That's better. You're not so bad," she said.

When he walked out, " 'Smatter? You look like a ghost," said Billy.

"I told you I wasn't feeling well."

"Gee, that's too bad. I didn't think you meant it. D'you feel awright now?"

"Not so very."

"I guess maybe you better go home or somethin'."

"I guess I better. Thanks a lot for asking me to your party. I liked it. Well, I guess I better go."

"Oh, that's awright. So long. Hey, ain't anybody ever goin' to call my number?"

IX FANTASIA

It was the stamp on a letter which his mother received from a cousin travelling in the Orient that aroused Drew's curiosity and led to his making a hobby of stamp-collecting. He seemed destined to be alone, from sickness, precocity, and the misfortunes that attended whenever he made advances toward the outside world. The love of books was already implanted deep, but he wearied at times of reading and sought other amusements. He had an allowance of a quarter a week. He eared another quarter by cutting the lawn, and sometimes more by trimming neighbors' yards. During the severe months of winter, there was snow to be shovelled. Usually he managed to obtain a dollar every week. He was not very fond of candy or toys. Most of his money he spent on magazines, movies, and books until he discovered the lure of stamps. To his early recreation was now added the love of beauty and of far places.

Tanganyika.... Dahomey.... Natal.... Borneo.... Newfoundland....San Salvador....Tasmania.... Senegal....Bosnia.... They were magic names to conjure with. Pictures of caribou, giraffes, full-bearded statesmen, temples, locomotives, cocoanut trees, and countless other subjects came under his scrutiny. He was not interested in rare stamps, or cancelled stamps, or damaged stamps. He wanted them fresh and pretty. The beauty of color and subject appealed to him. He would rather possess his gorgeous indigo and burnt orange stamp with the picture of the lake on it than the famous two-center of British Guiana which was of such crude design, in one color, and having no picture at all.

In addition to his reading and stamp-collecting, he developed another hobby for a rather odd reason. The profound shock of the tragedy which had killed Tomboy left its mark upon him. As the wintry months passed, he thought less often of that disaster, though it lay in the background of his experience and became a permanent if invisible or even forgotten influence. But he developed nervous habits; twitchings of his eyes, contortions of his lips, a trick of rubbing his arm rapidly across his forehead as if to brush something away. Once his mother rebuked him for tossing a caterpillar into a fire. He looked dazed and did not seem quite able to understand what he was doing. He stared with a puzzled expression at the fire. He jumped when his mother spoke, then saw a caterpillar writhing madly before it stiffened to charcoal. A sick, horrified, haunted appearance crept into his features. "Did I do that?" he sobbed, and ran.

He began to have terrible dreams. It became increasingly difficult to sleep. He would toss for hours restlessly. As a result, he took to wandering around after dark until he was so tired from walking that he fell asleep almost as soon as he crawled between the sheets. This practice, begun solely though unconsciously as a kind of natural sedative, grew into a new hobby of walking at night. He feared the dark more than ever, but late passersby, familiar houses, an occasional wagon or auto, gas lamps, and the light of the moon when it was out gave him a certain sense of not being alone or in absolute darkness. Then, too, he knew that his parents would always be up, waiting until he returned.

For some reason, he hated the sun. He was too young to understand the association with fire which he had made of it. He acquired a greater fondness for the moon. Especially on nights when the new moon was high, he liked to ramble along the avenues near his home, head up, eyes fixed upon the moon. He wondered sometimes if the moon itself was not an eye, a sort of eye of heaven which had become blind. He tried to make out the valleys, mountains, and sea-beds that books said were on its surface. In the cold light that poured from it, he found contentment. He took pleasure in watching its soft glow turn snow-crystals to palely sparkling diamonds. He delighted in the patterns it made through branches. When spring came around, and the nights grew shorter and warmer, he saw leafy arabesques appear where naked trees in winter had cast sharply defined shadows. Even after he had gone to bed, he often lay drowsily half-awake, watching the moonlight flood trough his window and trace the patterned curtains.

Can Such Things Be?.... Mozambique.... Guttering gas mantles and a moon rising beyond trees and roofs....

X PAIN

No one will ever like you with your teeth so crooked. You'll never be popular if you don't have them fixed. You might as well have it done now and get it over with. They'll hurt much worse later." So his mother said, month after month, Drew always protesting, until finally she took matters into her own hands and brought him to a dentst. Drew knew that his teeth were so badly out of place that they must be attended to. Their appearance had been partly responsible for his shyness. The fear of pain, however, made him resist persuasion until his parents acted.

For five long years the work continued. Bands were placed around every tooth. Hideous black bands whose metal cut into his gums. The torture of steady cutting. The torture of teeth that moved slowly into line. The torture of roots that revolved, of shrieking nerves. The nausea of liquid foods year after year. The derision of playmates. The mockery when he smiled and the ugly bands were visible for cruel comments. But that was easy to avoid — he solved it by rarely smiling. Not often could he have done so even had he wished.

The dentist said that the bands were necessary. A brace was put around both sets of teeth, inside. A little wire, "ligature" the dentist called it, was fastened around each tooth and the ends twisted tightly together on the brace. Small, strong rubber bands united the ends of the lower brace with those of the upper.

The teeth ground slowly, excruciatingly into line. What matter that the nightmares deepened and insomnia came? What matter that he shrivelled up inside, hating the ugliness of his mouth, trying not to smile, avoiding the few playmates he had and shunning all new ones? What matter that his nerves twitched day and night? There were times when he cried himself asleep, when mother came in and put her arms around him and tried to soothe his tortured mind and racked body with the only remedy she had — love. There were other times when the agony became a refined torment that exhausted him mentally and left him physically one raw wound. There were still other times when, in a kind of horrible delirium, he deliberately gnashed his teeth so that he felt a spurious relief when the surge of increased mad pain had settled again to the regular throb.

Five long years of pain, from the last term of grade-school, all through high-school, and into the first year of college. Five long years of loneliness and the shapes that walk by night. Five long years of soup, and mashed potatoes, and jello, and soft eggs, of macaroni and hash, of custards, gravies, canned tomatoes and apple sauce, until even food became a tasteless habit in a life whose only pleasures were stamps, books, and the moon.

Hatred of women — torture and agony — sleepless nights — and always the steady ache of teeth grinding through sore bone and inflamed flesh.

The delirium of dreams. Nightmares.

XI NIGHTMARE

When **Drew switched on the** cellar light, he felt uneasy, but his mother had asked him to fetch some potatoes for dinner and with her so near there could be no reason to hold back. Pail in hand, he walked down the short flight, turned the landing, and reached the basement after descending the long flight.

It was odd that the light went out just as he arrived. He became panicky. He froze rigid when that huge, swart, hairy arm with the curling talons crept out in mid-air from under the staircase. Slowly, with the paralysis of horror, Drew jerked back. Step by step he retreated. A fantastic glow illuminated the scene though the light was extinguished.

That clawing arm followed, swelling longer, pawing feverishly after him, but the dreadful thing did not emerge, and became more dreadful because he did not know what it was. Sick, numb with fright, he tripped on the landing and backed up the short flight. Those terrible talons that rippled like bluish snakes followed him still while he stared as in a cataleptic trance.

In the kitchen he turned with a glad cry to his mother.

She was not there. His scream rang through an empty house.

He awakened in a sweat to find his mother bending over him with frightened eyes. She asked what was wrong that had made him cry out so. He could hear his father turning over in bed, far away.

She comforted him and left. The dull agony of his teeth kept him awake. Restless, tortured, he finally gave up the attempt to sleep. He decided to get his chemical set from the attic. Quietly he climbed out of bed and opened the attic door.

It was dark on the stairs. He walked carefully lest he waken his parents again.

At the stair-head, he halted and fumbled uncertainly for the light cord. It must be farther along. He seemed to have misjudged its position. He took another step and fumbled again.

Hard, dry teeth champed on his wrist and a rustling came from the darkness. He tried to scream but his voice failed. He tried to jerk back, without success. Trembling, he clutched for the cord with his left hand. All at once he found it, and the bulb glowed.

They were skeleton's teeth clamped upon his wrist. A thing of bones swayed toward him, flapped its arms around him. He fought until he shoved it loose so that it tottered and rattled against a trunk. The trunk lid opened. A withered mummy sat up and turned its face toward him, a face corrupt, gummy, with liquid eyes that hungered. He ran, the two creatures in pursuit, ran for hours and ages before he reached the stairs and descended them and closed the door against two that clattered upon it. He awoke with fever-hot face and the agony of raw nerves that inflamed his mouth.

Fearing the dreams of slumber, he tossed around endeavoring not to sleep. He rubbed his jaws until the throb of nerves became audible. He ground his teeth with the deliberation of despair till their ache flamed into red torment.

He could see that red. It grew brighter, bathing the room in a ruddy glare. It occurred to him to look outside. He saw a house burning when he peered through his window. He slipped from bed and raced downstairs into the quiet of night.

The house was aflame. A woman's face peered from a pane on the second floor. She was crowned with fire and wrapped by curling tongues. Engines clanged to a halt, people rushed from everywhere. The woman looked straight at Drew and her eyes were wild. He sprang to help her but miscalculated and went drifting high over the house, through smoke and heat. From there he saw what the others had not seen, an airplane flying low along the horizon. Unaccountably it exploded and the dead flier shot across the heavens, falling like a comet to earth. When Drew alighted after his leap, he raced toward the body. Gigantic trees towered around him, trees whose enormous boles were whitish. A glare from the fire illuminated his path. He ran through the forest alone, all alone, and the trees soared higher until he was lost in their vastness. They became whiter and smoother. The red shadows were left beind. A pallor took their place. The trees had given way to a graveyard.

There lay the body of the flier, still smoking and broken. Drew looked at it. It lay against a giant tombstone. The block tilted and he averted his eyes as from a coming horror, but he saw a shadow spread across the body before the lid of the tomb closed. When the shadow was gone, it had taken with it the corpse.

He tried to run. Terror held him rigid. His legs would not obey. He looked down, and found that his feet were rooted in the earth. While he stood there, they had grown downward and he could not pull them out. He was trapped for ever in the graveyard. He struggled till he was exhausted. The moon rose, a dead, blind eye and poured a wave of pallor on the graveyard. Tombstones and wan moonlight merged. The moon curved across the sky and took the pallor with it as it sank. It took away the cemetery also. In blackness Drew strove to raise his rooted legs until a yellowish streak fell over him. He peered around. A gigantic dragon thundered toward him, belching smoke and yellow flame. It was so huge that trees and houses covered its back, and pygmies danced on its skin. Its maw was opened wide, its red tongue darting toward him. He turned helplessly around. A giantess lay behind him. Her legs were canyons on either side. A hot breath scorched his neck.

Mysteriously he was able to lumber forward. There was no place to hide except in a cave that loomed before him, hidden by bushes. He dragged his heavy legs and managed to stagger into the cave, with the dragon's breath still scorching his neck. He fell. He did not look behind but crawled wearily on till the cave ended in a solid wall. The wall bent like rubber when he tried to push his way through. He shoved harder but could not get through. A noise from behind forced him to look. A great white worm of snake writhed toward him. The white worm dragged him screaming out of the cave and past the legs of the giantess. The white worm reared up and flung him through the air. He hurtled amid whistling darkness until he crashed to earth.

He awakened racked by pain, and picked himself off the floor. He must have fallen out of bed. There was a bump on his skull, a throb in his head. The tortures of day and the terrors of darkness left him no hour of comfort.

XII WAR

"Why isn't there any more surgar?"

"It's war-time, son. We have to limit ourselves."

"Why?"

"Well, because the sugar is sent over for the soldiers and what we can get is awfully dear."

"Why are they fighting?"

"War was declared."

"Why?"

"Goodness me, I don't know. But we'll have to deny ourselves a lot of things. You'll get used to it."

"Couldn't we have them if there was no war?"

"Of course."

"Then why don't they stop?"

"You're too young to understand."

"That spoonful of sugar isn't enough for even cream of wheat and I don't like coffee without."

"Here, son, take mine. I don't need it."

"I don't like food without it so I don't see how you can."

"Never mind. I'm not very hungry and I'm used to doing without."

"No, I won't take yours, mother."

"Do as I say."

"When will they stop?"

"Pretty soon, we hope. Whenever peace is declared."

"Why don't they now?"

"Because it's war and they're fighting."

"What about?"

"Oh, a man was killed, so Germany declared war, and then some other country did until they were all fighting and now we are too for the Allies."

"Just because a man was killed?"

"There was more to it than that."

"Couldn't they settle it without fighting?"

"Why, I suppose so if they wanted."

"I never heard of anything so crazy. Yesterday we had to stand up and sing when a flag was raised in school. Is that what the flag means?"

"Yes, yes."

"There isn't any sense to it."

"You mustn't say that or you'll get arrested."

"Why?"

"For speaking like that about the flag. You mustn't. It stands for the country. You're a citizen and you've got to respect the flag."

"I don't see why if it means going hungry and getting killed."

"That's only because of war. It isn't like that most of the time."

"Then why is war?"

"Oh, it's a way of settling arguments."

"Does everybody want war?"

"No, I guess not."

"Then why do they fight?"

"Because the goverment declares war and they have to."

"Why?"

"Citizens have to support the government."

"But you said they didn't want war."

"Yes."

"Then why don't they get some other government?"

"You mustn't say that! It's treason."

"What's treason?"

"It means doing what the government doesn't want."

"Do people make the government?"

"Yes."

"You said they didn't want war."

"Yes."

"And the government declared war anyway."

"Yes."

"So now they get killed and we have to scrimp."

"Yes."

"It's all crazy. It's a rotten way. Why don't they stop?"

"Oh, stop asking questions. You don't understand. I never heard such questions from a boy your age."

"I don't care, it's all dippy. I wouldn't stand for a government like that."

"You'll have to be a solider when you're old enough."

"Why?"

"Because you're a citizen."

"I won't."

"They'll make you."

"Why?"

"They'll throw you in jail."

"That's better than getting killed. Do you see any sense to it?"

"Oh, stop asking questions and eat your breakfast."

XIII BERENICE

There was a lovely lady at the librarian's desk. She had great, dark, brown eyes, and an olive complexion, and a sensuous walk, and a voice like the caress of summer winds. She knew a good deal. She would talk to Drew by the hour after he had read stacks. Despite himself, he fell in love with her when he was fifteen, and she ten years his senior.

He hated her at first because she was a woman. Then he liked her because of the music in her voice. Then he loved her because she seemed remote and unreal, yet filled with the warmth of earth.

Rows of books stood, stack on stack, deck on deck, all around that vast and solitary room. Subdued light lent an atmosphere of dignity and quiet. Columns along the sides gave the suggestion of a Greek temple. Study tables of mahogany marched down the spacious floor. Far, far above, skylights blurred with the indigo of night. Here was a fitting shrine to commemorate the works of man.

To Drew, his first job at the library was an escape from bitter things; a flight to peace and the shadows of men who had walked long ago; a refuge in the magic of a voice and the mystery of siren eyes. He devoured a strange book on the great barrier reef of Australia. Sir Philip Sidney walked with him one evening, and old Ben Jonson. He was subtly poisoned by erotic pictures in a work on Pompeiian paintings. He read the

Satyricon, Apuleius, early issues of the *Transactions of the Royal Philosophical Society.* He was fascinated by a set on perfumes and perfumery. *The Decameron* bored him, a medical treatise with pictures of frightful diseases and human monsters entranced him. Socrates conversed with him one evening, the serenest words he ever heard. He devoured the *Dictionary of Occultism,* Sinistrari's *Demoniality,* a study of *Vampires and Vampirism.* And there was a wonderful group of books on astronomy with pictures of the mountains of the moon, and the nebulae, and flaming comets, and enormous promontories on the sun. Best of all he liked another set that showed extinct creatures browsing, fighting, roaming through the frondure and freakish arboration of bygone cycles. He read without direction or plan, as though he would swallow the whole sum of man's knowledge, if he had years enough to read. He lived in the past and the future, seldom in the present. Geologic ages and astronomical distances ran through his head. The imaginative sweep of *The Time-Machine* carried him breathlessly dreaming to the ultimate death of a world.

But ever there was the lovely lady at the far end of the room.

He wished the braces did not make his teeth so unattractive, or hurt so much.

XIV FIRST LOVE

The lovely lady spoke of far places, of New York, and Paris, California and Honolulu. Her voice was the singing of winds, the lapping of tides on alien shores, the sunlight on Southern cities.

High-school became a dreary routine. Drew was restless at home. He developed interest almost solely in his work, often arriving at the library before six o'clock. After the period of reading stacks, he had leisure to examine whatever book caught his fancy, volumes with pictures of flames from the sun, or the nude figures of models, or the infinite forms of snow-crystals.

Most pleasant of all was it to talk with Berenice — she must be Berenice, because so lovely and strange and enigmatic a woman could only have come from Poe — to hear music and to see beauty while watching those expressive features and being hypnotized by eyes that were a secret pool in which to drown for ever.

Drew would have liked to smile. He wanted to be Prince Charming, and carry the lovely lady off to his castle, and find that she was the youngest of the Three Princesses. But he could not smile, and the tumult within him was concealed by a wooden face. Prince Charming could not have had a thin, wasted body. Prince Charming must have been handsome. His face was gay, his mouth smiled, his eyes were filled with laughter. Prince Charming did not wear black bands, or possess crooked teeth.

Prince Charming would have laughed when the lovely lady said good-bye. He would have carried her away to his castle, instead of feeling miserable.

"You have been wonderfully helpful," said Berenice, her great eyes glowing mysterious.

"I-I had to be. That's what I was paid for." Prince Charming would not have made such a lame answer, or stammered.

"I am sure that you will like the new librarian, Miss Gerber."

"I hope so." Prince Charming would have been poetic.

"You have been a very helpful and pleasant assistant, Drew. This was my last evening here, you know. I wish you the very best of success."

The lovely lady bent over. A fragrance of far lands enveloped Drew. The Princess kissed him lightly on the forehead, the kiss of an angel, a spirit, a vision.

"There!" said the Princess. "Will you remember me? Come and see me in Church tomorrow at ten, if you wish, before I leave!"

And the lovely lady was gone, drifting through the door.

XV THIRD WITCH

What did Berenice mean by that remark, thought Drew. People do not ordinarily go to church upon a Saturday morning in May. Perhaps there was some special ceremony to be performed. He read through the morning paper, but could find no mention of weddings, rehearsals, religious ceremonies, rites, or meetings in which her name was mentioned.

A new interpretation occurred to him. The words were a secret message. This was to be a tryst. He was to attend church and there the lovely lady would met him behind a fluted column, and whisper the words of enchantment. They must be for him alone. They could not be told in evening at the doors of a library. They were holy words possessed of a mystery all their own, with the sorcery of magic casements opening on the foam of perilous seas in faery lands forlorn. They must be uttered where no other ears could hear. They must be spoken in sanctuary.

He loitered by the church at half past nine, and was inwardly pleased to find no strangers on its steps. He slipped inside and was disappointed on seeing several people seated in front pews. They talked with low tones which he could barely hear. He began to walk down the aisle, then reflected that he would attract attention if he rose again and left when Berenice came. So he turned, and crossed to his left, and stood between two pillars of the columned side-aisle.

Through stained glass windows shone a dim light. The Christ child, rosy and golden, lay in his manger. The sweet face of a woman smiled at him. She was idealized and lovely, but not so lovely as Berenice. In another window, rich with the deep blue of night and the reds and purples and golds of royal raiment, three wise men looked at a star that was like a new sun of glory, but Berenice would outshine that star. Angels, muted in the act of singing the songs of Paradise, spread their white wings across the ineffable radiance of heaven. Their song could not be so exquisite as the voice of Berenice.

Why must those persons remain, praying with inaudible but whispery words? Why must even a few others tread the aisles to make a scattering dozen worshippers? They were not for the lovely lady, nor she for them. Drew and she had a tryst to which none must be admitted.

The soft notes of the organ breathed forth. The wind and the sea and the moon and laughing leaves became vocal. There was quiet, until a princess arose to lilt a song for the break of day. There was silence, until the celebrants greeted the host with voices of gladness.

There was a sustained hush, a waiting hush, until the organ poured out the welcome of a stately melody that Drew had never heard. The dozen people turned their heads. Curious to see what interested them, he peered around a great column.

Berenice paced down the aisle with Prince Charming. Lovely as the light that flushes the eastern sky at dawn she looked, as she looked at Prince Charming. Rosy like the rose of Damask and ivory like the ivory that Marco Polo found, she stood at the altar where a man read from a book, and a strange man and a stranger woman stood at either side. Waiting like the tide at turn, a hush and a trembling, she gave her hand to Prince Charming. In her eyes was the glad light that warms the first day of spring.

Lovely, lovely and happy as a mating nightingale was Berenice as she left the church with Prince Charming....

Through the funereal silence of a colossal chamber, where figures in blurred outline stained the windows, and whence the worshippers had gone when the lovely lady and Prince Charming had fled to their castle, Drew walked. There was a weariness in the air. There was a heaviness in his heart.

The world is old, he thought; and he thought, the gods are dead.

XVI WHISPER IN DARKNESS

Two weeks after Miss Oran was married, school ended. A week later, Drew resigned his position. He could not endure the intolerable and dismal gloom which had crept into the library. He turned listlessly away from the long rows of books.

Neither of his parents raised objections or asked questions. Their hope of another child had never been fulfilled. Upon Drew they lavished everything they had. They were not well off, but they possessed a sufficiency. When pinching was necessary, Mary quietly did without things she wanted, and insisted at the table that she was not hungry in order to make him accept her piece of cake or dessert. The small salary which he earned had been a considerable help, but no protest came from them when he announced his intention of resigning.

Drew felt all the closer to them; to his mother because her self-sacrifices were limitless; to his father because he had undiminished faith in his strange son. There was a silent bond between the three that would never be destroyed though their lives pursued utterly different directions. In Mary's eyes the light of a personal God shone together with love for her child; an unthinking, unquestioning devotion to ideals which was impressive for its sincerity. Daniel, growing frailer and more disillusioned as the years passsed, and as he struggled along in the accountant's office waiting for preferment that did not come, looked ever more tired, and walked with an increasing erectness. He felt that his life was a failure from the high dreams of youth. To offset the inner weariness of spirit he assumed a jauntier outward bearing. Only in the privacy of his home did his face betray him, expressing the hope that he centered on his son's future, and regret over lost years which had not brought him success. They were both in their forties now. They realized that Drew would probably remain their only child. They realized too that he was definitely unusual. Whatever their secret desires, they allowed him to do much as he pleased.

That summer was the loneliest of his life. For long hours he would lie in his room, staring blankly while fantastic dreams coursed through his mind. He would imagine what he ought to have done with the lovely lady. He speculated about time, space, and god. He re-lived the nightmares of yestereve and tried to visualize the worst that might possibly afflict him tomorrow.

Always pain was present, racking his jaws and head. Continually his body craved more sustenance, but the torment of aching teeth was stronger than the dull emptiness of stomach. He pictured luxurious feasts that he would one day enjoy when the braces were removed. He idealized the Berenice that would some day come, bringing compassion, love, and understanding. He thought of the hosts of friends who would flock to his door, the wealth that would pour into his hands. He would build a huge mansion for himself. He would give millions to his parents so that they could travel the wide world over, live in luxury where they wished, and be rewarded for the years of denial.

A queer look gradually entered his gaze. His moodiness deepened. Growing like a bamboo, he was already tall as Daniel. He took to making long walks by himself, yet often could not recall where he had gone or what he had seen. In the face of a boy, he had the eyes of an ancient, sunken and shining as if with memory of childhood episodes or the splendor of a world to come, old griefs or fears of a future day.

It was from one of those walks to nowhere that he returned late on an evening in August and ate a dish of custard which Mary had left in the ice-box. He climbed exhausted, hungry, and pain-ridden to bed.

"Let me not be mad," he whispered behind his shut door. He held his burning head between his hands and rocked vaguely. "I shall go mad, mad, mad." There was no frenzy in his murmur. At his youthful age, he was already beyond despair. He spoke as a man in his dotage might mumble, weary of stale living yet fearful that a worse specter may approach.

"Ah, god, let me not be mad." Insanity would be a relief, but like all persons wavering on the dark line, he would withstand if he could.

Moonlight crept through the window to his bedstead. A ghostly pattern moved along the posts, on to the pillow, and finally crossed his face. It was hot as with fever through the pallor of his cheeks, and the lids flickered restlessly over gaunt eyes. The arm flung round the shadow of his hair twitched nervously. His lips were moving. They seemed, even in sleep, to say, "Let me not be mad."

XVII CLAVILUX

If **you will keep in** mind what I have just told you, ladies and gentlemen, I will proceed with the presentation. Remember, light, form, color, and motion are the components of this instrument which is played on keyboards like those of an organ. Perhaps some day we shall have Clavilux theaters as we now have motion-picture theaters. That day will come when enough people appreciate esthetics as a pure art, and find in the Clavilux their deepest spiritual needs and highest esthetic aspirations."

Now he goes to the keyboard and connects various switches. His fingers weave lightly across the keys, and abstract beauty made visible swirls across the screen. Geometric forms become mobile, cubes and spheres dissolve into the many-hued figures of a stranger geometry. Into the screen that miraculously acquires infinite depth, the stately procession drifts, a march of the conquering images. From the sides they float, in the tints of their innumerable splendor, and toward the endless they depart, shading to faintness and dying in darkness. It is the hymn of reason. It is the creations of the mind, for ever rising anew and for ever falling before the impregnable ramparts of the universe which it tries to encompass....

Torrents of light cascade like Niagaras from either side of the screen. Blinding hues and brilliant greens, capped with the dazzling white of sunfire, pour down abysmal gulfs there to dis-

sipate into the universal sea. The cascades pulse weaker and die. Across the sea stirs a troublous breath. Amber flecks brighten to orange, to red, to the sinister fire of creation. Each wave is tipped with flame, and the ocean boils restlessly. Out of steamy air comes a ball that dispels the clouds. Over darkling waters blows a breath of life. Softly stirs the sea, and the waves dance. Softly blows the wind and the white-caps rise. Softly shines the sun, and the breakers fall to foam on perilous seas...
.

The tetrahedrons march in imperial purple. They mount and form a pyramid. Far away beyond the infinite glows a sun. The topmost tetrahedron trembles, becomes pyramidal, spheral, and floats away transformed. The power of the sun is irresistible. It draws the tetrahedrons one by one till all are gone, swallowed by the orb that burns faintly brighter in the black of space. But shadows encroach. Even a sun must pass. It burns pale like a dying star, dim like an afterglow, and flickers out before the void triumphant. It is the funeral dirge of the universe that builds toward life and is conquered by death, until even itself passes away long after life and reason perish. It is the death procession of the cosmos....

XVIII CONSTANT COMPANIONS

During the whole of a dull, dark, and soundless day in the autumn of the year, when the clouds hung oppressively low in the heavens, I had been passing alone, on horseback, through a singularly dreary tract of country, and at length found myself, as the shades of the evening drew on, within view of the melancholy House of Usher...."

"Arma virumque cano, Troiae qui primus ab oris
Italiam, fato profugus Laviniaque venit
Litora, multum ille et terris iactatus et alto
Vi superum, saevae memorem Iunonis ob iram,
Multa quoque et bello passus, dum conderet urbe,
Inferretque deos Latio, genus unde Latinum
Albanique patres atque altae moenia Romae...."

"In the beginning was the word, and the word was in the presence of God, and the word was God.... How long, oh Lord, how long.... Thy breasts are as twin moons, and thy belly an heap of wheat...."

"Pou moi ta rhoda, pou moi ta ia, pou moi ta kalla selina?
Tadi to ia, tadi ta rhoda, tadi ta kalla selina."

"Now since these dead bones have already out-lasted the living ones of Methusaleh, and in a yard under ground, and thin walls of clay, out-worn all the strong and specious buildings above it; and quietly rested under the drums and tramplings of three conquests; What Prince can promise such diuturnity unto his Reliques, or might not gladly say,

Si ego componi versus in ossa velim?

"What song the Syrens sang, or what name Achilles assumed when he hid himself among women, though puzzling questions are not beyond all conjecture.... But the iniquity of oblivion blindly scattereth her poppy.... Darkness and light divide the course of time, and oblivion shares with memory a great part even of our living beings.... To weep into stones are fables.... In vain do individuals hope for immortality, or any patent from oblivion, in preservations below the Moon: Men have deceived even in their flatteries above the Sun, and studied conceits to perpetuate their names in heaven.... Life is a pure flame, and we live by an invisible sun within us...."

Magic words! Drew found them in the books he loved, and they came to him in the loneliness of night and the desolation of day. They were his friends and he lived with them. They took him to far places. They led him to lands preceding Mu, supercessive of time, and that were post-historic unto the Western World. They assumed solidarity before him in fire that burned of itself. They took from him hunger and they gave to him warmth. They were constant companions, bearing splendor, purple, ecstasy, and sonorous.

He lived with them. In the dark hours of night, he tried to add to them. They dreamed beside his pen and urged him on, but their royal circle admitted no impostors. They were curious words, haunting phrases, a kingdom among themselves, and all who entered there were kings. Few were accepted. All that he offered was less than the least of their number, but he would not turn away. Night after night, he sat outside their empire and they watched him toil through the desolate later days of summer. The years of pain had left a mark of indelible black, but the tide of purple was rising.

XIX STATE UNIVERSITY

Drew felt no thrill when he entered State University at sixteen. His mother was proud that he had outstripped most boys of his age. She was happy that he could receive the education which had been denied her. He had graduated with honors from high school. It worried her that he made no friends and appeared to prefer being by himself. He was morose and taciturn. He smiled so rarely that when he did laugh, she loved the change which brightened his melancholy face. She hoped he would distinguish himself. She wished he would join a fraternity and become more friendly. Sometimes she felt that he was a stranger to her. He seemed so far away and dreamy, so enwrapped in some unearthly vision. Her heart went out to him. Often she regretted forcing him to visit that dentist. She would almost have undone the work if she could. She would have endured the suffering herself were it possible. She clung to a hope that the future would amply repay him for the misery through which he was passing.

But the university meant little to him except a continuation of studies begun in high school. He registered. He took a test in English. He stood third on a freshman class of fifteen hundred and was exempted from rhetoric, which meant that they immediately enrolled him in a special sophomore class of star students. The honor had no significance in his eyes. He endured the required physical examination. They strapped a band round his arm and inflated it. Blood pressure normal. They weighed and measured him. Sixteen years, five feet eleven, a hundred and twenty pounds; forty underweight. Slight stoop of shoulders, posture B. Chest expansion almost none. Heart good. No vaccinations. Eyesight phenomenal. Urine tests average. No venereal disease. Teeth fair. Bronchial spots on lungs. Undernourished. Recommended for drill, extra gymnasium, and human economics.

Drew objected to all three but was forced to submit under penalty of having his registration cancelled. He disliked the extra gym. Sweating bodies, relay races, and the chlorined swimming pool annoyed him. He was bored by the course in human economics. It concerned the values of foods which he could not eat, diseases which he had no likelihood of contracting, exercises that he considered a waste of time, and essential factors in marriage that he could not envision. His deepest hatred was levied against drill. The ill-fitting drab uniform irritated him. Goose-step formations and child-like commands disgusted him. He remembered those months when he had been denied sugar, comforts, necessities, because of war. He recalled the sacrifices of his parents, and the headlines in papers. He detested everything connected with the military. He threatened to leave university because the completion of two years military training was required before a male student could apply for graduation. He resigned himself to the daily nuisance only when he encountered the dismay of his parents.

Thereafter he shouldered his rifle, learned the rigmarole of formations, studied the mechanism of automatic rifles and submachine guns, and paraded like a veteran. At the end of the compulsory period, he was given a rating of A and formally requested to enroll for training in the non-compulsory, non-commissioned advance R.O.T.C.

He sent for reply, "Mr. Drew Gordon acknowledges receipt of your request to take additioal training in the R.O.T.C. He declines because he is convinced that the abbreviation should read R.O.T. He took compulsory drill under protest and hopes that he will never again be subjected to learning the niceties of legalized murder."

For this piece of folly, he received a certificate of censure. He could think of no better disposal than to use it one morning in place of tissue paper.

XX THE RED SNOW

Drew **arose that morning in** March, tired and only half-awake as always. Snow lay thick on the ground, and for days past the weather had been biting cold.

His parents were seated before the usual grapefruit, cereal, toast and coffee when he descended, but they were talking with unusual animation.

" — the strangest thing I've seen since I came to this town."

"What do you suppose causes it?"

Drew heard the snatches of conversation as he entered the dining-room.

"Good morning, son."

"Hello! What's the excitement about?"

"Why, it's this snowfall. Have you noticed it? Go outside and take a look for yourself."

Never was he to forget the shock of that moment. The first strange natural phenomenon which he had seen presented itself. Because it was first, and so violently opposed to past experience, it made an all the more vivid impression upon him. To his sensitive mind, what he witnessed seemed wholly wrong; evil in a kind of cosmic sense; as if the entire order of the universe had become deranged. Half-awake as he was, he had a delusion that the nightmares of darkness were returned by day to plague him still. Nowhere on earth did red snow fall.

Yet there it drifted down, a steady, quiet stream of flakes, not white, but a weird brownish-red, tinting the air with a terrifying blood color and carpeting old drifts and ice with a film of sinister red. It was an alien scene on an alien world. This must be a dream-fantasia, unreal.

But for half an hour, the phenomenon persisted before the red snow ceased falling. The thermometer rose. An early thaw came, and by noon the crimson carpet was melted into brick- and sand-colored slush.

The evening paper carried a box about the freakish snowfall which had covered most of Center City. Scientists at State University were appealed to for explanations. A geologist suggested that air-currents in the upper strata of atmosphere had brought from other regions dust that colored the precipitation. It was, however, nearly five hundred miles to the nearest large deposits of such dust, and scarcely credible that, during precipitation over a wide area, one localized section should have received the entire burden of the air current. An astronomer proposed that volcanic dust carried from the far west or even Pacific islands was responsible; or that cosmic dust had come from outer space. Again, it was inconceivable to Drew that the dust should be selectively deposited, or carried so great a distance in compact quantities; and no eruptions of importance had occurred for years. Then a biologist offered the solution that a rare organism which sometimes tinted arctic ice far north had flourished on the snow after it fell. But how had the organism leaped so distantly from its region? And there were thousands of witnesses besides Drew who saw that the flakes were colored even while they dropped.

Whatever the cause, however the phenomenon might be explained by scientists, it left an indelible influence on the web of his thinking. It destroyed for ever his belief in a universe regulated by inviolable laws. If red snow could fall, why might not water some time freeze instead of boil over a fire? Why might not the sun rise from the west, or fail to rise at all?

What perpetual truth was there in physics, or past records, or external nature, or the cosmos itself as comprehended through experience, when a startling reversal of all that was normal had occurred? Was there any normal? He could not doubt his senses, because every one talked of the red snow, the newspapers carried accounts of it, and authorities gave explanations. He did not believe in any theistic religion. Now he was denied the belief in a universe that functioned in accordance with predictable, unchanging laws. What was left? In what could he believe if a simple and natural event like white snow materialized as something else, a deposit of blood-red crystals?

As a result of this one experience, his philosophy underwent a radical change. Often he had attempted to comprehend both the outer universe and the inner transitory world that was life. He did not believe in a deity, simply because he could not imagine the creation of something from nothing, and because it seemed an equally inexplicable evasion to say that a god was eternal and existed before the universe. He had believed in a system that functioned according to constants and certainties that were interpreted as laws; but now he was faced with a phenomenon that upset prediction. He began to wonder about other supposed facts. What proof was there that earth revolved around the sun? What proof of the attraction of gravity? What proof of the age of the earth? Fossils were judged by the estimated age of the rocks in which they were imbedded. The strata were computed according to the date of the fossils that they contained. Scientists forecast the return of the Leonids, and no Leonids came. They announced the order of the planets, and a new planet was discovered. Yet they also predicted the time and path of an eclipse to an exactness of above ninety-nine per cent. They foretold accurately when the tides would rise and fall, when sunrise and sunset would occur. But suppose that some day the eclipse failed, no tides came, and the sun stood still?

The product of this flux of speculation, begun by the red snowfall, was a new, half-mystical philosophy. The gods he had abandoned. The universe had tricked him. There were two alternatives left — to believe in nothing, because life was a sound and fury into which one was projected without wanting and from which one was sent against his deepest desires, and during which no striving achieved the goals one longed for except by chance, fate, accident, call it as one will; or to believe in change, paradoxically, as the only constant of an otherwise inconstant, unpredictable, and unintelligible existence.

During the weeks that he reflected, his thoughts were underlain by a concern with mutability. Nothing remained the same. Old friends passed. Houses disintegrated. Pavements wore away. Summer and autumn came, but winter effaced them, and in recurring spring the old year was dead. Never did the sun shine exactly as it had shone yesterday. No man's life paralleled another's. No two chairs were ever identical, and no day duplicated a day which was over. Indeed nothing remained the same. Each new experience was different from all others. Every man stood apart from his fellow beings. What if everything was closely or remotely related to everything else in the world? What if the wages the laborer received went for food, and clothing, and rent, and thus minutely influenced the course of a hundred industries and ever so faintly the balance of empires or of the world? Still there was no true identity; all things were interlocked, yet different; and human faces were never alike, and no two trees repeated each other, and never the same snow fell. Change only was sure. The universe crept on, from what to what? No man could say. That it existed at all became for a while the keynote of his philosophy; not why it existed, or what was its purpose, but merely that it existed. And the world could be understood only in the light of variation, mutability, change. Too sincere to adopt the subterfuge of a god in which he did not believe, too reflective and observant to accept the mechanics of a system that sometimes departed from certainty, he was left without recourse except the belief in a constant of change. The philosophy of futility, the acceptance of despair often entered his thoughts.

Trees, houses, birds, people, sunlight, books, mechanical appliances, the blush of color on a flower petal, the sigh of wind across dead leaves, those were real. The testimony of his senses was corroborated by the testimony of other people and by great men whose works he read. He could accept the reality of things, but that was not enough. Somewhere behind lay a riddle of no solution.

So he came to believe in things as they are, with the knowledge that they would not be, and the assumption that beneath them and above them was a mystery he would never solve. But did it matter whether he found an answer? For its own sake he loved the mystery of things, and echoed with one of his mental companions, there were not enough mysteries in heaven or earth to satisfy him.

XXI SVEN

Toward the close of his freshman year, Drew met the poet. They had been sitting next each other for some weeks in Romantic Origins before their greetings became more than casual.

For the first time in ten years, Drew established a friendship, all the deeper because it came at a time when the fantasies of loneliness had almost wholly usurped the place of reality. He found the warmth he craved at the period when he needed it most. It marked a turning-point in his life.

Perhaps the friendship began because the poet was not unlike himself in general appearance. He was a long, rangy fellow, well-built without being plump. He had gnarled hands that often twisted as if with an existence of their own while a faraway look came into his eyes. They were dreamy eyes, so dark as to appear coal-black. They usually seemed tired, sometimes haunted. They were the eyes of a man who beheld a vision which was constantly being shattered by experience and limited by the world. His was a Byronic face, distinctive after the manner of some old Norse deity; a strong yet gentle face. He was probably the worst dressed student on the campus. It seemed unlikely that his suits had ever been pressed. He achieved genius in his shirts which were invariably soiled. Drew watched him for weeks in the belief that some day he must appear in a clean shirt, but the day never came. It

remained an unsolved mystery how he managed to have an inexhaustible supply of dirty shirts, but the days were about equally divided in which he sprouted a stubble of beard that harmonized with the shirts, or was smooth shaven and freshened in contrast with the collar. A sprinkling of dandruff dusted his coat, always to the same amount. It might have been a relic from years back, for Drew never saw him brush it away, nor did its quantity ever vary in the slightest. He walked with a lazy slouch, though he was not round-shouldered. At different times, he wore disreputable felt hats of black, green, brown, and gray, with the brims pulled far down across his eyes; a blue beret and a tan one; a derby with a cigarette hole burned through the rear brim. All the coverings were in various stages of discoloration, deterioration, and wear. During warm months, he went bare-headed, but the result was even more striking because of the odd way in which he let his hair grow. It fell across his forehead in short, silky bangs, and circled his skull at about the level of his eyes. It was thick, soft, short hair, a nondescript dark. The effect was medieval, as though a prince had taken the disguise of a serf.

There was an unseen bond between them. One was outcast because he did not care, the other because circumstance had prevailed. Sven wanted only the reality of his vision, Drew sought a vision that would be reality. In lines that Drew loved, Sven gave the substance of his dream; and Drew, in the quiet of night, tried to turn his own ideal to prose wrought as a silversmith fashions a vessel.

Their friendship deepened to its full capacity virtually as soon as the advance was made. One conversation about books, people, experience, poetry, standards, and aspirations was sufficient to weld them. They became inseparable, lunching together, attending concerts and plays, strolling to classes and pairing off at drill. They became legendary. Striding across the snow-swept campus in a howling gale, Drew with his black hat pulled across his eyes and his cloak flapping behind like the wings of a demon, a tense expression on his features; Sven ambling beside him with an old felt similarly turned down and a long overcoat that seemed to increase his height, a glow of mystical pleasure upon his countenance, they were a sight to be remembered. Many a student and co-ed wondered who the two were who were seldom seen in the company of any one else, and who were so absorbed in their own discussion that they paid no attention to even the prettiest girls in the same tea-room, and who looked as though they might be interesting to know.

XXII END OF PAIN

"I suppose you'll be glad to get these braces off."

"Yes, Doctor, I should say I will."

"How long is it that you've had them?"

"About five years, I guess."

"That's a long time."

"A long time."

"You'll always be glad you had 'em straightened when you were young. Most people wait till they're grown. Then it's harder, and more painful."

"I'm glad it's over with."

"When they finally get around — just open your mouth a little wider, there, that's fine — why, it interferes with their lives, privately, socially, and in business."

"They ought to have it attended to."

"Keep quiet for just a minute more and we'll have this last band off in a jiffy. As I was saying, and when they do get around to having the orthodontia begun, they're often careless. I've had several patients who developed cavities because they didn't bother to brush their teeth thoroughly while they were wearing the braces. Did you?"

"Yes, morning and night."

"That's fine. I know it's harder to keep them clean when the bands and ligatures are in the way. Ah, there goes the last one."

"It feels good."

"Hmmm, this looks bad. You'll need some attention. No matter how careful you are, it often happens that cavities develop under the bands, especially down under the gums. Let's see, there are one, two, three, four, five, six big cavities. It's a good thing we got those bands off when we did. Now, when can you come for an appointment?"

XXIII ANGEL-FOOD

"Why, this looks like a Sunday dinner!" Drew exclaimed as he sat down at the table.

His mother beamed. "It's just to celebrate getting those horrid braces off," she said. "I thought I'd make you all the things you've been missing." A happy expression lighted her face. She was growing plump, and the gray hairs had begun to appear, but never had she looked so pleased as when Drew sat at the banquet she had prepared.

There was chicken-bone soup, boiling hot and rich. A wonderful salad of chopped pineapple, green pepper, grated carrot, and pimento, all in jello, sat temptingly upon lettuce, crisp and cool, with a crown of mayonnaise. The biggest and juiciest T-bone steak he had ever seen reposed upon a platter, garlanded with parsley and smothered with luscious morels. There were baked potatoes and fresh corn on the cob, asparagus in creamy gravy. A bowl of stuffed olives winked at him. Newly done cinnamon rolls lay steaming upon a plate. Beside them stood an angel-food cake, delicate, fluffy, and perfect. For dessert, there were mince pie as only she could make it, and strawberry shortcake with whipped cream. The feast was topped with aromatic coffee, and a goblet of the champagne that remained from her wedding.

Had the dishes been turnips and cabbage, Drew felt that he would have enjoyed it just the same. So great was his relief at having the braces removed that even left-overs would have seemed a luxury. His mother watched him anxiously. The smile that gradually crept across his features, the starved look that faded out of his eyes, the pleasure and content that were symbolized by his full partaking of the feast were ample reward to her for the years of his pain and hunger.

"Do you like it?" she asked.

"Perfect," he answered. "There isn't anything else that I want or could eat if I did. I'd almost be willing to go through the dental work again if I could count on something like this at the end."

Mary looked her happiness.

It was only in the seclusion of his room that Drew flung himself down hours later and buried his face in the pillows. "...She will never know," he whispered. "After all these years, and now I can't even enjoy good things. I suppose it's because I looked forward to it so much that there wasn't anything left when the time came. The reality couldn't live up to my anticipation."

...He wakened with a start. Dawn had broken long since. He was lying on the bed, his clothing rumpled, just as he had thrown himself the night before. A cloud seemed to have lifted from his head, a weight from his shoulders.

He tried to puzzle out why he should feel refreshed. As he was descending the stairs, the explanation occurred to him. For the first time in years he had not dreamed. No nightmares had tortured his sleep. Gone were the mental terrors with the physical pain.

He rushed to the great mirror above the mantel. His parents, seated at breakfast, were astonished when they saw him erupt into the parlor and stand grinning like an imbecile at his reflection. A long forefinger delicately poked its way across teeth and gums.

"How does it feel?" called Mary.

"All wrong," he replied candidly. "I got so used to the junk that now it's gone my mouth feels like the Mammoth Cavern!"

XXIV EBONY AND CRYSTAL

One afternoon, when Drew was striding through the heart of Center City, he passed a magazine store. Impulsively he swung around and entered. He examined the counters on which periodicals from all parts of the world were displayed. Here and there he opened a journal as he browsed through the array. Pretty girls, diving girls, smiling girls, girls' heads, girls in all stages of raiment from evening gowns to lingerie decorated the majority of covers. He passed them by. Popular weeklies and monthlies he wholly ignored, because they catered to the lowest common denominator of taste in which he had no interest whatever. They represented an average. Perhaps they attained a high level of mediocrity, but mediocrity in any form was not for him. He desired always and only the exceptional, the unusual.

He found it in a magazine tucked away among the rearmost counters. The magazine had a frightening cover in which a living skeleton figured. The cover instantly reminded him of a nightmare he had once experienced. The surprise of finding such a cover illustration among the average run made him pause to look over its contents. In the end, he bought a copy and took it home.

Before reading the stories which promised a feast of the morbid and bizarre, he browsed through its features. They included a page of editorial comments, a section devoted to reader reactions, a checklist of who the authors were,

announcements of stories to come, and invitations for criticism. During this perusal, he changed upon reference to a
book of "mad, strange, haunted" verse by a California poet.
The nature of the reference caught his attention. He read it
several times, fascinated by the description. Sven had begun to
make him feel the beauties of poetry. Moved by a sudden decision, he wrote to the publisher and inclosed a money-order for
a copy of the poet's volume.

The book arrived ten days later. He unwrapped it and
regarded it with disappointment. "I guess I wasted the money,"
he thought. The book was cheaply bound. It had staples
instead of sewn signatures. It bore pen corrections on many
pages. The printing was poor. There were no end papers at all.
Mistakes were frequent, and its general appearance miserable.
Altogether, it was the most unattractive book he had ever seen.

Indifferently, he glanced insde. The first poem was an odd
little lyric called *Arabesque*. Somehow, though its words were
simple, it achieved the impressive symmetry of a temple, a
chiselled and classic perfection, yet suggestive of beauty
touched with strangeness. Drew read on, and the book
became a living empire through which he wandered. A magic
casement had opened. The familiar world passed away. In its
place rose a kingdom of fantasy and glory, of haunted pools
and alien spires. The wind sang to him and the sea gave up its
secrets. The opulence of the Arabian Nights unfolded; ornate
decorations were scrolled upon these leaves. It was poetry that
ached with the burden of a wonderful vision that life must
always fall short of. It was the cry of a dead man. Lost Atlantis
appeared from fabulous waters; and lands above the sun were
travelled. Gods became vocal, and fens glimmered with were-
light. Sonorous as the music of Homer were some of these
lines; and others as sad as the web of Penelope.

These were not songs for the many, or lyrics for the few.
They were the language of hierophants, couched in cryptical
symbols. Often they were so cryptic as to be meaningless; but

often, too, they were instinct with magic. They were a sorcery breathed by only witches, and read by neophytes alone. They were ebony and crystal.

Drew exhaled a long sigh when he had finished the book. A tremendous vista had opened up to him. He felt as though he had gone beyond the limits of imagination and the ends of the universe. That prose poem called *The Shadows* with its funereal and enormous rhythm, its stately cadences, its melancholy splendors and eccentric purple, was only one among many that immediately assumed front rank among his invisible companions. Here was indeed a plenitude of beauty touched with strangeness; an extravagance of the remote, the unearthly, the distant and dreaming regions he longed for.

Clark Ashton Smith. It was a name he had never before heard of. Ebony and Crystal. It was a book that no one knew. Its very oblivion was an added pleasure for Drew. He possessed something denied to other mortals; he owned a magic key of whose existence none were aware. He read the poems again and again, until they became inherent in his mental web. Many of them he knew by heart, but he kept them to himself. Average people would not understand. He would, and so would a handful of worshippers; but here could the multitude never come to worship, for this was a shrine apart.

XXV JENNIFER

"Hello, Sven, I wondered why you weren't in class today."

"Oh, I had other things to do. Where are you headed?"

"The library. I've got to catch up in my assignments. What about lunch this noon?"

"Why, I'm having lunch with Jennifer but — "

"Jenifer?"

"She's a girl I met in Art Appreciation and — "

"Oh. That's too bad. Well, maybe we can have lunch tomorrow."

"Why don't you come along? She's a damn' fine kid. You'll probably see a lot of her from now on so you might as well meet her now as later."

"Well, I don't know. I'd like to see you but — "

"Oh, forget your woman-hating business for once. I know you'll like Jennifer. She won't bite you."

Drew smiled despite himself. His imagination sometimes tricked him by transforming into a faithful picture the remarks or comments of Sven. This particular projection was so grotesque that it amused him; and because he was, he decided to accompany Sven though ordinarily no amount of persuasion would have induced him to include a girl in any engagement.

He met them on the steps of Founders Hall after his fourth hour. Sven waved a gnarled paw above the host crowding out. Drew slid around co-eds and between jostling students until he reached them.

"Let's hurry before all the booths are taken," suggested Sven. "Jene, this is Mr. Gordon. Drew, Miss Dane."

Drew looked about him in some surprise. A big man wih a couple of cronies drifted away, and there stood Jennifer smiling shyly up at him. She was one of the smallest women he had ever seen and she possessed the largest pair of brown eyes. He noticed only that her complexion was rich, dark, and warm, and that she acknowledged the introduction in a voice whose depth rivalled its sweetness before they hurried off.

Drew was silent during the walk to Hangout. A conflict of emotions upset him. He resented the presence of the girl because she interfered with his friendship. He looked down on her because she was member of a sex that he despised. He regretted Sven's obvious interest because he feared a break-up in their own relation. At the same time, he respected the choice of his friend simply because he had taken Sven wholly into his life, and what Sven did was right. To these currents was added the personality of the girl with her warmth, friendliness, and enthusiasms.

XXVI SVEN, JENNIFER, AND DREW

Sven — My main objection to this place is that it's so damn' noisy.

Jene — They all are. Let's grab a booth before someone else takes it. Anyway, I've heard you speak so much about Drew that I want to know what he's like. I won't have a chance to know him if we waste the whole hour looking for a quiet tearoom.

Sven — You won't know him even if we do stay here. He hates women.

Jene — Do you? That sounds promising. I'm sure we're going to like each other, Drew — do you mind if I call you that?

Drew — Not at all.

Jene — You sit opposite me so that I can look at you. Ooooooh, what a beautiful blush!

Sven — Well, now, Mr. Gordon, would you mind telling us why you've gone in for that lovely beet effect?

Drew — I can't help it if —

Jene — Oh, Sven, don't you want to sit beside me? I can't look at both of you two tall men at once.

Sven — Don't ever fall for a girl, Drew. See what's happened to me? I'm ordered around just like that.

Jene — You know it isn't so. Do you think that's fair, Drew?

Drew — Well, I don't see why not.

Sven — Ha! Mr. Gordon is in his usual form.

Jene — I don't care. I think he's awfully nice and I know he would agree with me if you didn't lord it over him.

Sven — Is that what you'd like to do to me, Jene?

Drew — So that's what you think of me? Well, for a girl —

Jene — It isn't polite to fight before lunch. Let's order first. Are you wealthy today?

Sven — Not any more than usual. I guess you can have the lunch special if you want it.

Drew — I have a dollar.

Sven — Here's where we all eat. Somebody must have left you a fortune.

Jene — No, I'll do with a sandwich and coffee. It isn't fair to make Drew pay.

Drew — Sven and I often pool resources, don't we?

Sven — I'll admit I'm usually broke. Don't rub it in.

Drew — Oh, I'm sorry, I didn't mean it that way.

Sven — Damn it, now we'll have to spend the whole hour trying to smooth Mr. Gordon's ruffled feelings.

Jene — Is he as sensitive as all that?

Sven — More.

Drew — Let's all have the regular lunch and worry about paying afterwards.

Jene — That was sweet of you. You are nice when you want to be.

Sven — Notice that when you want to be.

Drew — I did. You must have been telling tales.

Sven — Me? Ha! You are too suspicious.

Jene — Very wise of him, I would say. Tell me, Drew, what do you do?

Drew — Oh, nothing much. Study, read, and sometimes write.

Jene — Don't tell me you write poetry too?

Drew — No, I wish I could. I go in for stories. Do you write?

Jene — No, I sometimes do sketches.

Drew — I'd rather be an artist than anything else.

Jene — Thank you, she said shyly. That was very well put.

Sven — He didn't mean it. That was unconscious.

Jene — How in the world have you managed to get along with him?

Drew — How have you?

Jene — That isn't fair. I asked first.

Drew — I know you did but —

Sven — Here's the food. Let's stop the argument till later.

Jene — It wasn't an argument.

Sven — It was too.

Jene — It wasn't so.

Drew — I'm hungry. Do you mind if I go ahead while you two fight it out?

Jene — Oh, do you think we were fighting?

Sven — Himmel, can't we even talk without you accusing us of fighting?

Drew — This soup is good.

Sven — Dog. Pig. Writer. Yah, writer. Trying to change the subject.

Drew — It's a nice day today all day.

Sven — That's the profoundest remark you've ever made.

Drew — What do you think of geology?

Sven — Well, now, I'll tell you. I think —

Jene — As long as you're talking and I've finished my soup do you care if I try out yours, Sven?

Sven — Yes, I do, dammit, I merely wanted to convince this — hey, let my soup alone!

Jene — Oh, all right, she said sadly. If you insist on being that way.

Sven — Well, Jene, what sort of girl is it that finishes her soup before anyone else and then wants to start in on theirs?

Jene — Was that a nice thing to say? Just for that I'll talk to Drew and you can go ahead sip your darn old soup.

Sven — For goodness sake, will you stop talking about soup? I'll be so sick of hearing the word pretty soon that I won't be able to finish it.

Jene — Goody. Soup, soup, soup, soup, soup, soup —

Sven — Slurp, slurp, slurp, slurp —

Jene — Oh, what awful sounds. I'm sure that Drew must be enjoying this.

Drew — I am. It was good soup.

Jene — That wasn't what I meant. I meant us and me.

Drew — I know it wasn't but I deal with important problems first.

Jene — Ouch! Do you hate women as bad as all that?

Drew — No. Worse.

Jene — But I'm such a little harmless one. I don't care, I think you're nice.

Drew — Is that one of your favorite words?

Sven — Oh, stop being sarcastic.

Drew — Why?

Sven — You aren't old enough to know better.

Jene — How old is he?

Sven — Eighteen, almost.

Jene — Hmmm. A mere infant.

Drew — I am not, I would have you know. Age doesn't matter. I'm a lot older in other ways.

Jene — What ways?

Drew — In, well, I guess I won't say. It would sound like bragging.

Sven — That's a hell of an excuse. Come again.

Drew — How old are you, Miss Dane?

Jene — The name is Jennifer, Jene to you, if you please. Twenty.

Drew — Hmmm. A mere babe in arms.

Jene — I like that! I —

Drew — I hoped you would. When you're as mature —

Sven — As what?

Drew — As mature as —

Sven — That's what I thought you said but I didn't think you knew the word.

Drew — I never believed I'd live to see the day when we would squabble.

Sven — Now we've hurt his damn' feelings again. What's the matter? Here you start out in better form than I've ever seen you show before and every once in a while you fold up like a pup. Nothing personal is meant, Drew. We're just kidding.

Drew — Don't take me seriously.

Sven — For gosh sake, don't look so mad then.

Drew — Did I? Oh — here's the Spanish steak.

Jene — I just knew it would turn out to be hamburger. Oh, well, I'll pretend it's turkey. Turkey yesterday and turkey tomorrow but never today.

Drew — That sounds like a quotation.

Jene — It is, from Alice in Wonderland, or it would be if I hadn't changed it. Don't tell me you haven't read it?

Drew — No, I'm afraid I haven't.

Jene — Drew Gordon! You ought to be ashamed of yourself! Weren't you ever young? How can you pretend to be grown up when you haven't read it?

Drew — I can't read everything.

Sven — All right, go ahead and sulk. I'm going to eat.

Waitress — Will you have coffee now or later?

Jene — Later, please, and tea with lemon instead.

Sven — Black coffee, now.

Drew — Yes.

Sven — What kind of an answer do you call that?

Drew — I mean, yes, now and later. Black with cream on the side.

Sven — What's the point of that?

Drew — Oh, I'll drink the cream and then drink the coffee.

Sven — He is completely out of his head. Pay no attention to him, Jene.

Jene — I can't anyway. I'm too busy eating.

Sven — That's a good idea. I better start before you cast hungry eyes on my alleged steak.

Drew — Aren't you staking a lot on that?

Sven — For god's sake, are you going to start punning again?

Jene — I hope you're mistaken.

Sven — Let's take time out.

Jene — All right, I'm cowed.

Drew — Bully of you, I'd say.

Sven — Who asked you to horn in?

Jene — He was only trying a flank attack.

Sven — I move that we call a halt before we're all milcontent.

Drew — Phooey. Those last two were putrid.

Jene — I think so too. You haven't seen him at his worst though. If it keeps up long enough it gets to the point where only one letter is the same.

Drew — Thank heaven, I've missed that.

Sven — You won't for long.

Waitress — Who is the coffee with cream on the side?

Drew — Madam, *I* am the coffee. Do you not recognize my bean?

Sven — Don't mind him, he's bein' sarcastic.

Waitress — I beg your pardon?

Jene — You'll do nothing of the sort, Drew.

Sven — Of course not. He's just as albeeno.

Jene — The word is albeyeno.

Sven — It was white of you to put me wise.

Jene — Why do you insist on making such puns?

Waitress — Who is the black coffee?

Drew — That must be you, Sven, you're such a blackguard.

Jene — This is too much for me. I'm going to black my steak.

Sven — Oh my god, did you hear that? And I dragged you into this! Well, Drew, you know that my intentions were of the best.

Drew — I know darn well they weren't.

Sven — You think so, uh? I don't know but what you're right.

Drew — Of course. I always am.

Jene — I'm glad to hear you say that. I love modesty.

Drew — Too bad we have to start out by being bitter enemies.

Jene — Isn't it pleasant? Tell me, are you always like this when you first meet a girl?

Drew — Always.

Sven — That's easy to say when you're about the first he's known.

Jene — Am I really?

Drew — Certainly, except for the others.

Jene — You must know lots and lots about women. Tell me, how did you like the first woman you knew? Did you love her? Was she blonde or brunette? Do you enjoy being kissed? Are your intentions honorable? Have you always done the decent thing?

Drew — Come, come, that isn't fair.

Jene — Just like a man, trying to dodge the issue.

Drew — I'm not.

Sven — While you're fighting, I'm going to eat this damn' pie.

Jene — We're not fighting.

Drew — We are too. What kind of pie is it?

Sven — It's supposed to be apricot.

Drew — Well, I never before saw apricots that looked like peaches.

Waitress — Sorry, sir, but we're all out of apricot. Would you like ice-cream instead?

Drew — No, I guess not, I'll take the peach.

Sven — Ha! You've been holding out on us. Who is she?

Drew — I mean, the peach pie.

Sven — You can't slide out of it that easily. The secret is out.

Jene — And you told me he was a woman-hater. I'm so disappointed in you, Drew. To think that you've deliberately misled me and all this while you've had a peach. You're just like Lee.

Drew — Who is he?

Jene — It isn't a he. It's Helione Forrest, a friend of mine. She likes peaches, and Walter jam Mare, and De Bussy, and cats. I think you'd like her.

Drew — I don't. I'm not interested in women.

Sven — See? I told you.

Jene — I don't care, I think he's awfully misunderstood. You must meet her some time, Drew. She's at art school now but I think she'll be back at the U for fall term. I know that you two will — Drew — My word, it's time for class. Do you all have one-thirties?

Sven — Sure, but we're cutting them. Why don't you stay and keep us company.

Jene — Do stay. It'll be fun.

Drew — No, I've got to go.

Jene — I hope we'll see more of you, Drew. I heard so much about you from Sven that I was pleased to meet you and have you join us.

Drew — I'm sorry I have to dash but I'll be late as it is. So long!

XXVII BLUE SUN

It was a hot, dry summer. The American [*sic*] sank to the lowest level in history. Yellow grass drooped on lawns in July. August found leaves crisping on trees. Outside the city, corn burnt on its stalk, and earth baked to a hardness in which nothing could thrive. So early, there was a forest fire in the north woods. A pall of smoke drifted across the city, and for days the air was fogged with fumes of a disaster two hundred miles away.

August blazed into September. The parched soil became dusty from drought. A deluge of rain soaked the ground early in September before the dry spell continued. The moisture came too late to save most crops. The melon crop might be good, but grains, vegetables, and most fruits were ruined.

Even livestock felt the abnormal heat. Cows lolled in whatever shade they could find. Hogs waddled in vain around mud holes that had turned to sun-hardened clay. Historic lakes dried up. Wild fowl flew south earlier than ever before. A haze blurred the atmosphere, and trees were powdery with dust. Along the country roads, leaves of oak and maple assumed a silver-whitish aspect from the fine coating. By moonlight they shone ghostly, and a myriad particles glittered faintly.

Toward the end of September, autumn winds began to blow. No matter how tightly windows were closed, deposits as soft as talcum crept into houses and covered all objects. The sun glowed murky. On many days, walking was a perilous venture, so filled with dirt and debris was the air. Breathing became unpleasant. Grit caused innumerable smarting eyes. A cake gathered around his mouth-corners before Drew was outside for five minutes, on frequent occasions.

The leaves, russet and amber and brown, cinnamon colored and red sinister, curled on sidewalk and street. They made a whispery rustle, dry as bones, when stirred. They voiced a thin rasp when they drifted across the dead grass of lawns.

It was a week after school opened that Drew witnessed the second of those natural phenomena which so deeply impressed his imagination. He had lunched with Sven and Jennifer, but the talk was curiously dull, as though the long drought had finally affected even conversation. For the most part, the three sat toying with utensils, or looking glumly at food, or uttering commonplaces.

Drew had classes for two periods after the noon hour. The professors droned on with lectures that did not hold his attention. The shifting of students was as restless as the leaves outside. Drew, staring through windows that were dim with grime, could see that a dust-storm was brewing, for the air darkened, and the wind wailed around cornices. He felt moodier than he had in a long while. His thoughts kept straying from the lecture, and the far away look of a dreamer filmed his eyes. He was spiritually weary, yet became enwrapped in a vision of time and space. It was a day to remember *Ebony and Crystal*, to recall *The Time Machine*, to think of the *Ode to the West Wind*, and to murmur the closing stanzas of *The Garden of Proserpine*.

When his last class ended, Drew followed the current of students pouring out. Hardly conscious of their purpose, he let himself be jostled along. Despite his friendship with Sven, and the warmth of Jene's personality, he felt alone, and as lonely as though he were a Crusoe upon a desert island. By the accidents of life, he was separated from the crowds pushing around him. His undefined ideal, which was yet supreme for all its vagueness, ruled his thoughts. He dreamed of a future that he could not know; the future of a million years hence; and of a past that was dead as the leaves that fell; the past of Greece and Rome, of Egypt, Atlantis, and Mu, and Lemuria, of the Dawn Age and the Carboniferous Period. What was it he longed for? He did not know. Something beyond life, perhaps; a dream of perfection; a vision of immortality against which the figures of men were as shadows groping in gloom, and the substance of things as mist.

He waked from his reverie to find himself crossing the Memorial Grounds, alone. Vast clouds of dust whirled through the air. It was mid-afternoon, yet darkness as of sunset hung over him. An infinite whisper was abroad, a suggestion of far, gigantic wings beating across voids. The wind shrilled around unseen buildings. He looked up, and the sky was smouldering. A huge, bloody red pall curtained all the heavens above, as though they themselves were burning, or a universal holocaust flamed beyond; it was like a visible prophecy of doomsday and vengeance to be. From the midst of that enormous conflagration peered a dull-blue sun. By some freak of atmosphere, its rays were distorted by dust; and like the fantastic orb in a nightmare, or of a star undiscovered, it glared sullenly through smoking clouds; sullen and old; old and weary; a dim, antique sun that was dying. It gave no light or life, this eerie ball that somehow suggested evil in a cosmic sense. It was a staring eye, but its peculiar blue was like nothing Drew had ever witnessed.

All the way home, he sat brooding, and peered through street-car windows at the dust, the burning sky, and the unnatural sun. He was unconscious of the grime that covered his face while he walked those final few blocks to his home. In a kind of sad ecstasy, he lay on his bed, watching the fantastic sun, the wildly driven dust, and the sky that smouldered as though a whole universe was about to flame.

XXVIII HELIONE

As Drew was striding across the campus toward his p.o. box one day not long after the dust storm, he met Sven, Jennifer, and a strange girl emerging from the Control Building.

"Hello, we were just looking for you!" Sven shouted through the passersby.

"This is Drew — Drew Gordon — you've heard me speak of him, Lee. Drew, do you know Miss Forrest?" asked Jennifer as Drew swung out of the stream of hurrying students.

"How do you do?" he acknowledged awkwardly, bowing.

"We're going over to Hangout for malteds. Come along," Sven urged cheerily.

"I can't. I have a class in five minutes."

"Oh, cut it."

"Thanks, but I guess I won't. See you later. I'm very glad to have met you, Miss Forrest, sorry I have to rush away."

He hastened to his p.o. box and collected mail — the student daily which he dropped in a waste-paper receptacle, notices of college events, and a note from Sven asking him to come to Hangout if he received the message before five.

"Oh, well," he shrugged. "I'll have to travel some to make that class." He stalked out.

Sven, Jennifer and Miss Forrest were standing where he had left them.

"We knew you wouldn't keep us waiting," began Sven blithely.

"Sorry, Sven, but I've got to rush to class."

"Let the damn' class go," the poet swore disgustedly. "Don't you ever cut them? We've all got classes and we're all walking out. You'd better join us and talk to Lee while we get our malteds."

Sven stuck an arm through Drew's left arm and unceremoniously led him off, the two girls on either side.

"What's wrong with this picture?" Jennifer asked gayly.

"Drew of course," Sven assured her. "He's cutting his first class and it hurts like a wisdom tooth."

The new girl laughed, a genuine, throaty, innocent, and yet oddly mirthless laugh. "His first class? Goodness, is he a freshman?"

"No, junior."

"Well, Drew, I hope you don't mind my calling you Drew but I've heard Sven and Jene speak of you so often that I feel as if I'd know you, don't let us lure you away from the righteous path to halls of learning."

"It's not that. It's just that I — that I — haven't cut any classes before," he concluded lamely.

"Do come with us and be wicked."

He could not decide whether she was serious or ironical. Her voice had an ambiguous inflection.

He cast sidewise glances at her as they walked toward Hangout, having corrected the picture. She seemed like an unusual girl. Physically, the feature that impressed him most was the scar which ran white down her left cheek. It did not seem like a disfigurement. The fine line was barely noticeable against the texture of skin, yet it subtly emphasized her features. He was in a quandary as to whether the mark detracted from or brought out her loveliness of countenance, for she possessed one of the loveliest faces he had ever seen, with a complexion of exquisite delicacy, eyes of indefinable green, long black lashes, and a nose classic in profile, the whole line from forehead to chin attractive, except that her upper lip slightly over-arched the lower. She had a peculiar walk, a sort of swinging glide, lithe, voluptuous, and natural. Her lips were a delight to watch, tender, rosy-soft, and with a suggestion of virginity that was naively appealing. They made a perfect curve, and their corners turned neither up nor down, but inward. She owned hair of coppery splendor, unbobbed, a crown of flame in which the sunlight ran riot. She wore an odd dress that almost harmonized with her. Mostly red, a flary, violent red, it had a kind of totem design around the waist. It seemed a bit incongruous with her appearance, but its incongruity somehow emphasized her beauty of figure. She was rather tall, he saw as she swung easily along in stride with him, sensuously developed, and her teeth were dazzling when she smiled. She was apparently a person of contrasts. He had already, so soon, decided that she was one of those rare women who are gifted with both great personal charm and intellectual ability. He seemed to remember that Sven or Jene had mentioned the girl to him at some time or other.

He remained silent as they walked on. Jene crossed to Miss Forrest and they began an animated conversation. Sven again held his arm as if he feared that Drew would escape.

"I really ought to be in class," was Drew's last, feeble protest.

"We all ought to be, but what's the sense of being so damned religious about attendance? You learn facts that you can find for yourself if you study. You're asked questions that you can answer if you've read the assignments. From now on, you are going to be led astray and like it. You're coming with us. It's about time you knew Lee, the two of you have so much in common and anyway you've pulled this woman-hating business too long. I'm tired of it."

"Are you lecturing Drew again, you bully?" interrupted Jennifer.

"Go right on talking to Lee and I won't mind in the least. As I was saying before I was so rudely interrupted — "

"Who's being rude now?"

"Can't a couple of helpless girls even ask a question if they want to?" broke in Miss Forrest with a mock mask.

Drew regarded her curiously. In her question and expression was the trace of a guise.

XXIX A WOMAN LIKE THE SUN

You have an interesting face," exclaimed the new girl. "A little bit like Stevenson, and with a sort of romantic melancholy. And you've got the oldest eyes I've ever seen in a man! No, don't move. Sit still while I sketch you."

Startled by this sudden appraisal, Drew did as he was told. They had barely taken seats in a booth at Hangout and given their orders. She seized the stub of a pencil, slipped a paper napkin from its container, and with quick, sure strokes caught his head. Her hands fascinated him. They were small, of patrician grace, and the fingers, which tapered, were wonderfully supple. Their skin was of a milky texture against which her veins were faintly outlined. And yet they were old hands, with tiny wrinkles, and cold hands, that seemed almost bloodless. But once, when her pencil broke and Drew offered his, their fingers touched. He tingled from the contact as though from an electric shock, and a glow simultaneously fleeted through her green eyes. He divined that a similar expression was in his. As if each had opened a door, and had psychically crossed a threshold.

"Hmmm, it isn't very good," she candidly judged as she surveyed her work. "Would you like to see it?"

He studied the portrait. It gave him a strange sensation thus to scrutinize his features interpreted through the vision of one who had known him so short a time. He saw dark sockets with

lids half-veiling the eyes, an ascetic forehead, finely modelled cheeks, and a bitter mouth. It was a sensitive face, expressive of intolerance, weariness, and pride. It was an old-young face. Its lips, he noted, matched those of the artist to a surprising degree. They curved inward at the corners and were only full enough to escape being sensual. It was almost a woman's mouth. All in all, a contrasty face, where intellectual powers of maturity vied with the weaknesses of delayed adolescence. In a way, he resented the sketch. The new girl had no right to read him so accurately on a first meeting. And despite her assertion, the drawing showed talent in its mastery of line.

"It's not too bad. For a woman," he remarked coldly.

The girl looked as if she were going to cry, then she seemed angry. She started to speak but surprised him by breaking into a sophisticated laugh. That silvery sound was a paradox to her naiveté, of countenance.

"I'll do another of you sometime, and with more truth," she retorted.

"Oh, for goodness' sake, are you going to be crabby already? After all, you've just met the girl," Sven chided Drew with disgust. Sven, seeing only the external, did not realize that Drew's remark was an outer defense to conceal his inner approval. For Drew instantly liked the girl. In that moment, intuition told him all that his mind later accepted. He knew why she had looked hurt — she was sensitive as he, and somewhere in her unknown past she had suffered a loneliness or unhappiness such as he had endured. She had reacted with a first instinct to defend herself by striking back. She had resorted to a mask of coolness as he would have done, to hide the inner hurt. All this he guessed, and guessed also that she had within her depths of fire, now as frozen as his, waiting only for the magic touch to awaken her. Already he felt as though he had known her for a long time, perhaps mystically in another existence, he fancied idly; and that the bleak course of his life had been set to make him realize more keenly the importance of her coming.

He became aware that she was regarding him with an intent, puzzled expression, like that preceding recognition. A coincidence occurred. Both opened their mouths and spoke as one.

"I feel as if I'd met you before," exclaimed Helione.

"Somewhere, sometime, I must have known you, long ago," said Drew.

"What is this, a rehearsal? Or a reincarnation?" Jene accused.

"Neither," answered Sven. "It's merely the beginning of what I prophesied."

Helione and Drew blushed in unison. It was the only time he ever saw her face color. He warmed with disproportionate pleasure that he was not alone a subject for comment.

"Himmel," Sven remarked with interested eyes. "What do you two call that effect? I hadn't realized we were taking a couple of chameleons to tea."

Helione turned to him with an indignant, "Do you think it's quite fair to criticize him for – ", just as Drew faced him and began, "You shouldn't be so personal about Helione's changing – "…. Both stopped abruptly, realizing that each had sprung to the other's defense.

Jennifer and Sven regarded them, surprised by the unity of their reactions. Drew and Helione looked at each other in silence. The ice had begun to melt. An unseen current was playing between them, a magnet more powerful than mind or emotion.

Spontaneously a ripple of delight amused them as they appreciated the unusual episode. Four interlocking friendships were established.

XXX SECOND LOVE

that sounds like the postman at our box but i dont imagine he will leave anything for me and if there is its sure to be an ad or a bill from the college shop unless ive overdrawn my checking account again and they want me to fix it up ill see what there is and the rest of my ironing can wait but even if theres nothing i believe ill have a melachrino before i begin on the lingerie though theres no reason why anyone should be writing me since i never have time to answer letters and anyway its such a bother i wouldnt in the least mind receiving loads of letters thats fun but i simply cant get around to answering so its no wonder that people stop sending me them i do believe i havent made more than six letters in my whole life up to now and they were all for jennifer on that lovely creamcolored stationery she gave me for my birthday but i suppose i used it mostly to prove how much i liked her since i never make letters otherwise my word there is something after all and its ages ago that anyone last remembered me i wonder who it can be for the handwriting isnt a bit familiar the tails of the letter curl up and backward so it must be maybe a love letter because that book on handwriting i once read what was its name damn i wouldnt be able to think of it now when i want to said that if the tails curl up and backwards it means great affection but thats all superstition even if it is a nice one which doesn't help much in knowing who it is except that its certainly male with jet black ink it looks like higgins waterproof and a heavy vellum envelope but who do you suppose its the boy i met yesterday at that it would just [?] his type such black determined ink and nervous strokes to the letters just imagine why im all over annoyed at me standing here like one of laurencins maidens looking so innocently sophisticated im sure and wondering who it is when all i need do is open it and find out why so it is that new boy whats he writing me for when i only met him once but then he did seem terribly interested even if he is a strange one and certainly seems different from the ones ive known still they werent many and they didnt last long because they couldnt bear my being so much more clever and not taking them seriously like the youngster from harvard who got so excited and i wouldnt let him kiss me but yawned politely and suggested he might learn a good deal if he went back to harvard for enough more years and he was mad oh well ill read what drew has to say and find out if he wants to see me again just possibly of course he doesnt but in a way i kind of like him and it would be sort of nice to do things with him and jennifer and sven

For Helione Forrest

For ever and for ever in our dreams we lived; beyond all time and all memory of things immemorial, through ages and epochs and aeons unknown. Our birth was with the stars when chaos flamed to splendor, and our life was with the cosmic march of stars that lived and died. We lived with the stars, but died not; and the stars passed in the celestial scroll of time, but change there was none in us. Only the ages changed, and they changed slowly; but the ceaseless birth and death, the flow and refluence, of stars saw us for ever young and for ever one with the white suns that burned anew. We know not when we came from the midnight gloom of old, if ever we came; for we rose with the stars, and the stars flamed out of the abyss so long ago that their birth is prememorial, a song of glory illuming the shadowy deep when it too was born. But that stellar song, if song it was, is buried deeply and for ever, while the phantoms of oblivion take from time a tale whose majesty was our majesty in the spheral song of birth.

Timeless we are, and deathless; without knowledge of the everlasting transition that marks all else save us; the mutation of stars that die, and systems that fade, and universes that flow back into the ancient dark; the impermanence of gloom to star-lit splendor back to gloom immutable and vacant for ever; the cycle of death to life and life to death till change have deepened to changeless death and the diuturnity of chaos absolves from being all to which it gave birth.

We only of that cosmic throng exist; only we walked abroad with the triumphal stars, equal, but more than equal, for they have passed, and we remain; we only perdure of those that lived and died. We were less than they, but more; for the emperors are buried in the cosmic grave, and their tomb is the nameless crypt of shadow; but we pass on, forgetful of the ghostly latter years of time; and our grave, if grave we have, shall be the deep and final change that brings all change to end.

Drew Gordon.

oh a melachrino quick now where did i leave them yes by the ironing board and the matches damn ive hurt me from those silly little splinters always breaking or flaring back but it isnt much of a burn so i guess i wont bother fixing it now gee i feel normal again or at least as much as ever theres a nice fra-grant pleasure about a turkish cigarette if you let the smoke purl out of your lips and dont inhale now ill read it more care-fully its the curiousest letter ive ever had me and if its what i think it is its the most amazing love letter i can imagine my but that boy can write if he would only come down to earth a bit it might do him good and hes so devilishly different i wonder what it would be like to be kissed by him no i wont think of it

thats odd now i remember ive never thought that before about
the boys ive met but he doesnt say a word about wanting to see
me again unless ive overlooked oh how did i happen to miss
this note i suppose because it was tucked away and shy like
lucian taylor he ought to read the hill of dreams if he hasnt
already for he does remind me a little bit of lucian

Dear Miss Forrest:

It annoys me to send you the inclosed trifle because I hate
women, but I trust that you will not understand it. If so, it was
pleasant to have met you. If otherwise, I regret to say that I
would like to see you again, for lunch tomorrow, in front of
Founders Hall, after the fourth hour. I do hope you will not be
able to come.

Drew Gordon.

well if that isnt the nastiest invitation ive ever received why
did he need to spoil such a poetic letter by sending a note like
this along with it just the same he sounds sort of lonely and
hurt and my word what a trifle as he calls it this is i think ill go
just to see what happens and find out more what hes like but i
must read the letter over again gee how exciting

XXXI FIRST KISS

"Let's get away from here. Do you realize that it's now after four, and we've been talking since twelve-thirty?" Drew smiled as he glanced at his watch.

"My word!" exclaimed Helione. "So it is, and we've had a sort of tea as well as lunch but after all it was I who did most of the talking. I suppose you must be tired of my voice and I know you have work to do. Gee, that reminds me, I forgot I was to do some more sketches for the College Shop and they told me to come in at three but it's too late now unless I hurry right over and anyway I could just as well do 'em tomorrow morning since they won't run 'em till next week. What a nice smile you have! You ought to use it oftener. Or do you really need to leave now? In that case, I'll go to the Shop and do the sketches," she coaxed.

Drew smiled again.

"Why are you laughing at me?"

"I'm not. I was laughing with you, Helione. I was amused by the way you covered about six subjects in one breath. Now that you and Sven have corrupted me away from duty, I might just as well make a good job of it. Let's both forget about things we ought to do and instead start off on what we want to do."

"I really shouldn't but I will. What would you like?"

"What would you? A movie? Or the Art Institute? We could look up Sven and Jennifer. I know what, let's walk awhile, if you don't mind. Curiously enough, I've never yet gone down the river bank and it's such a grand day out that I think I might like that or would you?"

"I was hoping you would suggest something of the sort. Haven't you gone riverbanking even once? I thought everyone went in for it before they left the U."

"Riverbanking? No, I haven't heard the expression before. Does it mean anything special?"

"You haven't? I'm amazed. You must be about the only boy, I mean man, in school who doesn't know. Oh, it's a euphemism for going off to neck in one of the secluded spots along the banks."

"No wonder I haven't heard the expression."

"I only know by hearsay. The girls at the house tell me about their, er, interludes, shall we say? some times. I've never gone in for that sort of thing myself."

"It's the eighth wonder of the world, with your good looks. How many sisters have you?"

"Do you think so? Thank you! I meant the sorority house, I'm a tri-Alph, not that it means anything, they rate pretty well at the top here but I never go to meetings and I hardly even know who most of them are, isn't that terrible of me? They've been ready to throw me out several times but they probably won't because they know I don't care much and besides, it's good publicity when I have a story in the State Student Monthly or do a poster for the Thespians. What are you, or didn't you affiliate?"

"No. There were a couple of bids when I matriculated but I didn't pay any attention to them. The family wanted me to pledge but I preferred to choose my own friends and go along in my own way, not that I have anything against them."

"They're all right the first year. They might have been worth while, at least you'd have had to be a good dancer and mixer, and you'd have met lots of people, but in the long run, I think you will be as well off without affiliating. They do want you to conform to type, and they're generally fatal to individuality, though that's truer of the fraternities rather than the sororities."

"Let's exit. We were going to wander down the riverbank before it's too dark, weren't we?"

"That's the time most of the girls like! Wait a minute till I fix my face."

Drew was fully as interested in the process as the girl herself. She powdered her nose with a deft gesture. She put a fruity-flavored dab of lipstick on the ball of her little finger and traced the curve of her lips with meticulous care, heightening their color. "I've always thought that nature should imitate art!" she remarked while she surveyed the result in a vanity case mirror. "Hope you don't mind me but I feel so much better when I'm all freshed up and exactly right." An almost colorless rouge softened the glow of her cheeks. A pencil stroked the slender line of her eyebrows. She restored her hair, though he could not see a strand out of place; yet she found several which required shifting a few millimeters. Light pouring through the window brought riches of sherry and henna and coppery gold into her hair before she fitted her hat. She found a phial of perfume in her magician's bag, and unstoppered it to place a tiny drop on the lobe of each ear. It was a perfume of subtle suggestion, a bit spicy, and quite alluring.

"What an odd place to put perfume!" said Drew. "What is it?"

"Not at all, a lot of the girls are wearing it there this season. Do you like it? It's l'origan."

"I love its fragrance. Somehow, it seems appropriate to you."

"Sure, what would be the point of using it unless it matched me?"

The question being unanswerable, he made no reply as they left the tea-room.

It was, indeed, a rare day of October. The campus lawns looked sere as they walked toward the river bank. Climbing masses of ivy were already drying to the color of the brown-

stone facades which they covered. A scattering of leaves loitered across the grass. They strolled beyond the Women's
Dorm, followed a lane to Center Highway, and ran over the
avenue during a lull in traffic. They continued on another lane
to the cliffs, and slid perilously down a steep path to reach the
narrow flats which lined each shore. Here the tall grass
swished and whispered against their ankles, and left a coating
of powdery dust that was part earthy and part vegetation. The
sun shone warm, with the warmth of Indian summer, underlain
by an indefinable implication of frost; a warmth that seems
prophetic of cold days ahead, so unlike the full and unqualified
heat of July. The leaves lay thicker along the shore, and all up
the banks that were flaming with autumnal colors. Through
the oaks and aspens and birches, the elms and hickory, the
poplars, the maples, the cottonwoods and spruce, the melancholy tones of fall held revel with decay. An occasional tree was
naked of leaves thus early because of the drought, others
looked forlorn in vestiges of crisped greenery, but most of the
oaks and maples wore proud raiment still, though each stir of
wind showered the air with crackling leaves. Yellow and chestnut brown and tawny and tan, they rustled on the ground; gold-
en, cinnamon, flushing red, ochre, and umber, and blackening
scarlet, they sun-dried upon branches. But the season was distinctive for things that were absent as well as characteristics
present. The hum of mosquitoes, the buzzing of flies, the
drone of honey bees; the vivid splash of a wild rose and the reticence of a violet, or the virginal white of mimosa; the streak of
an oriole, and the clear, piercing sweetness of a meadowlark
singing afar; the dive of startled frogs, scurry of chipmunks
and chatter of squirrels; scent of lilacs and odor of flowing sap,
the heavy, vital freshness of woods after a rain; fragrance of
clover and pungency of mint; caress of southern breezes and
the velvety feel of pussywillows — all these had departed with
spring and summer, and hardly any sounds except the dry
death murmur of leaves and the lowly lapping of water dis-

turbed the air. Upon tree and grasses, river and banks, fell the sunlight of autumn whose quality is peculiar to itself, with a tone of maturity, of mellowness, of over-passed ripeness and fulfillment now on their way to the desolation of November, the leaden light of December.

"Have you ever noticed the distinctive quality of autumnal sunlight?" Drew broke the silence.

"I wondered what you were thinking all this while. I should say so, I've tried to capture it in a watercolor without much success. I used to think it came from the tawny of woods but it's the same on lakes and pavements. Might it be a result of the sun getting farther toward the winter solstice? Or something in the atmosphere? I haven't been noticing it so much recently, I can't see well, you know."

"Oh, I'm sorry. Is it serious?"

"After about ten feet, everything is blurry and jumps up and down."

"You ought to have an eye specialist examine them. Perhaps you need glasses."

"I have, but they aren't much help. I can see better and farther, but everything still jumps up and down. I'm afraid there's nothing to be done about that, so the doctors say."

"I can't tell you how I sympathize, not that my eyes are bad, I've always had phenomenal vision, but I'm obsessed by the most dreadful fear of going blind. I think I'd kill myself if that ever happened."

"No you wouldn't, you'd get used to it, just like me. I really don't much mind. You see, I prefer to do without glasses, then everything becomes blurry beyond what's around me, and I decide the world is far better than it actually is. It's quite a nice sensation, I don't find the flaws and the ugly side of life, and I imagine all sorts of lovely things past the limit of my vision. You needn't be sorry for me, I've made the best of it."

"Even so, I don't think I'd care for the experience."

"I don't too, if you haven't been used to poor sight from a child. Guess I'll have me a cigarette. Care for one?"

"No, thanks, I don't smoke."

"What? Dear me, I'd been told such men existed but I never thought to meet one. They're a charming habit. Oscar Wilde says something about their being so pleasant because they leave you unsatisfied. Do accept and join me, these are rather good."

"What are they?"

"Melachrinos, and cork-tipped, if you please. Jene and I always buy 'em when we're flush enough. Come, do be wicked and break another principle as long as we began the afternoon that way by cutting classes and letting our work go."

"All right."

Drew puffed on the cylinder somewhat awkwardly until Helione gave him a few suggestions on how to be more casual, more graceful, and more efficient.

"You seem to have smoking down to both a science and art."

"The girls at the house practise in front of mirrors so they'll know just how to wear 'em. Jene and I are naturally the best, and it makes 'em mad when we criticize but they copy our style."

To his surprise, he enjoyed the taste and the aroma. "Goodness knows how I missed such an agreeable vice for all these years!" he exclaimed. "I want some more."

"I've only a few left but you're welcome to them if you like. Aren't you afraid you'll be unwell?"

"No, not if the habit comes as easily as the first. Thanks, but I won't smoke all yours. I'll buy enough for us both. Is there a store around here?"

"Sure, right ahead. The path ends and we have to climb up again. There's a little lunch-room at the top by the end of the bridge. Race you up!"

With a quick laugh, she ran. Drew, taken by surprise, was slow in starting, and could not overtake her. He had an exasperating view of silk ankles and fleet-footed legs always just ahead of him.

"Gee, that was fun, but I've lost my breath!" she gasped.

"I'm glad you found it so."

"Do you resent that I'm ahead? Don't. You weren't ready and I wasn't fair, next time we'll start even and I know you'll win. Where is that nice smile of yours? I'll be frightened if you wear your glum face longer. Try a new one!"

He obliged. The spontaneous and immediate perception of the girl, her gay mood, made it difficult for him to sulk.

"It's passing six," he remarked. "Let's have a bite before we continue."

"I'm not terribly hungry but I would relish a sandwich and coffee if you feel you can afford. I have a little money."

"You shall take sandwiches, soups, and desserts. No, I've sufficient."

"Aren't I expensive?"

"Cheap at a million times the price! And after all, this is a long date."

"Are you becoming bored? We can go home if you like."

"I should say not. You know I hate women, and this being my first date, I've only had time to hate you for about six hours so far. It isn't enough. I insist on hating you all evening as well!"

Helione flashed him an instant look of pleasure, appreciation, and feminine challenge. He tingled as when their fingers had touched yesterday.

The restaurant was a dingy place, but her presence brightened it. Sandwiches, ice-cream, and coffee comprised the menu. He enjoyed the plain fare and smoked incessantly over the coffee.

"My word, I ought never have offered you a melachrino, but who would think you to become such a cigarette fiend all at once?"

"I love it. You must teach me some more vices!"

"I'll have to learn 'em myself first."

"Hmm, maybe we can learn together."

"An interesting idea, if practicable."

"I don't know a better one at the moment."

"I don't too!"

He delighted in the flippancy. The girl was electric. She adopted his moods as quickly as they came, and he responded to hers with a rapidity he had not deemed possible.

"Have you a pencil?" she asked.

"I'm sorry, no."

"Some other time, then. I wanted to sketch you with your first or practically the first cigarette. You handle it well. I once saw in a window a type that would suit you, twice as long as the average, gold-tipped, but with black paper."

"It sounds good. I'll look them up."

"Do. You remind me a bit of Lucian Taylor with that expression."

"Who is he?"

"Haven't you read *The Hill of Dreams*? You should. It's a book by Arthur Machen that I think you'd like. Lucian is the protagonist. I won't tell you what the novel's about, you must find for yourself, but it has a decadent style, like the flavor of a ripe persimmon."

"I'll read it when I have time. It sounds interesting."

"It's depressing in a way like Ryder's *The Race Track* or Odilon Redon's oils and watercolors."

"I'm not familiar with them."

"I just happen to be because I've been studying art. I think it's my line, as I gather that writing is yours from what Sven and Jene tell me."

"I suppose so."

"Or rather, judging from the letter you wrote me. I was so thrilled when it came. I'm not sure I understand it all, but you write remarkably for a boy your age."

"I'm not a boy. How old are you?"

"You should never ask that question of a woman, most of 'em won't tell you the right answer, but I don't mind. I'm eighteen. What about yourself?"

"The same. I'm surprised. I thought you were older."

"Jene will tell you if you doubt me."

"I'll take your word for it. You look candid."

"I thought you were much older too when I met you and your letter sounds frightfully ancient, like one of Blake's drawings, or a Bible prophet writing of doomsday."

"I think our lives are going to cross, Helione. I'm not egotistic, yes I am too, but how many other people are there at the U or in the whole country for that matter do you suppose who have the vision or imagination or whatever you want to call it that we do?"

"Not many, or are we merely young and presumptuous?"

"No, young and more, young in years, old in thought."

"Perhaps."

"I feel restless. Let's start again. Would you like to see a movie or the stock company or shall we keep on along the river bank?"

"Let's cross the bridge and follow the other side to where I catch my car. There are always shows and dances, but there won't be many more days like this before winter."

He paid the check and bought another package of cigarettes.

"Gee, you'll need a lot of money if you're going to adopt other habits as fast as this!" commented Helione.

"I'll make it, and won't I like it!"

They walked over the bridge. Already its lights were on, though a rim of the sun still showed, smoky red, above the horizon. The air held a tang, and an odor of smudge and grass fires made it pungent.

"It's getting dark. I wonder if there will be a moon?" she asked.

"Yes, about eight o'clock. Are you warm enough?"

"Sure, it's only a cloth coat but it's enough till snow comes. Look back up the river toward the dam — isn't that a marvellous modern scene for a print? I'm going to do one sometime, with the bridge segmenting the sky, and the power plant ablaze with lights squatting beside the dam, and the thick smoke and orange flame leaping out of the smokestack. Doesn't it impress you?"

"Yes, though I'm not very interested in the smoke and steel phase of modern civilization."

"I like the view from here, all that power and strength and solid vitality — oh! I almost tripped. Mind if I take your arm?"

They walked down-stream. A strange, new warmth filled him as she slipped an arm under his. A stranger unrest disturbed his thoughts. He desperately wanted to kiss her, to savor the tempting lips, the virginal face; but a picture of flame and witches rose, their spell prevailed. His mind was a flux of remembered pain, anticipated desire, and forgetful appreciation of the moment. The moon swam up, and swathed the river, and delineated their path in arabesques of ebony filigreed with silver. Trees became prescient with mysteries of being. The river gurgled. Midway between high ground and water level, they approached a wooden trestle that spanned a dry ravine.

"Let's rest a minute," said Helione.

The rising moon shone in the river. A chill frosted the air. Curls of fog began to drift eerily and ghostly in the moonlight. Silence hushed the world.

He gripped the rail, leaning toward the gully and the river beyond. She moved closer. He turned his gaze from the vague and gloomy shadows of river against the bank, to look down at the girl. Her face was lifted to his, like a flower of night, and her eyes, so innocent, were smiling so doubtfully, so hopefully, so happily.

"You are beautiful," he spoke simply.

Her eyes lighted with pleasure, but she did not answer. She looked desirable, and as if she would not mind being kissed.

"We had better continue, before I forget that I hate women."

Curiously, an expression of triumph mingled with disappointment flitted across her countenance, though he had given no sign of response or affection.

For a long while they followed the path as it dipped and rose along the bank, now wholly in darkness, now dim in tree-patterns, now plain by the full moonlight. When they finally arrived at the next bridge where the carline ran, it was toward ten, and before they reached her home, ten-thirty had struck.

"I wonder what State we're in?" he asked ironically.

"I do live in a most inconvenient place, pretty far from anywhere, don't I?"

"I should say so. Is this your house?"

"Yes, won't you come in for a cup of tea?"

"Well, it's rather late."

"Oh, mother will still be up, and I never retire before one, we keep late hours. At least, the kids will all be in bed now."

"How many of them are there? You make it sound like a houseful."

"That's exactly what it is. I've two older brothers and a sister married, they live away of course, but there's about ten of us left altogether."

"About ten? Don't you know?"

"I never can remember unless I count 'em."

"Good God, what a life!"

"It's sort of crowded, I'll admit. I have to sleep downstairs. I've turned what used to be a side-room into my own bedroom, because the children take up everywhere else. Hmmm, counting the six or seven kids, me, my parents, and the three married, it makes thirteen, more or less. Gee, it wouldn't be so bad if they were older, but they're all at the worst age, from three to twelve. Do come in and have tea with me."

"Thank you, I will."

The living-room looked as though several cyclones had playfully swept through it. Horns, drums, whistles, dolls, carts, roller-skates, and miscellaneous toys festooned the floor, hung from chairs, and were draped upon the radiators. Magazines lay all over. There were even a few on the table intended to hold them. Newspapers littered the davenport.

"Isn't it awful? It's always like this no matter how often mother and I straighten the mess, the kids wreck it again in five minutes. Hello, mother, this is the boy I was telling you about last night, Drew Gordon. We're going to make some tea, will you join us? Are there any cookies?"

"Why, thank you, I was on my way to bed. There are some teacakes. I hope you will not think it rude of me, Mr. Gordon, for retiring and you must visit us again. Lee has been saying what an interesting person you are and I look forward to talking with you the next time you come."

The middle-aged woman, who had been rising as they entered, bade them goodnight. Mrs. Forrest was a gray-haired matron, large, plump, and dignified. Her eyes were very green and fathomless like Helione's. She had obviously possessed beauty in her youth. The bearing of many children had aged her and tired her. Her voice was still young, and her mind active as ever. She stammered slightly, as if her thoughts outran her words and she must return to finish a dangling sentence. She wore an expression of dulled pain; the untidy room appeared to hurt her. Although she had become inured to its disorder, she would never excuse it or feel at peace until the children were grown and she could again hold afternoon teas with substantial, conventional, socially acceptable guests.

Helione brought out a tray of tea and cakes.

"I'll straighten up a little so there will at least be a place for you to sit!"

"Don't bother." Drew dropped a pillow at his feet, took a cup of tea in one hand and a cake in the other, crossed his ankles, and sank Buddha-like to the floor.

"My goodness, how in the world did you do that?" she asked, staring at him in surprise.

"It's a convenient trick to know. Now you can occupy the unencumbered chair and it won't be necessary to spend time straightening things."

She adopted his suggestion and sat precisely erect in the chair. The glossy green dress she was wearing darkened the luster of her eyes and subdued her figure.

"One advantage of this position is that I can safely admire the perfection of your limbs!"

The girl laughed. "They aren't so bad, are they?" she flexed them and appraised them. She had fine ankles and small, exquisite feet, and a wonderful curve from ankle to inner knee.

"Is this how you always hate women?" she asked maliciously.

"No, thanks for reminding me. The tea was good. I must go now."

He rose and donned his coat. She overlooked his sudden change of mood.

"I enjoyed the afternoon and evening so much," she said. She walked to the door with him and opened it. There she stood, her lovely face lifted again like a flower. One hand, he noticed, against the jamb steadied her. The look in her eyes was wealth. Wistfulness, appeal, warmth, innocence, disappointment, hope, pleasure — they all mingled. He returned her gaze and unconsciously leaned his own right hand against the jamb. She raised an eyebrow in a quizzical arch that might have betokened invitation. Hesitantly, he closed his left arm around her and drew her close. Her eyes cleared, and half-shut, and an invisible smile trembled her lips faintly apart.

For a long instant he kissed her. The embrace was a gentle and lyrical blessing in which the hunger, the loneliness, and the dream of his life crept out, and were defeated by a surge of delirious blood, a bounty of beauty, through the paradox of a fierce, soft kiss.

He breathed a deep sigh, like a sleeper wakening. A bloom had entered her cheeks, a bright gladness her eyes. Not a word spoke either, for they knew by intuition. She was silhouetted against the doorway, and he remembered her hand and the sidewise repose of her head as he turned away.

He walked on the fields of eden, unearthly rapture made his features radiant. His being was breathless with exaltation, his mind soared winged to the stars. He felt mysteriously expanded like space unending, but all was the glory of paradise. Adoration invested his spirit. Every tree shone luminous, a wonder, a fable, and an ecstasy lay behind each leaf.

XXXII ENTER THE FOOL

"Who is that man?" asked Drew.

"Where?"

Drew nodded toward the Memorial Grounds on their left and Sven followed the direction of his gaze. A misshapen figure was staggering across the field. At times he walked, at times he broke into a lope, again he shambled in diagonals. He looked grotesque, like a dwarf, and crippled, like a hunchback, and ever his head nodded from side to side as though his neck were too feeble to carry the huge thing. Once he shouted aloud, but Drew could not understand the words of that cry.

It was late in a cold afternoon of November. The skies hung lead gray; a few flakes of snow had fallen earlier, and a chill wind moaned around the campus. Only a handful of students were hastening homeward. Paths and walks were almost deserted. But the stranger of the twisted child's body wore no overcoat, and his shirt was open at the throat. Tie and vest he had none. His head was hatless, and its mop of hair unkempt. The head, of enormous size, and shaped like a watermelon, seemed even more deformed because it was bald on the front half whereas thick, black locks tangled from behind and fell forward across the dome. The creature gibbered when it saw them. It halted. Drew's scalp prickled as he watched the monster crouch in the gathering shadows. Then its head began to sway on its shoulders. It cried out again in child's voice. It ran crazily across the field and disappeared behind Founders Hall.

"He acts like a madman!" exclaimed Drew. "Who is he?"

"That's The Fool," Sven remarked. "How long have you been in school?"

"I'm starting my junior year now."

"And you haven't seen him before?"

"No."

"I thought every one knew him. He's been around for years, ever since I've been here. I did know his name but I've forgotten it. They call him simply The Fool."

"Isn't it dangerous to let him run loose like that?"

"No, I guess not. He's harmless. Something went wrong and he was born all crooked and ugly."

"He gives me the creeps."

"I don't blame you the first time. You'll get used to him."

"How old is he?"

"Ask somebody who knows. Twenty or twenty-five, maybe."

"Why don't they put him away in an asylum?"

"The story goes that he was brilliant in school. His parents are supposed to have been a high-school teacher and a college professor. I gather that they were both wizards in their lines. Anyhow, they thought sure they'd breed a prodigy, I mean a mental one, a child wonder. I guess they succeeded as far as his brain is concerned. They say he was a marvel up to the end of high school. He could do all sorts of figures in his head, give you the cube of any number you mentioned, even up in the millions, quick as a flash, and all that sort of thing. He knew Latin and Greek as well as I know English — "

"That isn't saying much."

"Oh, you think so? Well, we'll let that pass."

"Sorry, I didn't mean to interrupt but I couldn't resist the temptation. Go on."

"Where was I? Oh yes, the Latin and Greek. He graduated from high school at twelve with the highest average ever made at that particular school, whatever it was. He was a shark at math and languages, but strangely enough a dud at logic and everything else. They thought sure he was going to be famous in spite of his handicap. He was always under a doctor's care. I understand the parents spent every cent they had getting the best specialists to see what they could do about him, but I guess it was hopeless.

"He started out like a demon here at the U and burnt up the old records as fast as they'd let him go ahead. He got his B.A. in two years, the quickest anyone ever finished here, and was all set to start after his Ph.D. though he was only fourteen then. Come to think of it, I believe he did put in a year or so of work, but then something happened. His head had kept on growing faster than the rest of him. Maybe that's why he was so brilliant, he had such a big brain. Well, it began hurting him, and the doctors didn't seem able to figure out why or what to do about it. Something happened. Something snapped, and he's never been the same since. They were going to take him away to a private sanitarium but it seems he had a sort of doglike love for the U. He kept crying and moaning until they brought him to school one day and then he quieted down, so they let him go on. I don't think he's ever attended classes after that. Apparently he was satisfied if they would just let him hang around.

"A couple of years ago, both of his parents died, heart-broken, so they say, because he was their only child and had turned out to be a kind of monster and a fool. Nobody seems to know how he's managed to live since, or where he stays. Maybe friends look after him, or maybe he gets along by himself, I don't know. They say he hasn't long to live, but he should have been dead years ago if the docs were right. He doesn't bother anyone much, though once in a while he'll stop you and ask you some ungodly question that you can't answer. All the professors know him, and the cops around here treat him as gentle as a babe. I'm not sure why, unless it's because they feel sorry for him or just think he's a half-wit. You know, that's a funny thing."

"Funny?"

"I mean queer. Most people are afraid of what they don't understand. They resent anything different from what they're used to. In the old days, they used to hound the crazy ones to death, or else treat them as a sort of prophet. The kings had court fools. Remember the fools in Shakespeare? I guess they still feel that way. They've found out that he's harmless even if he does have a screw loose so instead of locking him up they're kind to him. I sometimes wonder if it isn't because most of us feel that it wouldn't take much to push us across the line. Most everybody has a little of the fool or the half-wit in him. It's an old idea that madness and sanity are pretty close to each other."

"Where did you pick up all that information?"

"Oh, I don't remember. It's the story you hear if you ask. I ran into him once when I was a freshman. Something about him caught my fancy and I wrote a jingle about him."

"How does it go?"

"I don't know if I can recall, it's so long since I've thought of it. Let me see…. I've probably forgotten parts but it went something like this,

I am as mad as mad can be,
Nothing on earth can bother me,
Great big moonfaced politicians,
The cat on the fence, and world conditions,
Emily Post, and thieves in state;
Working hard for pieces-of-eight,
Finding that life from end to end
Means ditched by your girl and left by your friend,
None of these things can bother me
For I am as mad as mad can be.

That's all I can remember of it."

"It's a queer jingle."

"Yeah. It's about as crazy as he is."

XXXIII CHRISTMAS EVE

When they returned from the Symphony and an hour's dancing at the Peacock Club, Drew watched Helione and some of her family busy themselves with Christmas Eve preparations. It was nearly midnight. The kids had long retired. As he placed his briefcase by the door and removed his overcoat while Lee retired to rid herself of wraps, Mr. Forrest, Mrs. Forrest, and Alice continued working about the tree.

They greeted him perfunctorily, except Mrs. Forrest who paused long enough to approach him and ask, "Would you like a cup of tea?"

"Thank you, but Lee and I just had a bite at the Peacock."

"Just as you like. You'll excuse me, won't you, while I go ahead wrapping?"

"Of course, but can't I be of help?"

"We're almost finished, and I don't suppose you two have any desire whatever to be alone." She had an ironic chuckle, not quite so dry as Mr. Forrest who looked up to remark, "Hello, Drew, is it cold enough for you? Don't mind us because we haven't time to mind you until this drudgery is done."

"Go right ahead, I'm used to it."

Mr. Forrest glanced at him sharply but returned to his labors without replying.

Drew had never seen so many parcels under a Christmas tree. Small ones and large ones, fat ones and thin ones, in brightly colored papers and glittering ribbons, they lay piled under the tree, and the hill grew steadily higher. To be sure, when you figured it out, there were ten in the family, and if each gave a present to the others, it made a total of ninety. Toys, games, books, candy, cosmetics, inexpensive jewellery, lingerie, stationery, mysterious boxes and enigmatic packages all formed part of the mountain. Mrs. Forrest, her usual English drawl crispened by enthusiasm, opened several of the unwrapped parcels to ask him what he thought of a toy golf set, or whether little Patsy would like the picture books, and if Chubby would go for the drum. They chattered and joked, until Mr. Forrest bade them a reedlike Merry Christmas before retiring, and Alice followed suit in the current slang of her high-school crowd, and Mrs. Forrest departed last. "Don't stay long," she admonished. Then her plump figure creaked the stairway steps.

Lee had again gone to her room. Before she reappeared, Drew took a heavy package from his briefcase and added it to the mountain already under the tree. He was warming himself by a radiator when she came forth. She had been wearing a dress of glossy green, but she had changed to her fiery red frock with the totem design around its waist. She looked at him with an odd lift of one eyebrow that she seldom employed, and seated herself on the arm of an overstuffed chair.

"Gee!" she exclaimed as though a tension had gone. "Christmas Eve is so much fun but it takes all my energy away."

"I know just how you feel," he answered. The lure of her face, the indefinable green of her eyes, the appeal of her voice, the silken charm of a leg that swung, the patch of white peeping between a garter and the edge of her dress which had slipped up as she leaned back, soothed his senses. But they were as wine, too, and her whole self a magnet that brought him beside her. The sound of her voice, the raising of an eyelid, the repose of hands, every gesture of hers held infinite meanings, and the ebb and flow of an unseen tide seemed to unite him with her. He had long known that he loved her. He had struggled against his emotion, denying it, suppressing it, through the weeks that he had seen her oftener and oftener. Even when he first partook of the soft fruit of her lips, he refused to admit his interest. But on subsequent nights, his caresses became more lyrical, and it was increasingly hard for him to leave.

Now, he slipped into the chair and put an arm around her waist. Many-colored lights on the Christmas tree were reflected in her hair. It shone like a wondrous flame, and the modulations of red from crimson to mahogany shimmered within it. He became hypnotized, intoxicated, from looking into her eyes which surveyed him so disconcertingly and held such depths. He felt that his own must be burning darkly in their sockets. Gently, he tightened his hold, and she sank into his lap. Without a word, the lovely face lifted, and the luscious lips parted, and her countenance transfigured. For the first time, Drew saw the unmistakable expression of a woman who is loved, and who loves in return. The kiss was a mute blessing, a caress that defied analysis, communion with paradise. As in a dream, like one come home to harbor after years of wandering upon odysseys across fretful seas and perilous, he held her closelier. No word they spoke, for their eyes and their faces were eloquent, until a stirring upstairs warned him he must go. Then he inhaled a long, shaken breath, and ceased his gentle appreciation of hair and countenance and figure, and trembled in the flux of a madness that possessed him with divinity.

"You are the sun that dispelled darkness," he whispered. "You are the vision I sought. Would you like to hear something?" The essence of a smile from his spirit fleeted ghostlike in his eyes as she relaxed closer against him for answer. "I love you, Helione. You have done what I thought no woman would.

I shall wake tomorrow, and it will be like a vision of sleep, till I see you again and know that it was heart's desire come true. I do not know why I love you, but I love you, and that is enough."

There was, in the kiss to which she surrendered, a mysterious quality that none others had possessed. It was warmer, deeper, richer, fuller. In ways eluding thought, and beyond the intuitions of emotion, it expressed her innumerable response, and the immeasurable wealth he brought.

Slowly he rose, regretting to leave, yet wearing an ecstasy that made his face godlike. Only for a moment that look of exaltation prevailed. Then he fronted reality, and the rapture crept inward as he turned toward his briefcase.

"Will you bring me a glass of water before you go?" asked Helione. "Let it run a moment till it's cold."

Obediently he went, and when the water ran cold, he filled a tumbler.

"Thank you," she murmured. There was a new light in her eyes that puzzled him. She seemed pleased. Hardly tasting the water, she set the glass aside.

"It has been a marvellous evening," he said. Straight and tall he stood, as he smiled down at her with dark, appreciating eyes, haunted by dreams; and her face answered him with its glowing beauty. She clung to him in a profound embrace, until another stir above sent him striding out to a blizzard.

XXXIV CHRISTMAS DAY

Lazily he opened his eyes. The alarm-clock on his bureau indicated nine. He felt very tired still — ah yes, he had not arrived home till past two because he had stayed so late with Lee. His features became happy as he remembered. He heard Mary preparing breakfast, and the sound of Daniel descending the stairs — why, this was Christmas! He bounded out of bed, flung a dressing gown around him, and wriggled into slippers.

"Merry Christmas!" he shouted as he cleared the steps four at a time. Daniel had just reached Mary. All three indulged in a hug that almost ruined them before Drew dragged them to the Christmas tree. Beneath I lay a small pile of packages.

"Well, well, I'm too old to believe in Santa Claus but by George it looks as if he'd been here," Daniel commented.

"What do you suppose is in these?" asked Mary. Her countenance beamed.

"I haven't the slightest idea," answered Drew with a wholly unconvincing lie. "Anyway, I'm too busy."

The parcels produced a rhinestone bracelet, a beautiful handbag, and six pairs of silk hose for Mary; a set of the *Bibelot,* Tossella's *Serenade,* and a trio of fine broadcloth shirts for Daniel; three satin ties — maroon, iridescent indigo, and small-figured tan — a collector's copy of *Hydrotaphia,* and a portable typewriter for Drew.

"You shouldn't have spent your money on such expensive things," Mary reproached, without conviction.

"What about you and dad!" exclaimed Drew, bubbling with glee. "Anyway, I couldn't think of a better way to spend the checks I got for that essay and article than on Christmas presents for you and Lee."

"What did you give her?"

"A copy of Poe's *Tales of Mystery and Imagination* in a marvellous new edition with color plates and black and white illustrations by Harry Clarke. It's a sumptuous book and I'm sure she'll like the plates even if they are weird."

"What did she give you?"

"Oh, she hasn't much money and couldn't afford presents this year, I don't mind." Nothing in his voice betrayed the slight disappointment he felt. It was gone as quickly as it came.

Breakfast tasted never so good as today. Sausages sizzled to crackly brown, waffles golden and crisp, with either home-preserved peaches or maple syrup to accompany them — he tried both — and coffee piping hot, these were nectar and ambrosia.

As he left the table, he saw his briefcase against the hall radiator, where he had placed it last night. "Might as well empty it till school opens again," he decided, and unstrapped it. Among other things, inside was a flat parcel in green, tied neatly with thread of metallic gold and red. "Where did that come from?" he wondered, as he unwrapped it, but a suspicion was forming.

In his hands, he held a watercolor, and on its back was written, "For my friend, Drew Gordon. Christmas, 1926. Helione Forrest."

He studied the picture with growing love.

A nude maiden with bright orange hair sat primly facing left front on a draped bench. Her head was turned coyly toward the lower right. One arm lay along her left thigh, the other rested on a table. From under that arm, a lush green scarf trailed down and crossed her right thigh, and fell to the floor. In the background, on the table, stood a two-handed amphora in jade, out of which rose three plumes, with scarlet fringed stems and blades as purple as plums, which curved behind the girl's head. The plumes might have been feathers or leaves, it did not matter. The vase stood in front of the farthest background which was covered with orange-checked lemon wallpaper. A vertical fringe, juicy red as pomegranates, dropped behind the girl's left side. At the extreme right, pistachio paralleled the red. The girl's left leg was bent back, resting lightly on its toes toward the lower right, where a corner of magenta floor showed. The girl's body was apricot. It was a full-breasted figure, but her face seemed child-like, belied by heavy-lidded eyes and polite ennui. The bold use of warm and hot colors, the composition, and the brilliant technique, would themselves have appealed to him. It was a distinctive watercolor, if not a great one, but he appreciated it the more because the artist had made it individual and given to it her vivid personality.

The day was memorable throughout, a day of cheer, and bliss, and love of good living. After he telephoned Lee to rave about her creation, to receive her own enthusiasm for the Poe, and to enjoy the song of her voice, he lazed in idle talk with his parents until the Christmas dinner materialized under Mary's genius.

That was a feast for the gods. After a goblet of mellow sauterne, it began with a fruit-cup of fresh pineapple, orange, grapefruit, apple, and banana, topped with a big, winking, maraschino cherry. Chicken broth of unrivalled richness and flavor followed. Then entered the bird, and he was greeted like the prodigal son. It made your mouth water to look at him, this fat goose, basted to a turn and filled with savory sage and hickory stuffing. His giblets and gizzard and inwards bordered him. He had a host of good companions — crushed cranberry sauce, steaming biscuits jump from the oven, gravy that Trimalchio missed, baked sweet potatoes such as butter was made for, succulent artichokes, pepper hash relish, crunchy celery, honey that Hybla never surpassed, grape jelly sweet with the south, and stuffed olives that you couldn't pop in fast enough. You murmured a prayer for each mouthful, and quoted an ode for the salad. It had a gelatine base, and it enclosed a fabulous array of shredded pineapple, green pepper, pimento, onion, carrot, walnuts, and cheese nodules, and it would have drowned under mayonnese except for the crisp lettuce that upheld it. After these, oh rare plum pudding, and you couldn't leave it alone though you were already as stuffed as a ballot-box, not when you sniffed the brandy that saturated it, and tasted the lavishly lusciously fruity miracle of its contents. You didn't wonder how it was made. You marvelled that human inspiration could have created it at all.

And then the aroma of a demitasse, thick coffee, black coffee, syrupy coffee.

And then the liqueur, cherry rum.

"Give us the toast!" asked Daniel.

And Drew responded, "To a perfect day, a perfect dinner, a perfect home!"

The goblets went up, and the rum laughed down.

XXXV FLOWER OF WINTER

"I enjoyed the evening so much, Drew, thank you. But won't you come in and get warm before catching a car? I'll make some tea if you like."

"I would like that if it isn't too much bother. I'm simply frozen."

A bitter wind was howling that January night. It cut through the cloth coat that Lee was wearing. Its fur collar and cuffs were inadequate. Even Drew suffered, despite his heavy overcoat, wool muffler, thick gloves, and the black hat pulled low over his brow. He looked a sinister figure, with his eyes burning forth from a face that seemed haunted.

They had braved the cold to rush the gallery for one of those rare treats that reached Center City. George Arliss was heading a star cast in *Old English*. Of all forms of art, Drew cared most for drama, but it was enough if Lee became excited with enthusiasm. It was pleasant to watch her pleasure, and the thrill of her proximity would have made even a wretched production bearable.

Lee complained of the cold as they rode home. "I can stand any amount of heat," she said. "I love to lie around on the beach on the hottest summer days but this cold wears me all out. I just won't be any good until spring comes again."

The temperature had dropped below zero. High banks of snow lined the sidewalks. Ice glinted brilliant beneath street lamp and head-light. A shrill wind swept abroad, a wind that bit through the warmest clothing. Breath froze as it emerged. A lining of frost deepened where Drew exhaled through the flaps of his collar.

Once inside, he began to thaw out, not rapidly, because the Forrests' house was always underheated. Lee retired to her room to remove her wraps. A clock crept toward twelve. Drew listened with the pleasure he derived from little, familiar things to its regular tick, to the sounds Lee made as she moved about, to an occasional creaking from upstairs, and to the lonely howl of the wind as it soughed around eaves and naked trees. Truly it was a bad night out, a night to be thankful for shelter and warmth and food. He edged closer to a radiator and warmed his numb fingers on its coils.

Lee interrupted his reflections. He heard a click as she turned her light off, and a protest as her door opened. He looked up. She had taken off the bright red dress she was wearing, the red dress with the totem design. He caught a glimpse of slip and lingerie before she folded a wrapper closelier around her. She had left her glasses behind. He was amazed at the change in her appearance. Ordinarily, her face looked a bit severe because of the silver rimmed English glasses. They were a kind of visible barrier. They made her seem prim, studious; material for a school-teacher when she wore them. True, she also looked arty or intellectual, and slightly incongruous because of the beauty, delicacy, and softness of her face, with the scar a pale line down her rosy-satin cheeks. Now that loveliness emerged enhanced. Drew forgot to be shocked by her removing the dress, he was so delighted with the lure of her features. She paused in the doorway as if undecided whether to continue across the dining-room to him, or turn aside to the kitchen. He knew that, with her glasses off, she could not see him except as a blur. He solved the problem by rising and walking swiftly toward her.

"You look lovelier than I've ever seen you, lovelier than I thought you could be!" he exclaimed. She glowed in answer to the naive conviction and sincerity of his words. He bent over and kissed her, softly, longly, quietly, pouring the whole bounty of himself into that embrace. He could have been fierce for his hunger but was gentle for his love. The fragrance of her and the perfume she used, l'origan she had once said it was, enveloped her with an unseen aura.

"I'll go and make some tea," she suggested, gently pushing him back. "I don't want to, darling, but it might sound better in case anyone's awake."

Regretfully he released her. "I'll watch you," he offered. Arm around her, he accompanied her to the kitchen.

"There aren't any cookies," she apologized. "There isn't anything except bread. Would you like some cinnamon toast?"

Drew was hungry, but he knew the Forrests had to watch their budget closely. "No, thanks," he answered. "Just some tea to warm me. You are a sufficient feast for my eyes."

For answer, she looked at him with that shy invitation which he could never resist. There was a depth to his kiss that satisfied and hurt her, disturbed and excited her at the same time. She lay soft in his arms, clinging to him.

"You're sweet," she whispered; and then added mischievously, with one of those mysterious changes of mood which were wont to pass swiftly over her, "when you try to be!" She danced away.

"I did start to make some tea," she accused.

"Curses! Foiled again! I shall have you yet, fair lady!" He fell in with her mood.

"Mmmmm, can I depend on that?"

Drew blushed. He hated himself for it, but he could not help it. Every time he was asked an embarrassing question, a surge of blood betrayed him. Lee studied him critically.

"You look awfully nice with that lovely beet-colored effect," she said mercilessly, and laughed with a friendly malice. "I wonder how you'd be in blue, or say a slightly glazed magenta?"

"Don't! You're positively diabolical. I can't help the tricks that nature plays on me."

"It's sort of interesting to know that anybody, any man, I should say, can still blush."

"Well, I don't think it's polite of you to laugh."

"I don't too, darling," and with another sudden change of mood she forced her face into a frozen and ghastly mask. Drew chuckled one of his inaudible laughs, so weird was her expression.

"There," she pouted. "Now you're laughing at me. Is that fair?"

"No, and this isn't either, wretch!" whereat he bent to her lips. She was not a small girl, yet there was a curious pleasure in coming down from his height to embrace the upturned face. A pale flush tinged the scar.

"The tea is boiling," she murmured.

"How do you know? You aren't watching it. You are enjoying the pleasure of being loved."

"Sure, but I can hear, can't I?"

"Alas, the perfidy of woman. Even when kissed, she must listen to the kettle boil."

"You're a hell of a Hamlet," said Lee. "You don't sound a bit tragic. Or convincing."

"Tush, Miss, your language!"

"Oh, all right. You're a damn' poor actor."

"Let's drink the tea before I am shocked to a daze."

Lee parted her lips with feline ease and clicked her teeth voluptuously. It was a curious gesture that he had never before seen her employ. It stirred him profoundly. Then she undulated to the stove. He did not understand why her walk had such a sensual appeal. It was a sort of lithe, swinging gait; deliberate, yet graceful, and wholly individual; with toes pointing faintly inward, and an innate rhythm to her motion, the effect was hypnotizing.

"What's the matter with my legs?" she asked with mock truculence. "Aren't I all right?"

"For God's sake, will you stop saying aren't I and I don't too?"

"No, aren't I the best judge of that?" she teased. "You don't really believe you ought to decide on my phrases and I don't too."

"Oh, gosh, I give up," he groaned.

"You didn't tell me what was wrong with my legs."

"Why, uh, nothing. I like them."

"Hmm, he likes them. Just like that. Dear me, I am overwhelmed by this enthusiasm."

Delighting in the persiflage, which was a kind of intellectual game with them, to be indulged in whenever occasion warranted, they moved to the parlor and sat on the worn davenport while sipping tea.

"Damn," said Lee. "This room is always a mess. I wish the kids would learn to stop leaving their junk around." She gathered up toys from the floor, newspapers and magazines left in convenient chairs, and miscellaneous play things, all of which she heaped upon the under rungs of a table. "There, that's a little bit better."

"Oh!" she exclaimed before resuming her seat, "I just remembered, would you like to see some sketches I did today?"

"Well, I don't know — "

"Why, Drew! I'm always interested in everything you do." A disappointed and hurt expression clouded her eyes.

"Darling, you didn't let me finish. What I started to say was that I don't know whether I could appreciate them with you around. You take all my attention and I don't have eyes for anything else."

She smiled at him, happy again, and tip-toed to her room. She returned with a pencil sketch and a sheet of finished pen-and-inks.

"What do you think of them?" she asked. "It was my first big order and I worked just hours at it, all day. I had to cut my classes, and I didn't have time for lunch — my word, I only had time for a sandwich at dinner too now that I remember — no, I'm not hungry, I'm pleased, anyway, don't you think this child looks quite cute in that snaky hat — "

"Yes, because she looks so much like you!"

" — and this one has such ravishing lines, don't you think, or do you? I always did want to do lingerie ads if I could get 'em."

Drew examined the figures critically. He liked them simply because they were something that Lee had done. They were stylized, of course, and made to conform with commercial requirements, but he considered them well-done.

"They're good," he said wistfully. His plain statement bore a world of meaning. "More than anything else, I wish I could draw."

"But you write so well."

"That doesn't matter, I'd rather be an artist, like you. That girl — my, I could go for her, because she's exactly like you!" He set his tea cup down. "In fact," he added, "I am going to appreciate her."

With a dainty, seductive motion, Lee placed her cup and saucer precisely upon the edge of the window-sill behind, her sketches upon the end of a piano-bench, and sank back toward the cushions, but near Drew. Lightly he ran his finger-tips across her brow, her soft cheeks, the lobe of her ears, the exquisite curve of her lips.

"I do not know why I love you," he murmured, "but I love you more than the whole rest of the world." The splendor of her mouth came to his, and she was folded in his arms. The same strange feeling that had attended past occasions when he held her boiled up within him; a kind of fever, a kind of madness, shown by physical trembling and a glow that deepened his eyes; a love that was the more profound because of the loneliness he had known.

"Listen to the wind!" he whispered. An eerie, high wail sounded from frozen trees, he heard the crackle of ice afar.

"I'm cold, and you're so warm," she voiced. She clung to him as to fire. She drew up her knees and curled against him, a child and a woman, trusting, lovely and soft. Lightly, so lightly, he stroked the calf of her leg, and slid off her slippers.

"Don't," she murmured, but there was no command in her words, and her limbs flexed as he removed the stockings. A dizziness swept through him. Never before had he dared go so far, or had she seemed so willing. Never had she appeared so seductive, nor ever had he been so drunk with love and the rapture of her beauty.

"I'll be cold," she said, and he helped her arms from the wrapper.

"Is that nice?" she pleaded, and the slip was gone.

"You shouldn't," she sighed, as he unhooked the brassiere.

"Darling! Careful!" she cried and the last garment fell.

Lovely she was, lovely, all feverish, in her white and rose glory of body. The blood welled up in his veins, and boiled higher, and overboiled, and a frenzy shook him visibly.

"Why are you trembling?" she asked, but he did not answer.

"Don't take off your clothes — here. Someone might come." Still he did not answer.

"If you must," she whispered, "come to my room. Be quiet."

In a kind of delirium, intolerable because it was to perfect, they gathered clothing and paced softly to her room. There was no light, and no light was needed for his eyes shone with a luminous glow from within. Even in the dark, as she lay warm upon the bed, he could see the voluptuous smile that parted her lips, the ecstasy that pulsed like a bloom upon her cheeks.

"Careful!" she cried. "You're hurting me!"

"I'm sorry," in a husky voice, while the melting splendor of her body united with his in the driving passion of his love.

The wind whooped around the chimney. Cold crept through the room. Not even ice and cold and a wild wind could chill the flame of that first union, or darken the invisible sun that burned within them.

"I'm afraid, darling I'm afraid!" There was a catch of breath in her shaken whisper.

Peace and comfort and frenzy were answer in the gentle fierceness of his embrace. Gone were the snows of winter in that fury. She unfolded like a flower of night and her arms encompassed him drawing him deep toward her even as she murmured. Forgotten was the glint of ice and the reign of frost in the supreme ecstasy of that first profound caress that dissolved into one the dual fires of their being.

XXXVI RIDDLE THE FOOL

Drew hurried from the Library that evening in February
with guilty haste. He had been reading all afternoon. For an
hour, he had caught up on assignments, then he had turned
to *Hydrotaphia* for pleasure. Soaring among those crooked
splendors and those cadences whose music rivalled that of
the celestial spheres or the ocean or the winds that walk the
earth, he had grown forgetful of time. From the purple of
ecstasy, he emerged, and it was six o'clock. He was to have
met Lee downtown for dinner at that hour. She would probably be late. She always was. But he for ever expected her
to be on time; and he had visions of her, numb with cold, or
waiting irritably inside the drug store, or departing in
anger.

As he swung through the door, cold struck him like a blow,
and he shivered. Icy blasts howled along the ground. Packed
though the snows of winter were already, the wind found
loose grains. They scurried in thin rows over drifts. They
crept out in ledges under every lea. They pelted through the
air and stung like hot ice. There was no cheer in laps that
stood iron-naked and chill. Neither stars nor moon were visible in a black sky. Zero weather would have been bearable
except for this freezing wind that drove underneath the heav-
iest garments, and made his eyes ache and his flesh grow
numb as it cut into him. He turned his collar up and uncon-

sciously curled his long body like a hibernating bear as he hurried toward the trolley. He rounded the library building and was knocked sprawling.

"I beg your pardon," he mumbled as his dazed senses recovered. He picked himself up. "I was in a hurry and didn't watch where I was going — oh! It's The Fool!" The exclamation broke out before he could check it.

The creature looked monstrous, there in the darkness and cold. The pupils of its eyes were pinpoints shining into his. Weirdly they dilated, until they were of abnormal size, with a mad, red tinge, and they glowed like coals. A child's arm clutched his.

"What is the infinite cube of one?" It was a squeaky mouse-voice to be coming from so huge a head.

"Why, I, I, I don't, well, I guess it's one," stammered Drew.

"Ha-ha! Trying to confuse me, were you? You know that that's not the answer. If you put cubes against each other for ever — "

"Oh, that's different. Then the answer is infinity. But I've got to hurry or — "

"No, no, that's not it, because eventually the cubes would fill the universe and then there would not be room for more."

"Sorry, I can't help you. I don't know the answer."

"Yes you do, brother. You called me *The Fool.* We know the answer. I can see in your eyes that you do. Aren't we brothers?"

"You must be mistaken. I've got to go. There is no answer."

"I knew you knew, brother! That is the answer."

The Fool chuckled and put his tiny hands up to the vast head. The head rolled, and the red coals in its eyes shone brighter.

"Riddle me this!" he cried. "Only the cardinal numbers have a beginning but no end. What has an end but no beginning?"

Like a misshapen shadow, The Fool was away and gone before Drew could answer. It almost seemed to him that the creature scuttled, or was that a toad-like hop that carried it squatly off?

Cold to the bone, anxious to keep his appointment, still hearing the magnificent periods of Sir Thomas, and baffled by his encounter, he hurried on his way.

What has an end but no beginning?

XXXVII CIRCE

There was a fever in Drew's caresses that cold, March morning. All day he had walked lost in his thoughts, a many-colored flux among which the physical appeal of Helione, the mad love she elicited, the vision of her loveliness, the memory of other nights in which the hours had run too swiftly to satiate rapture, disturbing recollections of his childhood dreams, the play upon which he had neglected work for weeks, speculation about what career he should pursue after graduation, and all the mental web of his experiences ebbed and flowed. He knew at last that this woman had become the dominant theme in the symphony of his life. He would endure any ignominy, suffer any hurt, forgive any action of hers because of his love. He could not control it. He could reason out what he ought to do, but she influenced every movement he made and every thought. At no time was she absent. Vividly she came in imagination, until spiritual and physical hunger drove him irresistibly to find her, to see her, to be with her. He knew also that the direction of his life would never be settled until he had fixed permanently her place. In his heart she was fixed for ever, but he wanted her, all of her, as the other half of his being. Like the lover in Plato, he thought of her and of himself as two halves of an ideal one. It was a whole that must be pure and complete in itself. There was not room for others. Out of that deep love, half mystical and half earthly, partaking of the divine and the humble, grew the seeds of what Lee said was jealousy. Himself he had gladly surrendered, but he wanted her entire being to unite with his in the perfect sphere that he visioned. Above all, he wanted the certainty of her response, the stability of her acceptance. So it was that, after he had escorted her home from *The Thief of Bagdad,* he sat very quiet, yet tense, beside her on the sofa. She had gone to her room to hang up her frock, "because you are awfully hard on clothes and I have to have something to wear," she had once explained. Clad in her Chinese wrap, hands folded in the loose sleeves, she sat, head on knees, looking sidewise toward him.

"I'm cold," she murmured.

Silently he placed an arm around her and held her closer, kissing away the chill on her cheeks. Her hair spilled across his lap, a wine dark mass with glints of bronze. He caressed the silken luxury of its disarray. Fragrant with l'origan, and the exquisite art of her make-up, lovely in the soft lines of the wrapper, she lay in his arms.

"Why do you look at me like that?" she asked.

"I was thinking."

"Of what?"

"Oh, something that I wanted to say to you."

"Tell me."

"Well, I don't know."

She sat up as though an electric current had passed through her. With the intuition that is given to some few mortals, she guessed what was coming.

"Tell me, I want to hear."

"I'm not so sure."

Her arms crept around him. "Tell me," she tempted, a color in her cheeks. All at once, and mysteriously, she had become warm. A visible murmur undulated along the curves of her body. She lifted her legs to the sofa and relaxed upon it, voluptuously curled, her head in his lap. Se pulled his head downward with gentle insistence. Like the wings of a moth was his kiss, fleeting across her lips in a second. She could feel his tenseness.

"Tell me what you were going to say, darling."

His dark eyes, their hazel lost in the wells of the sockets, with a sad, hungry, and yet wild light in them, looked into hers, all bright and innocent. Her upturned face was like a lush, tropic orchid, with petalled lips, and her satiny smoothness of complexion, and the heavy green of her pupils, and the long, black lashes, and the mahogany red wealth of her hair.

"More than anything else in the world, I love you," he whispered. She clung to him with an instinctive response.

"You occupy all my thoughts and rule me from morning to night. Lovely, so lovely. I only live for the times when I see you. Nothing else matters."

She lay soft and passive, with the ghost of a smile on her mouth.

He hesitated, peered into her eyes a long minute. "I can't say it, Helione. There aren't enough words to tell you what you mean to me. I had it all in mind but I can't think when you look at me like that and when you are so close. All I know is that I will always love you, no matter what happens Will — will you marry me, some day?"

A tremble softened her body. The smile, so faint, so pleased, so enigmatic, parted her lips.

"I love you," she murmured, almost inaudibly. He embraced her in a kind of frenzy. He caressed the silk of her robe, and it slipped open. Save for slippers and hose, she lay nude upon the sofa.

"I guessed what you were going to say," she whispered. "Are you shocked?"

He did not reply. The polished calves of her limbs gleamed into view. There was a ritual to be performed at the altar of love, the mounds and curves and hollows that she cared for with such pride that they might win such worship; the ritual of tender caresses, and finger-tips upon eyelids and cheeks and mouth and lobe of ear and depression of throat; the rite of lip against lip and tongue to tongue; the adoration of breast and armpit and stomach; the mystery of thigh, and the increasing fierce ecstasy of union. Her eyes closed as in some intolerable rapture. They opened again and looked forth, luminous with unseeing delirium. Strokes of fire caressed nipple and mount. His coming was the splendor that dissolved her being. Her eyes rolled up, up, up, until only the whites showed. She radiated a glow like the sun, a warmth as of summer. In the fullness of that embrace, they held a high communion of body and spirit and dream. The deepest wells within were tapped. And from temple to chin, the scar turned into a line of pulsing crimson as the blood alternately rushed and drained away. As never before, Drew experienced the exaltation of consummated love; as never in the past, Helione responded with the opulence of her radiant beauty. Lyrical and perfect was that commingling; all the poetry, music, depth, and wealth of life entered that love caress, while the unheeded minutes lengthened to hours....

"You had better go now," whispered Helione. "It's after three and I think I hear someone moving."

Slowly he returned from the high places, the great places, to earth.

"You didn't answer my question," he said huskily.

She wakened from a deep dream and her eyes opened lazily.

"You don't want any other answer now."

"Yes, I do. It means so much to me."

"But I can't answer, darling. I want to live my own life. I want independence and freedom. I don't want to be tied down yet. Besides, you haven't enough money for yourself even. Let's wait."

"That doesn't matter, Lee. All I want to know is that you'll say yes, and some day when we are able we'll get married."

"I don't believe in long engagements."

"Don't you love me at all? Good God, I would do anything for you, Lee."

"I know you would, darling, but it isn't that. Something might happen. You could fall in love with somebody else, — "

"I won't."

" — or I might get interested in another man. Oh, don't look so hurt. I probably won't, but I just mentioned it. Let's go on as we are for a while at least."

"I only want your acceptance, Lee. It will settle so much. Then I won't have to worry and I can do more work and maybe we can arrange things to be married that much sooner."

"You had better wait, Drew, till you know more about it."

"Wait! Wait! You always say that! I worry and worry about us, Lee. It would help so much if you would only be definite, one way or the other."

"I can't be sure. I like you a lot, Drew, more than any one I've ever known else. But I don't want to marry and have to settle down and raise children, not yet. I want to live first."

"But Lee, you could say yes even if you didn't mean it and that would be something to go on."

"I won't mislead you if I can help it. I like you too much for that."

"But you don't love me."

"Well, I don't know. You're awfully hard to get along with some times. Maybe I'll marry someone else and have you for a lover. Don't you think that that would be perfect?"

"No. I couldn't be interested in you if you were married."

"What difference does it make as long as you love me?"

"A lot of difference. Oh Lee, why do you change so quickly? One minute you're heaven, and then you're hell."

"Why not accept me as I am and stop worrying? I'll never be any different. I can't help the way I was made."

"No, I suppose not. Then your answer is no?"

"I didn't say that, darling. I just said I didn't want to be definite yet."

"I want to know now!"

"You'll miss your car if you don't hurry. Let's talk about it some other time. You'd better go."

Savagely he embraced her; all the longing, love, despair, doubt, and misery of his life blended in that caress. With a strange gesture of approach and retreat, his fingers trailed across her thighs, her breasts, her face; fiercely he turned from her and ran into the night.

He had only a minute to reach the car-line. He sped down icy walks and the slippery hill. He heard the trolley grind from its wye. He hurried as fast as his legs would move. He saw the street-car roll on its way. He shouted, but it flashed by while he was still half a block distant. Gasping for breath, his ears freezing and his lungs tortured by zero weather, he walked to the corner. It would be an hour before the next car came. He could not return to Lee without rousing her family. There were no stores open in this lonely outskirt of Center City. He flapped his numb arms indecisively and puffed on a cigarette. There was nothing to build a fire with. It was a full three miles to his transfer point, but if he hastened, he might arrive before that trolley left its wye in forty minutes. Exhausted from the turmoil of the day, and from his emotional outpouring, bitter with disappointment, depressed with frustration and yet exalted by the memory of rapturous hours with Lee, and now stiffening in the frigid air, he began following the rails.

Stores, homes, and warehouses crept by. Walking was difficult because a blanket of grain-snow lay over the ice underneath. A chill moon sank whitely in the west. Sinister shadows were cast by tree and house. No other person was abroad. His ears and hands and face, even his feet, congealed in the frost. Not a wind stirred. A dog howled far away, an eerie and lonely wail that shivered through the air. From farther still rose the mournful whistle of a train. He picked his way between ties, occasionally sliding on a patch of ice, ploughing in loose snow, frozen externally but alternately seething and stiffening from the tempest of his thoughts.

Unconsciously, he began to run. He must make his connection at the transfer-point or his walk would be wasted and he would shiver for an hour. He ran faster and faster, like a specter fleeing from disaster or racing toward its haven. The ties flew under his feet. A crackle was in the air. He slowed when his breath came in painful gulps, ran when he felt rested. The outskirts and the lake and the woods passed behind him. Patterns of snow and trees, arabesques of moonlight and shadow sprawled for ever ahead beyond the gleaming rails. The moon westered, low against the horizon. Cold bit into him. He raced faster, gasping for breath, running, running, running, as though his legs could not move swiftly enough for the urge that drove him.

The cemetery loomed on his right. Tombstones rose ghostly in the moonlight, and a filigree of black shadows lay across graves and by trees. The old experience on the farm came to mind, and he remembered nightmares. His legs flew beneath him. He dashed through moonlight and cold and darkness past the terror of a graveyard.

A gulf opened below. He leaped wildly but without success. He saw the culvert yawn, saw the cement flanges approach, felt himself hurtle through space. His shins cracked against stone and he clawed vainly for support. There came the dreadful sensation of falling....

Slowly, dazed, he opened his eyes. Where was he? A stream gurgled beside him. One leg hung in icy water, the rest of him lay on iron-hard soil and packed snow. He sat up, head throbbing.... He gradually understood.... The running, the fall through a culvert.... A wave of horror sickened him as he realized that this must be the stream that emptied into Twilight Cemetery, curious in that its flow continued the year around, however cold the weather.... A shudder seized him.... The pain in his legs was excruciating, and a fluid trickled from his head.... He ignored it.... The edge of the culvert was eight feet above him.... He made a frenzied leap, caught, hauled himself wearily out.... How long had he lain there?.... He did not know, for his watch was broken....

Running, racing, flying, he sped down the blue-glinting steel. His breath became fire and ice and torture. The fingers of skeletons were on his neck. Moonlight whitened the cemetery and cast fantastic shadows. The burial ground swirled away behind. Like the wind he ran, gasping, tripping, plunging onward.... Rows of houses.... A street-car ahead, its doors closing.... He stumbled through.... Curled on a seat, he choked for breath, and relaxed in a fatigue of despair, frustration, love fulfilled, and physical exhaustion.... A trickle of blood stained one cheek....

XXXVIII FOUR AT TEA

Lee — I believe I would like a salad, if you feel you can stand it.

Drew — I'd love to buy you one! But you'd better order something further. That isn't much.

Lee — Well, if you really don't mind, I will. I've been rather strapped this week and I had to do without lunch today.

Drew — Strapped?

Lee — Sure, you know, broke, hard-up, without funds.

Drew — You poor kid. But it's an ugly word.

Lee — Oh, it's all right. But I won't use it if you object, my lord and master.

Drew — She said, sweetly. Brrr. Have some tea.

Lee — I was just going to. And maybe a teeny, weeny piece of chocolate cake with ice-cream. They have lovely ice-cream here and the most delicious cake. What are you having?

Drew — I haven't quite decided. There seem to be several things I haven't tried.

Lee — Why do you always choose the exotic things that nobody ever heard of on the menu before?

Drew — That's a hell of a sentence. I suppose I could answer if I thought long enough but I can't say offhand. Probably it has something to do with some part of my past life.

Lee — Sure. Everything does, but you always pick out such weird items.

Drew — That's my privilege, isn't it?

Lee — You don't need to be so truculent. I was only asking.

Drew — I'm going to order lichee nuts, herring marinierte, and mate.

Lee — It sounds dreadful, all except the lichee nuts. They're rather good.

Waitress — Orders, please.

Drew — One lobster salad, chocolate cake with double chocolate ice-cream, pot of tea, and I'll have friandises, herring marinierte, and mate.

Lee — Why did you change from lichee nuts?

Drew — Oh, I suppose just because you knew they were good, and I wanted things that are all new to find out for myself.

Lee — You're a bit childish in some ways.

Drew — Thanks. I like the charm of novelty.

Lee — It isn't necessary to be quite so sarcastic, is it?

Drew — I'm sorry. I've been doing a lot of work lately and I guess it's making me irritable.

Lee — What have you been doing?

Drew — Writing, mostly.

Lee — What? Tell me about it.

Drew — Why, it's a play that —

Lee — How exciting! Am I in it?

Drew — What a question to ask, darling. You know you're the heroine. Who else would be?

Lee — You might put in one of those cute young Gammas that I hear are so crazy about you.

Drew — The tail of a scorpion, and so forth.

Lee — Don't be nasty. I've heard rumors.

Drew — Let 'em pass. What have you been doing?

Lee — Tell me, first. I asked first. What is your play about?

Drew — About two hours.

Lee — That wasn't worthy of you.

Drew — Oh, I'm not sure yet.

Lee — You mean you don't know? Dear me, it must certainly be a queer play if the budding young playwright himself does not know what it's about. How do you expect anyone else to know?

Drew — I don't. I merely meant that I'm not sure how I'll go on with it. I've got the first two acts done but there are about three more yet.

Lee — You haven't told me what's in it.

Drew — Would you really like to know?

Lee — Of course I would, darling. Oh — how can I ever think if you do that? A waitress might pass. What makes you want to trail your fingers across my hand?

Drew — You!

Lee — Sir, unhand my ankle.

Drew — That wasn't my hand. Don't you know a hand from a foot?

Lee — Not now, I don't. I don't know why it is but you make me all weak when you just touch me.

Drew — Huh, what do you think happens to me? I can't help it, Lee, I simply can't control anything when I'm seeing you. It's like a fire running wild — an invisible sun.

Lee — You're sweet, Drew.

Drew — Good Lord, Lee, I —

Lee — Hush. Our orders are coming. You were going to tell me about your play.

Drew — Oh. Yes. Well, I don't know quite how to begin, it's such a queer sort of play. It's about a girl who is a man —

Lee — A girl who is a man? What do you mean by that? It sounds Freudian.

Drew — Wait, let me finish. She is a lovely creature, like a princess, and she looks a good deal like you. From sunset to sunrise, she is a woman, a strange, mysterious woman like those in Poe, Morella, Ligeia, Berenice, Helen, you know them. Well, she is in love with a ghost and the ghost comes to her every night at midnight. He is an awful ghost, all ugly and deformed and shadowy, but she knows he is a prince in disguise and he is under a spell, and when her love burns high enough he will be released from the enchantment and become himself, a handsome young prince, beautiful as a god. But every morning, when she wakes up, she is a man, the handsome young prince, and he lives up in his castle in the mountains, and he wants to go down to the valley becase he has heard that a woman like the sun lives down there. So he disguises himself as an old crone because he knows that if the woman is what he thinks she is, she will be all kindness no matter how miserable the visitor looks, and it won't make any difference to her if he is man or woman, rich or poor, handsome or ugly. So he disguises himself and hobbles off down the mountain, but it's a long way, and by the time he gets to see the woman's hut, or rather, to where he can see it way in the distance, night has come, and he feels so weary and tired that he stops under a tree to rest a minute and he falls asleep. The princess wakes up and vaguely recalls a dream she had about being a prince and starting down a mountain but she can't remember all of it and anyway the ghost is at the door and she lets him in. That's as far as I've got.

Lee — Hmm. It sounds awfully interesting. It's allegorical, of course, or at least symbolic, isn't it?

Drew — Why, I don't know. I'm writing it just because I thought of it and it appealed to my imagination.

Lee — I don't think you had better tell it to many people. It's a bit, shall we say, revealing?

Drew — What do you mean by that?

Lee — If you don't know, it doesn't matter. How does it go from then on, or did you say you hadn't decided?

Drew — I haven't worked it out yet except for the end.

Lee — Tell me about the end.

Drew — Why, just at sunrise one morning, the moon eclipses the sun, and as a result, the prince finds himself walking up the staircase of his castle and it was all a dream. He hears a sound, a slow drip, drip, drip, and he notices a little stream pushing its way step by step downward. He doesn't pay any attention to it but the drip becomes louder the higher he climbs until he drives him wild. Then he looks down and discovers that it is not water but blood that is dripping. He starts going faster until he is running and the drip is like thunder in his ears. When he reaches the top, he rushes to the door that the stain is coming from under and bursts it open. There is the woman of the valley, the woman like the sun, lying dead, with his sword in her heart, and she is all naked, but her face looks like his. Just then the eclipse passes, and he wakes in his room, and he gets his disguise to don and go down into the valley.

Lee — Hm. It's interesting. But weird. I don't think many people would understand it.

Drew — Who cares? I'm writing it for my own amusement. Anyway, it has no meaning. It's just an idea of mine that I —

Lee — Ooooh, the salad looks luscious.

Drew — So this is herring marinierte?

Lee — You ordered it.

Drew — I know, but it looks rather formidable.

Lee — Mmmm, pardon me for sounding so pleased but this salad is simply divine and I was so hungry.

Drew — I'm glad you like it. I'm going to try the pimento. I have a suspicion that this piece of fish was pickled raw and I do not like fish pickled raw. Oh well, the spices look good and I love pimento. Ah…. Oh, my God, water!

Lee — What's the matter?

Drew — Give me your water too!

Lee — Why, surely, but what —

Drew — Hahh, hhhh, haah, hhhhh, haah —

Lee — What on earth do those awful sounds mean? What happened?

Drew — I'm sorry I have to breathe so hard. That blankety blank pimento was a hunk of raw red pepper.

Lee — Oh! That's too bad. Did it burn you?

Drew — Oh, no, I was only (gulp) trying to give you my interpretation of the Mad Monk of Morocco.

Lee — It isn't necessary to be quite so sarcastic, aren't I right?

Sven — Hullo! I didn't expect to see you here.

Lee — Hello, Sven, this is a pleasant surprise. Won't you join us?

Drew — Yes, do, oh my God.

Sven — What's the matter with him? He looks sick.

Lee — He ate some red pepper.

Sven — If he hasn't any more sense than that, he ought to look sick.

Lee — Won't you sit down?

Sven — I might as well. I was supposed to meet Jennifer here at three-thirty.

Lee — It's only three twenty-five. She'll be along soon and you can all join us. Why not wait for her here?

Sven — That's not a bad idea. Have an oval?

Lee — Not now, thanks, later. I'm enjoying the salad. Mind if we continue?

Sven — Go to it. As for you, Mr. Gordon —

Drew — For God's sake, my name is Drew!

Sven — All right. As I was saying, as for you, Mr. Gordon, when did you develop this passion for red pepper?

Drew — I didn't. It was a mistake. I thought it was pimento.

Sven — That's a hell of an excuse. They're both just as bad. I wouldn't —

Jene — Dear me, I didn't expect to find such a reception committee.

Sven — Hello, Jennifer, it's about time you came.

Lee — You're looking marvellous. Where did you get that cute scarf?

Jene — Wurf, wurf, wurf. Hello, everybody. It's nice to see you again — no, go on with you things, Sven and I will be with you right away, won't we?

Sven — Sure, sure.

Jene — I picked it up the other day when I was looking through the Mart. I saw the loveliest slippers there and —

Lee — That's where I bought my last pair, remember the ones with —

Sven — They're off again. We might just as well be in China the next half hour for all the attention we'll get. I'll talk to you — no, go on, you can answer between bites.

Drew — It's no use. My throat is so scorched from that pepper that I won't even be able to taste anything until it cools off. Anyway, these aren't hot dishes. They'll keep. How's yourself?

Sven — So-so. Wishing I had my term papers done.

Drew — So do I. Aside from them, have you written any more poems lately?

Sven — No, not for months. I've outgrown it. Just now I'm planning a novel.

Drew — Outgrown it? One never outgrows poetry. I'm still pleased and I'll always enjoy it when I read Kubla Khan for instance.

Sven — That's another question. You're talking about reading poetry which is a sort of passive pleasure. I meant the active one of writing poetry which is a different thing. You can outgrow the mood or condition that makes you write it. Then you turn to something else.

Drew — I should think you would always want to write lyrics, or at least be able to.

Sven — Be able to, perhaps, but not want to. I *suppose* I could sit down and dash off a quatrain or sonnet at any time, but that isn't what I meant either. All the good poems that I've written practically wrote themselves. A gesture, an episode, parting from a friend, a thought that suddenly came to me, the sound of Jene's voice, a love I had, or a grief I experienced, there used to be a lot of things like those that I felt so keenly or that impressed my imagination so that I tried to capture them in songs. It isn't wholly or even largely a conscious process. The feeling grips you. You get a sudden desire to catch your vision and set it down just as you saw it, though of course it's always idealized or heightened or it wouldn't have seized your imagination so. That's why I only wrote lyrics and never long poems. You can put so much in a lyric. You can concentrate the intensity of your dream or whatever it was that inspired you. You don't have to think or plan. You have the vision, it overflows, and you set it down, and if the vision is great enough and if you are sensitive enough and if you are naturally gifted in being able to express yourself, then you write an immortal song. But you don't care whether you do or not. You write first because you have to, you aren't happy until you do. You don't think about words or what you intend to say, or what people will think, or even whether anyone is ever going to read the poem. Not while writing, you don't. Afterwards, after it's done, then you may want to show it around, or publish it and let the world have it. Then you may hope that you become famous or get royalties. Those desires may even help build up your mood or your wish to write, but it takes The Fool or the flash of a girl diving from a springboard or a woodpecker tatting away on a stump to set you going, and when that happens everything else is driven out of your head and all you have left is a clear vision and a powerful need to put it down, in a lyric if you're a poet, or a theme if you're a musician, or on canvas if you paint.

Drew — I don't see how you can say you've outgrown poetry if you can still be so enthusiastic.

Sven — That's evidence in itself that I have. I couldn't be so critical otherwise. I'd be emotional perhaps, but the minute you become analytical you're lost.

Drew — Oh, that's not entirely true. Look at Swinburne and his critical essays.

Sven — I suppose there are exceptions, but I still think it's a sound rule. When you become analytical, you tear down, or build up, and those are different habits of mind than the one where you don't either tear apart or put together, but merely tell what impressed you. At least, I think the great lyrics are like that. They present. Like Kubla Khan, or La Belle Dame, or Full Fathom Five. They don't analyse. That's left for the reader or scholar to do if he wants to.

Drew — It sounds plausible enough, but I don't yet see why you are abandoning poetry. If everything you say is true as I presume it is since you are better qualified to speak than I am, I should think you would be proud to write poems. I should think you would want to continue.

Sven — Not necessarily. Perhaps others do, for that matter I know that a lot of poets have spent all their lives at it, but with me it's different. To tell the truth, I haven't thought much about it until you started me going just now, but I guess it's because I've said all I had to say in lyrics. Or rather, I've written so many poems that they present about all the types and kinds of incidents or pictures that appeal to me. I could go on writing them, surely, but it would only be varying earlier moods I've had, and not so well. Probably that's part of it. The more esthetic and emotional the experience, well, for that matter the more experience of all sorts that you have, the less any one of them catches your imagination. On the other hand, their total begins to mean something.

Drew — Is that why you are turning to novels?

Sven — I guess so. Yes, I'm sure that's part of the reason. In a novel I can gather all the variety of experience.

Drew — But you could do that in a book of poems. You did it in this last volume of yours, the fourth one, I mean, I forget its title.

Sven — Windows? Well, perhaps, but not in the same way. You might make a collection of lyrics that would come near the scope of life. A narrative poem might come closer still. But in one case you'd have a series of highly colored presentations and in the other you'd have to sacrifice some of your exactness and realness just for the sake of meter and rhyme.

Drew — I see. What it comes down to then is that you want a broader scope.

Sven — Exactly.

Drew — You want to build up and present aspects of life that ordinarily wouldn't impress you as material for poetry. You want to give the whole sweep of it and have all sorts of moods and experiences closely tied together as you couldn't in a lyric. And I suppose, speaking from my own efforts, that you'll find more subtle and flexible rhythms in prose than you do in even the freest lyric.

Sven — Perhaps.

Drew — That was a noncommittal answer. What's your novel about?

Sven — I don't know.

Drew — Ye Gods, are you pulling my leg?

Sven — Now, now, don't get a hemorrhage. I never said I was writing a novel. I merely said that I was thinking of it. I may never get around to writing it.

Lee — What are you two talking about? Can't we be in on it?

Sven — Himmel, now we're going to be in hot water just because we went ahead and talked instead of staying quiet while they talked about shoes or something. Let's order before we have to go all over the same ground or get involved in an argument.

Lee — I was only asking, she said plaintively.

Jene — That's my she said. They were probably discussing just poetry.

Sven — Just. Huh, I like that. What's the use?

Lee — There isn't any with two beautiful and heartless girls like us against you.

Sven — Well, now, let's all have an oval, order something, and call a truce for the time being. Suppose you tell us about yourselves for a change. What have you been doing?

XXXIX THE SCAR

"You are exquisite, Helione."

"Except for the scar."

"It makes you the lovelier. Beauty is emphasized the more when it has a flaw or defect. If it were pure, there would be nothing beyond, and I would care for you less if you were absolutely perfect. How did it happen, if I may ask? Don't answer if the memory pains you."

"Not at all. I was sledding one winter when I was a girl, and we lived in Montreal then, and a youngster with me tried to kiss me. I wouldn't let him, I've always been able to take care of myself, so I simply ran off and started down the slide again. He wanted to frighten me, I imagine, for he slung his sled, it was fastened to a rope in his hand, out on the chute as I was coming down. He didn't quite manage to jerk it away in time and a runner cut my face open. They took me to a hospital but I've had the scar ever since. It was curious, I didn't shed even one tear, and he stood there crying as if he had killed me."

"That was tragic, I'm sorry the accident happened, no, I'm not, in a way, because I think you look more beautiful now. The day I met you I was sure you had suffered a deep hurt in the past, it was one of the things that made me like you."

"Well, you're right, but that wasn't the real hurt."

"Tell me."

"No, you would feel bad."

"I won't. Tell me, I'm curious."

"I think not, it might make you angry, you're so sensitive and jealous."

"I promise I won't be. Do tell me."

"All right, if you insist, but remember, you asked."

"I'll remember."

"It was about two years ago. I had graduated from high school and I thought I'd rather study art than enter the U, so I began Art School, that was where I met Jennifer, but this was before. I'd known a girl in high school and we were pretty close chums, she was in one of my classes and we used to talk a lot. She kept telling me about a friend of hers, he's a well-known artist, by the way, and wanted me to meet him, of course I was pleased to. She took me to his studio one day and suggested that I'd be a good model with my figure and coloring. I felt embarrassed and didn't know what to say but he seemed anxious and asked if I'd mind posing for him and I said yes, I felt flattered, you can imagine. He set a time, and when I came, he told me it was to be a figure oil, a nude. I've always been proud of my figure, so I had no objections. About the third time, during a rest, he offered me a drink, it was the first I'd had, and like a fool I accepted and took another. They went to my head. The next thing I knew, I was lying on the studio couch, and — oh well, why go on? You can guess the rest."

"Did he succeed?"

"Yes. But what hurt me most was that next day my friend cut me cold, absolutely ignored me, and I've never seen her since, and I've never known why — Drew, you're crying. I'm so sorry, darling, I was afraid you'd be hurt if I told you but you wanted to know and you promised you wouldn't be angry."

"I can't help it, Lee."

"Forget about it, darling, I have. It didn't mean anything to me and I've never gone back, of course."

"That isn't what hurts."

"What is then?"

"A dream."

"Are you as metaphysical as the man that only an idea could hurt?"

"No, I'm sorry, forgive me for being a damned baby. I'll know better than to ask hereafter."

"It's a wise thought. Come, smile that nice smile of yours and kiss me. I'll have the apartment just another week before Marion returns, it was generous of her to let us use it."

"A dream blasted."

"Don't think of it. The whole place is to ourselves. Aren't you glad?"

"Yes, Helione, as glad as I can be...."

"The beauty of your face is rivalled only by the beauty of your body...."

"Helione, Helione, this is madness, God! for more madness."

"Don't talk, darling, keep on. Oh! Your hands are lyrical...."

XL THE ATMOSPHERE OF HOUSES

By Drew Gordon

Houses, like people, possess a character of their own. Each person whom one meets, each stranger one passes upon the streets, belongs to the category of human beings, yet is distinct from all others. He is a new world to be explored, a little world, perhaps, but he is undeniably different from all the millions who are like him; and though one lived with him, studied him, identified oneself with him, he would always retain still further secrets. What reason is there, then, that any individual may ever hope to comprehend another individual in all his infinite variations? One's own experiences are peculiar to himself, and serve at least only as an approximate guide to the understanding of other people. If that be true of man to man, or woman to woman, how much less chance is there that a member of one sex may even approach comprehension of a member of the opposite sex, where a fundamental difference in structure and nature adds its complication to the isolation of the individual? I am separated from Sven. I do not know him. I can never be wholly him, nor live his life, nor understand him in his multiform aspects. But he too is man, and I therefore deduce that he reasons as I do, suffers as I have suffered, desires goals like those that I desire, loves as I would love, and pursues in a general way paths akin to those which I follow. But neither he nor I are as Jene and Lee. Our natures are separate from theirs. Because our very physical being is opposed to theirs, it ensues that their mental processes, their lines of reasoning, their hopes in life, their emotional and intellectual reactions, must derive from sources at variance with ours. Our most vivid imagination will fall short of success in any attempt to identify ourselves with them. Conversely, their deepest striving to grasp our natures must always fall upon their side of the barrier. We are parted by visible walls that we can not scale. To a large degree, we do not even attempt to understand. We love and we desire, we are loved and we are desired, for physical reasons. We satisfy the requirements of our respective natures, woman to man and man to woman. But few indeed are they who go deeper, who try also to feel the psychical makeup and the inner contrasts of the other sex. And those who try are doomed to failure. "He understands women", or "she does not understand men", are equally futile generalities. Both statements are partly true. They are true to the extent that every man understands how different from himself are all women; and does not understand fully how they are different. That is the everlasting riddle. One hopes that the puzzle may never be solved, for the attempt to explain it adds interest to life and intensity to existence. One hopes — I hope. I am not sorry that the sexes are two, however great the pains of misunderstanding. Would that the sexes were three, or five, or twenty, to increase the already myriad mysteries of living. Life could not be too complex for my desire; there are not enough secrets to challenge my wits. It is an empty pleasure to obviate a difficulty; the charm lies all in the trying; and the greatest allure is invested in problems that are insoluble: why man differs from woman; what came before birth and what succeeds death; whence the universe originated and whither it is going; why the planets are eight; whether there is a god; that things are at all; the nature of seeds; the flush of color in the face of a woman loved; the sparkle of an emerald, the smoulder of a ruby by candlelight; fire; where did Ophir lie. These were not such splendid conjectures did they permit certain solution.

XLI THE ATMOSPHERE OF HOUSES, PART II

By Drew Gordon

Last night, I commenced an essay on the subject indicated by my title. My attempt wandered from its purpose, and I wrote of many things except the atmosphere of houses. Today, I examined my piece, but I do not wholly condemn it for its divagations. Is not life itself so devious, and so errant? We leave a friend, expecting to greet him tomorrow, and read by the night's paper that he died in an automobile accident. We invest our money in securities, that we may be free of economic worry, and the corporation goes into receivership. We love, and we marry, and we beget children; and we are saddened by the unloveliness of our wives, or the increasing stoutness of our husbands. We dream of far places, but they are never as we picture them. Their strangeness disappears when we arrive, and they are like our old haunts. We toil for rewards, and are passed by while newcovers receive the fruits of our labor. We help a friend and are repaid with enmity. We give to the old man shivering on the street, and receive a bequest in his will. We arrange for a little gathering of friends on a week-end; a letter arrives telling that cousin John and Aunt Jane are on their way with their five children to pay us a visit. We return from our office, expecting a dinner, and the greetings of family, but find that our house is reduced to ashes by fire, cause unknown. We save a thousand dollars for a luxury — a car, books, a trip, a fur coat; pneumonia or appendicits erases the hope. We are desperate with hunger and find a gold watch that has fallen from a woman's wrist. We sow wheat, and the plague of locusts descend upon it. We buy tickets to a lottery, and a fortune is ours. We strive for fame, and the world forgets before we are dead. We think of a way to make the old bus go farther on less gas, and wealth floods us from the patent. War takes our son, tuberculosis our daughter, and the Black Sheep discovers a silver mine in Ontario. We go off on a picnic, and the ants enjoy our food after the rain has soaked our clothes. The man we trusted absconds, while eloping with the woman we loved and to whom we introduced him. We cross Main Street and meet an acquaintance whom we have not seen in ten years, an acquaintance who was last reported in Egypt. We invite ten persons to a party. Four arrive, and the viands we prepared are wasted, unless we wish to dine for a week on left-overs. We invite twenty guests for our next soirée, and they all come bringing some friends who are in town overnight; our offerings are inadequate and they depart disgruntled. We look at a log burning in the fireplace and dream great dreams. They materialize, or they remain but dreams, and only blind chance, fate, accident, fortune, determines which will prevail. Who can say what geniuses were denied existence because of contraceptives? For ourselves, there was only a chance in millions that we were born at all, but whether we would have wished to be, or not, here we are. When I think thusly, would that I could achieve the dispassionate attitude of Montaigne — no, would that I may never. To be the detached observer at times is splendid, but solely as relief from a passionate entering into the multiform elements of reality. I would know everything, try everything, be everything, do everything. I am glad that I can not, for thereby will my existence never grow stale. And ever the finger of fate intervenes. I am reminded of this by a remarkable coincidence that befell me today. After my last class at two-thirty, I felt a desire to have tea with Helione. I telephoned her residence and her business address, but she was at neither place, nor could they suggest where she might be found. This being a restless day of April, the stir of wakening life excited me. I wanted to get away from school, and people, and city. I went to the shores of Maple Lake, and walked along its deserted paths, and wandered among the wet freshness of its great trees, with the little green buds opening all over their branches. As I rounded a turn, there I saw Lee, pacing slowly down the path. We walked on, commenting on the chance that brought us together. She remarked that it would be pleasant if Sven and Jennifer were with us to enjoy the afternoon outdoors. Who should approach us then but Sven and Jene, driven like ourselves to escape for the day! The strangest coincidence was yet to come. We sat on a bench and thought of plans for the evening. Sven and I had less than two dollars between us, and the two girls who offered their slender resources had barely a quarter each; altogether, insufficient to pay for dinners and a movie or play. At that moment, Sven turned around to toss his cigarette. I heard him exclaim. He lunged across the back of the bench — to Lee's and Jene's alarm — and returned holding three dull silver dollars. It was providential that he found a sum which sufficed for our evening. I would have been less surprised had it been a bill, or even a five- or ten-dollar bill. But it is a mystery how three silver dollars, which obviously had lain there a long while, perhaps all winter, came to be lost behind that particular lake bench, and discovered by us particular four, under the most fortuitous circumstances. There were actually three coincidences, but they succeeded each other so quickly as to seem parts of one.

This last bit of luck stimulated us to speculation about coincidence. "Why is it," I remember Sven asking, "that readers object to coincidences in novels though they are common enough in life?"

"Perhaps they don't want life or reality in the fiction they read," I answered.

"I'm not sure that they do object," said Jennifer. "Thomas Hardy often used them in the best of his novels, *Jude* and *Tess* and *The Return of the Native.*"

"I wouldn't say that," began Helione, interrupting us both. With her usual intuitive logic, she went straight to what I now consider the truth. "I think they object to coincidences, first because they want more than life merely in art, and because they subconsciously want at least the illusion that mind or man is superior to fate. They want to believe that they control destiny instead of the reverse. When they read a book or see a painting, they have a vicarious experience but at the same time they pit their own life and imagination against the artist. Too, they anticipate what is coming next, and since they have only the logical developments or the dramatic unity of the artist to judge by, they feel cheated if coincidence breaks the ideal line of progress. Of course, it seems silly to me, that attitude. I don't object to coincidence in novels like Hardy's, it's part of life, but I resent it in the hands of insincere artists who use it as an arbitrary solution of problems. I've always said that life sould imitate art and it would be much more satisfying!"

XLII THE ATMOSPHERE OF HOUSES, PART III

By Drew Gordon

I like and dislike houses as I like or dislike persons for they too have a character no less individual. The first time I entered Lee's home, I was impressed by its coldness. It was untidy, humble, underheated, but these things had nothing to do with its psychical nature. That essence is imparted by the people who inhabit the dwelling; and though they die or abandon the place, their atmosphere persists. And the house of Helione is inhospitable. It questions you when you arrive, and urges you begone upon your way. No, it is not quite that even; it really pays no attention to you. It is aloof, separate, and it does not let you in. That is its character: absolute indifference, an atmosphere that is the more chilling because it persists without distinction between visitors and occupants. The unfastened door — unlocked that you may come and go because you are neither welcome nor turned away; the hall book-case with glass panes — glassed for separateness; the objects fallen carelessly around, newspapers and toys and trinkets — careless because it does not matter that you come; the windows without blinds — blindness because there is nothing to attract or repel attention; the chairs that creak; the clock that is never on time since your presence has no meaning; the piano with its back toward the living-room so that you will not feel inclined to play it even if you approach it; the floor lamp whose long shade prevents a glow from reaching out to you: these are a few of the traits that indicate the structure's personality. Indifference.

I remember too the occasion when I went to Jene's residence. Lee and I and Sven were invited to dinner. I had not previously encountered her parents. Her father is a wizened man wrapped in unknown thoughts. Mrs. Dane has signs of dementia; a woman with smoky veils to her eyes who utters frenzied atrocities in a voice of culture with a soft inflection. There was a tenseness in the atmosphere, but the vagaries of the parents could not wholly obliterate the dominance of Jene. They had built the mansion, and their handiwork assumed their traits, but Jene had given to it her impress. A cheery fire crackled in the fireplace. Tall ivory candles illumined the dinner-table. The cuisine was faultless. Severe stiff chairs were a trial to comfort. Sterling plates with filigree ornamented the wainscotting with high disdain. There was a reticence about the vast parlor in whose recesses were lost the outlines of a grandfather's clock, the three-dimensional shadow of a Steinway, a built-in bookcase filled with sets in morocco and calf, divans and chairs and tables. Out of this opposition — cold and warmth — emerged an atmosphere that is predominantly Jene's: the leap of flames; the drip of wax into formations modelled weirdly by currents of air; the rich coloring of a Sarouk; pillows tossed carelessly before the open fireplace; highlights on mahogany moulding; vivid sketches of nudes, watercolors of hills and ancient buildings, still-lifes of fruit and vase — the work of Jene — splashed upon the walls; Pater and De La Mare and Kenneth Grahame lying opened, back upwards, upon table and floor. A house of drama; fire assaulting ice.

Dora's house is a lewd house. The weeping willows of its lawn are meretricious; a spurious protection; a sentimental cloak. As you enter, there is a lobby so small that you must virtually rape your hostess before you are admitted to the living-room. Waxen calla lilies flaunt upon the mantel-piece. Innumerable pillows of purple and henna and green and burnt orange and ravenous blue promise a sensuous content. The

rug is enticement to seduction, so thick its nap, and so yield-
ing. Chairs can not be found. Only a tremendous davenport
and the pillows that allure offer ease. The blinds are always
down, and the curtains never drawn. Upon the one side-table
reposes one book, *The Memoirs of Fanny Hill*. When logs
ember in the fireplace, no other lights are used; but in summer,
one amber bulb hides in a corner, or one candle languishes
upon the mantel-piece; and the heavy odors of incense, magno-
lia, sandalwood, orange-blossom and rose, are ever present,
scenting the languid air. A house of eastern sin; harlot's den.

I received an interesting confirmation of my estimate of
Sven upon that evening when I first visited his home. Like
Helione's, his residence was either freakishly planned, or was
modified by exigency, for his bedroom-den also occupies front
on the ground floor. As one enters, his room is on one's right,
parlor to left, dining-room in left rear, and kitchen to right
back. His quarter is apotheosis of himself and of the rest of the
house. Papers, letters, books, bottles of ink, stationery, rubber
bands, typewriter, carbon-, copy-, and bond-paper, pencils, wire
clips, rolls of manuscript, and miscellaneous debris conceal his
desk. A Japanese print snubs a Beardsley drawing upon the
walls. The book-case is stacked with Swinburne, Brooke,
Millay, Wylie, Whitman, Blake, Masefield, Robinson, Ibsen,
Sudermann, and similar poets and other Scandinavian authors
whose names I do not recall. On the top shelf, an oboe scowls
beside a clarinet. A steam-engine in miniature rusts against a
baseboard. Cannisters of tobacco line a table. Battalions of
pipes — meerschaum, briar, corncob, and thorn; amber and
composition, bakelite and ebony cigarette holders; a colossal
house pipe that must hold at least a tin of tobacco; and a
cracked hookah: these adorn the same table. Everything is
clean except the floorboards, which are decorated with fluffs of
dust. A cactus plant rules the sill by virtue of spike threat,
defeating the water hyacinth that can not decide on whether to
bloom. There is a microscope inclosed by a glass dome on a

stand beside his desk, and near it lie some strange odds and
ends: a Mayan figurine, an Egyptian scarab, a Roman coin; a
pair of chop-sticks; several pieces of quartzite, jade, onyx, and
tourmaline; a phial of quicksilver; and other bric a brac.
Museum. Poet's house, mind's house, that takes all life for its
province. Not the atmosphere of a house, but the house of
atmospheres.

I recall now what it was that first attracted my attention to
the aura that pervades human residences. Many years ago,
when I was a boy of ten or eleven, I accompanied a group of
youngsters when they explored an abandoned house. As I
remember, this occurred during afternoon, and the deserted
structure was flanked by occupied homes, but for some reason
it had stood unlived in for hosts of seasons. The grass grew
rank on its lawn, and weeds rioted where the garden had
bloomed in its backyard. Only a few daisies and a few yellow
lanterns and one dwarfed oriental poppy won a starved exs-
tence from the tangle of weeds. There was a fat caterpillar,
glossy green as a rubber plant, eating away against the vivid
scarlet of the poppy. Late summer sunlight outlined the house
with dusty gold. Its windows were boarded, but the back door
was unlocked. Someone before us had broken its latch. We
entered bravely, jeering at each other, proclaiming our fear-
lessness, for all abandoned houses were ghost houses in our
minds. The interior was not quite bare. I recall an old rocking-
chair that rotted in the parlor. I remember rusty tines in the
pantry. I am sure that a pile of rags lay in some room upstairs.
But everywhere lay a fine silt of dust, and the sunlight came
antique through slatted windows. I will never forget the wallpaper with its pattern of bluebells faded almost to tan, peeling in
enormous patches, or the stain where moisture from rains of
unknown years had bred a mould on part of the ceiling. Most
prominent of all was the silence. No fearsome solitude. No
creepy isolation. But the sad, lonely desert of a house that
broods, awaiting the return of those whom it sheltered, but

who will never come back. A desolation where the steps of intruders echo hollowly, through declining years, and yet do not disturb the psychoplasm left by the occupants. Of course, I had no such thoughts at the time. I was merely awed, and a trifle chilled by the emptiness; but as I see it in retrospect, I see also why I felt as I did, and what significance the house held. Atmosphere of decay. Vain regret that the years of ago are not the years of now. Acquiescence to dissolution.

In the apartment of Miss Tibbs, everything has its exact position from which it may not be shifted so much as a millimeter. Waxen lilies occupy the precise middle of the mantle. Old maid's house. Virginal death in life.

A surprising residence which I have visited is the artist Clemaut's. His studio is in violent disorder. Canvases, oils, paints, brushes, waste, frames, tubes, and miscellaneous items are flung without reason into corners already possessed. Bottles of wine, liqueurs, and cordials march upon a table, but there are neither goblets nor glasses. If you sit in a chair, it usually collapses beneath you. If you examine the floor, you find that you have stepped on the nose of Narcissus, the delta of a brown wench, or the neck of some unknown contemporary, perhaps an enemy of Clemaut's. These are some of the patchwork of types and scenes with which Clemaut has elivened his under-standing, so to speak. An amazing plant startles you from its position near the front skylight. It appears to have been designated an apple-tree by nature. At least, so its trunk and a couple of branches with absurdly small apples would indicate. But Clemaut has trimmed here and grafted there with inspired perverseness. A pomegranate looks unhappily at a pear blossom. A sprig of oak leaves can not quite reconcile themselves to kinship with a mass that hopes to become bananas, but has doubts when it surveys the pine needles bristling beside it from the same branch. And the coconut apparently ruling is a study in brown discouragement at the top of this botanical nightmare. Studio of revolt. Pagany triumphant.

Varied are the atmospheres of houses, as innumerable as the people who exist, and as many as there are residences upon earth, but among those which I have known, I like best the aura of my birthplace. There is nothing to distinguish it. Never is it immaculate, nor ever wholly in disorder. It remains in the genial disarray that associates with a home well lived in. Bowls of nuts, cookies, fruits, and candies are ever upon tables, offering refreshment at all times to whoever enters, for whoever enters is guest. Casually lie magazines and books, to be skimmed if there be delay in the arrival of the host. A tin of cigarettes, whose ranks have been disturbed, suggests that further assaults are welcomed. The door to the kitchen stands ajar. If the visitor would go there, he may at will. Pillows are carelessly strewn on the davenport. If he would sit, let him, or lie, he need but do so. Does he prefer to recline on the floor, there is no hindrance. The doors of the victrola are spread, its top up, and displayed are the albums of records; his choice is his own. There are easy chairs and hard chairs, he takes which he wishes. A fire burns lowly in the grate; he may increase it from the waiting logs, or open an unlatched window, as he prefers. A decanter occupies a nook, with goblets beside it for his selection. He is king. Nothing is forced upon him, and he need partake only of what he selects. House of warmth, house of comfort, house of friendliness. Atmosphere of hospitality. Psychotone of welcome to good living.

XLIII APRIL NIGHT

the woods are awake and the buds are out and the young grass
waves on the lawn the world is asleep but the new world wakes
and my love is waiting life blows up from the south on a warm
sweet breeze the flowers of june creep out of the mould of april
the soft shoots rise by day and sleep by night but she does not
sleep even as i she waits in the dark of night pleading that i
must come that i must come the world is a flame and the night
is a song sleep falls over the weary but not for her she places
a candle beside her bed and unrobes but she does not sleep
she is white as the stars are white she is pure as they she is
rosy all rosy and waiting for me and me alone i must go i must
go

In the late hours, Drew rose, and dressed, and went forth.
The mystery of love and night, of spring and beauty possessed
him. the way is long, he thought, and the car goes slow though
i do not see her i shall have come i shall have blessed and been
blessed i am mad mad mad for only love could be such happy
madness but i will be mad again and again for her her kisses of
yesternight were sweet but tonight will be sweeter the light in
her eyes was glory but tonight shall paradise be mine

Full bloomed flowers were yet unopened in field and mead-
ow but floral shops were rich with blossoms and the florist
must have known that this was the night of love for why else
would his shop be open at nearly midnight?

"A — a gardenia," said Drew shyly.

"Yes, sir," answered the florist, happy in the coming of spring and wakening love. "How many?"

Drew fingered his change wistfully.

"Just one, a perfect gardenia."

The florist looked at him and the night prevailed. From his stock he selected a gardenia, lovely and fragrant and exquisite, and beside it placed a single rose whose petals were like a blush but whose heart was all a fire.

"For the price of the gardenia," he smiled as one who thought of another girl and another night.

"Thank you," stammered Drew, in his eyes the appreciation he could not express as he fled upon his way for this was the night of bounty, this was the night of love, and all were ready to aid him in his quest. He gathered the gardenia and the rose and transferred to his last car.

she waits for me in her room, he thought, i shall come to her arms, he dreamed. her mouth will be soft and red like the rose but her face and her body will be as the rose and the gardenia and her fragrance as the gardenia it is late but not too late it is late but the darkness and quiet the night and love were made for us it is late but she waits and i come

The long hour's ride was over. Drew paced up the hill, quickly and silently, past the dark houses and along the deserted street.

There is a light in her room, he saw, and his heart sang within him thus in the night for love we two alone while the whole world sleeps thus in the night for love

is her family awake or not yet returned, he thought, but no car was parked by the house.

they are not home, he thought, and he thought of the rose and the gardenia, and the caress, however brief, that was worth tramping the world across and looting the vaults of time.

shall i ring or shall i knock upon her window, he thought, and he thought, i must come secretly as the traveller in the listeners for his tryst i must come like the breath of the wind

"Are you sure that it's safe, darling?" Drew did not recognize the man's voice.

"The family is away for the night, there are only the kids and they're asleep." That sounded like Helione.

The whispers came to Drew even as he reached her window, even as he was about to tap, even as his eyes saw through that space where the curtain had not been pulled completely down.

Drew did not recognize the naked man who was laying himself beside the waiting, naked loveliness of Helione.

XLIV SUICIDE

It was an old revolver, and faintly stamped on its stock was the symbol .32....

"A package of .32's, any make," said Drew to the man behind the counter....

the chambers do not close yet the stock says thirty two and the bullets say thirty two it must work though the barrel and stock do not click shut above the chamber but the hammer will fall when i pull the trigger

Click

a dent in the rim of the bullet but not in the cap the chamber does not revolve i must revolve it it will not fail this time it will *not* fail

Click

a dent in the rim of the bullet but not in the cap the chamber will not close beneath the stock and barrel the gun will not work

stuffing beneath the doors rags around the window sashes and all the windows down i must put out the pilot light and turn the burners on how strange to hear them hiss and see no flame a horrible odor i thought gas was odorless nasty smell but it wont be for long and it wont matter what it smells like vile stuff oh my poor head never had a headache and now i have to get one at the last minute i should be glad because i wont be able to think of anything not ever again how it hisses and smells

Knock, knock

delusions already it must be quicker than i thought but it has an awful odor oh my poor head i hope im not going to be sick why does it hiss so ill go mad if it doesnt stop

Knock, knock, knock

death at the door knocking already or is my spirit knocking i wonder the traveller at the door in the listeners it cant be long now i wish id known gas made you so dizzy and nauseous i hope they wont feel too bad how it hisses and hisses i hop*e* i dont

Knock, knock, knock, knock. "Milkman! Anybody home? Milkman! How much milk today?"

both windows open burners turned off rags under the table there maybe he wont notice

"Just a minute, please."

now i guess the rooms clear awful taste that cant be the gas hissing i just turned it off my head must be buzzing oh my poor head like the toothache years ago

"Two quarts of milk and a pint of cream."

Do not use except under the direction of a physician. Maximum dose, two capsules. Deadly in overdose. Antidote: mustard and warm water, or salt and warm water, or tickle throat to induce retching immediately. Call physician. Keep patient moving at any cost.

Drew read the instructions carefully before slipping the bottle into his pocket. But where to go? Mary was now at home. It was a sad, drizzly day, no day to find a lonely spot in the woods, and the wind swished mournfully through trees and rain dripped from sodden leaves. In his pocket there was not enough money left even to take a hotel room. At most, he could order a sandwich or sundae at some grille. Ah, that was it, Hangout, to whose inner room no one ever came at this time of day. By evening, even earlier, the damage would be done....

When the sandwich and coffee were brought, "Do you mind if I sit here the rest of the afternoon? I have some studying to do," Drew asked, his rare, friendly smile breaking forth.

"Not at all, there won't be anyone else in here till five probably. You can have the place to yourself. Do you wish anything more?"

"No, thank you." The waitress departed, returned with a check, left again.

Drew waited until he was sure that she was not coming back. A hopeless, joyless gloom quieted him with the peace of decision and ultimate despair. The sandwich lay untasted. He did not remember what kind he had ordered. His coffee cooled untouched.

Carefully he emptied the bottle into his hand, and swallowed the ten pellets at a gulp, washing them down with water.

For a long time, nothing happened. The coffee became entirely cold. His sandwich began to dry out. The top slice of bread curled up and he saw that jelly and roast beef comprised its filling. A radio blared raucous jazz in the main room. His hand, clutching the empty bottle, lay listlessly across the table. It seemed too great an effort to put the bottle in his pocket. Would suffering attend? Probably not. Drugs that were intended as sedatives for pain would be certain to offer a soothing sleep, for ever. And no physical hurt could compare with the torture of spirit, the inferno within, black flames and sun of blood.... His head nodded.... He ought to hide the phial or do something with it but it was such an effort to move.... He had not felt so drowsily content in years....

"Hello, Drew, I didn't expect to find you here at this time of day. Mind if I sit with you for a malted?"

It must be Sven but he could not raise his nodding head to make sure. Anyway, it didn't matter. He was awfully sleepy and content.

"What's the matter? Aren't you feeling well?"

i ought to say im all right but its too much bother why did he have to come i wish hed go away so i can sleep

"Been drinking?"

of course not you silly ass not in the afternoon is it afternoon no matter go way i want to be alone oh so you want the bottle thats your game well i want it myself "Give it to me. Give it to me, I say!" if i wasnt so sleepy id take it away from you take it away take it take oh well if you want it as bad as all that take it i dont care sleepy sleep

"Drew! Come with me! We're going for a walk!"

"Go way. Don't walk to walk....Tired...."

"You're going to get the hell out of here right now and you're going with me. Come on, damn you, even if I have to haul you."

"No. Wanta sleep. Tired....Go way....Leave me alone.... Won't walk.... If I wasn't so tired I'd show you....... Do — wanna — go........ Oh, well, 'stoo much....trouble....to argue... .....Don' wanna go.......Go way........Sleepy........ Sleep........ Only wanna.... sleep........"

"Keep moving, you damned idiot!"

"Dowanna...... . Sleepy....... . Where are we?...."

"Down town!"

"Wha time's it?...."

"Nine o'clock. Keep going. Come on, get up and keep going, I said. You heard me!"

"Sure....But what's...use...of...living......Leave me alone... . No use going...on......"

"Shut up. We're going on, get me? Keep moving or I'll break that damn' head of yours."

"Don't...care......Leave me alone...... Wanna sleep.... sleep...... sleep......"

"Keep moving!"

"Keep going!"

"Goddammit, the next time you try to fall I'll rub your stupid face on the walk. Come on."

"Keep moving. Keep moving. Keep moving."

XLV WHATSOEVER A MAN THINKETH

she is late she is always late i must not let her know will she
guess i must not let her know that i saw i should not have
called her but i could not help it will she say anything about it
of course not no woman would and it would only cause trouble
if she did i do not want to see her i do not want the date but i
could not help it i wonder if she will be as she was when i saw
her last she was so sweet and cruel she is always sweet and
cruel i wonder who he was i never saw him before and she
hasnt said anything to me about anyone she goes out with but
i must not say anything i must not let her know that i know
three times and out why did sven have to come along then i
must be meant to keep on living though i dont know why
theres nothing to live for it only hurts and hurts and hurts you
i dont want to see her i cant i do i do twelve forty ten minutes
late is she coming maybe she forgot she is always forgetting
maybe she knows if she does she wouldnt come she must she
must now that ive gone to this trouble they must think it funny
that i keep on standing here why dont they look at someone
else do they suspect do they know no they couldnt they must
be waiting for somebody they know wouldnt it be crazy if they
were all waiting for her maybe they are waiting for her waiting
to see what happens when she comes wouldnt they be startled
if i pulled out a gun and shot her and shot myself as if it were
the most natural thing in the world to do everybody would

scream and faint and start running and they would never know why i did it nobody would know not even lee they would say i was crazy and they would all feel sorry for the poor girl killed by a jealous man or a mad man without any reason that they could see i wont even if i had a gun i wouldnt i wouldnt give you the satisfaction of not knowing even if i had a gun i wouldnt three times and out i must be meant to live i wonder why i dont believe in god i dont believe in anything i dont count much in the scheme of things so why dont they let me go my way id rather be dead than this i dont want to live and yet i have to go on strange that i should want to see her again after that i wont see her again just this once and it will be all over and she can sleep with him the rest of her life for all i care he mustnt she mustnt i hope he has leprosy i wish theyd go away instead of standing around watching they just hope that ill do something but i wont ill fool them well just meet and walk away as if nothing had happened that is if she comes if she doesnt ill find her and shell wish she had come no i wont i mustnt think like that she will come shes always late she says she forgets i wonder if thats all i mean to her is that her it looks like her walk my shes in a hurry i wonder why damn somebody else imitating her walk where can she be twelve fifty and she said shed be here at twelve thirty maybe i ought to walk over to the p o and see if shes left a note in my box saying she cant come or something but she might come while i was gone and go away thinking i got tired of waiting maybe she wants it to happen ill fool her ill stay right here until she comes even if i have to wait all day then she cant say she came and i wasnt here to meet her because i was here all the time i wonder why she said yes so quickly when i called just as if she was anxious to see me and i know he must mean lots more to her than i do why should she want to see me if she likes him so much maybe he didnt ask her to lunch i bet thats it she only said yes shed love to because he didnt ask her and i did im better than nothing at all so she said yes that must be it well its the last time shell ever see me shell wonder and wonder why i dont call again and shell never know i dont care its her own fault still if i hadnt been so dreamy id never have gone out that night and id never have known so id still be just as happy as i was i should have stayed home that night but i went it was such a perfect night and i kept thinking what a pleasant surprise it would be for her to see me when she wasnt expecting it and the gardenia to symbolize her and how much i thought of her and instead i wonder how many times she has seen him it wouldnt surprise me if its happened before only i didnt know about it that couldnt have been the first because he was so easy and sure and she didnt seem to mind she seemed to expect it i mustnt let her know that i saw i mustnt let her know that anything has happened does she know she couldn't have seen she was too occupied with him and he couldnt either because his back was to me he was awfully good and expert as if hed had lots of experience i wonder how much he has had probably a good deal who is he and how long has she known him i might try to find out but it would probably make her suspicious if i began asking questions anyway it doesnt matter now because im not going to see her again after today shes never said anything to me about him but that doesnt mean anything i suppose because she knows how much i love her so she thinks she can do anything and ill still love her but i wasnt supposed to know or see i dont i dont i couldnt even like her after that i only want to see her this once just to prove how casual i can be ill talk about art and writing and things and after lunch i wont say anything about seeing her again but just dash off suddenly because i have a class at one thirty one oclock if she doesnt come pretty soon there wont be time for lunch ill go and show her im independent and wont hang around waiting for ever for her still she might come just as i went off ill wait a few minutes more ill wait till one five im glad those people have gone i dont want anyone around when i see her yes i do too i dont care at all how many of her sorority sisters or my friends or anyone else are around im just seeing her

because i have a date and i never break dates thats all because
she isnt really worth waiting for ive just idealized her ive
romanticized her and pretended she was something she isnt
shes just like all women you expect something fine and noble
and then youre disappointed because they turn out to be animals she only exists in my mind like i see her now all lovely
and radiant and unearthly like the women in poe and faithful as
penelope but its only a dream ive built up around her because
she isnt actually like that and now the spells broken so im simply going to forget and not have anything more to do with her
ill get over it after a while and i wont remember the bad parts
only the good and shell always be with me in mind as id like
her to be its better that way because then it wont hurt and hurt
so inside and truth wont ever interfere to spoil the dream sven
says you should look at life and build up your dream from that
but i dont think he does or even believes it himself because if
you started out youd never get as far as a dream or at least not
the pure dream that i want like platos and brownes why doesnt
she come she isnt usually as late as this she might have had an
accident on the way or got hit by an automobile shes so near-
sighted and cant see where shes going without her glasses
maybe i ought to call her home or the shop just to make sure
she left it would be terrible if she really was hurt i dont think
id ever get over it still it would serve her right after what shes
done only id never have known if i hadn't gone out that night
she may be late because she had to work though and she
wouldnt have any way of letting me know so it wouldnt be her
fault really that she was late or couldnt come and she may be
hurrying now to keep the date that would be nice of her even
if she didnt succeed she can be so damned nice when she
wants to be just like the other night when she was so nice to
him i hope they enjoyed it because shell never enjoy it with me
again i dont intend to see her at all and shell be all by herself
except for him and shell wonder why i dont call and shell never
know but it will be her own fault unless there are others good

god i wonder how many of them there are and if shes accepted them all i wont think of it damn this active imagination of mine the moment i think of a thing i can see it as clearly as if it had already happened and it probably has for that matter what can be keeping her one ten i may as well go i suppose ill just have time to grab a sandwich and run to class i cant wait for ever and anyway it will serve her right for not being on time when she said she would i wish she had come for this last date because i certainly wont call her again or see her or have anything to do with her i almost wish shed still come but i guess she wont and it serves her right maybe hell wait for you but i wont these steps are awfully wide i wonder why they made them so wide its a good thing ive got such long legs or id be as bad off as other people and couldnt take them one at a time lets see ive only got about fifteen minutes left of the lunch hour ill have to go to a hamburger shop which doesnt take long id never get waited on in time at the grille or the canopy or hangout or tallowick and i do so hate the smell of onions and pickles and raw hamburgers but i guess its the only thing i can do now there wasnt much sense to making this last step twice as wide as the others i wonder why they did the architect must have been on a jag when he drew up the plans gee id better watch where im going or ill be bumping into somebody before i know it "Oh, hello, Lee, I was just going. I was afraid you weren't coming." *"Is it late? I'm terribly sorry, Drew, I had some work at the shop and couldn't get away sooner but I hurried and now I'm all out of breath because I ran all the way from the trolley."* "Oh, that's all right, I just got here myself and was afraid I'd missed you. Where would you like to go?"...why did i say that i shouldnt be making excuses when its she whos late *"It doesn't matter much. I finished my work and I'm in no hurry because I have all the rest of the day to myself. Or are you? Do you have a one-thirty?"* "Not at all, there's plenty of time. Let's go to the Tallowick for a change. I don't feel like Hangout today." i do have a class and i said i didnt what on earth made me say i didnt but i cant back out of it now i must be cold i wont weaken i wont weaken *"That would be pleasant. How have you been?"* "Quite well, thanks. Working hard and studying and running around." is she suspicious does she think that i saw and know maybe shes trying to sound me out to find out if i know anything *"Naughty boy, don't you know you shouldn't play around nights?"* "Oh, yes, but it's spring and I get tired of studying. But tell me about yourself." *"Ah ha, trying to shift the subject to conceal your escapades? Drew, Drew, I'm sure you have been up to something or even found, shall we say, a soulmate? No, I haven't been doing much. When did I see you last? Tuesday? And it's now Friday. Well, Tuesday night I did some fashions for the Print Shop and Wednesday I stayed in watching the children and put them to bed while the family was out and last night I went to see a movie with Jennifer. Just the usual dull routine, waiting until I saw you again."* i am glad she said that even if she doesnt mean it that was sweet of her no i must not weaken i do not love her now i do not even like her or want her but oh she looks lovely and her eyes so innocent stayed in and watched the children and put him to bed "Is that all you've been doing? It sounds sort of dull." *"Oh, I've managed to live but it was not nearly as exciting as it would have been if you had called. I kept wishing you would."* a lie a lie but i will not tell her i will not "I've had a lot on my mind lately and — " *"Oh! Before I forget, what do you think? Jennifer said she was having a party next Saturday and she asked me to come and she wants me to bring you. Won't it be loads of fun? Sven will be there, of course, and Jerry and Karl and Dora and lots of other people. You'll come, won't you?"* who are they i guess ive heard her mention some of them before "I should say so. It sounds interesting and I'd love to take you. What time do you want me to call?" that isnt what I meant to say but i cant back out now i dont want to go i dont want to see her ever again not after that but the sun shines red in her hair so lovely and the green eyes of her and the curve of her cheeks and those luscious lips and all the appeal of her *"Oh, come about eight."* "That means eight-thirty."…*"You shouldn't have told me, now of course I won't be ready till nine."* "Is that all you think of me? Well, in that case — " *"Don't be silly, darling, you know it's only because I take such extra special pains to look my best when you're coming that I'm slow."* dont touch me dont dont ah i can't help it im weak when she only touches me and i meant to be so firm and not see her again and i cant do it but i wont give in and ill never forget or forgive never never never and i wont make love to her not ever again and i dont care what she thinks "But you always look your best, Lee. It's one of the nicest things about you that you look as if you had just stepped from a style show no matter what time of day I run into you."

XLVI AFTERMATH

He was an old man, and he sat on the walk as though too weary to stand. He leaned against the stone coping behind him. A cap lay in his knees. His right hand tiredly clutched a bunch of pencils.

He was an old man, and the beard that streamed from his chin had not been combed in days. Tobacco stains yellowed it, though the brows over his discouraged eyes were white.

He was an old man, and he did not ask for alms. His appearance was sufficiently vocal. He might have been dumb. Muteness would explain the despair in eyes that were as thinly blue as skim milk. He might have been blind, for his eyes peered at the pencils with an unseeing look. His cheeks were hollows.

He was an old man, and he paid no attention to passing crowds. They ignored him. A relic of time, he sat in expectation of nothing except slow death, and the slower bounty of human beings, for the prolonging of life, with poverty to accompany him, and bread alone to feed him regrets.

He was an old man, and Drew dropped a quarter in his cap. He hurried on, knowing that the derelict gazed blankly as before at his pencils, unaware of contempt, pity, kindness, or indifference, while he dreamed of the years that the locust hath eaten.

XLVII BEACH VIEW

"Oh, damn!"

"What's the matter, Lee?"

"I've ruined the picture, that's all. Some insect hurt me and when I jerked, a dab of magenta streaked the orchid and peach. Well, that's that."

"Don't worry. You'll do another and a better one, though you had a splendid start on this."

"That's the trouble, something always happens, whether I'm painting a picture or writing a sonnet."

"You ought to be thankful that you have so many talents. I envy you."

"I scatter my time over 'em so I'll probably never get anywhere with even one, but you concentrate on writing and you'll succeed."

"I'm not so sure."

"Of course you will. You always manage to get what you want. I never knew a man with such persistence and power to center his attention. I don't have it. Instead, I play at several things and won't master one."

"I think you have already, only you won't admit it. The real difficulty is that it's so hard for you to get started, not that you haven't the talent because you do."

"It's sweet of you to say so."

"I mean it, Lee. Aside from the great physical appeal that your beauty makes to me, and the charm of your personality, I love you because you represent what I regard as the highest type of woman. You are brilliant in conversation, your mind works like a flash, you think for yourself, and you're always filled with ideas. But even above these, you are rarely gifted. You write excellent lyrics, and the sonnet you sent me rivals some of Edna Saint Vee's. Few women or men either of your age have the promise you hold in graphic art. I may exaggerate a little, because I love you, but even so, you know yourself that your instructors have raved about your work, and put your watercolors and woodcuts and line drawings on exhibition. You dance, I mean abstract, esthetic, or rather kinesthetic dancing, with spontaneous originality. You could make a name for yourself if you wanted to, with your supple figure, and the facile, significant mastery of gesture which seems to come naturally to you. You sing passing well. With study and training, you could at least become a high-salaried singer of blues, not that that's a high goal. I wouldn't be surprised if you could act, I'm going to center my next play around you. But any one of these would be a rare gift to most people, and it's sheer genius that you possess them all."

"That's what Mr. Ekstrom told me when I had him for Elizabethan Lyrists."

"He was right. Take everything together, and you're the type of woman whom poets dream of and artists idealize."

"Don't put me on a pedestal, Drew. I'm human. I don't want to be held up like a statue in a museum."

"Be that as it may, you are treasure for any man, I'll never cease marveling why no one found you before I did — if I did."

"Yes, you were the first to apprciate me. But I'm not surprised. Most men want to patronize the girl. They don't want her to be clever or intellectual or brilliant, or better than they. They want her to look up to them, but I'm not made that way. I've always been myself, I won't play up to them, so I suppose it's no wonder that those I met before you simply couldn't stand me."

"Why do you put up with me?"

"Because I like you, sort of. About as much as from here to the diving board, that's a good middle distance, isn't it? Too, you do apprciate me, and that helps. You're an enfant terrible, like myself. You don't give a darn what people think, and you do about as you please. You talk well. You're original, and I've not yet been bored a minute when we've been together, not even that time I met you for breakfast and we talked and did things and went places until three in the morning, a whole unbroken fifteen hours and I wasn't bored even a second nor were you. You look romantic, and you have an interesting outlook on life which is rather uncommon nowadays. Too, you do exert the most extraordinary sexual attraction — "

"Ugly word."

"All right, amorous fascination, to be candid. When you come down to it, I wouldn't be surprised if that's what's held me to you as long as this."

"I don't like the sound of that. Are you losing interest?"

"Well, no, but one's interests expand."

"Have yours, recently?"

"Ask me no questions, darling!"

"Then I'm sure they have."

"Think so if you like, I'm not responsible."

"Don't I know it!"

"That isn't the way I meant it."

"To be sure, but it was a good moment to be literal. My, you look seductive, desirable, and beautiful in that bathing-suit, or what there is of it."

"I wish there were less!"

"What a remark! Let's wander up the beach. People might come around even in this remote part, and it is a gorgeous day, and I'd love to kiss you where no one can see. July, oh July!"

"Sir, are your intentions honorable?"

"Of course not! I intend to satisfy your desire about the bathing-suit!"

"Oh, not here!"

"Right! That's why I suggested walking up the beach. Do you see that patch of woods? Well, they go on for quite a ways, and they're very secluded, and nobody ever enters them. I assure you, my purposes are of the most satisfactorily sinister nature!"

"In that case, let's start."

XLVIII ANTS

Good wine was scarce in these days of prohibition, but good wine was companion to living well. When Drew obtained the recipe for sake, he promptly proceeded to experiment. You took three pounds of rice, six pounds of raisins, nine pounds of sugar, three cakes of compressed yeast, six lemons sliced, and six oranges sliced. You mixed the ingredients all together in four gallons of warm water. You put that combination in a covered stone crock and let it ferment. You stirred it once a day. At the end of ten days, you strained it through cheese cloth and pressed the juice out of the solids. You added the juice to the fluid already obtained and threw away the mash. You also added four pounds of sugar dissolved in a couple of quarts of warm water. You let the mixture settle for eleven days more. Then you bottled it and began drinking it at the end of two weeks.

The bottling was a nuisance. You had to wash the bottles in boiling water until they were spotless. You must siphon the fluid off ever so carefully, to avoid stirring the sediment and lees. You could use filter paper, but hours and days were required, during which time much of the alcoholic content and bouquet would have disappeared unless you owned special filter apparatus.

Drew did not greatly mind the labor, except for the ants. There had been that summer a plague of red ants in Center City. They over-ran houses, were found everywhere food lay, crept into pantry, fruit-cellar, and coal-bin. They dug holes wherever dirt was plentiful outside, erected mounds between the pavement blocks on sidewalks, and tunneled the mortar out of old foundation stones inside.

Drew worked in the fruit-cellar. Ants crawled on floor and walls. They investigated the shelves where rumbles of jelly and jars of canned fruits and vegetables had been stored away. They crept around him as he bottled industriously. From time to time, he slapped or blew them out of his vicinity. Until the last few bottles, he managed quite well. It was really no fault of his that, in attempting to bend over and blow a battalion of the red pests out of his way, the bottle which he was filling tipped over. Since he had no mop handy, he completed his work rather than interrupt it to sop up the mess.

Dinner was called before he had quite finished. He hurried his operations. He barely had time to dash upstairs and wash his hands when the meal was served. As always, the expert hands of Mary made it seem like a banquet. She was one of those talented women, the product of an older day when initiative, resourcefulness, and courageous imagination were required, who could make the humblest viand taste luscious.

For tonight, there were only hash, soup from the bones of Sunday's chicken, mashed potatoes, left-over carrots, last week's cookies, and the staple trimmings. But the chicken-bone soup was a triumph, flavored with celery, salt, cayenne, and a few sprigs of parsley. To the hash had been added a little sage, and some bread-crumbs, and it had been baked an appetizing brown, so that the sage and the hash mutually emphasized each other to advantage. The potatoes were royally crowned with the superior gravies of that same defunct fowl. The carrots had been alchemically treated with a cream sauce. Last week's cookies, crisped in the oven, tasted as though they had freshly come from gifted hands.

For dessert, there was an epitome of left-overs. The pineapple fragments from Sunday, the green pepper from Saturday, a raw carrot that had escaped Sunday's feast, and a table onion that had languished for days, were chopped and imbedded in lemon jello, served with lettuce, and deluged with mayonnaise. There was a crisp, delicate flavor, almost a tang, to the dessert that made it seem an inspiration, a hitherto unknown luxury. And then the fragrant coffee.

Drew enjoyed the meal so completely that it was not till an hour later when he remembered the mess he had left in the fruit-cellar. He hunted up a mop and descended to the basement. He was forced to fumble a moment before he found the cord that turned on the fruit-cellar light.

Almost paralyzed with astonishment, he stared at the scene which sprang into view.

Thousands and thousands of ants covered the floor. A red mass of them was drinking the spilled sake. They raced around in wild and eccentric circles. They sprawled upon their tiny stomachs with collapsing legs. They staggered away in erratic lines. Here and there lay one completely at peace with the world. New ants continually arrived to join the spree. Their predecessors lurched off in whatever happy dreams of intoxication the ant-kingdom is subject to.

If ants had voices, Drew thought he surely would have heard a symphony of bliss.

XLIX THE HILL OF DREAMS

The autumn of his senior year, Drew read the second of those two books that so profoundly gripped his imagination, influenced the cast of his thoughts, and even to some extent altered the course of his life. Jennifer had often referred to the book, Lee had repeatedly urged him to read it. He withdrew it finally from the library but it lay unopened in his room during a feverish two weeks which were incessantly occupied with classes, studies, and Helione. He would arrive home at three or four in the morning, sleep till eight, and snatch a hasty breakfast before the long ride to State University. He would return in mid-afternoon to study until dinner time. Then he would start out on the tedious journey to Lee's home and accompany her to a movie or party. Afterwards, they would sit in a cafe and talk of plans, people, art, life, books, everything, until midnight, when he would escort her home. There would be a few priceless minutes with her, or a voluptuous hour of lazing and love, in which the whole fire of his being and the warmth of her blended to radiant splendor, ineffable as the breath of gods. But the strain of study and continuous activity, the burning of nervous energy combined with too little sleep, his many worries and insufficient nourishment snatched at irregular hours, undermined his health. Always tired, haggard almost to emaciation, living on little more than the strange, apparently inexhaustible store of mystical power within him, he yet grew irritable and his reactions more puzzling than ever to his friends. His relations with Helione he jealously guarded as a rare secret. Others might guess, but they would not know.

He began to flare up at trifles. He walked so enwrapped in his thoughts that he was accused of snubbing friends and acquaintances. He could not answer the simplest questions in class, but made brilliant responses on vague or abstruse points. Often he sat in moody silence, his mind far away. He was annoyed because he was ignored, but did not realize that his own abstraction and the respect of his friends for his apparent desire to be alone were responsible for their neglect. The secret preying upon him, the vision of that night indelibly etched, he vainly strove to forget or to suppress from his thoughts. As a result, it manifested itself in devious ways — bitterness, irritability, day-dreaming, and subtly caustic remarks when he was with Lee. He could not prevent them. He would desperately determine on the way over to be polite, kindly, considerate. And within a few minutes after he arrived, the resentment he felt, the devil within, goaded him to comments that did not always fall short of insult. He could no more help it than he could help loving her. He could no more sever his relations with her and turn elsewhere than he could stop his having been born. The inner fire was running wild. All the loneliness, despair, terror, frustration, hunger, and longing of past years burst their bonds at last. The floodgates of his being were opened. The emotional depths of his nature swept away the restraints of reason and the suppressions of intellect. The pure flame blazed high by day and higher by night. The invisible sun never set. But Lee, knowing little of all those long, lost years, and seeing him only as a fretful lover who became increasingly difficult to get along with, came to the conclusion that he was losing interest in her and adopting this indirect method of causing a break. Her pride rebelled, but the power of his personality, his deep passion, the love that verged on frenzy and that seemed almost a monomania, bound her to him. She could not really love, for all her love was devoted to herself and to the stylization of herself. Every gesture, thought, and outward aspect was precisioned to conform with her egocentric pattern. But she craved being loved, as proof of her success and support for her purpose. She liked to bask in the warm sun of the boundless appreciation of Drew. No man she had yet known possessed so many enthusiasms, such infinite capacities to sympathize, so varied a character, and such strange, conflicting, paradoxical facets of personality. They were all centered on her, the bad with the good. She minimized the bad because the good were day-long pleasures for reflection, and evening raptures in which she, through some mysterious and divine dissolution, melted only to be re-created in the white flame that he brought.

The increasing bitterness of his remarks, she resented. They were not to be endured. She accepted them for a time since they were of gradual development, but the crazed union of sarcasm and passion, of conversational antagonism and personal eroticism, became more than she could understand, or accept. He expressed on a Friday as he was leaving the belief that he would see her tomorrow. "Well, I'm afraid not, I have other plans," she answered. "Oh," he exclaimed, in a voice that sounded hurt, "I'm sorry you're going to be busy." She relented. "I'm not doing anything Sunday. Would you like to see me then?" "No, I've got to study," he replied curtly, jealousy and disappointment dominating him with a surge of perverseness. "That's too bad. However, it doesn't make much difference, as Jennifer said she might have some people over to tea then and I'm to hear from her tomorrow." "I hope you enjoy it." Yet he kissed her goodnight with a savage fury that left her weak, and strode out to catch his car as though he intended never again to see her. She could not understand his mood. The very anomalies of his make-up were a tie; his unpredictable responses were a bond, though he did not know it.

Thus he was not to see her Saturday, and the offer of Sunday he had refused. He had his choice of studying one day and of amusing himself the other. He decided to vary his usual custom and to enjoy the earlier occasion. He thought of seeing a movie, or calling up Sven, or listening to an operatic broadcast over the radio — the second act of *Tristan* — of writing a play or finishing one of the various plays and essays which lay in different stages of incompletion. Then he remembered the book he had drawn. It was due Monday. He finally determined to read part of it during the afternoon, and to indulge in some other entertainment for the evening.

About three o'clock, he settled himself in a great, over-stuffed chair and opened the volume. He had not previously met the author's name, but the title was attractive enough except for the faint implication that the novel might be sentimental. It was to some extent that implication which had kept him from opening the book sooner.

There was a glow in the sky as if great furnace doors were opened.

With that opening sentence, a thrill tingled every nerve in his body. He never could say why, but he knew instantly that he had found a book that was to be like a Bible. As through a psychic sense, he identified himself with Lucian Taylor. As through a glass darkly, he saw his own dreams and hopes and despairs parade before him. The afternoon passed, and he came from a new star to the humble earth when dinner was called. He dined silently, and briefly, before returning to those elfin pages.

It was not merely that the novel paralleled his aspirations. The author was a master of style, an apostle of beauty. Each word was as carefully chosen as the bit of a mosaic. But this was a living mosaic, as subtle as music, as flexible as the fabric of life. The words possessed an evocative magic, like childhood dreams, or the luster of old jade. They burned with a glory all their own. They were like an instrument whose rhythmic repetition has the cumulative power of x raised to infinity. There is, in the ritual of some savage tribes, a certain drum-beat that gains by persistence an added intensity though the note and the beat and the interval are never varied. The incessant, steady, unchanging throb of the drum becomes a kind of hypnotic pulse. A flute, however, has the advantage of controlled mudulations. It may pipe, now loud, now soft, now shrill, now low, upon always the same note with the same regularity. It may shade gradually into minor, it may wail into a high, piercing scream, or subside to the sough of sodden leaves in rain. This book had a beat like the throbbing drum, but more like a flute. Strangely, it repeated a monotonous note that varied only in its intensity; a terrible note of pain allied with beauty; yet at the same time it sank to the dead frustration of the world and rose to the ecstasy of a supernatal heaven, and wandered across the foam of perilous seas. It was a terrifying work of splendor and torment, a narrative in which the suffering of the flesh combined with the torture of the spirit, and blended with that intolerable perfection which is so deeply agonizing because it can never be attained, and so deeply desired because it is beyond life. It was that immortal longing which both satisfies and assuages the spirit, tantalizes and appeases the flesh with its presentaton of the sadness of things as they are and its paradise of the dream that all men hunger after. What it told seemed like the resurrection of his experience to Drew, and implicative of universes beyond. Its style was an esthetic triumph enriching it with felicity. Somehow, and somewhere, it achieved the great mystery of life as well as the material of life. It found the extragalactic sun that has attended the course of humanity since Socrates walked through the streets of Athens, and Christ in the thoroughfares of Jerusalem, and Shakespeare in the byeways of London. If there be no soul in men, there was yet soul in this book. Life may be futile and beauty an idle dream, but in these pages was a life fulfilled and a dream begotten beside which the world that is and the days that are became components of a lesser unreality.

Sensuous, mysterious, enchanting, the pages of this record unfolded to his eyes. He shivered as in the spell of nightmare, or a surpassing vision of loveliness. He dreamed great dreams, pity and aversion came to him. He trembled on the brinks of precipices and ascended with wings of the infinite. He loved and hated, feared and desired, longed for and rejected, through the crucible of this chronicle. It was like an open fire, in which all emotions are fused and molten, until the slag is drawn away and only the vaporised purity of quintessential being remains.

There was a passage about the charm of medieval manu-scripts, those exquisite old works illuminated with raised uncials and gold-leafed decorations. There was a long and sym-bolic legend of the woman and the rose. There was an elfin description of dark woods and a hill that reminded Drew of the forests of his childhood fears. There was a persistent presence of suffering, so acutely allied with the unhappiness of his own brief years that they seemed again to unfold before him, as though, detached, he witnessed the succession anew of wasted yesteryears. Pain and desire and the love of all things lovely, fear and despair and loneliness, unassuaged longing and the pursuit of the ideal which must ever be frustrated in life, a feel-ing for the deep enigma that lies even in the thorn-bushes of the hedge and the earth-grains of the hill, hunger and the crav-ing for a pure white sanctity beyond life, for a flame above the moon and a sorcery under the sun — these were the keynotes of that story, and of Lucian Taylor, even as they were the keynotes of Drew's life. When he read past the pages of that wild, last chapter, in which, as on the open-stops of an organ made of the winds and the waves, the full horror and the full beauty and the full tragedy of Lucian Taylor's aspirations were unloosed and yet consummated in a kind of dreadful tone-poem until only the shrill, frantic piping of the flute finally reigns supreme, and the shrill scream of the wind is answered by the melancholy roar of riven forest-wood, Drew ceased altogether to read. He felt, he lived, he endured the crucible of those final pages as a personal experience, until there came the stoic peace that follows the cleansing purification afforded by tragedy.

The profound influence of that volume remained with him. He bought a copy printed on blue rag linen paper, appropriate background for its atmosphere. Often he read it over. Often there came passages from it to mind. It entered as an integral part into the web of his thinking, and in the presence of a fourteenth century missal, or the dark and lonely woods of autumn, or the woman he lived, or apart with his strange and secret meditations, its phrases helped to mould his responses and to interpret his experiences.

L LOST GENERATION

"Yours is the lost generation, not mine," Sven remarked one evening after they had gone to a lecture by Miss Millay and returned to his home for coffee. "Rupert Brooke wrote some of the best of the war poems, though personally I like his other work more, and Edna Saint Vee has written some of the finest of the modern lyrics. In a way, he represents war which naturally hit men the hardest, and she represents women, whose lives were less directly cut off or violently changed. I suppose you could say he was timely, and she was timeless, though that's an unsatisfactory distinction and won't hold water. I'll admit that so far as I'm concerned, my attitude is warped by the year I served in France. But I'm a good ten years older than you, and I've got a foundation that your generation hasn't. Oh, I'm bitter at times, and I'll never forget horrors I've seen on the battlefield, but I still think that yours is the lost generation."

"That's a puzzling attitude," questioned Drew. "I don't quite follow you, I should think yours would be the generation hardest hit."

"No, mine, people who were born from eighteen-eighty to around nineteen-hundred, were the ones who experienced the world war most directly. We'd been brought up in a pretty civilized world. We had pretty definite standards of ethics, politics, education, and so on. The war was a terrible shock. It destroyed something in us, but just the same, we had traces of what we learned in our adolescence, and that's what counts most in forming character. The years from fifteen to twenty or twenty-five are the most important. Anyway, we were brought up in a fairly stable society. But what about your generation, the people who were born from nineteen-hundred to nineteen-ten or so? The war was a bad dream of your childhood. You began to reach adolescence or maturity about the time it was over, and then what? When your outlook should have been being formed, there wasn't anything to form it by. First you had post-war radicalism and confusion. Then you saw the fastest revolution of morals America has ever seen. They're still changing and God knows what the end will be. Old social principles died over night. New ones rose and died too. Then came the boom and inflation. Our whole structure of civilization, social, economic, and political, is going mad. A sort of cynical disillusion about the value of life, the worth of marriage, the honor of officials in public life, a general skepticism is prevalent. The wealthy are in a fair way to exceeding the decadence of later Rome. Luxury, extravagance, and waste are widespread. The poor multiply while you wonder at the paradox of enormous wealth and extreme poverty side by side. The result is that your generation had its adolescence in an unstable world. There was nothing to tie to. Monthly and yearly came vast changes which are still proceeding. No one knows what will come next, a panic maybe, or else the decay of civilization through a surfeit of luxury. What you found was instability, change, corruption, nothing you could depend on. That's why I say yours is the lost generation. If you have any philosophy, it must be that of mutability."

"I'm not so convinced, Sven. It seems to me we doubt more, we're ready to try anything once, but otherwise we're about the same as any generation."

"Generalities are poor arguments, I'll admit, but look at the Lotus Eaters Club, for instance, the place I took you to the other day. State U is a hotbed of cults, clubs, revolts, and fads of all sorts. It's probably a good thing because at least more students are thinking, but the point I had in mind is that they haven't much to develop an integrated outlook with and my generation had. Sure, I know I'm saying just the opposite of what most people believe, but I'm right. My generation was lost in the sense that it was killed, suffered a violent shock to its beliefs, but we had a solid foundation. Your class, Drew, is reaching its adolescence during a time of transition, when nothing is certain or constant. I don't speak of you, because you're an outstanding exception, but the general run aren't adjusted and never will be. They missed the war, but they got the after effects, the break-down. The direction of their life is being set in this period of collapse and flux, a time of chaos. Post-war prosperity, depression, speculation again, the disintegration of the social order, unrest and skepticism, no religion, the sanctity of marriage gone, crime universal, homosexualism increasing like mad, decay from the top down and the bottom up, that's what your generation is accustomed to, and the real results aren't beginning to show until now. Maybe in nineteen-forty or fifty, there will be some kind of stability on its way, I can't say, but it will be a harder, more futile, and lop-sided outlook than mine."

"Who are the Lotus Eaters?"

"Oh, they're a loose group of all the rebels here, barbs, intellectuals, outcasts, free-thinkers, homos, free-lovers, esthetes, and what have you. I don't pretend that they're typical of the student body, but they're the best cross-section of students who think for themselves and do things, and that's the only sort that's worth considering since they're the ones who'll be doing the world's brainwork and creation in a few years. Look at those I introduced you to, there's a Georgette, the French jewess, with a mind like a razor and no faith in anything except psychology that she's hipped on, sexual relations with every man she can get, and Marcel Proust whom she knows by heart in the original. Al will probably teach, but he questions even the value of education. Ruth doesn't know what it's all about and doesn't care. Sam Esper hasn't a dime and yet has seduced half a dozen girls I know. What difference does it make? is the only reply you can wangle out of him. Cal can't see anything but Joyce, Lawrence, and Gertrude Stein. Even Lee, you don't know from one minute to the next what she thinks. And Tad. He's been expelled several times but he keeps coming back with some new idea or what not. Len is as crazy as they come with that being hyper-civilized, a damn good sculptor, and a degenerate. He once told me the only thing he regretted was a nine-year-old girl he ruined in Italy. If they're examples of the intelligent post-war generation, two types predominate. Some, like Cal and Tad and Len, jump to extremes. They pick up a current fad or a sensation and make it the whole of their lives. Others, like Lee and Georgette and Thorn, simply drift. They dabble in everything, and the more they look around, the less they find to be sure of. When you've kicked religion out the back door, seen the social system go bust, watched the economic structure act like a drunken acrobat, found that politicians are crooks ruled by criminals and an insatiable lust for the public monies, discovered that the big industries bleed you and exploit you for what they can get, and now it's coming out that the warlords bloated us with deliberate lies, propaganda, and fake atrocities to make us mad so that we entered the insane mass murder overseas, is it any wonder that your generation is cynical? You've lost the old belief in a future life with its rewards and punishments. The theories and findings of science haven't offered a good cosmic philosophy yet. What's left? You've developed a peculiar sort of organized and carefully integrated philosophy, more or less mystical, that works for yourself, but that's an exception, what do the others possess? Nothing, except to get what they can in this world by any means. It isn't eat, drink, and be merry for tomorrow we die, it's gorge, pillage, and rape, for tomorrow we rot."

"In the long run, Sven, it will be good. People will cease to act like cattle. They're already thinking more, by your own admission."

"Yeah, for how long? They may be thinking more, but they're also ceasing to act at all. Why? Disillusion, doubt, disbelief. And because birth control is steadily decreasing the number of children that intelligent and racially valuable parents bear, but the oafs, the yokels, and the undesirables including idiots and criminals breed just as much as they always did. The days of great leaders are passing. The democratic ideal is winning, the mass level is coming to rule. And when that happens, the whole mass level itself will probably start to fall."

"You're too pessimistic."

"Only because I have such a high ideal of what humanity could achieve, like Dean Swift. At any rate, we're living in one of the most exciting periods of history even if we have passed out heyday, though I may be wrong. Read Spengler's Decline of the Land of Twilight or Twilight of the Western World, I forget which, if it's ever translated into English. Better still, read it in the German when you can.

"By the way, have you heard from Jene?"

"Not lately, why?"

"Well, keep Saturday night open, she's having a party and you'll probably get the invitation in a day or two, you must come. Now let's make some more coffee and forget the world for awhile. How's your play coming along?"

LI GREAT AMERICAN NOVEL

Terry sat toying with the keys of the piano. A huge man with a childlike face who did not seem to care whether anyone paid attention to him or not, so long as he could pound out jazz rhythms or popular songs. Oblivious of others, glad to be left alone, he rambled through *Abdul the Bul-Bul Amir* and *The Devil Is Afraid of Music.*

Jennifer darted about, parrying with one person, asking what another would like before explaining in a burst of laughter that she did not have it anyway. Golden-brown as a south sea maid she looked tonight, and the rich coloring of her complexion was rivalled by the richness of her voice. She was the spirit of Christopher Robin in the body of Alice grown up.

Lee had deserted Drew as soon as they arrived, and he followed her with wistful eyes as she circulated. Now she talked of many things with Bob and Dora Fash. They were a couple of friends of hers, so she had said. Bob had black, oily hair and a weak mouth whose corners went down. Like Lee's, they also curved inward. His wife was taller than he, a big brunette with big, brown eyes, a sensuous mouth, and a Slavic cast to her features. But the complexion was excellent and her figure, if heavy, attractively proportioned. She had a catty voice.

Lee drifted on from them to a fat little man who was looking over Terry's shoulder. Pudge O'Tief, so he had been introduced to Drew. He was round like a ball, plump like a toad, and he had thick jowls. His eyes shifted restlessly. His lips were thin and cruel. He gave an impression of energy and drive, but Drew did not like his eyes that shifted, or the lines of his mouth. Jene had said he was studying piano. Drew glanced at his squat fingers and became doubtful about what he could accomplish. The grubby one fulfilled his skepticism by taking a seat beside Terry and doing the rhythmic background for Ravel's *Bolero,* while Terry swung into the melod. Drew was secretly pleased. The squidgy one played accurately, and without distinction. His part was faithfully done, and uninspired.

Lee must have thought so too. She passed on to Thorn Rebble, a man who looked faintly like James Joyce. He wore a sandy moustache and was of slight build. His hair was combed back from a high forehead. Glasses protected his eyes. He had an odd, infectious laugh that tinkled frequently. It was a dry laugh, yet genuine, appreciative, with reservations. When Lee approached him, he was talking to a platinum blonde of doll-like appearance. Helen Engel possessed marvellous hair and a marvellous voice. Her hair was paler than ripe wheat, paler than the lower part of corn-tassels, and it seemed unique with its kind of colorless color, silky and soft. It hung low, a mass bobbed below the nape of her neck. Her voice was music, the whisper of a woodwind. It caressed one's ears. She had high, small breasts, and genuinely naive eyes. She could have been Peter Pan wishing to be Anna Pavlowa.

"I'm sorry," said Drew. "My attention strayed to the rest of the party. What were you saying?"

The girl looked at him with obvious disappointment. She owned a slightly crooked nose that came straight from her forehead like the classical Greek, but her lips were oriental in their fullness, and long lashes intensified the green of her eyes. Her legs were slender as a faun's, but she stood as tall as Lee, and she possessed beautiful breasts. Her teeth were magnificent, of extraordinary whiteness, evenness, and harmony. Her fingers were tapering and exquisitely set off her hands. The pearls that hung from her ears drew attention to their delicacy. Her hair could hardly be classified. It seemed golden like her skin but had overtones of yellow and undertones of chestnut. It combined the qualities of light and medium blonde. Altogether, with the oblique slant of her eyes, she looked as if the East and the West had met at last.

"I asked what you said."

"Oh. Yes. I was so stunned by your appearance that I looked at the rest of the party to recover my senses As a result, I probably have forfeited your good will for ever and ever, amen."

The smile that was turned upon him gave immediate forgiveness. And invitation. What was her name? Ah yes, Diana Harmon.

"Oh, I don't do much. Write when I feel like it, which isn't often. I'm puttering around with a play now. Tell me about yourself."

"I do a little of everything, big boy. At present I'm giving fashions the good old s.a."

"Essay? Do you write too?"

"Step it up, you're a couple of numbers behind! I meant s.a., sex appeal, must I go into detail?"

"Oh. You ought to be a success at it with your figure."

"Not so fast! I know my own limitations. But I like the work and there are plenty of parties that are nobody's business."

"I dare say."

"Dear me, what's going on here, an incipient romance?" Jennifer interrupted gaily. "Come and have some nibbles."

"May I bring you a plate, Miss Harmon?"

"The name is Diana — to you. Plate? And how! The boy friend seems to have washed out. Go strong on the nuts, if there are any."

"I'm sure there's symbolism of some sort in that request!"

"Oh yeah? Well, don't miss the train while I'm waiting."

Drew walked to the table where the buffet dinner was spread. Absnt-mindedly, he prepared a plate for the undecided blonde. He was still struggling with the peculiarities of her lingo as he turned from the table.

"Oh, Drew, how thoughtful of you! And so many nuts! How did I know I just adore salted almonds?"

He wakened from his reverie. Lee was sauntering off with the plate, the blonde was regarding him with disgust and her with spite, and Sven was studying the expression of his face with amused but sympathetic eyes. Feeling foolish, Drew prepared another plate for Diana.

A few minutes later, Sven dropped into a chair beside him where he sat on the floor near Diana. Drew interrupted the pleasant manoeuvre of surrounding a battalion of stuffed olives long enough to ask, "How's your novel coming along? Or haven't you begun it yet?"

"Weeks ago. I've got it pretty well laid out."

"Are you actually writing a novel?" interrupted Thorn, and added with a quick laugh, "You would pick out a field that is untouched except for several hundred thousand others."

"Well, now, how's your own novel coming along?"

The laugh was on Thorn. His novel had become a standing joke. Ever since he entered State U, and all these years since he had graduated and taught, he referred to the novel he was going to write. It had, for hundreds of reasons, all duly explained by Thorn, never been commenced. He carried in his pocket a piece of paper, tattered and worn, which he exhibited to the skeptical. At its head was typed, "THE OLD AND THE NEW. A Novel by Thorn Rebble." Probably when he died, there would be found among his effects the Great American Novel in the shape of a single page bearing the legend, "THE OLD AND THE NEW. A Novel by Thorn Rebble."

While they conversed, Terry continued his tireless manipulation of piano keys. Sometimes he ad libbed, sometimes he pounded out the rhythms of *St. Louis Blues, Chloe, Old Man*

River, St. James Infirmary, and again he improvised. A silent man, he communicated by notes rather than words. They were his medium, his speech, his life. Against the subdued background of his playing, the circle gathered around Sven, carried on the discussion begun by Drew's question, and faced the poet turned novelist, who sat forward on the edge of his chair, smoking innumerable cigarettes, his hair rumpled from a gesture he often employed when thoughtful. He would absently run his gnarled fingers through his hair. At his feet sat Drew cross-legged, and Helione, under-priestess of the arts, like disciples listening to the master. Jennifer curled up in an overstuffed armchair beside Sven. From time to time, other guests joined the circle or were replaced by still others, but the central group remained.

"What's the plot of your novel?" asked Thorn.

Sven — Himmel, I couldn't explain that without practically telling you the whole story in detail.

Thorn — Why?

Sven — Because it really hasn't a plot, or at least, no more than there is in life itself. From another standpoint, you could say that it has several plots or plot-themes, but they develop and end spontaneously just as the little dramas of everyday life arise, sometimes by chance and sometimes by plan.

Drew — But don't you need a central theme? Something to unify the novel? Otherwise, I don't see that it would get anywhere.

Sven — Yes, but plot is not the only answer. There is a kind of abstract or ideal unity in life even though it is composed of a multitude of details and little things.

Lee — There would be no unity, though, if it weren't for the perceiving mind. You experience things and you create a sort of unity for the sake of clarifying or understanding experience.

Sven — You shouldn't worry such a pretty head with such abstract thoughts.

Lee — But I'm right, aren't I?

Sven — Of course. That's exactly what I'm doing in the novel.

Thorn — Aren't you making the mistake of starting with an idea and trying to illustrate or prove it with the novel?

Sven — I don't think so. The idea and the novel developed together. I've been thinking about it for several years. As a matter of fact, I've begun it half a dozen times, but I always stopped because the usual ways of writing a novel were inadequate for my material. The result is that the material shaped the form, while the material and the purpose were mutually derivative.

Drew — I'm all at sea. Can't you be more specific?

Lee — Yes, tell us the plan or whatever it is of your novel. This pretty head is more than worried with the present abstractions.

Sven — You expect me to believe that? I know you better, Lee. Sure, I'm willing to talk about it if you think you won't be bored.

Chorus — No. Go ahead. I want to hear. Tell us about it. Quit stalling. What is your subject? Come on, we're listening.

Sven — Well, now, I guess I ought to go into the lecture business or something. Anyway, you brought this on yourselves. Let me see, where shall I begin? I suppose I might as well start by reminding you of some obvious truths. In life, for instance, there is rarely a full development of any given situation that corresponds to the plot in a novel. I mean, a development which brings in nothing extraneous and which ceases after the denouement. In life, all sorts of coincidences interfere with the dramatic occasion. Things happen that have no real bearing on it, and things continue to happen, or at any rate the flow of human experience, of life as a whole, even of the individual life, continues after the tragedy or denouement or climactic moment. Realness is greatly to be desired in art, of course, but mere realness will not do, that is what life itself offers. Thus you have the primary basis for art, that it must resemble life, but differ from it. The details and extraneous matter must be left out. A selective principle enters of necessity into the making of any work in any art. The principle may be ethical, religious, aesthetic, utilitarian, philosophic, or any of a dozen others. A corollary of this principle is that truth and imagination, or fact and fancy, or objective and subjective elements, also enter the composition. That is, you begin with reality, but your mind and thoughts play across the experience, take it apart, leave out some of it, and make additions to it. This play may be rational as in the writing of a philosophic novel; emotional as in the painting of a picture or the creation of a lyric; or rational-emotional as in the making of a symphony.

Thorn — Few works of art, if any, could be classed as purely emotional or purely rational. Isn't the combination always present?

Sven — I imagine so, at least I can't think of exceptions off-hand. However, I only meant that one or the other usually predominates. That's enough for generalizations, they're too easy to become lost in and they won't get us anywhere, but I did want to give you the broad background behind my novel. Before I go into it, let's take one look at a more specific kind of generalization. All experience is, of course, transmitted through the senses and absorbed, sifted, or comprehended by the mind, leaving aside the question of whether emotion or reason predominates, and also leaving out the question of sense deficiencies and physical defects. We'll assume that reason usually predominates, though some people are guided primarily by emotion or intuition. The point I am trying to make is that all of us, you, Thorn, and Drew, here, and Lee, and Jennifer, and myself, and the rest of you, each of us is almost wholly guided by his own special, individual, and particular experiences. I may assume that you think like me, but I know each of you has had particular experiences that I have not, and that I in turn have had some that you have missed. None of us can ever hope to understand fully the nature of another person, or why he does what he does. Each of us regards life from a special viewpoint colored and created and moulded by our past experiences. And by experience I don't mean simply happenings like falling in love or going to school or working in an office or being robbed. Books and dinner and sunset and old Greek statues are quite as valid and real experiences as birth, accident, or death. People who want to Live with a capital L give me a pain in the neck. I hold that you can live fully without ever having been subject to rape, murder, starvation, or oppression, to put it baldly. To get back to the subject —

Drew — Just what was the subject?

Sven — That will be enough from you, Mr. Gordon. If you don't take care, I'll put you in my novel.

Lee and Jennifer — Just what was the subject?

Sven — That sounded suspiciously as if you wanted me to carry out my threat. Anyway, the subject — yes, don't look so skeptical, Thorn, and that's a hell of a way to laugh, by the way — I did have a subject, which was my novel. I've given you a sort of background, now I'll show you how it works out in this specific case. I start with a situation, the most important in the protagonist's life, that is, my purpose begins there though the situation actually concludes the novel. No, I won't tell you what the situation is. We'll assume that the hero is Mr. X. The great crisis of his life is Y, a decision, we'll also assume, to drop out of sight and go to some remote place to live in oblivion the rest of his days. When X is making this decision, all the influences of his past experiences would be brought to bear. In the white heat of extremity, the extraneous parts of his life would be shorn away, but everything that contributed to his decision or that would be affected by it would stand out clearly in his mind, or at least they would form an undercurrent in his thoughts. These past experiences would come as flashes of memory, pictures of old occurrences, but they would probably be in a sort of confused flux. That is where I would depart from life, I would present the images in chronological succession, for the sake of the possible reader, and for the sake of artistic unity.

The flux and catastrophe conclude the novel. The novel would begin with the first and earliest of these experiences bearing on the crisis, but each scene or memory picture, for the sake of unity and art again as well as life, would be presented immediately, as it happened when it was in the process of happening, and with no hint of the catastrophe which I, as the artist, know already. An apparent irrelevance might be presumed by the reader during the early pictures and episodes, in that they might seem disconnected, but as he read on, he would begin to see the design above the threads. After a fashion, such a novel would be not unlike a symphony, with many themes introduced one at a time, the themes gradually attaining deeper significance by reintroduction, by their bearing on each other, and by their relation to the whole, all the themes being interwoven, unified, and consummated in the climactic chord. The result would be —

Thorn — A series of high-spots only, with none of the balance of either art or life.

Sven — No, I don't think so. Both important occasions, and trivial instances, would be necessary, for one remembers both, and both influence our major decisions. Thus one might have heard Debussy's Afternoon of a Faun on some occasion when he was experiencing a profound grief. Ever after, in another sorrow, he would recall the music, and conversely, hearing the music would remind him of his past grief. Thus a little thing might have a great influence on the protagonist. No, Thorn, the trivial and the great both have their place. You would have had a better case if you had raised the objection that such a novel would tend to give equal values to both the large and the small, but then that is a commonplace of life itself. And you must not forget that there would be a weight of implication in each episode. It would bear not only the value and significance it possessed to the protagonist at the time it occurred and while it was occurring, it would also be prophetic of the importance it is to have later in memory, and still later in its final relation to the climax.

Thorn — In other words, you are merely writing an autobiography.

Lee — Oh, I don't think that's what he meant.

Drew — Neither do I, but tell us yourself, Sven.

Sven — You two are right. Other people's lives are more interesting to me than my own because I know my own experience and undersand it, but I do not know theirs. Egobiographical the novel might be, but not, or at most only partly, autobiographical. If you reduced it to sources, I suppose it would be about one-third personal experience, about one-third experience which I have heard about or which various persons have told me of, and about one-third imagination, again for the sake of achieving artistic unity as well as fidelity to life, and for the sake of trying to understand how another person acts and why, by creating hypothetical experience. Furthermore, it would make use of everything that I assume enters into the experience of the highest type of man — poetry, prose, and the drama, love and hate and pain, disappointment and aspiration, dreams and hopes, literature and art, persons, places, objects; but it would make selective use of them, to illustrate life and to illuminate it without reproducing it in every detail. It would be projected against an implied basic assumption, a vision of all humanity, a dream of the great potentialities which exist in man at his best.

Thorn — Another great American novel.

Sven — You wear sarcasm well, don't you? The answer to your comment is no. I would not limit myself to one class, one type, one country. I do not want to represent a section or a period. I do not wish to be the voice of an age, or the spokesman of my time. My purpose is far larger. I want to present as well as I can a story of the civilized man; not the average man, for God knows I have only disgust for the average and only detestation for anything lower. By civilized man, I mean the top rank of humanity, the man of culture, education, and ability who carries within him an ideal to be achieved and a vision of how to achieve it; but a man who also bears within him the seeds of evil, traces of the mire from which he rose, and the capacities for his own undoing; a man influenced by mortality; a man whose vision is so clear that the reality of things must ever seem cruel and ever ready to drag him down, as he always is dragged down because in life he can not ever hope to experience or to realize his ideal. No, the novel might just as well center around an Englishman, a German, a Russian, a Chinese, or a citizen of any country or any race, except for the chance that I was born an American and that therefore, I suppose, my outlook may differ from theirs; but I can not help feeling that there is some sort of universality or similarity of experience and nature common to every man. I have little sympathy for any artist who limits himself to one phase, and that among the lowest or most ephemeral or least important, of existence, without a larger vision. Hardy had the larger vision even though his materials derived from a particular section of England. From that standpoint, the artist could use any phase of experience, if he has the whole vision necessary and gives to that phase no more than its proper place and no more than its comparative value. If he does not, he is neither an artist nor anything except a crooked mirror. To carry out the simile, you might say that the lowest degree of art is to distort or misrepresent life, like a crooked mirror. The second level is to reflect life, like a true mirror,. The third level is to focalize life, as in a lens. And the highest level of all — well, there is no equivalent in the simile, but it would be like a lens which was also a filter and allowed only the purest and most enduring values to come through.

Pudge — I don't suppose your novel would fall in the fourth class?

Sven — I wish it would, but the third type is nearer my plan.

Pudge — Ever hear of Pollyanna?

Sven — If you're referring to my remarks about the purest values, you've either mistaken my meaning or your education has been neglected. There is no pure value unless its opposite exists. There are no great men unless they have been to the depths and known the ultimate of evil and yet gone onward, or upward, if you prefer.

Lee — Gee, it sounds exciting. I'd like to see it when it's done. It certainly ought to be interesting with your poetic approach. I hope it's as good as it promises to be.

Sven — It doesn't matter much to me whether it is or not. The purpose is high. My enthusiasm exists only while creating. Afterwards, I'll become interested in some new project.

Lee — Maybe I'll try to do a novel too. I'd like to work in such a fluid medium for a change from kinesthetic and graphic arts. Do you think it will be published?

Sven — No.

Drew — That was a surprising answer. Why not?

Lee — Aren't you going to submit it?

Jene — Dear me, why this confident pessimism?

Sven — Well, now, I can't give you the whole explanation, but it's briefly this. I have no morals to preach. I want to focalize the important elements of existence preceding a crisis, with whatever veridity experience or life such as I know it affords. Naturally, such a novel would be long even when compressed as much as possible. I do not want to omit anything which is prominent among the components of reality. But among those come the many aspects of sexual experience, or biological experience, if you prefer. After all, food, representing self-preservation, is the primary essential of life. Sex, representing race-preservation, is the secondary essential. The rational mind, representing the interpretation, appreciation, and evaluation of life, is the third essential. They would be the basic categories from which all values arise in the case of any given individual. But it will not be within my lifetime that the censors would allow the parts of the novel creating of sexual experience to be published. Which means that the novel will probably appear in incomplete form if it is ever printed at all.

Lee — Gee, Drew, I'm glad you're not writing the novel.

Drew — Ssh. What a remark to make, darling.

Sven — I seem to detect small side voices, what? Supposing you —

Thorn — Won't you be cheapening yourself or your work if you let it be published not as you wish it?

Sven — I don't think so. As I said, I have no ethical or other purpose, no special axe to grind. My interest will cease when the work is done. I will satisfy my urge to write an artistic unit, and I will complete so far as I am able to what I intended to accomplish. Then my interest will either become passive, or die out entirely. I have never looked at any of my poems after they were printed. Usually, I begin planning something new, so I suppose the same thing will happen when the novel is done. Therefore, I won't care much what the fate of the novel is.

Lee — I like that. You remind me of a phrase I've read, cacoethes scribendi. As if the writing were a kind of madness, an ecstasy in itself, and after you've passed through, instead of looking back you go on until you have another attack of cacoethes scribendi.

Sven — I suppose so, though it sounds deadly.

Lee — Will you let me do some illustrations for your novel?

Jene — I'd like to too, she said awkwardly.

Sven — Well, now, Mrs. Egerson, we'll see about that.

Chorus — Mrs. Egerson!

Jene — We saved it as a surprise for the last. Sven and I were married this afternoon. Won't you wish us luck, and now I'll go get the wedding cake so we can cut it and all have a piece to celebrate, she said merrily as she hastened away from it all!

LII HELIONE WITHIN

there that damn drawings done and i hope he likes it but if he
doesnt he can get some one else to make his poster even if i do
lose the publicity which i dont need so im not going to spend
any more time on it i always did hate to draw children the little
brats i loathe em i suppose mister alden will object to the jew-
ish noses ive put on em but he can object all he wants to and
he probably will to that cute expression ive put in their eyes
hell think they look like illegitimate children wicked offspring
of wicked parents and they are wicked children thats the trouble with em mister alden will say i dont think these will quite
do miss forrest and ill have to admit i dont too hell say i should
have made em more innocent and ill have to do em over but i
wont well ill not fuss any more with em tonight maybe theyll
get by though i certainly did the job in a hurry let me see its
only ten thirty if i could work so fast all the time it wouldnt be
so bad ten thirty drawing board goes there ink in the drawer
tacks in the tack box i must remember to buy more thumb
tacks pencils and crayon in the box that rubber eraser isnt
much good it always leaves such a mess im afraid ill have to
clean up my room again tomorrow ten thirty i wish drew would
call though i feel tired but it would be pleasant to dance for
awhile and forget all this commercial stuff at the fire room in
the lafayette id like that but he wont call because its ten thirty
and too late for him i wonder why he never calls after nine

when he knows i never get to bed before one and hes often told
me he doesnt too oh well he doesnt care much about dancing
though hes awfully good and fits like a glove thats a nice
wicked description i must remember it but just the same its
true and he does if only he would phone or suddenly walk in
and even just talk or make love to me again no a good girl
wouldnt think that but i dont care he does make love so well i
wonder why it is he isnt what youd call handsome he doesnt
care to dance he doesnt seem to enjoy the frivolous things i
like to do but theres something attractive about him like the
strange way he kisses me so intense like a boy and a man and
a fire all at once he hurts and yet id rather see him than anyone
else or almost anyone else ten forty five he wont call because
he never does this late i suppose i could go to bed but i dont
feel sleepy and besides bill might phone or maybe some other
man i know no he said he would be working late all this week
and he isnt as pleasant as drew i dont really like him much
especially that awful moustache of his i wish hed get rid of it or
be like drew so soft and so fierce i wish he would come but he
wont because he never does this late wish i had someone to
talk to after working so hard and he would be the most interesting as he usually is if he werent so mean to me at times id
like him lots more i wonder why hes so mean or if its just that
he hasnt got over hating women yet he seems to resent me but
hes always calling for dates and wanting to see me again and
most of the time i will but id be more willing if he wasnt so bitter except for the letters and theyre so sweet and lyrical and
passionate that theyd be ruinous if i ever wanted to do him dirt
goodness what put that thought into my head its queer that he
should be so bitter when hes only nineteen enough to make
me think something must have happened to him when he was
young still that cant be he would have told me im sure but
maybe not what could it be not a love affair because if hed had
one hed never kiss me the way he does and hes often said he
never kissed any girl before me i shouldnt have told him about

the men whove kissed me except that i wanted to tease him and whod have thought hed be so hurt its his own fault for being so sensitive since it certainly isnt mine that im attractive and men want me he has no more right than anyone else eleven no he wont call tonight nobody will now its too late i could read vanity fair but i dont feel in the mood for it and im not sleepy oh i remember i forgot to take supper because i was too busy drawing why doesnt drew phone and ask me to the grille for a sandwich or a salad and coffee but he wont its too late i guess ill have to help myself and i know there wont be a thing in the icebox there never is but ill go and look the kids have probably eaten up everything in sight like they always do when i have a place of my own there wont be any kids around not even if i get married never never never i wont have any children not even one i wonder what drews would be like that might be fun no i wont even think of it goodness they would be queer children if they had his build and intensity and strangeness and my beauty and genius i dont care im not egotistic mister ekstrom said i was the only genius he had ever had in his classes and drew says im his inspiration and if it werent for the scar i would be a famous beauty ill bet i wont ever say anything about it to drew if he thinks its all right it is its pleasant to hear him say im beautiful more pleasant than bill i do wish drew were here now hes such a silly boy at times but he is so passionate ive never known anyone quite like him if only he would Ouch! wheres that switch it ought to be right inside the door instead of clear across the kitchen i suppose it serves me right for bumping into something while trying to find my way in the dark but how can i help it with the switch way over here oh my last pair of hose and such a nasty run i wont be able to afford new ones till they pay me next week there that stops the run though it looks pretty bad i dont know if i can darn it so it wont show and even if i do i wont feel as nice in em because ill know theyre darned well it cant be helped ill just forget about it those damn kids are always leaving their junk around for me to trip over i wonder why i trip so much even when theres nothing in the way of course they would eat up all the apples the little pigs there isnt a one left not even a teeny weeny piece of one ah some left over pie i wonder how they happened to miss it ill have that and some tea wish i were at drews now his mother makes such lovely things that lobster salad and those date bars the other night were simply divine and she always has so many good cakes and cookies and candies on hand our house isnt ever like theirs but i suppose mother doesnt have time what with the kids around and so many other things to do but then i dont often seem to be here for dinner and theres never anything left over there isnt much now but ill pretend im not very hungry and i wont be hmmm there isnt lots of tea left but ill buy some tomorrow and try oolong or jasmine for a change im getting sort of tired of orange pekoe and green tea now what was the name of that tea drew mentioned oom ool oos oopon i cant remember it but ill ask him again the next time i see him he would find some outlandish tea that no one ever heard of before strange where he gets his exotic tastes when his parents arent a bit like that gee id hate to be married to such a man thered be no pleasing him with his finicky tastes and i think id become awfully tired of oo whatever it is and anchovies and caviar and kumquats and pomegranates and tortillas and halvah and bacclava and chinese duck and all the other queer things he likes but still it would be an interesting life and awfully wearing i dont see how id ever get my work done or he would either after hed made love to me all night long so id be just all worn out the next day like i always am after i see him or maybe he wouldnt be so intense after we were married and had slept together awhile but i wouldnt like that and i wouldnt like him then too maybe thats how he keeps his hold on me because i dont love him not really i couldnt i couldnt love a man whose tongue is so sharp and he has such a wild temper anyway theyre supposed to love me and all i need to do is take it goodness i dont see how a bundle of oppo-

sites ever got thrown together like drew too bad he isnt better
looking at that hes no so bad and he certainly looks interesting
a bit like stevenson with a sort of hamlet effect people always
stare when we go any place i suppose its because hes so thin
and tall and excited and wears a black hat but its mostly me
though because they turn around to look when im just by
myself its nice to be with him though hes so tall that hes just
right for me or maybe hes a little too tall just a little just about
as much as whats left of this pie from there to there i dont suppose it would do much good to look again because theres nothing else in the icebox a piece of pie and two cups of tea arent
so very much but theyll have to do until tomorrow breakfast
guess i wont bother washing just a cup and saucer and pan still
i might as well rinse em it only takes a minute dear me what a
mess this kitchen is i dont believe i will after all goodness
knows how i could have stood it for all of fifteen minutes when
it hurts not really but mentally if everything doesnt look just
right ill turn the light off and pretend i wasnt here and forget it
must go carefully so i wont trip again let me see what can i do
now i dont feel the least bit sleepy yet i could play the golliwog
cake walk or the hungarian rhasody or le cathedrale engloutie
no i wont either now that the familys all gone to bed and theyd
object so i cant play the victrola its so nice and quiet guess ill
dance dancing without music is so much purer an art but still
kreutzbarg and georgi were marvellous and even drew said he
thought it was the finest recital he had seen but wigman was
better whether he agrees or not id like to dance like her without music or anything except just the pure form and pure
rhythm and pure line her hands were so graceful like the
stalks of fluid lilies in the face of night but her expresson was
part of it too i remember i bet i could have been as good an
interpreter of kinesthetic art as drawing or writing or singing
if i concentrated but i dont suppose i ever will because i want
everything but drew concentrates on only writing and hell be
better at it than i will at anything i suppose i dont care mister

ekstrom said i was a genius and its just too darn much effort or id do more i suppose i ought to take my slippers off so i wont make any noise gee its warm guess ill take em all off while im about it ill have to hang the frock up but that wont take a minute i must remember to send my dresses to the cleaners tomorrow or i wont have anything to wear ouch this door creaks badly when i think of it sometime ill remember to find the sewing machine oil and fix it so we wont wake the family some night when i ask drew in my word i forgot to do my laundering and im sure these are the last scanties ive got and my stepins are all soiled oh bother ill look when i come back if i dont dance now that i feel in the mood for it ill simply waste an hour fussing around here wouldnt drew be surprised if he were to walk in now and see me coming out with nothing on for that matter i guess the family would be pretty shocked too if they knew i was dancing naked in the living room i dont care i do have such a good figure and whats the use of having it if you dont show it off for everybody to admire theres nothing wrong with mine and its so refreshing to float like this to inaudible music just the pattern and the abstract supple line just the flexing of fingers the cupping of palms and weaving and swaying like a lily in the wind just the rhythm and the pale pistachio kiss of wind as i pass clothes are such a nuisance i think all dancers ought to appear nude so that costumes and clothing and colors wouldnt interfere with the fluid lines of their bodies and the unsexed purity of kinesthetic pattern gee what a good phrase i must think to use it the next time anybody talks to me about dancing i bet theres a wicked come hither look on my face now wish someone were here to see it and tell me where did i learn this tricky effect of approach and retreat oh i know from those two boys who were giving lessons in dalcroze eurhythmics here last fall they were funny no drew doesnt like that expression ill change it to they were odd even for inverts they danced like women unfolding and opening and retreating instead of having the drive and thrust of male dancers how shocked dora was when i told her that but its true too bad they were fairies they might have been awfully interesting if they werent and they were so handsome but their dancing was good even if it did have the receptive quality of women instead of the phallic drive of men ill remind drew of that when i see him tomorrow hell be so startled to hear frank phrases like that come from such a beautiful naive face as he calls mine that it will be loads of fun to tease him oh gee im beginning to feel tired and warm guess ill take a shower and freshen me up its all of since this morning that i last had a tub but it makes me feel so clean people ought to be forced to take at least two baths a day thats one of the nicest things about drew that he takes such pains about personal cleanliness just like me but then so does bill or at least he does most of the time if only he or no drew had seen me dance then it would have been so much more fun with an appreciative audience and especially drew because hes so enthusiastic only i know id never have done any dancing if he were present and i was all undressed like this hed have wanted only one kiss and id have told him he could have only one and then id have melted and instead of dancing wed have just lazed and loved until he had to leave but that would have been so much more satisfying or at least exciting than dancing even now where did i put my bathing cap im sure i left it here on the towel rods to dry i know i did this morning but it isnt here now it would be typical of alice to borrow it herself and then throw it somewhere where i cant find it as if it belonged to her damn when i make enough money im going to rent a room or studio of my own where there wont be sisters and brothers and kids always taking my things and leaving them where i never can find em though i never touch anything of theirs its the penalty of being the oldest girl i suppose youve got to sort of see that all the others have everything they want and let em take anything of yours if they ask but they help themselves without asking oh so thats where it was i dont care im going to speak to mother

about alice borrowing my things and throwing it or at least letting it fall behind the radiator where it gets all dirty that isnt
fair now ill have to rinse the dirt off it just like the time when
she took my lorigan and cerise lipstick with the luscious fruity
taste a week ago and i had to ask for em before she gave em
back ouch the waters hot why dont they invent a shower thats
just the way you like instead of always being too hot or too cold
and changing when youre in the midst of it no matter how carefully you adjust the faucets what a clean fresh pleasure there is
about a shower it pinks your back and runs down your breasts
and stomach and legs and leaves you feeling new and cool like
crisp lettuce leaves it feels as if it were making love to you
caressing you with soft impersonal fingers that are gone before
you know it and ambiguous as though they couldnt decide
whether to stay or run off but go because its their nature to
like drew except that he isnt ambiguous and stays and caresses you over and over until you cant bear it any longer but
havent the strength to resist i guess thats enough for tonight i
feel so much better already theres something delightful about
a towel after a shower its a rough male kiss as brooke said of
the blankets and it leaves you glowing all over and your skin
actually blushes like an american beauty rose come to life how
nice i look in the mirror all bare and lovely and soft and warm
like a woman but firm like a man thats a cinnamon thought but
its true and im sure its why drew and i get along so well together hes a man but he has lots of feminine traits and im a girl but
i should have been a man because im so determined and
strong and individual so i suppose we click because we sort of
fit on everything the cap looks out of place though you either
ought to be all naked or else all dressed to be appropriate wearing merely a cap or shoes and stockings or a bracelet and necklace looks obscene i wonder why oh well theres the cap back
on the rack but i just know that when i look for it tomorrow
alice or somebody will have borrowed it and ill need to hunt
again before i find it now where did i kick those mules not that

theyre much good but theyll serve until i can afford some new ones oh there you are gee i bet i look like a streetwalker coming down the stairs with this without a thing on except a pair of mules with big pom poms on em like the place dora was telling me about in paris where she went one night with that boy whatever his name was and they were let in and had to take all their clothes off and werent even allowed to go if they wanted to but once inside had to undress and walked through the dive looking at those naked men and women indulging all sorts of love and even homosexuals and lesbians and worse until they reached the other side where they paid to get their clothes back but anyway the women wore only shoes and stockings and sometimes a necklace and the men just sandals and socks and dora said it made them all look so much more depraved than if they hadnt been wearing anything at all i dont know whether id care to go through an experience like that unless drew were along but still it might be a terribly exciting thrill for once like the time al took me to the burlesque show and the stripper was so marvellous until shed got rid of everything but slippers and the audience was in such a frenzy i wonder if i look like that now just the same i know its a cute effect if i could see it i suppose i ought to put some pyjamas on just in case anyone comes maybe i will when i get back to my room that must be twelve thirty that just struck cant see without my glasses and im still not very sleepy i suppose i could read awhile but ive looked at the post and the new vanity fair and harpers havent come yet and ive read all my books dozens of times i might leaf through my clipping file again no i did that a few nights ago or i could mend my hose and the tear in my black lace formal but i guess ill let em go till some other time i could do some sketches cant do that either i worked so hard earlier this evening that i simply havent energy enough to get out my drawing board again and i dont feel much in the mood for writing and ive already danced i suppose theres no help for it if i do anything at all except just lie down and think it will

have to be reading darn that creak it squeaks when you open
it and it squeaks when you close it but ill oil it tomorrow oh
dear what a mess my books are in Letters to Women they were
good i like auslanders phrases if i hadnt read it so many times
id go over it now Tales of Mystery and Imagination that was a
lovely christmas present from drew but i dont feel much like
looking at those weird drawings of clarkes now Angels and
Earthly Creatures she writes the most curious poems like
mine so that you know a woman wrote em but they have a kind
of fragile strength thats more like a man writing Human
Anatomy i dont want even to look at a book on drawing
Modern French Short Stories i wonder if this is the book that
has that story in it about the man who went to a house of love
one night and paid for a private room where he did things with
a beautiful circassian and months later was taken by a friend of
his to a peep show and he recognized the room and all at once
felt sick when he realized that he and the circassian must have
been the subject or rather object of the peep show watched by
other people that night he made love to the girl because it was
in this same room but i dont recall the title and it would take
too long to skim through all these stories to find out if its this
book Robes of Thespis that has some good plates in it but they
arent nearly as lovely as the ones in the bakst book i took back
to the library last week The Memoirs of Fanny Hill i must
return this to bill ive kept it for weeks and i dont like it that
evening when he brought it over and read me parts of it until i
was so weak i just couldnt help giving in to him and i know he
did it on purpose the pictures alone are so exciting even if they
are an imitation of beardsley like this first one especially its not
so badly done but its a plagiarism in style at least though i cant
imagine beardsley ever drawing a man like that showing his
phallus entering the womans delta where did i get that word oh
yes from drew when he was studying greek but then he says
he once saw some illustrations by beardsley for lysistrata that
were pretty erotic do we look like this when hes making love

to me i bet we look a lot better the man reminds me of bill more than drew because of the way hes going about it and the expression on his face he doesnt look as if he had any thought about the girl at all but wanted to satisfy only himself like bill and of course its so much better when drew comes because he waits till im all fire and melted and then he enters and its perfect and yet thats such an ugly thing men have i cant imagine anything less attractive or esthetic and most of them dont even know how to make it seem pleasant except drew and its surely natural instinct with him because i know hes never had experience before me but he naturally makes an art of love and leads you to want to help like that night when he waited so long waking me and he was so warm and smooth and firm and i kissed it when i wouldnt even think of doing that with bill or any other man but drew is so clean and fierce and tender at the same time that he sweeps me away before i know it and there are only the two of us united and nothing else matters no no no i mustnt think such thoughts i wont look at any more books and besides its getting late and i really ought to put my pyjamas on that reminds me i forgot to see if i have some clean lingerie for tomorrow id better make sure because i certainly dont want to have to wash things in the morning or now either if i can help it good theres still this lovely pale rose one piece dansette though the flowers look a bit faded why theyre almost green instead of blue i guess theyve been washed so often or else its the light they dont look quite as nice as they did when i got em but drew wont notice in a half light and if he does i know it will be because he isnt as much in love with me as he says he is and my word what luck id forgotten all about these salted almonds that drew brought over the other night and i stuck em away here so the kids wouldnt find em and now here they are when i can appreciate em most gee but theyre good so crisp and firm and nutty and just the right tang of salt so they arent too sweet drew does have the best taste i wish he were wealthy because he understands me so well and knows exactly what i like and better still what is characteristic of him too so he always brings a perfect gift and if he only had millions instead of hardly anything i know id marry him right away not for his money but just because hed know how to spend it better than anyone else and we could travel and own cars and yachts and go to plays and entertain and buy stunning clothes and have places of our own but he isnt wealthy and hasnt any interest in money and with his dreamy ideals about art as an end in itself i dont suppose he ever will have much but even if he did i dont think id marry him because im going to live my own life away from kids and family besides hes such a difficult person to get along with sometimes that hed wear me out if we were married but its pleasant as we are now it would be perfect if i were to marry some rich man who had to go off on business often so i could keep drew for a lover that would be exciting with one to give me all the luxuries i like and the other all the love any girl could want but i know it wont be and some day when we have a fight or something happens itll be better to break off i suppose while everything is perfect and hell idealize me and write about me and ill try somebody new which is better than getting married and settling down and growing old while love cools even if he does say it never will but of course he doesnt know for sure and it always does my those nuts were good and i ate em all just imagine a whole pound of slated almonds helione helione you will never keep your figure if you gobble nuts like such a greedy pig i dont care i was so hungry and they were delicious and now im thirsty some of drews lovely sake would be the thing to take my thirst away but there isnt any so i suppose i might as well have me a glass of water oh bother with it im beginning to feel sleepy and the light is so brilliant now why didnt i think of lighting the candles before guess i will now or one of them anyway were are my cigarettes and matches i thought i put em in my oh i remember theyre in with my cold-creams why is my skin so dry that i have to buy more rubinstein and elizabeth arden than any girl i know while i think of it ill just take care of my face now before i forget where did i put the skin food or has alice borrowed it too here you are but there isnt much left only enough for tonight it feels so soft and its so fragrant and tomorrow my skin will be as tender as ever and drew will love it just the same i bet i look a sight now but i wont even turn to the mirror to see whether its so still i do have such a luscious appearance what was it that drew said was so nice about my breasts theyre just the right fullness and tip a little toward the sides which he said was perfect and it is but i wonder how he knew come to think of it only a man with a lot of experience would know that still drew is instinctively a good amorist and he might guess without really having had the experience one melachrino and ill turn out the light no ill light the candle and smoke in the almost dark what a decadent shape the candles have they must have got soft during the warm weather until they bent over why they look just like a phallus or rather a pair of em dear me is it my imagination or are they really like that but ill light one how palely it burns but when the electricitys off oh how exquisite all curled over and the flame burning up from the tip and the room so dim and the cigarette smoke so fragrant and i so lovely waiting here alone and no drew beside me to make it perfect there must be a slight draught a very very slight draught or the candle wouldnt gutter unless its my blowing out smoke that makes it flicker so but i dont mind the shadows dance so vaguely like dancers in a fluid bas relief or moving frieze and the other candle curved and dead i suppose i should have lighted it too while i was about it standing like an ivory ghost and curled up like a phallus and shiny i wonder i wonder yes i think i will but wouldnt drew be shocked if he knew maybe ill tell him sometime at that how soft the sheets feel tonight like the embrace of a quiet lover and the candle oh

LIII SPRING DAY

"Are you going on a picnic, son?"

"Well, not exactly, Mother. Lee and I are taking a canoe-trip this afternoon and I'm putting up the eats."

"I didn't know you could canoe."

"I can't, but she's going to teach me. Don't worry about us, we can both swim, you know."

"Do be careful. I wouldn't want anything to happen to you."

Drew went ahead with his preparations and checked off the items: picnic-kit, thermos of coffee, sugar lumps, cream, boiled eggs, salt and pepper, bread, lettuce, tomatoes, butter, mayonnaise, mason jar of shrimp salad that his mother insisted on fixing, a couple of oranges, and a box of big, red strawberries.

A sense of excitement and expectation animated him. This would be great fun, and something new. It was a wonderful spring day, with nature in the full burst of awakening. The leaves were already green on poplar and oak and elm, the young shoots of tulips budded, and the early violets bloomed in pastures and forest mold. Orioles mated and baby robins had begun to appear. The morels were out in orchard and forest, puffballs and fairy-rings outcropped in fields. The June bugs were hatching, the black bats flying by night, but the plague of flies by day and the pestilence of gnats and mosquitoes at dusk had not yet arrived from the south.

Drew was a bit late and hurried, perspiring under a hot sun, to catch his trolley. He was to meet Lee at the transfer point at two o'clock. He arrived at two-fifteen. She was nowhere in sight. Wondering if he had missed her, worried about her absence, he fidgeted on the corner within reach of his kit. When the time limit on his transfer expired, he tore it to shreds absently. He peered at each girl who passed, and compared all the clocks he could see with his own watch. She was always late, he sighed, and kept on waiting. Two-forty-five came. The afternoon waned. He regretted every moment of this perfect day that was snatched from his plans. He wanted to be away from people, and noise, and the business activities of a mechanized civilization. The passing of trolleys, the grinding of brakes when autos halted on red, the chatter of dowdy human beings irritated him. He longed for the companionship of Lee, and the clean freshness of river and wood.

Three o'clock came. He had often waited an hour or longer for Lee, but today was to be so special a treat that he determined to hurry her. Stepping into the drug-store, he telephoned her home. There was no answer.

"Good! She must be on the way," he muttered.

Fifteen more minutes passed, and still she did not arrive. He finally decided to call her office and find when she had left.

"Oh, hello, I was wondering if you would call," came her voice to his surprised ears. "Gee, I'm sorry, Drew, but I have to work today and we won't be able to go canoeing after all."

LIV PAGAN HOLIDAY

"Won't this be fun? Dip your paddle in, haul it back, lift it out, and then bring it forward again, like this, see? And do it regularly. Follow my stroke if you can. Well, let's see, suppose you count six from beginning to end — there, that's it! After awhile, maybe I'll let you take the stern."

Drew, enjoying the novelty of canoeing, obeyed instructions as well as he could, and proved an apt pupil. Forgotten was the disappointment of a week ago. Out of mind were the careful preparations, the vain waiting, the bitterness of learning that Lee had to work. Another date was made — and now he put aside the past for the immediate pleasure of setting forth up Sun River.

The waters lazed by, sluggish, muddy with the sediment of rains. A tangle of cottonwood, vines, hemlock, poplar, maple, oak, miscellaneous underbrush and wild grasses lined the banks they passed. The season was yet early and they appeared to have the river all to themselves. A farmhouse drifted into view occasionally. They paddled around frequent bends and turns. Civilization faded behind. The water-tower perched high on the first cliffs passed from sight. The bridge became lost behind foliage and hills. The noise of cars died away, the chatter of men and women, the shouts of children, subsided. Between leafy aisles, with the dank smell of the river in their nostrils, the song of invisible larks in their ears, and the warmth of a northward-swinging sun dappling the banks in patterns of light and shadow, and ever a south wind gentle against their faces, they stroked along.

"Do you like it?" called Lee from the stern.

"I should say so! But I'd like it better if I saw you in front so I could watch you."

"I'll change if you wish."

"No, after all I've never canoed before. Maybe I'll try paddling you back by myself tonight while you take it easy and loaf."

"Well, I won't object!"

She was as gay and animated as he had ever seen her. Paradox of culture and paganism, of the hyper-civilized woman and the child of nature, sophisticate and naivette, her personality showed yet another new facet in these surroundings. Gone was the world of Cezanne, Kreutzbarg, Woolf, *Vanity Fair,* the neck line of a frock, Prokofieff, the Fire Room at the Lafayette, Advanced Fashion 94s, business, and studies. The esthetic blessings of art were forgotten in this primitive immediacy.

"Mind if I take my shirt off?" called Drew, perspiring from the warm sun and the exertion.

"Go right ahead. D'you mind if I put my blouse aside?"

"Yes."

"Good, I knew you wouldn't care! I'll slip it on again if anybody comes," Lee answered cheerily from behind. The adjustments were made while the canoe drifted slowly in the current.

"Ready?" asked Drew, looking around. "My word! What an immoral and seductive picture you make! You might just as well remove the brassiere too — it doesn't help much."

"You aren't supposed to look! No thanks, I guess I'll keep it. I've got to have some protection, don't I?"

"Protection? You're a liability. How can you expect me to keep my eyes ahead now?"

"You'd better, darling, or — else — we'll — drift — back," she emphasized each word with a dainty bite and click of her teeth.

The kiss of the sun was a golden blessing upon his shoulders and arms. The rhythm of motion and the exercise of paddling gave him the comfort of physical content. Under the warm benison of sunlight, he paused again to remove his under-shirt.

"Dear me, what's going on up there?" Lee chided.

Lean, yet with skin glowing in the soft light and cooled by the wind of their passing, he stroked happily forward. He was not so supple and lithe as Lee, but as much as he had ever been, he was at peace with the world, and content to bask in sensuous relaxation while enjoying the muscular pattern.

"When you feel tired, just say so and we'll stop. It's hard work, isn't it?"

"Sure, but it's perfect!" he replied without turning.

The canoe glided onward. Miles drifted behind them. They avoided snags, and sunken trees, and sand-bars. Through the drowsy afternoon, they headed upstream, until the last farmhouse had disappeared to their rear, and only green walls lined their course. A stillness lay over the world, though crickets chirped and meadowlarks warbled and humming-birds darted across wild roses. A muskrat splashed along shore. Frogs leaped as they swished past. Turtles plopped from stumps and logs at their approach. Leaves rustled in the stir of a breeze. Their paddles made a steady dip, and sometimes when they swung close to shore, they forced a way through alders and trailing aspens. Many sounds were abroad, yet the valley seemed quiet after the activity of town.

"I could relish an orange — I didn't have time for lunch," suggested Lee in a plaintive voice.

"Fine! How did you guess I brought some?"

"Oh, I knew you knew that I liked 'em, and felt you would think to bring 'em along."

"We'll head in wherever the next good landing-place appears."

Drew had been weary for some time but hesitated to interfere with her pleasure, or admit himself so easily fatigued.
Now, consoled, he watched for a break in the vegetation, and a
path up the steep banks. A few minutes later, they floated
toward a partly submerged log jutting off shore, where
grooves in the mud and the outlines of a path indicated that
previous campers had landed.

"I'm absolutely ravenous," he confessed as they carried pillows and supplies up the bank.

"So am I, darling. I began to wonder if you would ever
decide to halt."

For answer, he swept her to him and kissed the tempting
mouth. "Dear me!" she exclaimed in mock alarm, breaking
away. "Is there no safety for a hungry and helpless and practically undressed lady?"

"I'm afraid not!" he blithely answered.

It was fun building a fire. They searched along the shores
and in the forest stretching away from the banks for last year's
leaves and fallen branches and dead longs, all of which were
plentiful. Near their landing-place, they found stones remaining from the fires of previous campers. Already the sun was
westering when they made a tiny pile of leaves, covered it with
twigs, and stacked it with dry sticks. Gay, carefree, bandying
conversation, and poking with eager inquisitiveness into the
picnic things he had brought, they sprawled by the fire.

An hour later, filled with the content of remarkably appetizing foodstuffs, and somnolent in the hush of twilight, they
reclined side by side before the fire.

"Now we shall drink to Bacchus and Ceres and Pan," suggested Drew, "and as a testament to one of the most perfect
days I've ever had. Will you have Tokay or sake first?"

Lee preferred Tokay. He poured out the winking wine, and
they sipped appreciatively while the bed of coals glowed. A
great stillness hung across the valley. The sun was low on the
western horizon. In an hour, it would be dark, but as always at

twilight in the secluded outdoors, there came an eerie hush; after flowers have folded to rest until another day; when the wind is momentarily stilled; while the flaming colors of sunset vie with the growing blue and silver of night; after the thrushes and pipers have sung their evensong; and before the night insects begin to hum, or the black bats to circle.

"Cigarette?" asked Drew.

"Yes, thank you." When he had lighted it for her, she parted her lips and let the smoke drift out as from a censer. It was a curious gesture which she invariably employed when smoking, a trick that for all its simplicity looked wickedly decadent, perhaps because it was uncommon, more likely because of the seductive lips and the deliberately sensuous pleasure which she obtained from the act. She tilted her glass for another sip of the mellow Tokay.

"My, that wine is lovely," she drawled, a throaty timbre to her voice. "I suppose this is some that your mother made?"

"Right! I'm glad you like it."

"I do. It seems the appropriate thing, if not the only thing, to follow a picnic lunch like this outdoors. Your mother does make heavenly wines and salads and everything. Like that mushroom souffle when you had me over the other night."

"Did you like it? Well, you'll have mushrooms of all kinds and prepared in a million ways now that the season is on. That reminds me, the car that Dad bought was delivered a few days ago, I guess I told you that, anyway, he and Mother were going mushrooming tonight after he left the office. You must come over to Sunday dinner — they'll probably bring back pecks and sacks of mushrooms when they return this evening. Does it seem a little cool for you? Perhaps I had better throw some more sticks on."

"What a nice crackle they make. The wine and the fire certainly ought to keep us warm even if it does turn chilly later."

Drew looked dreamily across the darkening river.

"I don't know," he whispered in a low voice. "I think I would always be warm with you around."

"That's your romantic nature showing itself, silly. Of course it isn't so, even though it does sound flattering."

"It *is* so. You are like the fire, or the sun, to me. 'Su phileo, kai su erao, kai su ereso aei,' " he quoted.

"What does that mean?"

"It means — oh, I'll tell you some time."

"Tell me now!" she leaned toward him, and placed a palm upon his arm. In that tactile gesture, a current of the emotional excitement of love flowed into him. The flames danced up, and the trees trembled as from an eddy of wind, and an afterglow illuminated the river. Drew, deeply and mysteriously moved by that passive caress, gazed into her lovely face, and shadowed eyes, and noticed the rosier color of her cheeks, and the overtones of light, copper and henna and mahogany and wine and fire-red, that played across her hair.

"It means, I love you, I love you deeply, and I shall always love you." A faint smile soothed her features, and she swayed to him for a caress whose gentleness could not disguise its profound significance. Adoration of the beloved, appreciation of her beauty, physical and spiritual communion, surrender of self, the psychical desire to protect her, they were all symbolized in the complex subtlety of his kiss.

"Enough, sweet tempter!" she chided and broke away. "Either I must put more clothes on, or else — !"

"Take 'em off!" he finished with a smiling sigh, characteristic of the confusion which her sudden reversals of mood momentarily occasioned in him. "I sometimes wonder whether you are serious or only playing."

"Playing, of course! I'm going for a swim. Won't you join me?"

"We haven't any bathing suits."

"Don't need any."

"It's getting dark."

"That's a grand time to splash around."

"And swimming after dining and drinking isn't supposed to be healthy."

"That was a long, long time ago. Besides, I'm careful, and I've done it before."

"The river is treacherous. Dirty, too. And I don't swim very well."

"Take the canoe if you like and follow me. It's exciting to feel the water slip around you, so cool and refreshing, after you have sipped such warm wine, and lazed by a fire. Come on!"

"No, I think it would be safer if I watched," he said, after a few moments' hesitation. "I'm really a poor swimmer. I couldn't help if anything happened to you. I'll take the canoe and stand by in case of accident. Must you go in?"

"Why not?" She set her empty glass by the kit, and swiftly stripped.

Drew walked with her to the canoe. He shoved off till they were clear of the muddy shore. Then he let the canoe drift. He watched her with admiring eyes, a turmoil of love and desire and esthetic appreciation as she stood, a naked nymph, poised for an instant, in the prow. Then she was gone, flashing into the waters, and striking out with easy, lithe strokes. A ruddy tint made a swath from the setting sun. She crossed to the opposite bank in that lane of crimson and dark; she waved at him gaily, turned, and swam luxuriously back. Her face laughed up at him from the side. "Gee, that was fun! I'm all sobered up now and just a trifle cool."

"Want to climb in?"

"No — paddle toward shore and I'll come overboard then."

Near the landing-place, she entered like Aphrodite rising from the waves, a glistening wet glow emphasizing her beauty of body.

"We haven't any towels," he reminded her, "much as I dislike mentioning the obvious."

"That's all right. I'll dry out by the fire."

"You can use my blanket to wrap around you. And I think you'd better have another drink to help keep you warm. We'll open the bottle of sake."

"That's a noble idea, darling. One of your best!"

She huddled by the fire while he heaped sticks and boughs upon it until it blazed up fiercely. She sipped amber delight from the glass which he handed her. Together they stared at the blaze, absorbing its visible flames, enjoying the wine, and experiencing the invisible warmth from within.

"Lovely one," Drew murmured, "come closer that I may adore you as you deserve to be loved."

The flushed face enticed him from across the fire. "You'll get your clothes wet!"

"That is easily remedied, he said as he went native," replied Drew.

"And I will *not* come to you, my lord and master."

"Then I will come to you, he said, suiting the action to the word."

"Ooooh, a naked man approaches with evil intent. But I will be brave. I will not flee."

Splendidly, their minds were attuned, and welcoming, their bodies came together. Like children of an ancient day — and Drew wondered if life was naturally simple and happy like this in the primitive years of man, when civilization was yet to come — they lay by the flaring embers. Night fell. Stars came out with a brilliance that they never displayed in the city. Chirp of crickets and whisper of leaves and laughing gurgle of water softened the stillness. A woodchuck or prowling raccoon snapped a twig somewhere off among the woods. An owl hooted afar. Vaguely they perceived their surroundungs, hardly aware of them, for deep in his arms she lay, relaxed yet responsive to the infinite modulations of his love, and the caresses she returned were as lyrical as those she yielded to, the tender blessing of lips, light-fingered play upon throat and back and arms and thigh, a fleeting kiss upon eyelids and cheeks and breast.

LV MORNING SONG

It was nearly four o'clock when Drew let himself in. He still remembered the pagan holiday of a few hours ago, and weary though he was, he felt a full content and an exhilaration that made him oblivious of fatigue. He was not thinking in words as he usually did; rather, his mental continuum flashed pictures and images – the trip up Sun River, picnic lunch on its banks, a setting sun, and a girl who was like a brighter sun, the soft submission of Helione, and deep, lyrical hours of love. Gone was winter, and over the months of snow, past, past were the days of cold. Spring had come and the world waked anew. Warm winds blew up from the south, and already he heard the singing of unseen birds as dawn flushed eastern skies. It had been a magic night, a night that atoned by its wealth and completion for the sadness of yesteryear. His eyes exhibited a luminous quality, as though they looked on things far away, or were lit by a torch in his brain, and his face was transfigured by dream. Yet he remembered to walk quietly in order not to disturb the slumber of his parents; with care he unlocked the door, gently he closed it behind him.

Chairs and tables merged in gray dusk; they looked ghostly in the shadow of dawn. But these were familiar ghosts, and even in that gloom, there was an atmosphere of friendliness, the atmosphere of welcome which had always been inherent in his home.

He tiptoed through the hallway, and still without turning lights on, deposited the picnic-kit against a baseboard in the kitchen. He stood motionless for an instant, debating whether to clean it and wash its utensils now, or to let it go until morning. If he fixed it immediately, he would save Mary from extra work. On the other hand, the noise he must necessarily make would disturb the rest of both parents. He decided that it would be more considerate if he did not waken them. As he stood, a great hush seemed to pass across the world. The singing of birds was stilled. The south wind paused in its coming. A gray, uniform dusk prevailed. From within himself alone, a pure flame appeared to flow out, illuminating every object and investing lifeless things with a supermundane reality. As if nothing mattered, or had a meaning, until that invisible sun rose above it and bestowed upon it life, purpose, and ideal existence. He tingled in the sway of a mystical exaltation.

The telephone rang.

Its jangle came harsh in the silence, unpleasant as it broke the spell. He hurried toward it, bumping into chairs. His thoughts were confused, so unexpected and so incongruous was this interruption. He must reach it before it rang again, lest his parents wake. Probably it was a wrong number. Who could be calling at this hour? It could only be Lee. Why was she calling? It must be of great importance for he had left her scarcely an hour and a half before. What could have happened in the interval? For surely, she would have told him everything of value when he had seen her, or would save it till tomorrow if it had slipped from her mind. What could it be? He disengaged the receiver just as the ringing began anew. Fumbling in half-darkness, he raised it to his ear and spoke as softly as he could into the mouthpiece, "Yes, what is it?"

"Is this the Gordons' residence?" It had a tired, gruff voice which he did not recognize.

"Yes, who is this? What do you want?"

"Are you one of the Gordons?"

"I am Drew Gordon, their son. What is it you want?"

"I'm sorry to have to inform you. Can you come to the Polyclinic Hospital as soon as possible?"

"Polyclinic — what — has something happened? Is it serious? Who is it?"

"Mr. and Mrs. Daniel Gordon were brought here after an automobile accident last evening — "

"And they are — ?"

"Dead."

.... Dazedly, Drew stared before him, a dumb, fierce torture writhing within, anguishing every nerve. Why had he come to the kitchen? His face was wet with tears, and he was washing the dishes of the picnic-kit over and over and over again in a house of soundless sounds....

LVI EPITAPH

REQUIESCAT IN PACE
TO DANIEL GORDON, MARCH 19, 1880 –
JVNE 4, 1930
AND MARY GORDON, OCTOBER 1, 1888 –
JVNE 4, 1930
FAREWELL AND PEACE

EVER KIND IN ADVERSITY
CONSIDERATE OF ALL SAVE THEMSELVES
SELF-DENYING THAT THEIR OFFSPRING MIGHT HAVE
ALL
FORGETTING YESTERDAY
AND ACCEPTING TODAY
IN THE HOPE THAT TOMORROW WOVLD BRING
THEM BLESSING
THEY WERE A GRACE TO EARTH
AND AN IDEAL OF HVMANITY
THOVGH VNSVNG BY POETS
AND VNKNOWN BY THE WORLD.
IN THESE ASHES REPOSE
TWO SPIRITS LINKED AS ONE
THROVGH ALL ETERNITY
AS THROVGH THE COMPLETED SEASONS
OF THEIR DAYS VPON EARTH.

HAIL TO THEM
AND TO THEM FAREWELL.
LIVING WE SHALL REMEMBER THEM
AND DEAD WE SHALL GO TO THEM GLADLY
KNOWING THAT THE INEXTINGVISHABLE SVN OF
THEIR BEING
WILL BE THERE TO WELCOME VS.

AVE ATQVE VALE

LVII EMPTY HOUSE

From attic to basement, Drew wandered through the house, their house, his house. It was quiet as a tomb. He looked wistfully at unfinished needlework in his mother's room. He stared blankly at the big books on accounting at the head of Daniel's bed. He riffled tintypes and yellowing photographs of ancestors filling a trunk in the attic. He looked hungrily at cookies which Mary had baked only a day before the accident, but a lump rose in his throat and he left them untouched. He walked softly where twin caskets had lain in the parlor.

Silence and weariness and pain.

But the atmosphere of friendliness lingered on. He would never abandon this house, never leave it or move away. As he flung himself on the davenport, he almost felt a twin presence beside him, and the murmur of ghostly voices. They were gone, but their psychotone remained.

It was little comfort. In the poignant realization that living individual and material identity had perished, though their aura continued, he suffered a black depression. One living and two dead, or was it two living and one dead?

The room blurred.

From far away came the slow, inexorable ticking of a grandfather's clock.

LVIII WALL WITHIN A CIRCLE

"Why won't you marry me, Helione?"

"I've told you before. I like you a great deal but I want to be independent and live my own life."

"Then why do you let me keep on seeing you?"

"Well, you don't have to call up, do you? All you need do is stop asking me for dates."

"That was unfeeling — "

"I didn't mean it so. You know what I had in mind."

"More than ever before, I need you, Helione, now that I have no one else. What mother and dad left would be enough for us to live on three or four years till I make a name for myself and they liked you so much I know they'd want us to keep on."

"I know they would too, darling, but it isn't that. It's — oh, can't you see, I don't ever want to marry, or not yet anyway. There've always been kids around at home and I don't want any at all, never, and — "

"What does that matter? I don't either. I'm like you. God knows I wouldn't take the responsibility of passing as futile an existence as this on to anybody who didn't ask for it and that's impossible so I don't intend to have any children either. And with birth control helps as efficient as they are now, women needn't bear children if they don't wish to."

"You can't be sure just the same. Nature has a way of playing tricks when you don't expect it. Besides, if that's the way you feel, what's the use of getting married?"

"You know as well as I. Freedom from worry and jealousy. To be always with you. To love you, to be playmates and companions, to give you things you want. I don't want to possess you like a piece of property but to enjoy living with you as equals and we can still keep our independent existences except that they'll run parallel more often than they otherwise would."

"But you love me now. If you were sure of me, you'd be free from jealousy as you say. Then what? I'd be tied to you, and next you wouldn't worry about other rivals, and pretty soon you'd accept me as a matter of course, and that would be the end. I'm frank with you, darling, because I like you so much. I'm afraid that you'd take me for granted as soon as we were married and that would spoil it. I want to be free. I want to live my own life. I want to be loved and have men admire me, but you know that after you've been married awhile, you fall in a rut. Just think of all the people we've known who got married and now look at them. There's Dora and Bob, and Lucy and Ned, and Ivy and Thorn, and a dozen more. The wives become dumpy, the husbands crabby, or the kids squall all night, and they have to worry about jobs and insurance and bills and everything but they all started out like you."

"Oh, Lee, you're wrong, can't you see? It's bad enough to judge others by yourself but it's worse to judge yourself by others and that's exactly what you're doing. I don't pretend to be conventional. You've known me two years now and you ought to realize that we've got something most people haven't. Ours is one of those rare loves that occurs once in a century, like Catullus and Lesbia, or Dante and Beatrice, or Heloise and Abelard, or Tristan and Isolde. I'll grant you that the majority of people make a failure of marriage but what does that prove? We can't tell until we try for ourselves. They weren't prepared, or they hadn't known each other well enough, or they were simply motivated by physical desire. Can't you see? It's far more than that with us. It's similarity of tastes, liking the same things, fitting each other perfectly from just the standpoint of love, and beyond that even there's a sort of madness about us, a frenzy that I know our friends have never experienced when they got married because they didn't have the dream or the vision or the fire that we have, not even Sven and Jennifer, and you'd surely have thought they would — "

"That's just it. They're not so different from us. They weren't going to have any children either, but just the same, it'll only be a couple of months now till Jennifer — "

"Their lives aren't ours. They may have changed their minds and decided to have a baby. We don't know. How can we tell for ourselves unless we try it? I'll admit that most marriages are failures. Men idealize women and women idealize men and they don't find out what they're really like until it's too late, after they've been married, but we've been going along for two years now seeing each other constantly and going to parties and shows and dances and teas together, and there's never been a single minute of boredom and every time I see you there's a new delight and I find something new in you because we're both inexhaustible and yet we've been living almost as if we were married — "

"Why not go on then just as we are?"

"Because we're taking chances and if anything happened where would we be? And that's the least of it, Helione, I'm sick of worry and doubt. I can't explain it any better. I want permanence or at least as much as you can ever get in this world. Why won't you be definite and say yes or no? Marriage is the natural thing, it's inevitable for a full life whether it's official or not. You know I'd live with you if you preferred it that way because I love you enough to accept any condition but as long as society is organized as it is now I'd rather marry you and not risk your happiness with the rest of the world. If you'd say no

I'd be so hurt that I'd probably go crazy but I'd get over it at least to all appearances and if you'd say yes you know how immeasurably happy it would make me, but you won't say either. You keep putting me off and evading the question and — "

"I won't listen any more if you're going to be abusive."

"I'm sorry. I've been so broken up about my parents' death that — "

"Oh Drew, darling, you mustn't think of that."

"What's the answer, Helione? They're gone, and I'm left. You're here, but a million miles away. The only sure thing is that I've loved you since the day we met, and I keep on loving you deeper like an immortal flower unfolding — "

"That's sweet of you, but then, why bring marriage on? If you feel like that, what difference does it make what I do?"

"Don't be perverse in giving what I said the wrong interpretation, Lee. As nearly as I can express it in words, I feel as if you and I were the halves that must unite in order to form a perfect whole. Do you remember the allegory of Plato's in The Symposium — "

"The two lovers trying to come together as one because they were originally one? Sure, but that was a bit of myth that he used, a mystical doctrine and not a pragmatic one."

"It doesn't matter how it originated. I only wanted to make you realize how much you mean to me and why I feel as I do. Perhaps it is mystical, but I have never loved you merely because you have beautiful hair, lovely eyes, attractive arms and legs, talk well, draw well, write poetry, and have sex appeal. I love you because I must, I don't know why. You are an exception to the ordinary run of women and I stand apart from men but it's more than that. It's an inexhaustible fire pouring out of us. It's an invisible sun that burns within us, life and love lighting each other. It's a pure flame that leaped into being the day we met. I felt it and you felt it and you remember how we instantly realized that we were destined to be together."

"That was years ago, Drew, and we've changed since."

"In what way? Do you love someone else?"

"I can't say."

"Would you rather I walked out and never returned?"

"Don't do anything rash."

"Evasions, equivocal answers, all! What's happened to you, Lee? If you're tired of me, say so. I'll take it hard but I can take it. You act as though being favored with so much love had gone to your head and you wanted to keep me always in doubt so you'd be sure things continued as they are now and — "

"I've got some work to do and I resent your attitude."

"I'm sorry, Lee. My emotion carried me away."

"That's better. Kiss me and then run along, darling, and I'll see you Saturday night."

LIX EXIT THE FOOL

Daydreaming, and oblivious of where his feet led him,
Drew was crossing the campus one morning in June when he
sensed rather than heard himself hailed. The blank light in his
eyes died out. They focussed again on reality. Before him stood
The Fool, capering in the sunshine.

"Brother, what time is it?"

Irritably, Drew glanced at his wrist-watch.

"It is just eleven."

The Fool danced up and down. The two previous occasions
when Drew saw him had been in winter, late one afternoon
and after dark on a cold night. Then The Fool seemed weird,
like the grotesque figure of a nightmare. Now it was daylight,
and spring approaching summer, and The Fool appeared enigmatic as ever, but he also aroused pity for the tragedy of his
misshape, as well as fear because of his deformed aspect. His
enormous head rolled on his shoulders incessantly. His neck
could not support its weight. It lay on his right shoulder, it
wobbled to his left, and his weak child's arms tried in vain to
hold it erect. But his eyes were unconquerable. They widened
into Drew's. He squeaked answer in a voice like that of a
mouse.

"You are not telling the truth. It is a quarter of twelve."

"I'm sorry to disagree, but I set my watch by the official
clock only a few minutes ago."

The Fool leaned closer. The squawk became a shrill whisper.

"You are counting by time. I was asking about eternity. It is a quarter of twelve, ten minutes of twelve, or sooner."

"Sooner than what? Do you mean later?"

"That is for you to say.

> Dig and delve
> Till a quarter of twelve,
> Then away, away,
> It's the break of day,
> Or twilight's fall
> Which is better than all,
> And you and I
> Alone know why,
> So dig and delve,
> It's a quarter of twelve,
> Away, away."

The Fool's voice grew fainter as he danced across the campus.

LX COMMENCEMENT

The line of graduating seniors was already assembling in front of Founders Hall. College by college, the robed figures gathered, white tassels for the Arts, red tassels for the Scences, green tassels for the Professions, yellow tassels for Agriculture, and brown tassels for the Unclasseds. The years of youth and dreams were over for them. Behind them lay books and love and gayety. Before they lay struggle and children and reality.

Drew halted before ever he reached their ranks. Into his mind came a memory of the proud hopes that Daniel and Mary had entertained for him. He stood third in his class, ranking next to the Salutatorian and Valedictorian. They had idolized him. They would have been in the auditorium, smiling happily as he stepped forward to receive his diploma. There would have been a gift waiting his return home – a watch, a book, a check, whatever they had planned, but something above monetary values whether it were small or great.

Instead, they would not be present, for they rested in Sunset Cemetery, nor would they ever know that he had walked tall and erect to the president, or ever hear the applause of class and spectators. And barely ten minutes ago The Fool had upset him with his cryptic gibberish.

Some distance ahead of him, he distinguished Sven and Jennifer. Elsewhere were others whom he knew.

His somber eyes envisaged the scene, solemn faces and laughing faces, lovers and companions, coeds and men, groups and singles, graduates and onlookers, beneath a splendid sun or June and a sky of peacock blue. Founders Hall, ivy covered Library, Political Sciences, Women's Dorm — all the buildings rose clear and sharp against the bright sky.

He turned to go, cap held loosely under one arm, gown flowing behind him. He would apply for his degree in absentia. He could not partake of the ceremony, for the black mountain of his thoughts crushed him. His melancholy demanded solitude, his misery needed aloneness. As in a mist, the countenances of Mary and Daniel materialized, rejoicing that his college years were crowned with success....

He turned again. Donning his cap, he took his place as the band blared forth the Commemoration March.

LXI PYJAMA PARTY

"**What do you think, Drew,** I received an invitation from Dora this morning to a pyjama party that she and Bob are throwing next Saturday. She said I could bring any man I wished but they'd like to have you."

Something froze inside Drew as he looked across the table at Lee. Instantly he thought of that physical beauty he loved so deeply, visualized it seductive in silky things, all too intimately on display for other eyes. The tightening around his heart passed with a surge of emotion in which doubt, jealousy, love, and bitterness commingled. He hesitated to reply, conscious of her voice babbling on.

"Have you answered yet?" he finally interrupted.

"Sure. I called her right away as soon as I got the invitation and told her I'd love to come. I said I'd phone again later and let her know who I was bringing. What's the matter? Don't you want to go? Or have you something else on? If you have, just say so and I'll get another man. It'll be loads of fun and Dora's parties are always so interesting and I'd just adore the chance to show off those lovely new pyjamas that I haven't even worn yet, you know, the ones I showed you, pale pistachio almost apple green with the ever so tiny border of burnt umber to match my hair and the cute neck line that looks so tricky as if it were simply going to melt away only it never quite does fortunately for me and — "

"Are you really going to wear those?"

"Sure, why not?"

"I thought they were rather transparent."

"Not quite, they're only translucent, but they'll have to do. After all, darling, I'm not going to be the only girl present and I certainly intend to look my best and be just as cute as they will."

"Just the same, I think you ought to wear something under them."

"Don't be medieval, Drew, this isn't eighteen-fifty. Besides, is there anything wrong with 'em? Didn't you yourself tell me they were stunning when I bought 'em? And I haven't any others that are new enough to wear. I suppose I could buy another pair for the party but I'm pretty strapped right now and don't think I could afford to buy more new ones. Really, they're all right. They probably won't look half as wicked as some of the other girls'. At least mine are silk but I know Dora's going to wear that beautiful chiffon outfit she bought for her wedding and if you think mine are too light wait till you see hers and believe me, you'll open your eyes. I'm awfully fond of 'em, mine I mean. That cool, pastel pistachio is the shade I've always wanted to wear and it suits my coloring so exactly and it's such a lovely pair even if it was expensive. Do you remember that print of Cezanne's I showed you? And the water-color of the girl I did at the beach last summer? You know, the one with the girl in the green bathing suit and the tawny hair? Well, these pyjamas — "

Her voice went on but Drew swirled into a reverie of unhappy thoughts. He did not want anyone else to admire Lee's loveliness. She would somehow be cheapened in his eyes if she went thus to the party. He could not have said why or how, except in some indefinable way as though a humming-bird with soaked wings dropped to earth and lay draggled among weeds. Their relationship was so deep, so personal, so fulfilled in itself, that even a casual gift of the slightest favor to others took away from her a little of the glory in which he had invested her. Was it the curse of Iago that corrupted him, and was it himself at fault instead of her? Fear that something might happen at the party? He had never been to such a soiree, but he had heard of others and they seemed to have been the excuses to disguise wild parties that degenerated into God-knows-what. Or did he hesitate lest he be the dark specter present, partaking without pleasure and watching without the carefree geyety expected? He wished that Lee had never told him about the party or asked him to escort her. He could not be unhappy about what he did not know. Still, he admitted he would have been deeply hurt if he had found out later that she went, without asking him or telling him. But now he knew, and if he pleaded a prior engagement, Saturday evening would find him as past occasions had found him, wondering what she was doing and who she was with. He would be at the bottom of a depressive cycle. He would be in a kind of sick despair. His imagination would riot, tormenting him with exquisite fears. He would turn to writing and pour out his love and his disappointment, his sorrow and regret, in prose of nervous or hectic beauty, unreal yet quivering with the surge of uncontrolled emotions, that expressed by its very style his driving complex without even slightly relieving him of the burden. If he accepted and went, he would be made unhappy by any of a hundred so insignificant moments — the touch of a hand, the dropping of a casual word, a stray reference with hidden implications — that yet meant so much.

"Well, all right, Drew, if that's the way you feel about it and aren't any more interested in taking me than you seem to be, why — "

Resolutely he thrust from mind the fears and suspicions of Othello. Helione had come to him vivacious and excited with enthusiasm, and he had responded by sulking like a child. Contrition dominated him as suddenly as he kicked the fears out of mind.

"Oh, no, it isn't that at all, Lee. I was thinking about what I'd wear. You know I'll be delighted to take you and it sounds as if it would be a grand party. What time shall I call?"

"Oh, I suppose about eight-thirty. How will you come? We can't exactly go wandering around town in pyjamas on street-cars, don't you think?"

"Leave that to me. I'll arrange transportation somehow. I might rent a car from one of these Drive Yourself agencies or borrow Sven's or whoever else feels like loaning me his. I'll solve it one way or another."

"You always do, Drew. That's one of the nice things about you. Gee, I'm all excited! I have a feeling it's going to be a good fast party from what I know of her crowd. Aren't you thrilled?"

"I wonder what they'll do for amusement?"

"Oh, dance, I suppose, or play games, or drink, or whatever Dora and Bob suggest. It's customary, you know, for the hosts to do something about seeing that their guests have a good time."

"You wouldn't kid me, would you? Now, I never would have thought so myself. Anyway — "...

LXII LAOCOON

As usual, Helione was not ready when Drew called for her. She would hurry and be out in a few minutes. Wouldn't he sit down while she finished her dressing? Mrs. Forrest sounded polite and slightly ironic, though she sympathized with Drew because Helione always managed to keep him waiting at least half an hour.

"My, aren't we gorgeous?" she approved as she surveyed his Russian pyjamas. They were blood scarlet, and a bizarre black design figured the blouse.

Drew colored. However he resented the prank of nature that made him blush at slight provocation, he had never been able to master these sudden rushes to his head.

"Are you trying to match the costume?" suggested Mrs. Forrest. "I'm sure all the other men will be jealous as soon as you walk in. The girls can't help falling for you," she continued mercilessly.

Drew resorted to the only effective retort he knew. He met her on her own grounds. "Oh, I'll simply knock 'em dead and carry 'em off one by one," he promised.

"My, isn't he bold!"

"You don't know the half of it. Casanova had nothing on me! Don Juan'll turn in his grave after I get to the party!"

"And is he modest!"

"Far be it from me to contradict a woman of your discerning taste, Mrs. Forrest!"

The persiflage ended when Lee came out, to Drew's relief. She looked charming, though a long jade wrap concealed her costume.

"Be as good as you can," Mrs. Forrest called, lightly mocking, after them. "And don't stay out too late!"

Drew helped Helione into the roadster.

"Isn't it a gorgeous night?" she exclaimed. "I'm glad it's June. That's a good month for a pyjama party. And with a big, white moon, isn't it perfect?"

Drew agreed as the car accelerated.

"What's the matter? You don't sound very enthusiastic."

"I have to watch where I'm driving."

Lee sat still for a moment. Then she slid gently closer and put her left hand on Drew's arm. "...Do you still like me?" she coaxed.

The car wobbled. Inaudibly, Drew sighed, but what could he do against the inevitable? She had only to touch him, and he trembled visibly; only to look at him, and his eyes lighted with the feeling his voice could never express. To hold her in arms were miracles.

"Don't do that!" he commanded. His spirit belied his words.

"Why not?" She moved closer. "Don't you even want to kiss me?" Her question was wicked in its innocence. The appeal of her mind and body, beauty of face and figure, whelmed him. She was the dark side of the moon, mysterious and compelling. She was the inner fire which one could never know because it lay so near.

He halted the car on a side street of vacant lots. "How do you expect me to drive?" he began sternly. She did not answer. She looked at him from half-closed eyes, and the faintest of smiles hung upon the crimson lure of her lips.

"Lovely lady, Helione, you are about to be seduced!" He tried to be impersonal.

"Oh, not that," she protested softly. "Not yet, anyway. Wait till after the party."

"I shall remind you then."

"Can I depend on it?"

He leaned and kissed her, slowly, deeply, sensuously, for a long minute. She yielded until her breasts were exciting against him, and the sun of her being lighted the darkness of his soul. Or was it the pure flame within him that illuminated her?

"That's enough," she whispered, moving gently apart.

"You are never enough."

"It is sweet of you to think so. I only wanted to make sure that you still like me."

"Like you? Great God, if you call this liking, what do you suppose love would be like? First you set me on fire, then — "

"Please, Drew, not here. Wait till after the party."

"The only trouble with you, Lee, is that you're beautiful, desirable, talented, and full of the Devil."

"Sure, I know it."

He threw the car into gear and drove on. Her mood was strange tonight, unpredictable. She could not have been merely curious to test his emotions, or was she making certain of him while she laid other plans? Her hazel green eyes told nothing. They were guileless. Perhaps, like a luxuriating cat, she only wished to be contented by a stroke, reassured by a caress. Would he ever know what thoughts ruled her?

She did not speak, or again try to distract his attention, during the ten-mile trip. Half against the cushion, half against him, she lay back in the seductive ease of a woman loved. The turmoil of his mind increased. Contact with her aroused him. He could neither think nor act rationally when in her presence. By ways he would never comprehend, she dominated his emotional and mental lives. The craving for love, the worship of beauty, need of intellectual companionship — they all united in her, and he was helpless. Whatever she did, he would forgive because he must. However she erred, he would forget, at whatever sacrifice, because he loved her with that mad, supercessive, immeasurable passion which the cynical gods, who alone are capable of deific attainments, destroy some few mortals with, and fewer women. Catullus and Lesbia. *A thousand and a thousand and ten* thousand.... Dante and Beatrice. *Abandon hope, all ye who en*ter here.... Shakespeare and the lad and the dark lady. *How like a winter hath my absence been From thee.... Ruin hath taught me thus to ruminate That time will come and take my love away. This thought is as a death which can not choose But weep to have that which it fears to lose....* Rossetti and The House of Life. *Look in my face; my name is Might-have-been; I am also called No-more, Too-late, Farewell; Unto thine ear I hold the dead-sea shell Cast up thy Life's foam-fretted feet between; Unto thine eyes the glass where that is seen Which had Life's form and Love's, but by my spell Is now a shaken shadow intolerable, Or ultimate things unuttered the frail screen. Mark me, how still I am. But should there dart One moment through thy soul the soft surprise Of that winged Peace which lulls the bridge of sighs, — Then shalt thou see me smile and turn apart Thy visage to mine ambush at thy heart Sleepless with cold commemorative eyes....*

"Well, here we are."

Drew descended from the high places of his reverie. How the deuce had he managed to drive these last few miles unseeing? It was as if he had withdrawn into himself, literally. As if his eyes became blind. As if the back of the pupils held a picture-screen upon which his thoughts projected visible realities. As if he saw the screen instead of the world familiar to normal people....

"What's the matter, Drew? You look so blank!"

"I'm sorry, but I can't help it. I'm always a blank when I see you. You do things to me."

"So do you to me, darling." She pressed his arm. Blood boiled in his veins.

"No — not now! I just repaired my makeup. Let's go in."

Dora answered their ring. "We were just beginning to wonder what had happened to you! Hello, Drew, it's good to see you again. You know the way to the guest room, don't you? Lee, come to my room and take off your things."

Drew wondered if the party were to be no larger. As he passed the living room, he saw five or six persons, but did not pause for greetings. He hurried on to the guest-room and surveyed himself. Yes, his appearance seemed to be all right, except for the haggard circles under his eyes, and the tenseness of his facial muscles.

"I suppose I ought to take it easy for awhile," he thought. "One of these days I'll be having a breakdown if I'm not careful. After tonight, I'm going to take a long rest."

He flung his wrapper on the bed where other capes and coats already lay. Fortunately, he had not torn his pyjamas or got grease on them from the car. "But if there were any, I could claim that the spots formed part of the design," he decided, and "I wonder who the people are?" Probably he knew them all.

Lee and their hostess were coming from Dora's room as he emerged. He could not suppress a momentary start at the vision of loveliness presented, though a storm brewed within him.

Silk the color of chartreuse clung to Lee like gossamer. Wickedly attractive she looked, voluptuous and alluring. The silk was so sheer that her nipples blurred through, rosy and tempting, and the suggestion of a shadow darkened her trousers. Beside her, Dora, enchanting in flame of grenadine, walked yet more unconcealed. The chiffon riffled around her, a haze of fire through which her body glowed. Lustre of blue-black hair capped her. Nymphs they were, blonde nymph and brunette, Circe and Cleopatra, and Drew's heart leaped out to them, while he tightened strangely. He wanted to love her, to love them, to turn and flee. But he must not make a fool of himself, he must not leave, he must not embarrass his hosts.

"That's a stunning outfit you're wearing," Dora cheerily approved. Her eyes flicked him from head to foot as though she visually stripped him, with a caress the more erotic because imaginary. "It's exactly the thing to bring out your saturnine expression!"

Drew made a powerful attempt to meet exigency. "Thanks! I'd have complimented you first but I was simply bowled over by the two of you. I can only admire in silence knowing that my vocabulary is insufficient and that I'll be blind to all else for the rest of my days!"

"That will do very nicely," Dora smiled as she led them in. "And now that we're here, we can start the drinks. Lee, you and Drew know all these people, don't you? And this is Bill Gavin — "

Drew turned to ice. The man faced him. That man whom he had seen, one horrible evening more than a year ago —

"How do you do?" he bowed impassively, thus preventing himself from seeing the outstretched hand.

Winey colors rioted in the group. Dora and Lee were living dreams with their grenadine and chartreuse not quite costumes. Helen Engel wore a port mauve. Muscatel intensified the statuesque proportions of Diana. The resplendent rayon clung like her native skin until he belled loosely toward her ankles. Pudge O'Tief suffered by contrast, perhaps because of his plumpness. Then, too, rye was not the most becoming shade he could have chosen. It looked unhappily like the color of a substance rather less aromatic. For the others, Bob turned up in a superb sherry effect, verging on royal purple, that separated the almost pallid white of his complexion from the blackness of his hair. And the stranger of that night suggested an orange-and-bitters. A swastika ornamented his blouse, his trousers were dark as fernet. Drew disliked him because the costume resembled his own, because it did not quite suit him, and because he represented death come to life. Covertly he studied him. Gavin was shaped like a clothespin; with a Hebraic nose, a womanish face, and dark eyes the color of figs; hair of thick, flaxen blond; rather short of six feet; possibly twenty-eight; apparently intelligent; and bearing the traits of easy success. Drew would not have missed Gavin, and he knew without a word beng spoken that the antipathy was mutual.

Lee betrayed no emotion when she saw her seducer. "Hello, Bill, how are you?" she called. "I'm glad to see you here."

"Yes, it's been a long time," Bill remarked ambiguously. He slurred his words with a caress for each.

"Now that you've held up the drinks so long," Bob interrupted, addressing Lee and Drew, "you can set yourselves right by downing the first round fast. To the success of the evening!"

"Dora certainly knows how to pick the good-looking ones, and people that fit," Lee commented to Drew as goblets arrived. He wondered whether her words implied more than they expressed.

Glasses went up. The julep, fragrant with mint and musical with ice, slid into gullets like water into blotters. The initial round had scarcely disappeared before Bob was back with another. "Late start, we have to make up for lost time," he announced. The drinks hastened after their predecessors. Drew felt a glow already permeate him.

"Let's see what's on the radio," said Dora. She whirled the dials. Advertising, speeches, a symphonic broadcast, a play, and several popular bands blared forth briefly before she tuned in a hot orchestra. "If this isn't Duke Ellington, it ought to be. Kick the rug away, Bob!"

Drew, interested in the procedure and warmed by the highball, had been watching. It dawned on him that he should ask Lee for the first dance. He located her, and saw with a jealous pang that she was talking to Gavin.

"Excuse me for breaking in," he began, "but would you like to dance? They're just starting."

"Oh, I'm sorry, Drew. Bill spoke for this one only a moment ago and you weren't around so I said yes. Would you care for the next?"

"No, thanks," he answered curtly. "It's already taken." He instantly regretted his words. He ought to have concealed his temper, but hurt pride brought his resentment into the open.

"Too bad. Perhaps we might have a later one."

His moody eyes followed them as Gavin swung her into a sexy glide. Since the others were now dancing, politeness compelled him to ask Diana. They swayed to the weird laziness of *Mood Indigo,* thus making the reversal complete. None had her original escort.

Drew did a masterful job of hiding his disappointment.

"You could dance to this on a twenty-five cent piece," he murmured.

"A dime would be more like it," she shot back. Her face enticed him.

"How do you expect me to dance?" he asked in mock helplessness. "I'm a mere man at the mercy of a Come-Hither."

"I don't! You're only supposed to admire."

"Taken for granted!" The appeal of her lightly clad body, the fragrance of a tantalizing perfume she used, the slow delirium of the music, the heady warmth of the drinks, and the still more heady languour of a June night went to his brain.

"Do you like to be kissed?"

"I don't know. I never think about it before and what's the use of thinking after?"

"I meant, just as a preliminary."

"Why bother with preliminaries?"

"It's an old French custom."

"Personally, I like the new French customs, if you get what I mean."

"Madam, I was born yesterday."

"Yeah? Well, at this rate, you'll die tomorrow."

"A pleasant prospect. May I count on your assistance?"

"You've certainly improved your technique since I met you! It was at Jennifer's party, wasn't it?"

"Good memory! Wait till my technique goes into action!"

The music wailed to a fantastic end before she could answer, but her face promised experiments.

The next number on the program will be Chant of the Jungle. Stand by for station announcements.

During the short wait, Bob like a magician produced more drinks.

Lee drifted over to Drew. "What dance are we having?"

"If any, I suppose the usual last one," he replied bitterly.

"If that's the way you feel about it, why bother at all?"

"True. There's no point in forsaking new fields for leftovers."

She floated off. Momentary regret filled him when he saw that she was evidently beginning to feel the alcohol, but then, a haze, not all cigarette smoke, cast a pleasant veil over the party.

Several dances passed. The stimulus of rhythms and cocktails increased. The party was growing freer.

"Damn!" said Dora when the announcer cooed that Soandso's orchestra had played the last number on their program. Idly she twirled the dials. Snatches of inferior jazz muddled out. "I can't get anything good. Let's have another drink."

Bob complied. "The scenery from kitchen to here is becoming monotonous. I bet if you look you can find I've worn a path a foot deep for you camels." He produced a tray of pelicans.

"What're you trying to do, kill us?" asked Pudge. "What did you put in this?"

"Equal parts of gin, honey, and lemon juice."

"Awwww, it doesn't make sense!"

"The honey sweetens the lemon juice, the lemon juice tartens the honey, and the gin slides down on the back of them both!"

The drink pursued its ancestors. A delightful warmth crept through Drew's veins. Past worries and future troubles clouded into fog.

"Anybody still want to dance?" called Bob.

"Who could?" That was the silky voice of Gavin.

Dora set the radio low on an ordinary program while Bob shook another drink. "Hope you all can mix 'em or it's going to be too bad," he spoke thickly when he returned. "This is an alexandrine."

"What's that?"

"Whipping cream, creme de cacao, and gin."

"Jeeze Chris'!" Pudge swore feelingly, though his enunciation became a hope rather than a fact.

The drink dived like Weissmuller. Bliss entered Drew's life. Lee was entrancing. Dora was lovely. Everybody had charm. Even Bill possessed a vague attractiveness. If he wasn't quite as disagreeable as he had seemed at first, at least you could tolerate him.

"There isn't any good dance music, now," announced Bob. "Let's do something else."

"What?"

"Anything exciting, like sardines, or post-office, or strip poker."

"Post-office? That's a child's game, and sardines is just an excuse for private necking." Boredom crept into his eyes which glistened as water crept out.

"All right, strip poker then, I'm not particular. Or does anyone have a better suggestion?"

"Why not cards or dice?" Drew offered, through the tightness of his heart and the ebullient looseness of his mind.

"Well, gambling with friends doesn't exactly give me the biggest of kicks," protested Bob.

"I mean, for forfeits. Strip poker seems rather futile. It wouldn't last long because it couldn't with our present garb."

He felt a great relief when they accepted his suggestion; relief of the kind that would be experienced by a man who, saved from falling over a precipice, could not quite haul himself back to solid earth, or as if he drowned, until someone threw him a shingle. While they were making preparations, he cornered Lee. "Let's leave after the game's over," he whispered.

"Right when the party's getting gay? I should say not!"

"There's no telling what will happen next with this mob in its present state. Let's decamp while the going's good. It's pretty late, but we can drive to a lake and cool off if you like."

"I think I'd prefer to stay."

"But Lee — "

"Run along, I won't keep you. I'm enjoying myself and you needn't worry about my reaching home. I've already had two invitations."

"I couldn't possibly guess who."

"Don't try to be funny."

"Sorry, Lee. Of course I'll stay until you're ready."

"Good idea, darling, that's better. Let's join 'em, they're calling us."

A clock bonged midnight. Drew was developing an odd belief that he dreamed all this — that he partook of a vivid but unreal nightmare. Twelve o'clock. He should not have drunk so much. Yet he accepted the mixture that Bob brought out before play began. The intoxicant numbed and soothed. It gave a labored beat to his pulse. At the same time, it delineated the pinnacles of his thoughts. Hmmm. Pointed thoughts. Big, rocky thoughts. Maybe, if they got bigger, they would pierce through and then everyone could see what he was thinking. Lee would read them. They would all gather and stare at the pointed thoughts. They —

"Hey, Drew, wake up! It's your turn."

"What are we playing?"

"Dice, are you blind? Bill, Diana, and I have shaken. You've got to beat four sixes in two."

Drew rolled. The best he could throw was three sixes. The dice passed. Helen tied Bob. In the play-off, Bob won.

"Here's where hell begins!" he promised. "Wait till you hear these forfeits and have to pay 'em!"

"Whoa, wait a minute! Nobody's decided whether to have forfeits after each game or play for awhile and pay them off in a bunch at the end."

"Let's have 'em now," Pudge suggested. "We'd forget how many we had after a couple of games. Woof! What did you put in these drinks? It's all I can do to remember my own forfeit!"

"O.K. Get ready for the axe!"

Helen, the soberest of the group, wrote the names of all except Bob on separate pieces of paper, folded the scraps, and juggled them. Bob sat in a chair. Standing behind him, she selected a strip at random and asked, "What shall he do to redeem it?" As he named a forfeit, she jotted it on the outside of the slip, until all were tallied.

"Hope you can read my writing, I know I can't!" She chuckled boyishly as she wobbled to a chair. She had a nice chuckle. Amused and ho-hum.

Bob picked up the slips. The first read, "Pluck three of your own hairs and braid them in your fingers. Pudge."

"Jeez'!" the victim grunted with a violet jerk of his head. "Do you want to drive me nuts? Braid three hairs, and I had a haircut this week! Awww, it doesn't make sense." He ran his hand through his scalp and pulled out several strands. Holding the three longest between thumb and forefinger of his left hand, he began the impossible by attempting to braid them with fat fingers. He looped the outer hairs in. The moment he attempted to loop the middle hair over, the other two sprang back like millimetric bamboo.

"Haw!" Pudge drunkenly burpled. The rest of the party howled as he fumbled with the infinitesimal strands: a ludicrous figure, fat and foolish, solemnly attempting to braid hairs that he probably could not see.

"If male, pose as the Apollo Belvidere; if female, as the Venus de Milo," continued Bob. Drew's heart tightened. "Diana! Well, if your name's any indication, you ought to be a success!"

"Not so fast!" asked the muscatel blonde. "Is this supposed to be with or without?"

"Without," said Bob pitilessly. "How do you think the dame became famous?"

"O.K., big boy! I'll be laying for you later." Six voices caught up her words as one and bandied them around. She gasped as she suddenly realized the double entendre which they had given her phrase. "Speaking of the lion's den of thieves," she began confusedly.

"Now which is it? Be specific while you pay the forfeit!" Lee chided.

Diana took what little refuge there was in silence. She wriggled from her golden slip-on blouse and kicked her sandals aside. The trousers fell at her feet. For a moment, noble in the splendor of her body, arms coyly held across her full breasts and milk-white thighs, she posed. To Drew she seemed sexless, for she caught the mood of another classic statue which she had evidently confused with the Venus de Milo. Then she stooped for her garments and became again a woman desirable, when, like a goddess disappearing, she reclad herself.

"Hell, I'll be barging into a madhouse before I'm done," swore Pudge as the strands recoiled. Intent on his task, he had missed Diana's posing. Several guests kindly informed him of his loss. He scowled in sarcastic gratitude and resumed his braiding.

"Sing Old Man River while standing on your head," recited the winner. "Drew!"

"Good God, that's a penalty on all of us!" Bill objected sourly.

With a great effort, Drew raised himself from his seat and swayed against a wall. His initial attempt to stand upside down resulted in general collapse. The party cheered as his long legs came down like folding telephone poles.

"That was swell! Do it again. I haven't seen anything like it since Pisa started to lean!" Bob laughed.

In his second try, Drew managed to arch against the wall, though he felt giddy. He murdered the tune, wrecked the words in a whisky bass, and returned to his chair amid universal groans.

"Phew! I'll pick safer forfeits next time. Do an imitation of St. Denis or Shawn. Helen."

The girl in mauve arose and pirouetted through motions. Willowy, slight, and graceful, she possessed a sense of rhythm and a lightness of carriage that gave her exceptional success.

If tight, she did not show it. The fog lifted temporarily from Drew's mind as he watched her whirl to a bow, her scarf streaming around her.

"That was awfully well done," drawled Lee.

"Hey, where's my third hair?" Pudge muttered to himself. In despair, he pulled out another. "How long is this supposed to keep up?"

"Until they're braided," Bob insisted, and to Helen, "Very good. Let's see who's next. Stand in the middle of the room. Take off your costume. Tie something around you like Gandhi. Recite a poem. Bill."

His audience commented gleefully upon his topography as he stripped. Alcohol, hope, or embarrassment rose about ninety degrees due south. Gravely he looped the bottom of the pyjamas around his loins. He squatted Hindu fashion on the floor. Then he chanted,

> "There was a young woman I know
> Who liked it above or below,
> In front or behind,
> And she didn't mind,
> There always was farther to go."

He arose, dressed leisurely, and resumed his seat. Each reacted differently to his limerick. Helen looked as far from it all as a bowl of cherries. Dora and Bob asked him enthusiastically to repeat the verse for them to memorize. Pudge laughed heavily. Diana worse an expression of wise innocence. Lee twirled her goblet. She studied its lines. She admired its contents. She daintily removed a drop from its outer rim with the theory of a handkerchief. Drew stared at her.

Bob returned to his reading of forfeits, and presented a bomb as though it were candy. "Give a practical illustration of the high spot of a wedding night with the assistance of the winner."

Drew's heart came to an absolute standstill and he congealed like liquid air, as Bob opened the slip.

"Dora. Damn. I might have known it would be just my luck to draw my wife."

Dora regarded him oddly. "Must I?"

"Of course, since everyone else has redeemed, unless they'll release us."

The party was deaf to his plea.

"All right, I'm game."

"That's the spirit, though of course, since you're the host, you could declare the forfeit off or substitute a new one," drawled Bill. Drew thought he detected a covert sneer.

Whatever he meant, and however he intended his remark, his implication of poor sportsmanship stung Bob into action.

"No, the laugh's on me, I'm game."

Dora made no reply as she removed her fluffy chiffon ensemble and lay back on the studio-couch. Too many drinks had made her features feral, though they still exhibited a kind of demoralized harmony, like an atonal chord. The scar of an operation — probably appendicitis — nestled on her stomach. It startled Drew. He had a sudden terrible illusion that the face of Helione stared at him there. He looked on in wide-eyed delirium. Whispered comments came from afar —

"Good technique — "

"Ought to be, they've been married long enough — "

"Wish I were the winner — "

"Hey, one of you girls lend me three of your hairs, they're longer than mind and maybe I can for God's sake, what's going on — "

"Christ, she's beautiful — "

"Talk about sex appeal — "

The forfeit was consummated. A tremor disturbed Bob's voice as he read the last slip, "If male, kiss Dora; if female, kiss the winner. For at least five seconds. Lee."

The fantasy that was over had made Drew feel like one fascinated by a monstrosity; attentive but impersonal, a detached observer. Its very frenzy brought it the atmosphere of unreality. This final request sank into his heart with the force of lead. Shock paralyzed him. The other redemptions did not touch his life, but at these words, black abysses engulfed his inner self.

Lee did not look at him as she rose. She tripped to Bob and curtseyed modestly, "Please, sir, I was told never to make advances to men."

Bob bent over and kissed her full on the mouth, a long, luscious kiss.

Could they not hear his heart? thought Drew desperately. Pound, pound, pound — surely it must thunder through the room and deafen them all — thud, thud, thud — with triphammer blows — beat, beat, beat — drown them in airquakes — drown, drown — he would kill Bob — kill, kill, kill — and the red mists rose yet he could not move.

"Thank you, she said demurely," Lee gasped as she broke away. "Now I must return and pacify my lord and master."

"What? Drew get sore over a little thing like this? No, he won't."

Was that her sitting beside him?

"You don't mind, do you, honey? It's all in fun." Gone was the mystery of her voice and the sun in her eyes. She sounded drunk. Was she? Or he? Was that her hand falling upon his? No, it couldn't be, for if it were, he would thrill to the touch. He felt no emotion. It could not be her. Something had split him in two. Part of him lay sleepless with cold, commemorative eyes and he longed for the dead sanctuary of that other self, but part of him sat lifelessly quiet. He was the participant in a dream-horror who is also the onlooker, watching the torment of his true self. He would run, run, run, but as in a dream-horror, he could not start.

"My lord and master spurns me," a tipsy voice mocked lightly. Helione wandered away.

Bob was handing out the umpth drink.

"He maketh me sad," sang Lee. "Let's go on. I want more excitement or something to cheer me up!"

"Try this!" She took half the cocktail at a swallow, while Bob batted his eyes in awe.

"Well, we still haven't tried strip poker," Bill suggested casually.

"I want to play strip poker!" wailed Lee. The idea seemed to grow better the more she thought of it. Hope and new interest reanimated her face. She found enthusiastic support.

Drew tried to speak, but his throat constricted. He could not make a sound or think of the simplest word.

"Damn these hairs!" cursed Pudge wildly.

"Oh, throw them away. We'll call the forfeit paid," said Bob. "Anyway, we're going to play strip poker."

Drew found his voice. "Isn't it rather futile? I mean, after what we've already had."

"You're a pessimist. Nothing's futile," Bob remarked with vague conviction. "Where's the cards? You find the cards, Dora, while I fix another little drink."

Bong, bong, went a clock. Drew, imbedded in ice though the night was warm, took his cocktail at a gulp. Cigarette smoke, heat, odor of human flesh, and the smell of stale drinks fouled the room. He needed this bracer to rouse him from lethargy, give him strength to keep on.

"Attaboy."

"How about some food before we begin?"

"Too much trouble. We'll eat after this is over."

The game began. They tossed the pillows down and sat in a circle on the floor.

"Straight draw, one bet only, nothing wild," announced Bob as he filliped the cards.

The faces of the players came to Drew with savage clarity despite the fog from incessant cigarettes and innumerable drinks, and the madness of the evening. Bill was calculating; he wore unscrupulous urbanity like a suit. Bob flushed with drinks. Dora looked sensuously content; the forfeit heightened her color and softened her features. Sensuous discontent spoiled Lee's expression; she was amoralized. Envy of others' good fortunes combined with fatuous hope on the fat face of Pudge. Diana mirrored deviltries. Helen was naively curious. Himself, God knew what. And all merged in a kind of group hysteria, ready for anything. Couldn't he and Lee steal their exit? Couldn't they frame an excuse? What was the use of trying? She would rebel and insist on staying to the end. She always did. And she had asked for the game. He could have left, as he once walked out on a childhood part, but he would only make himself conspicuous or draw ridicule. Black settled upon him like a mountain.

He studied his cards.... Bill won with a trio of aces.... The deal passed.... Gavin won again.... Slippers, blouse.... On the fourth hand, he lost his wrist watch.... On the fifth, he wagered his last garment. He drew to an eight and miraculously filled with a nine.

"Lay 'em down," said Gavin.

Drew anxiously showed his hand.

"Full house wins. They're yours, Lee."

Drew and Diana went bankrupt on the pay-off. Their trousers increased Lee's pile of winnings, or rather his, for Diana's was an inflammatory one-piece affair.

"Shake!" Diana dropped easily beside him. "We're babes in the woods compared with these cut-throats. How does it feel to be an elk? Nice ribs on the north shore, eh what? I never yet have won at this game. My luck's terrible."

"Can't be worse than mine!" he consoled her and added slyly, "Nice moons near Polaris!"

The warmth of her so near disturbed him. A malicious gleam winked in her pupils. She brushed his shoulder in arranging some pillows. The two had withdrawn slightly from the main group. No one was paying attention to them. On impulse, as though he would thereby efface the memory of Lee's forfeit, or in some abstract sense atone for it, he leaned sidewise and kissed her tempting lips. He did not raise his hands from the

floor or try to hold her. It was a queer kiss of labial contact solely, but it became fraught with potentiality when the girl parted
her mouth and ran the tip of her tongue lightly across his lips.
"Some day — " he whispered, slowly returning to his position,
but he did not end the sentence. A crackle of electricity shot at
him from Lee. He glanced up, to find her watching his bye-play.
Was it hatred or jealousy that moulded her countenance? He
met her glance with a piercing response. He had evened the
balance. To know that she resented his kissing another than
her despite her own love gifts were talismans. She smoothed
her face save for a peculiar lowering of eyelids that buried a
glint. The incident passed unnoticed except by Diana who wisely kept silent while she smiled a satisfied smile.

He followed the game, and sipped a new cocktail that Bob
produced. Helen went nudist on the eighth hand. Drew lost
count thereafter; Dora was next to fall out; then Pudge and
finally Bob joined the shorn lambs.

Play settled between Lee and Bill, the remaining survivors.
Bill held a many-colored heap of winnings, and Lee was limited
to her costume.

"A sandal," she bet. Bill evened with somebody else's slip-
per. He won with jacks to nines and collected.

Lee wagered the other sandal and won. Two hands later,
Gavin had collected both.

"Aren't I nice feet? Do say so even if you don't agree," she
asked slurrily.

"They're divine," he agreed. "Like their owner."

"Aren't I though?" She nodded assent and laughed deliberately — ha, ha, ha — on a rising scale, like fragments of Chinese
glass tinkling in a wind. The gesture separated art from artifice.

She lost bracelet and ear-rings, pearl drops whose lustre
brought out the coral of her lobes.

"Wish I'd thought to wear all my jewellery, loads and loads
of things," she regretted flippantly. "My virtue won't be safe
much longer if you keep on winning!" But the next hand

returned the bracelet to her. She held a pair of fives, Bill's lay-out was a blank.

Again she lost, kings under three jacks.

"The uppers this time." Nonchalantly she hummed a bar from *St. James Infirmary* in a sexy baritone as she lifted her cards. "Where are you, Mrs. Luck?" Mrs. Luck had changed her address. Gavin won with a trio of tens against two pairs.

Drew followed her motions with a death mask as she paid. Her beauty of back and breasts and waist emerged, the beauty which he had loved so long and so deeply, but the crimson lit-ten coal mists grew, and he was numb.

"Lowers, of course, since I haven't any more," offered Lee with a throaty laugh of excitement. The fever of gambling gripped her and her voice was husky. She peered at Drew but turned quickly back to the cards. What did she speculate? He was unable to read her glance. Perhaps it meant nothing, though it had a devilish gleam.

"Too bad," murmured Gavin, laying down a flush to her queens. "You lose, I'm sorry to say."

"So I do," she answered sadly. She slid out of the lowers with a single deft movement. "Glad mine wasn't a one-piece like Diana's or you'd have had 'em before."

"Well, that ends it." The victor gatered his spoils.

Immobile, and all stony-still, Drew faced the unadorned glory of Lee. Somehow, it was less exalting than it had seemed on those nights.... Somehow, her body became a bare, a naked thing, its wonder lessened by the presence of six others.... Even though they were all, all except Bill, as innocent of clothes as she, a super-substantial glow had died out of her quintessential form.... Invisible sun within her....Within him....Within nobody....

"No, it isn't over yet, I've one more chance," Helione drawled leisurely. For a moment, and a moment in which a burst of blood roared through Drew's veins, ebbing away and leaving him finally dry, all dry and withered and ice, an awful expression whipped across her features, and she stared at Gavin, lust and cruelty, diabolism and hope, challenge and fear, pride, anxiety, sensuous stimulation and drunken bravado, feline initiative and softness and hardness, even shame, commingling with evil so transcendent that it was wholly extramoral into the awry oneness of her innumerable self.

"I'll wager divine me as you put it against your winnings and all your own things!"

Bill looked at her lazily. "I don't think so. You're not yourself and I won't accept the offer." Did he sneer to egg her on, wondered Drew.

"I know what I'm doing perfectly well. Of course, if you prefer to be sure of remaining the winner, I suppose you will, but I thought that gentleman gamblers always gave the loser another chance. I'm right, aren't I?" The polite timbre of her tone cut like a poisoned razor blade.

"O.K. with me. What do the rest of you think?"

"It's her funeral. Let her do what she wants," was the consensus of opinion. This promised a thrilling climax to the party. Bob and Dora, who had been about to prepare snacks and sandwiches, stopped in a hurry.

"It can't go on, she's under the weather. I'll take her home." Was that far voice his? Drew questioned himself.

"Speak for yourself. I'm gambling and I'll take care of me." Were those sharp words hers? he speculated. They had an alien ring, and they came from foreign spaces.

"Would you like to deal?" asked Bill.

"All right. Then it's understood I wager me — "

"Meaning?"

"I bet my, mmm, last favor, shall we say? against everything." Her voice vibrated, her tinkly laugh chimed up anew.

"To be paid, when?"

"Oh, I suppose it'll need to be here and now since it's part of the game. That is, if I lose."

"I don't expect you to."

"I don't too!"

She dealt slowly, precisely. Her old-young fingers dipped to her cards and raised them. Her face lighted as she examined the spread. "I'll take two," she decided.

"I'll have the same," answered Bill. He wore an appearance of casual interest. The cards fell neatly by his knees. He scooped them up.

"What do you have?" A tremor dwelt all over Lee.

"What's in your hand?"

They laid the cards down simultaneously. Lee held jacks and tens, Bill turned over three leering kings.

"Well, I'm very much afriad that it looks as if I lose me. Do be kind if you must collect," wailed Lee in confusion.

She glided to the studio-couch, falling upon it and rolling over on her back. The seducer followed. Beside the couch he tossed his orange and charcoal pyjamas with the swastika on the upper. Expertly, he proceeded. There was not even the movement of a muscle from the reclining girl. One arm hung across her forehead, and she seemed to be resting, but her breasts were taut, and tense the curves of stomach and thigh. Her face paled, then flooded with color. The scar leaped out, then faded away. On the glowing pallor of her cheeks, it now burned like a thread of corruption, and in the touseled waste of her hair, the myriad sherry and port and winey shades darkened against shadows on the wall.

Only the sound of heavy breathing. Only shadows that did not move. Gavin had a mole on his left shoulder. Someone stirred. Drew saw without turning that the scene had roused Pudge. While the others watched the decadent tableau, he busily induced an ipsation, with fingers like grubs.

"Enjoying yourself?" It was a reed-like whisper. Fury and madness and writhing torture deprived it of tone. Even thus, while whispering in darkness, Drew did not tear his eyes from the loathly frieze.

The fat one bared his teeth. "Yeah," came a vicious answer. "I'm enjoying myself, a lot more than you. How do you like it?"

Drew stared glassily ahead, as in those nightmares he had experienced long ago. This was the terror that walks by night, the evil dream from which there is no escape, the black void where no sun shines for no woman comes but she means nothing at all nothing to me and it is not she it is a lamia that has taken her form and i only dream hideous dreams and i know that i sleep yet suffer the horror of all that happens till i wake tomorrow glad that dreams do not come true if they did i would take to drink drinks like a lot of ants they rush around all ants on the floor drunk with fiery stuff burning around her and flames in the wind and her screams above it till she didnt have any clothes on what why little boys should never see a girl naked an hour or two in bed not meaning any harm othello no harm in a friendly game theres no reason to kill why youre not mad or youd kill you love each man kills the thing he loves and the gods whom the gods would destroy they first make mad with love but i do not love her i do not know her i never saw her before she would not deceive me if i knew her he knows her he has her she is his not mine he is the man mad men are deceived even in their flatteries above the sun invisible sun within us and a woman like the sun but the sun went out out damned spot red as blood on her face oh faces of darkness and light no they divide the course of time a quarter of twelve a quarter i should have dropped a dollar if i had it father time an hour or two not meaning any harm fooling around like the mad fool an end but no beginning plague his riddles an end has passed i did not see her i did not see them i did not see it i only dreamed all mad to kill in darkness they came fingers and talons out of the cellar fingers after her a pair of fives jacks no bill it was all his all of her so lovely if we had only left you can go if you like but im staying and she stayed if we had only gone gone gone her clothes and her body so fair and her hair bobbed bob kissed her bill bob kissed diana no i did diana her mouth was sweet like a plum i will phone her tomorrow and drive past lee and kiss her or sven no svens married now bill

can take her and ill get diana and well go on a picnic and there
ill leave them so diana and i will love while lee watches and
shell see what i saw till she goes mad well both be mad and ill
kill time kill him kill her kill kill kill three times and out i cant
kill not even myself ah thats it i was meant to live to kill them
and not myself alone so lee and ill be alone not alone with
dreams while i cant forget not alone well go together lets go
now its getting late you can go if you like but im staying its getting late a quarter of twelve ten minutes of twelve and sooner
too late to follow fool too late but if the car should have an accident daniel and mary waiting and who would know why off the
road or into a tree an accident so easy to kill all of them all of
her hair scar eyes breasts body teeth how it hurt and the
braces black as sin the bracers i shouldnt have drunk so much
all black forever and forever beyond the stars as black as sin
no sin shes not mine i dont own her ive no claim on her i only
love her no sin but its black as the braces for such a long time
year after year while it hurt black hurt and it still hurts i cant
bear it i cant berenice but shes gone gone all her clothes and
the flames around her as she lay on the couch and rolled over
and spread her legs for all to see as bill came bill kill it rhymes
bill kill but how not gas or poison or gun they wont work three
times and out if only they had worked so i wouldnt be here now
but im not here i dream im somewhere else asleep i didnt see
him i didnt see her i didnt see anything i only dreamed it was
bill kill not quick but slow for hours and days like the chinese
glass tinkling what a laugh ha ha ha up the scale chinese a slit
at a time paper thin and a drop of acid a minute and a hot iron
on his skin every hour till he howls and goes mad not that ill
not be mad ill make him mad while he dies for days with her
beside me but i do not want her i do not love her she is his
beside him a slice at a time shell watch him die with every drop
ill enter her till he howls and goes mad and when hes dead
shell follow a slice at a time to scar her scar like a line of fire
and the wind howled but they ran so i stayed till they came he

came and i watched fool that i was what time is it brother what has an end but no beginning he howled the wind whipped the flames poor girl poor flame life is a pure flame and life is a poor flame and we live by an invisible gun sun pun within us i guess its sun it doesnt matter now its too late unless i wake up but i wont it was too real for a dream and too mad for truth ill not go mad that would leave them together too long how long or lord no i don't believe in god how long has it gone on gone all her clothes and they watched while bill won kill one kill both kill kill kill for tomorrow we die no use living today so tonight we die and well sleep sleepless with cold commemorative eyes and then well be to be or not to be lee but diana shed be jealous if i loved diana tomorrow ill call her and diana and i will make love till shes mad but maybe shell turn to bill instead and leave me i dont believe it but nothing matters shes his already he won by chance its all chance from birth to death birth what if shes pregnant and comes to me but bills the one and she can go to him as he came to her if she is if she isnt she can go to him when her count shows trouble i didnt count i wont be missed in it but shell come to me she always does no i dont want her shes gone i dont love her she does not exist its a nightmare and ill wake tomorrow but i saw it the talons following and the trees like gravestones but ill wake from sleep only the sleep eternal in an eternal night not night not night like this and her so lovely waiting for him i couldnt bear it so bare and beautiful and all for him she didnt mind there always was farther to go no farther i cant go on forever i cant bear it bare barren pregnant if she is it serves her right for having the crust i asked for bread and they threw me a crust to preserve me preservations beneath the moon thy breasts are as twin moons and thy belly as an heap of wheat for im for him to reap for him to rape while the fool looks on for he loves her but i do not love her she loves him and the scar flaming scarlet harlot that she is and i the fool you were right brother i wont think of her for hes taken her steak smothered in mushrooms roast baby pig reminds me of pudge chops how he licked his chops when he won her and she paid she would she does what she says but she says what she wants and what she wants she gets i shouldnt have given so much she knows that im hers and whatever she does ill forgive ill not forgive or forget i was a fool to keep on after a year ago i should never have gone back on her back waiting all black like outer space the deeper you go the more there is the more you know her and shes never the same ill never know her but i dont want to now even if shes deep as the well of democritus and wise as the witch of endor and her hair flaming red red mists like the red snow all red as a harlots house atmosphere of lust even as the rug is enticement to seduction in doras house house of lust the color of madness all red ill not be mad id sooner die an accident so easy off the road into the ditch or a tree

"Drew! Watch where you're driving! You almost hit that wall!"

"Where?"

"Be careful. Watch the road."

"Oh, sure, where?"

Drew looked around, shaking his head to clear away the throbbing fog. A lamppost shone wobbily nearby. The car was halted. Must have stopped when she cried out. How did they happen to be here? Must be on the way home. Party break up? No memory. Must have drunk too much. Mouth burned. From black coffee? Funny if they had had food and coffee and he didn't remember taking any. Oh well.

"I'm frightened of the way you're driving, honey."

"I'll go careful, I'm all right."

"Are you sure? You don't sound as if you meant it."

"That's all right, never mind. My head's better."

He drove on. Lampposts blurred by in endless lines that met vaguely far ahead. Try as he would, he could not catch up with them. Their meeting point must be farther away than it seemed.

The fog in his mind slowly cleared. The weight of his heart deadened him and yet he could feel it pounding heavily again, thud, thud, thud, as the wild evening jumbled itself crazily in retrospect to snatches of conversation, the sweet lips of Lee, Diana, a girl posing as Venus, bits of memory, braidless hairs, Bob consummating the marriage ritual with someone, comments, rhapsodies about the girl's charms, feverish faces over cards, dancing to slinky rhythms, the seduction of Lee while they watched Bill and cauldrons boiled dry in the black inferno of his thoughts.

He became aware of pressure against his side. He saw without turning his head that Lee was leaning toward him. The smile of an angel or a panther, the unmistakable look of a woman who has been deeply loved glowed in her cheeks. She troubled him with eyes infinitely varied and amorous and abysses.

"You aren't mad at anything, are you?"

"Of course not. Why would I be?"

"Just wondered, I wanted to be sure. Do you like me?"

The lights rushed past. Drew did not answer.

"Why are you mad?"

He swung the car left, drove a little farther, and ground it to a halt in front of her house.

Before he could open the door she slid nearer and placed a hand upon him with fingers that crept erotically into his palm. "I wouldn't have gone through with it if you hadn't made me so angry when you kissed Diana. Why did you do that, honey?"

She lay against him, and a sad fire warmed the ice of his veins. He did not move. He trembled in utter demoralization. She gazed up into his face like a lithe animal waiting to be caressed.

"Kissed her? And who began that?"

No reply. A silken cheek stroked his shoulder.

"Good God, aren't you ever satisfied? Isn't one man enough for you in a night?" It was a strange sound, the tone of a howl that emerged as a whisper of discarnate fury.

Her eyes flickered in lazy protest. "Oh, that didn't count, darling, you know it. I don't like him. That was only part of the game. I had to play fair and be a sport, didn't I? Besides, it wouldn't have happened if you had taken me home earlier, that's what you should have done."

"I tried to for all the good it did."

"I don't remember. I would have loved it if it had been you. I made believe it was." Scent of perfume, siren eyes and lure of a lyrical voice, fragrance of her, body of passion and Circe.

He deliberately weakened. I will kiss her coldly and casually, then turn away and escort her to the door. I will say goodnight and make no mention of seeing her again. She will have the kiss she wants, and that is all, only that, he thought....

The pressure of her rich mouth, warm and full and inviting to a deep caress, brought the tide rising within him and the unseen incandescence. I might as well let it be a long kiss, he thought.

"Come, sit with me in the garden for a few minutes until it grows lighter. I feel a bit dizzy, thanks to you," she appealed in words as lush as persimmons with implications of ecstasy to come.

Silently he assisted her from the car. Hating his weakness, ceasing to strive desperately to break away, memory of the party a loathly worm eating at his brain, struggling until it seemed his veins would break and his heart burst and his body sunder to escape the solar fire within, he swept her into his arms. He carried her across the cool grass of the lawn and the cool stillness of preliminary dawn soothed the furnace of flesh. Still holding her, he moved to a little grassy arbor in the flower-garden. The moon paled low toward the west, a great, weary, enormous ball, like an eye dead from living and blind with dying. An eerie pallor whitened the grass to silver. The black arabesque thrown by oak and maple seemed almost to stir upon the ground. Tall and dreamlessly quiet stood the flowers. Aroma of huge peonies, spice of flowering crab, virginal narcissi, sweetness of climbing roses, fragrance of iris and black-eyed tiger-lily scented the air. Moonrays and shadow, darkness and light, mystery of fire and secret of pattern, they fused in the triumph of her eyes, or were they his that gave a spell to the world and a wonder to the good earth?

Fiercely he kissed her, and again, and more fiercely, while her arms twined around him, drawing him closer, closer, into coils of the serpent, until her breasts pressed him as though spirit and flesh attempted to merge him with her in some mystical unifaction, the frenzy of a divine oneness. Her cheeks were a blush of flame, her lips the petals of a hungry flower, her eyes the heart of an opal, herself the intoxication of the opening roses that blossomed in front of the oaks and the maples that guarded the house. He unfastened her blouse and slipped it from her, and even as he loosened the smooth suggestion that was the lower part of her pyjamas, her hands were fumbling at his waist, and the fire in her cheeks burned hotter, and with a kind of horror and madness and ecstasy, in which the desperate evening swept up like a great and terrifying blast of flame, he came to her and a sound like a dry seed-pod rattled in his throat, and the inexhaustible loveliness of Lee writhed into molten splendor beneath him, drawing him down, down, down to immeasurable gulfs and sucking him in, in to bottomless wells.

LXIII DAYBREAK

The milkman's cart was rattling down the alley when Drew reached home. The newsboy was already crossing lawns to deliver the morning paper. The sun was up and sparrows chattered.

He left the car in front. He was too exhausted to put it away. Wearily he entered the house and climbed upstairs. His pyjamas were half off when he arrived at the top. He walked to the bathroom and removed all of them. Knowing he would probably be freshened to an extent where he might find it impossible to sleep, he yet stood under a cold shower for several minutes. Needles like ice and fire drove against his skin. The water streamed out at full pressure. It poured off his shoulders and ran down his legs.

Like a symbol, the shower appeared to cleanse him without and within, as though he had washed away a dual coating of soot.

LXIV TONGUES

"Well, if it isn't Drew! How are you? I haven't seen you in weeks."

"Hello, Sven, how's yourself? What brought you downtown at this hour of the morning?"

"I'm fine, thanks. Jene wanted me to buy some things and here I am."

"Aren't you ever going to finish that novel of yours and begin seeing people again?"

"Sure, sure, but I'm also a married man, don't forget, and you know how it is."

"Not being married, I can't say that I do."

"Well, let that pass, but from all I hear, you don't need to be married."

"Yes?"

"Don't look so innocent, I'm no censor! Or if your feelings are hurt, I'm sorry I said anything. Forget it."

"Really, I don't quite follow you. What are you driving at?"

"Why, it was some damn party or other that you were at recently where you raised hell."

"This is getting interesting. What makes you think so? I was at a party all right, but it seems to me I did about as well as I could under the circumstances."

"I should say you did! You couldn't have done better!"

"I wish you would explain. We must be talking at cross purposes. Forget my feelings and tell me the answer to the riddle."

"As I got it, it was like this. Jene had a couple of girl friends over last night to talk about babies and things so I went down to hear the symphony while they were settling the milk and diaper problem and afterwards I ran into Pudge — Jack O'Tief, you know him. We both wanted a cup of coffee, so we wandered into a one-arm joint and got to talking about this and that. He was telling me about this party and it must have been just about the worst brawl thrown in these parts for some time from all I gather, what with strip poker and the Aphrodite business and the rest. Anyway, it seems you and Lee were pretty well fried to the gills and made a bet that you won and seduced her while they all cheered. You should have heard Pudge's description, I don't think the original lost a bit in his telling."

"Me?"

"That's the story I got."

"Are you sure?"

"Absolutely. Himmel, what would be the point of my trying to make you hot and bothered for nothing? Of course, I've only his say-so to go on, and since I wasn't among those present, that's all I know. Did he exaggerate?"

"Not as much as Munchausen, but enough. I won't mention any names though it's wasted effort if he's been yapping around, but the episode about me is a flat lie and I'm going to tell him so. I don't know what his game is but if that's his story there's going to be hell to pay and he'll dance to some music he doesn't like. You've only my unsupported word for it, but you've known me for a long time now and — "

"Your say-so is O.K. with me, it's good as gold. I don't know O'Tief very well, only met him a few weeks ago, so I took it for granted he knew what he was talking about since he said he was at the party but you certainly ought to know what you did."

"He was there, but he must have been cross-eyed, and aside from that, he hasn't any right to be slimy over back fences even if it were true. Wait till I corner him."

"Don't be too nasty, Drew. Your temper has pretty well ruined you a couple of times."

"Yes, I know it, but I can't let slander like that go unchallenged. I think I'll barge over to his place right now before he does any more damage."

"I can save you the trouble. When I was talking to him last night, he said something about having breakfast with Lee today at the Carson Grille. As a matter of fact, he seemed to be bragging about it. Personally, I can't see why a kid as fine as she is, whatever he says about the party, should bother with him, but you never can tell. Anyway, you might find them both there now, and I'll just forget that he said anything last night."

"Thanks for the tip, Sven, and I hope you make a good Sphinx."

"But watch your step. You look all in. And don't start something you can't finish. I don't want to be Sunday-schoolish but I've lived longer and I know the ropes a good deal better than you. Give me a ring or drop over if you want to talk about it or need any help."

"I will. I'll be dashing off now — see you later."

LXV JANUS

"Just a minute, Pudge, I'd like a word with you."

"I can't stop now. Breakfast took longer than I thought and I'm late for an appointment."

"All right, what are you doing for lunch?"

"I'm engaged."

"After lunch, then?"

"Sorry, but I'll be busy all afternoon."

"I'm anxious to see you some time today, for only a few minutes."

"I'm afraid it can't be managed. I've got a full day on my hands and I won't have a second to spare."

"I think it would be wise if you found time."

"Threats, hey? Well, threats don't go down with me."

"It was merely a suggestion for your own good."

"It doesn't make sense. What's eating you? What do you want to see me about?"

"You know damned well."

"If I did, I wouldn't ask."

"Did you tell Sven that I was the one who made Lee at the party a couple of nights ago?"

"Of course not. He must have balled the story all up."

"So you did tell him about the party and — "

"Nuts! I can't stop to talk now. I'm late already."

"When will you have time?"

"I'm awfully busy this week."

"How about Sunday?"

"We're moving out to the lake then for the summer."

"In other words, you're afraid to face the music."

"You must be crazy. You'll go haywire one of these days if you don't look out."

"If I do, it had better be you who watches out. Will you see me today?"

"No, I've got too much to do. I have to run along now."

Crack!

"There's plenty more where that came from. Now will you see me or must I knock the slime out of you?"

"You're as crazy as they come. I can't be bothered with a nut."

"You damned liar, you rat, you yellow-bellied snake, you cowardly garbage grub. Show some guts even if you haven't any. What's your game, trying to knife me behind my back?"

"So long. I'm late for my appointment already."

LXVI THUNDERBOLT

Monday

Mr. Drew Gordon:

There are some things which a gentleman will never do, no matter what the provocation. I will admit that I was — shall we say, indiscreet? — upon a certain occasion where others were present. Since those others were considerate enough to keep the occasion strictly a matter for ourselves, I can no longer regard you as a friend of mine. There was no excuse whatever for you to inform Sven or anyone else of what occurred. Doubtless he has now passed the story on to many people besides Pudge, but whether he has or not, the damage is done, thanks to your action. I regret that I must take this course. I see no other way to protect myself from possible future hurt at your hands. You will never never, never again have an opportunity to spread gossip about me. You may think that while men do not suffer when they are indiscreet, and if anything become a trifle more romantic, neither do women; but let a girl's reputation once be questioned, she can not regain it, and when you take from her that, you have taken from her all. I am glad that I find out the truth now, even at this late date, before I had committed myself more definitely to you, as I have occasionally — very, very infrequently — thought of doing. I trust that the knowledge of this loss will lead you to be more careful in whatever relations you may have hereafter. Pudge, at least, is a true friend in letting me know of your contemptible action. I am sorry, but I think it best to terminate our friendship. I will not be at home Tuesday evening. I have cancelled your date and accepted a new invitation. I also consider any and all other plans, which you might have made, in which I was concerned, to be definitely ended.

Helione Forrest

P.S. I have returned by parcel post the two books which you loaned me. Thank you for permitting me to read them.

H. F.

LXVII PETITION TO THE GODS

Tuesday

Dear Lee —

I beg of you to reconsider your decision. I have not informed anyone of the party, nor did I make a single reference about it to Sven, until he told me that Pudge had given him the story, and that Pudge had told him it was I, not Bill, who figured in the episode. If you doubt my word, ask Sven the source of his information. Surely you have known him long enough to accept the truth of his statement.

No man who loves you as deeply and completely as I do could be guilty of the caddish trick which you accuse me of. I can not understand why you credit the outrageous lies of Pudge, whom you have known so shortly, or why you use them as an excuse to throw me overboard. For they are lies. Do you not see that he is taking unscrupulous means to gain his end? That obviously he desires you, and is adopting without truth or honor the most underhanded means to break our relationship? If you realized how bitterly I was hurt, and surely you must realize it, you would understand that I could not possibly tell others of a situation wherein I appeared, if anything, as the queen's fool.

I do not mean to derogate you. Perhaps if I were wiser, or if I loved you less, the memory of that evening would turn me from you. God knows it ought to, but neither He nor anything on earth can obliterate my affection and esteem for you. I still hope that you will discover the truth, and that our strange, precious relation may continue as it has in the past. I have sacrificed pride, ideals, career, for you. Life itself I would gladly offer if the gift were necessary. You know this, as well as I do.

The reasons for Pudge's dishonesty, his mean and vicious falsehoods, I can only guess at, since I do not know, but there is one simple way of bringing the truth to light. I have sent notes inviting him and Sven, to join you and me at my home Friday evening. We will have complete privacy, of course, and the truth will obviously appear in short order. I invite you, for your own sake and for mine, to be present. I hope that you will be fair enough to come, and to judge impartially from the statements of all concerned who said what and to whom. This request was what I attempted to phone you about. I would think it ungracious of you to have slammed the receiver without permitting me time to say a word, but under the circumstances, I assume that you acted according to what you thought were valid reasons, as indeed they would be had I betrayed you.

Will you grant me the one last favor of accepting this invitation?

Drew

LXVIII CRUCIBLE

It was a wild morning when Drew went out to mail his letter. The latter part of June had brought a spell of hot weather. Day after day, the thermometer climbed toward a hundred, dry heat that parched lawns to yellow and made leaves droop limply on the poplars and elms. But last night it had turned cool when high winds blew out of the northeast, and now a driving rain squalled across Center City. He donned his slicker and an old hat before he left the house to itself. He walked for several blocks past rows of houses where spacious lawns, neat banks, and well-trimmed boulevards soaked up moisture, until he came to a branch post-office. He registered the letter and sent it by special delivery.

Rain whipped his face. It poured down his slicker. His trouser-cuffs were already soggy, and water sloshed in his shoes, but he paid no attention to discomfort. Driven by the maelstrom of his thoughts, goaded by the unattainable goal of his desire, tossed in tides of circumstance which had spun crazily out of his control, he stalked on, heedless of where he went, but not back to the house of desertion and death. Trees bowed in the storm, branches and leaves soughed with a sodden wail, and rain swirled endlessly out of dark skies. Hardly anyone was abroad. Like a specter he passed the few strayers, hat pulled low, and his eyes shining weirdly, and the rain glistening on his cheeks. Occasionally a lull came, occasionally the gigantic flare of lightning, and sometimes the cosmic bursting of thunder, then the rain slanted down anew, gusts tore along sidewalks, and the gutters ran full. The gale fitted his grief so well that he accepted it as natural. Here was his true home in this savage fury of sound and water.

His thoughts revolved in a closed circle. Why had Pudge lied to Sven? Pudge scarcely knew him, but knew that he and Drew were old friends. Did Pudge hope that the misinformation would carry back to Drew, as it had carried? Was he motivated solely by malice? By desire to win first favor with Lee? Why would he want her favor after that party? Or had he been so drunk that he actually confused persons and happenings? Did he seek retaliation for the caustic disgust that Drew had expressed about the exhibition which he fancied was unnoticed? Even so, why did Lee accept his assurances so readily? Why did she deny him, Drew, who had accompanied her for so long, the slightest opportunity to speak for himself? Had she tired of him? Did she seize on this as an immediate excuse to rid herself of him? Had she become so worried about her escapade that Pudge's fabrications fell on willing ears so that he was the more easily able to poison her against Drew? How could he know what their motives were? He would talk to Pudge, but Pudge took cowardly refuge in privacy. He would talk to Lee, but Lee would not listen to him. He must bring them all together. But would they come? If they came, would Pudge have won her confidence so well that she would refuse to believe even Sven? Why did she trust Pudge? What was the secret of the hold which he had suddenly obtained over her? Round and round his head whirled, seeking answers for vain questions. It would be so simple if he could only cease to love Helione. That mad eveing ought for ever to have stilled his passion. "Here lies love" should have been the words that ended it, but his emotion was stronger than reason, and truly nothing could quench the fire or power of that devotion. He had never felt that he found the full depths and recesses of her being;

always there was more to come, new facets, additional charms, the quirk of an odd belief, a flash of poetry or a lilt of song, a brilliant enthusiasm, an unexpected knowledge, appreciation of a painting, the birth of fresh ideas, the reactions of a rare and gifted intelligence, subtleties of emotional wealth, the mysterious play of brain and heart not only across the surfaces of things but true to their depths, a lyrical replenishment that made it impossible for him to exhaust her capacities; and the more he found, the farther he was drawn into her and enveloped in ever widening and closelier clinging webs; while the spontaneity of her responses, helped by her extraordinary physical appeal, united with their unpredictable variety, meeting his in a unifaction as innumerable as the suns of the universe.

Somewhere, sometime, he became aware of specific surroundings. He must have walked for miles. The blocks of houses lay behind, and behind him the stolid certainty of cities. Of persons or dwellings there were none in sight. He stood upon forested cliffs that banked the American River. He could not see the opposite shore. A solid wall of rain intervened, slashing from infinite wastes. In front of him the bank dropped steeply a hundred yards. All around was the sound of running water, the dreary swish of leaves, and the wail of grinding branches. A huge log lay beside him. It was green with moss. Angleworms crept at his feet. Aside from this one lowly creature, no other living things were in sight. Hidden were birds and insects, even the squirrels had taken sanctuary. The world was a desolation of mad rain. The wind lashed it against his face. Thunder muttered like the mirthless laughter of gods, the chuckle of a stone giant.

He was standing by an oak of enormous girth. Unconsciously he raised his fists and beat upon the wet bark, as if, like Chaucer's protagonist, he pounded at the door of mother earth, crying to let him in.

LXIX HERE LIES LOVE

Tuesday night

Mr. Drew Gordon:

Kindly do not attempt to communicate with me again.

I must reject your invitation.

I took the liberty of phoning Jack and found, as I suspected, that you and Sven are engaged in the dubious task of trying to scheme against us. I will not be a party to any such cheap tactics, coming, as they do, so closely after your recent scandal-mongering. Jack said that he would not even bother answering your note. He advised me to do the same, but I desire to make my attitude clear for all time.

It may interest you to know that, as a result of your malicious attitude, I have allowed him to read your love-letters and other communications to me, to speak of them wherever he pleases and however he pleases. I trust that this will serve as a lesson to you. If you wish to spread gossip, you will now understand that two may play the same game.

I never want to see you again or have anything further to do with you. Do I make myself sufficiently clear? Any communications from you will go unopened and unanswered. I consider the friendship closed.

Sincerely yours,
Helione Forrest

LXX PRELUDE TO IMMORTALITY

i havent any right to take her life but i tried to kill myself and it
didnt work so i must have been meant to live but there isnt any
use living without her so i must have been meant to kill us both
that would end it all and wed be together for ever and for ever
and no one could come between us through all eternity life is
a pure flame but death is eternal and there wont be any worries
and well both have peace and i wont know or care what people
think because ill be with her again for ever and for ever and
they cant do anything about it or stop me till were free of flesh
and evil and sorrow they might say i had no right to do it but
ill not hear them did she have a right to reject me for a pack of
lies when she knew what it would do to me but i have no right
to her only love and its neither right nor wrong it just is still i
ought to kill him but no if i began that there would be bill and
the artist and pudge and how many others the whole world
cant be wrong and i right though they believed ptolemy and he
was wrong round and round without end the fool an end but no
beginning there is no end and there was a beginning yes there
is an end and it will hurt them all and hurt him most to keep
on living when we are dead and she for ever beyond his reach
and i laughing laughing laughing at him madly from beyond
the grave where he wont have guts enough to follow to come
back and see the expression on his face while he goes through
hell but he wont hes too fat and will satisfy his desires else-

where while bill finds a new one and they both can but i cant
there is no other we two were alone and there is no coming
back she doesnt deserve to die so swiftly but slow death is torture and who am i to say that shes not been hurt as i have perhaps she has then it would be a blessing for us both and she
need not know to pass in sleep or dreams will she be awake or
asleep so late she must be sleeping her last sleep in sleep or
dreams she doesnt deserve to die nor i she does i do ah god
what else is there i cant go on or ill be mad perhaps i am
already i dont care im beyond caring i would kill myself but it
isnt even worth trying because ive already tried three times
and it didnt succeed i cant be meant to go on living because
theres nothing to live for without her and mary dead and
daniel dead and even married and there are no others alone
where can i turn where can i go alone but they would be waiting for us beyond they cant be far ahead so recently no i dont
believe in spiritualism and god there is no god there is nothing
beyond but blackness and that for ever is better than this for
even a day no worry no pain no sorrow no gladness no joy no
love no hope no faith no fear no lee no drew no anything all
black yet if i stayed here there might be hope she might relent
no hope ive tried everything and theres nothing left you infernal gods and demons of men and bitches parading as women
not lee she was so lovely and all this while two years but no it
was never meant to be with the artist i wonder who he was and
bill and pudge and myself so many a dog would be more than
i or less i dont know which a dog or a god but there is no god
and a blind universe cant really mean anything for life would
have meaning but it doesnt no god no purpose no reason i
might as well get rid of this hurt once and for all but why
should it hurt if there is no reason no answer but death what is
it like but it makes no difference for i dont know now and i
wont know then but there will be nothing to worry about and
no hurting within so that you cant sleep or eat or think and not
having nightmares or hating faithless friends not friends and

not breaking your heart for anyone you cant be with and not
believing people who betray you and not having anything
except sleep and peace and night for ever and for ever and her
there too it wuld be perfect if there was a hereafter of some
sort where we could always go on with nobody else around
and just us lying on hilltops and walking in fields of flowers
with sunny skies and laughing as we used to but i know it isnt
so i wish i could makebelieve it was but i know it isnt because
ive learned so much yet it would solve everything if i could
believe and shift the burden on to god like other people till i
ceased to worry but i dont believe and i wont deceive myself
only there is a mystery to things and why they are what they
are no help there ill have to settle it myself and theres only one
way i can except to forget her and start all over but ill never forget and it isnt once in a lifetime or a century that two like us
meet if only shed see me i could try to straighten things out
but she wont not after putting my letters in his hands the liar
the thief cruel cruel oh gods and demons and furies why do
you select me instead of him what hold can he have over her
and has he known her long but she believes him so she must
be tired of me i wonder why perhaps i loved her too well and
gave her so much that she took it as little and wanted more but
it doesnt matter for life will be over soon and ill never need
worry again why was i born i didn't ask to be and id rather not
ever have lived than gone through this hell i don't suppose it
was their fault but it wasnt mine either whose was it not gods
becuase there is no god not anybodys i guess just fate and an
ecstasy ending in pain just crazy chance in a world where anything happens except what you want and nobodys to blame not
i or pudge or lee or daniel and mary or bill or the artist or god
or other people or anybody or anything its just luck or accident
and mines been all bad but it wont be from now on theres no
other solution might admit of a wide solution not true whatever
sir thomas thought life is a pure flame and we live by an invisible sun within us but even the sun must die and what if the

other sun goes out theres nothing left unless you want to just be with the stamp of defeat on you whatever became of my stamp collection still in the attic i suppose where i put it away in the trunk those skeletons fingers when i turned the light on and the mummy rising an evil dream perhaps this all is and ill wake tomorrow and ill wake in eternity no i wont wake at all ever and that will be so much better no worries no pain no sorrows only the sleep eternal in an eternal night thats what it was an eternal night and the everlasting drinks and the atmosphere a lewd house house of eastern sin i should have known better than to go but lee asked me and i weakened then i shouldnt have taken so much till it paralyzed me and he won the bet why cant i go mad and jumble it all but ill never forget that picture no use to keep on with that in my mind and lee gone but well both be gone i shouldnt have sneered when he played with himself but no one else was watching and i had to say something or do something before i went mad perhaps this is his revenge if im not mad *"All out! End of the line!"* i wish id rented a car again so the trolley ride wouldnt be necessary but im almost there what if someones home the familys away for the night darling are you sure its safe the familys away for the night darling we have the place to ourselves till marion comes back what a lovely back she had nice moons around polaris perhaps i might have made lee jealous if id got interested in diana but no if she doesnt love me for my own sake i dont want her to for that reason and anyway its too late now *"Fares, please!"* good connections anyway like lee and bill or the artist or pudge if pudge is there or bill i wont think of it now ill wait and see and if they are ill decide what to do then i hate to do it but i dont see any other way out we could have had such a wonderful life together when my plays were successful travelling and writing and drawing and meeting interesting people and making names for ourselves and making love to her and having books and paintings and a house and things of our own and now it will never be that would have been nice maybe when we were fifty and had done what we wanted and experienced everything and our children were starting out in the world but theyd have had a better life no we wouldnt have any children oh well i guess whatever happens is for the best since it cant be worse i could still go back and think it over some more but i wont im tired of thinking and im worn out with feeling but what if she isnt home what if somebody else is there what if shes staying at miss tibbs place again oh well i wont worry till i see and find out and if everythings all right it will be over in a minute and i will never again hurt and hurt and hurt inside only the sleep eternal in an eternal night

LXXI INVISIBLE SUN

Quietly Drew entered the house. He felt as though the nightmares which he had lived long ago had returned to plague him, yet the bare, worn simplicity of the parlor, with its eternal light burning and papers carelessly scattered on lounge and floor, seemed real. He hesitated, but there was no sound except a snore from Mr. Forrest upstairs. More stealthily than he had ever thought possible, he paced across the dining-alcove to his right, until he stood at Lee's room. He lisened at the door. *Is there anybody there? said the traveller, and his horse champed the grasses of the forest's ferny floor.* He heard no movement, no stir within. Could she be away? He had seen from outside the light in her room, and she must be here. Had she heard his ghostly entrance? Did she wait with beating heart to see what intruder came in the dead of night? Was he about to interrupt another amour as on that evening ages past? Would it be Bill again? Or a newcomer? He drew the gun from his pocket, the automatic which he had bought only today. He held it, loaded and ready, in his hand as he opened the door.

Helione was lying on her bed, asleep, though fully dressed. Her drawing board with an unfinished sketch, bottles of ink, and materials lying in disorder, suggested that she had flung herself down for a rest. One arm lay palm up. With the acute perception that is sometimes active in circumstances of stress, he noticed that a spot of ink blackened her forefinger, and a cut

marred her thumb. The calm of slumber tranquillized her face. Gone was its mask of cosmetics. Vanished were the disguises of conscious control. The features of a child remained, innocent of wrong, devoid of guile. Even in the grip of the forces that drove him, he wondered how such purity could persist there, after these last five days. Within him rose a powerful impulse to bed over her and bless her with one kiss before eternity, but he knew that it would lead to others, and that his flesh would weaken until his spirit was lost.

A dreadful turmoil surged through him. As he raised the weapon, his hand trembled. Only by an exertion of greatest will did he steady himself, while the frantic boiling of cauldrons and screaming of gales inside him brought veins out on his forehead.

He pulled the trigger.

A roar as of infinite Niagaras burst forth and thundered in his ears. A dark stain appeared in Helione's right temple, and a quiver possessed her body. By some reflex, the lids of her eyes flew open, and her dying pupils looked at him. A faint, sweet smile, wholly free of earth and trouble, hovered upon her mouth. In a daze, he stooped over her still form. Tenderly and lovingly he kissed the lips from which no breath came. With that gesture, the storm and terrors and furies passed away. A radiance welled up, a white and searing fire that purified. He felt like one escaped from prison, knowing that no hunters will follow. *A quarter of twelve, ten minutes to twelve, and sooner.* Far away, echoing across eons of time and cosmic leagues of space, he detected the sound of running feet, a patter that approached but would never come nigh. The sadness, the suffering, and the loneliness dropped from his face like films. The light in his eyes burned brighter and intenser; and faded mysteriously, leaving only a coal on its way to a cinder and to ash. His face quieted to repose as gentle as that of the dead girl. All the burden and weary ways of living disappeared. Only the eternal and unquenchable spirit remained; and in that sole instant of his life, his countenance exceeded beauty, with a commemorative prelude to immortality, the implacable strength of being, and the dispassionate appraisal of deity.

Once more, he raised his weapon and fired.

Across the western world, an old moon sank, and on the eastern horizon, an old sun rose, but those who entered saw the rising and setting of an invisible sun.

September, 1932 — January, 1933.

NOTES

Abbreviations used in the notes:
- C   Donald Wandrei, *Colossus,* ed. Philip J. Rahman and Dennis E. Weiler (Minneapolis: Fedogan & Bremer, 1989)
- *CP*   Donald Wandrei, *Collected Poems,* ed. S. T. Joshi (West Warwick, RI: Necronomicon Press, 1988)
- *DD*   Donald Wandrei, *Don't Dream,* ed. Philip J. Rahman and Dennis E. Weiler (Minneapolis: Fedogan & Bremer, 1997)
- *SS*   Donald Wandrei, *Sanctity and Sin: The Collected Poems and Prose Poems of Donald Wandrei* (New York: Hippocampus Press, 2008)

Dead Titans, Waken!

p. 5: Via Dei and Via Diaboli are Latin for "God's highway" and "Devil's highway," respectively. The Latin was supplied by H. P. Lovecraft (see Afterword).

p. 6: The Great Plague occurred in England in 1664–65. Daniel Defoe's historical novel *A Journal of the Plague Year* (1722) treats of the event.

p. 14: The transformation of the Grants may have been suggested by the celebrated transformation of Helen Vaughan at the conclusion of Arthur Machen's "The Great God Pan": "The blackened face, the hideous form upon the bed, changing and melting before your eyes from woman to man, from man to beast, and from beast to worse than beast..." *Tales of Horror and the Supernatural* (New York: Knopf, 1948), p. 115.

p. 29: This chapter is a slightly altered version of "A Fragment of a Dream" (*Minnesota Quarterly*, January 1926; rpt. *Recluse*, 1927 and DD).

p. 32: *susurrous:* whispering.

p. 33: *concameration:* a vaulting or vaulted roof.

p. 34: Compare this episode to the conclusions of Wandrei's poems (*SS*) "The Captive" from *Sonnets of the Midnight Hours* ("The dark, walled city slowly came in view, / The magic towers, the skyward thrusting spires, ... one savage curse I cried, / And I, and all that phantom city, died"), and "The Challenger" ("He stood at last before the citadel / That rose from out the gulfs of utter night,... And on the doors of doom, disdainful, hurled / His cosmic challenge in an alien world").

p. 35: The image of a crater ringed by mountains, usually with a tower or object at its center, is a persistant one in Wandrei's fiction, and is utilized in "The Crater" (*DD*), "The Tree-Men of M'Bwa" (*DD*), "A Race Through Time" (*C*), as well as elsewhere in this novel.

p. 38: In *The Web of Easter Island*, the use of Graham's dream as the penultimate chapter eliminates the foreshadowing role it plays in *Dead Titans, Waken!* It is interesting to note that, although the dream chapter was composed independently several years prior to the bulk of *Dead Titans* (see Afterword), Wandrei was nonetheless able to utilize elements of its imagery as foreshadowings or recapitulations: the road to the hilltop necropolis (Vadia/Isling), the mountain hollow (Easter Island crater), the funnel-like maelstrom (return of the titans), etc. These correspondences may indicate that Wandrei consciously structured his novel around this early mood-piece.

Alternatively, perhaps the dream chapter was subsumed ex post facto into *Dead Titans*, on the basis of a shared use of imagery of long-standing appeal to Wandrei ("craters," for example).

p. 55: *bruskly*: alternative spelling of "brusquely."

p. 60: *Marie Celeste*: Actually the *Mary Celeste*. This ship was found sailing off the coast of the Azores in 1872 with no one on board. The mystery has never been explained.

p. 69: *eoliths*: Certain flints found in Tertiary deposits in England, France, and elsewhere, believed to be the earliest traces of human handiwork.

p. 69: *Predmost race*: Referring to a region in Moravia where the remains of Upper Paleolithic man were found. *Grimaldi race*: Remains of prehistoric man excavated at the Grimaldi cave near Menton, France, in 1901; they date to roughly 30,000 years ago. *Heidelberg man*: Remains found near Heidelberg, Germany, in 1907; they are thought to date to about 400,000 years ago. *Eoanthropus*: The name given to a member of a genus represented by what was formerly believed to be the remains of a prehistoric man; named initially as the genus of the Piltdown man. *Piltdown man*: A hoax perpetrated in 1912, when there was found near the small English town of Piltdown a human brain case remarkably like that of modern man but with a jawbone resembling an ape's (the jawbone was later ascertained to come from a different species). The hoax was not exposed until 1953.

p. 69: *Rhodesian man*: Fossil remains discovered at Broken Hill, Northern Rhodesia, in 1921, usually considered to be an early type of *Homo sapiens*. *Pithecanthropus Erectus*: A name formerly given to *Homo erectus*, which includes Java and Peking man. *Peking man*: Remains discovered in northern China in 1927; they date to roughly 500,000 years ago. *Sivapithecus*: The ancestor of the ourangutan.

p. 69: *Propliopithecus*: A name given by Ernst Haeckel to the earliest known forerunners of gibbons, from remains found in Fayûm, Egypt. *Notharctus*: Remains of a group of lemuroids from the Lower and Middle Eocene in North America.

p. 80: *Clavilux*: see note on *Invisible Sun* (p. 211).

p. 95: This image, eliminated in *The Web of Easter Island*, was foreshadowed by Graham's dream (Ch. III).

p. 102: Teuffelskopf: The compound in German would translate to "Devil's Head" — a rather peculiar name for an insane asylum.

p. 107: By the odd expression "what I fear to be and for ever chaos" Wandrei pesumably means: "…what I fear will for ever remain chaos."

p. 109: "Myrna" is an adaptation of the prose poem "The Delirium of the Dead," first published in *DD* (329–32).

p. 109: Christabel is the central figure in Samuel Taylor Coleridge's unfinished poem of that name. Lesbia is a character appearing in many of Catullus' poems; she is probably based upon Clodia, the wife of Q. Metellus Celer, with whom Catullus presumably had an actual affair.

p. 118: *manusensus*: Evidently a neologism coined here by Wandrei, meaning "touching by hand."

p. 121: *FRS*: Fellow of the Royal Society. *FRAS*: Fellow of the Royal Astronomical Society.

p. 122: This suggestive linkage to the fictional creations of Lovecraft was eliminated in *The Web of Easter Island*. See Wandrei's statement, "I've never written anything that could really be put in the Cthulhu Mythos…. The Web came closest with a couple of chapters vaguely Cthulhuan" (letter to August Derleth, 11 [17?] October 1967; ms., State Historical Society of Wisconsin).

p. 122: The conceptions expressed here (the notions of the relativity of time and the possibility that our universe is only an atom in a larger super-universe) are also found in Wandrei's landmark tale of science fiction, "Colossus" (1934).

p. 123: It is astonishing that the elegant explanation Wandrei provided in *The Web of Easter Island* for the subterranean mound of bones — that the chamber was used by the titans for sampling human life-plasm over the aeons, as a gauge of the progress of their great "experiment" — was not part of his original conception of the novel. Evidently the image of the bone-mound preceded, in Wandrei's imagination, any rationale for its existence.

p. 128: *anus*: Latin for "ring" (specifically, an iron ring for the feet), evidently referring to the fact that the statues are up in a circular or ringlike configuration.

p. 128: *Roggewein*: Jacob Roggeveen, a Dutch admiral who discovered Easter Island in 1722. He gave it its name because he came upon it on Easter Sunday.

p. 132: This scenario (of being an atom under observation in a microscope) is exactly the situation that the protagonist of "Colossus" finds himself: *"The White Bird reposed on the slide of a microscope!... He had burst through the atom that was his universe and had emerged on a planet of a greater universe, a superuniverse!"* (*C* 136).

p. 136: In Wandrei's "Something from Above," a story that once formed some part of *Dead Titans, Waken!*, an alien beam travels to earth and leaves a circular hole in the clouds in its wake.

p. 138: Compare this image to one found in "The Crystal Bullet," in which a mysterious object fallen from space is bathed in a spectral glow: "It was a pulsing light, rigid in outline, but through whose depths ebbed and returned a rhythmic wave that started from the crystaline object.... [T]he green tide pulsed out in mounting waves" (*C* 369). Later, through this light, "shapes and forms of things which had never walked upon earth by day or night or hovered in dreams were issuing forth..." (*C* 372).

p. 140: *color out of space*: An obvious reference to Lovecraft's celebrated 1927 story.

p. 144: *monopyre*: A neologism coined here by Wandrei; meaning uncertain, but presumably referring to the solitary statue at the center of the crater.

p. 145: *necrolith*: Another neologism, evidently meaning "death-rock."

p. 146: *milliard*: A thousand million [years].

p. 148: *rorgled* and *crarking*: Wandrei's neologisms, evidently intended onomatopoeically.

p. 158: The paragraph may reflect Wandrei's admiration for Olaf Stapledon's *Last and First Men* (1930), which depicts the history of the human race over the course of the next two billion years. In later years, Wandrei listed this book as "basic... in choosing a science fiction library," calling it "perhaps the best novel of science fiction thus far written" (letter to Derleth, 27 July 1948; ms., State Historical Society of Wisconsin).

p. 159: Wandrei employs the notion of "clouds from space" in "The Red Brain" (*C*) and "Black Fog" (*C*).

p. 159: A comet passing earth brings destruction in Wandrei's "The Fire Vampires" (*DD*); in "A Race Through Time" (*C*), he postulates the far-future annihilation of human civilization after the passage of a rogue "dark star."

p. 159: Wandrei uses this same inane notion, that calendar names and conventions will persist into the far future, in "A Race Through Time" (*C*), where an abandonded ruin yields up a newspaper dated September 1,995,851.

p. 159: suicide chamber: It is probable that this conception was inspired by Robert W. Chambers' "The Repairer of Reputations" (in *The King in Yellow,* 1895), a story set in a future New York where euthanasia chambers are commonplace.

p. 160: *triunarization*: Another neologism, presuambly derived from triune ("three in one") and referring evidently to the fusion of the three "tangibles" (length, breadth, and thickness) into one.

p. 160: Sir James Jeans and Arthur Eddington were British astrophysicists. Wandrei is probably referring to Jeans' *The Universe around Us* (1929) and Eddington's lecture, "The Expanding Universe" (delivered at the Physical Society on 6 November 1931 and published in the *Proceedings of the Physical Society* for 1 January 1932). Eddington's book, *The Expanding Universe* (1933), appeared after Wandrei had completed the first draft of his novel.

p. 161: five hundred milliards ago: This figure would actually be 500 billion years — somewhat of an exaggeration.

p. 162: *cryptoglyphics*: Another neologism, evidently meaning "secret hieroglyphics."

p. 165: Atalan: Perhaps intended to be seen as a corruption of Atlantis.

Invisible Sun

p. 175: "The King of the Golden River": A children's story by John Ruskin (1819–1900).

p. 177: Rolling Prairie is probably meant to stand for Le Sueur, Minnesota, where the maternal side of Wandrei's family, the Garnseys, lived, and where the Wandreis frequently visited. A favorite cousin of Wandrei's was Jack Garnsey, perhaps the model for Jake.

p. 180: *Grimm's Fairy Tales*: The celebrated compilation of fairy tales by the brothers Jakob Ludwig Karl Grimm and W. K. Grimm, first published in German in 1812–15. *The Treasure Seekers of the Andes*: A boys' book (1907) by Edward Stratemeyer. *Tales from Shakespeare*: The 1807 retelling of Shakespeare's plays for children by the English essayist Charles Lamb (1775–1834).

p. 180: *From the Earth to the Moon*: The science fiction novel by Jules Verne (1828–1905), first published in French as De la terre à la lune (1865).

p. 186: *Sea and Land*: Possibly a book (1887) by James W. Buel.

p. 191: *Can Such Things Be?*: The landmark 1893 collection of weird tales by Ambrose Bierce (1842–1914?). Howard Wandrei wrote a fine appreciation, "Bierce," *Minnesota Quarterly* 8, No. 3 (Spring 1931): 12–20; rpt. *Studies in Weird Fiction* No. 10 (Fall 1991): 31–34.

p. 194: This image appears elsewhere in the Wandrei canon, each time in conjunction with the description of a nightmare. Cf. the prose poem "Nightmare": "...in mid-air a great clawing arm reached toward him out of the darkness" (*DD* 321). Cf. also the poem "In the Attic" (*Sonnets of the Midnight Hours*): "... from out the greater dark, / The swart hand crawled, through mid-air lengthening..." (*SS* 97).

p. 195-197: A similar image can be found in the poem "The Woman at the Window" (*SS* 81) and the prose poem of the same name (*DD* 338–40). From the latter: "at dusk...the sun turned the window into fire...a sheet of blazing red...[and] limned with a hellish indistinctness the face of a woman peering out."

p. 202: *Satyricon*: The fragmentary Latin satirical novel by T. Petronius Arbiter (first century BCE). Apuleius: Lucius Apuleius (c. 123-c. 180), Latin author of the *Metamorphoses* (or *Golden Ass*) and other works. *Transactions of the Royal Philosophical Society*: Actually the *Philosophical Transactions of the Royal Society of London* (1665f.), a celebrated body of British scientific and philosophical writing. *Decameron*: The series of tales by Giovanni Boccaccio (1313–1375), written over many years but first assembled in 1349–51. *Dictionary of Occultism*: there does not appear to be any such work. Perhaps Wandrei is referring to Lewis Spence's *Encyclopedia of Occultism* (1920). Sinistrari's *Demoniality*: Luigi Maria

Sinistrari (1622–1701), *Demoniality; or, Incubi and Succubi* (first published in an English translation in 1879; translated by Montague Summers, 1927). The Latin text is available in *De la démonialité et des animaux incubes et succubes* (1875). *Vampires and Vampirism: A Book* (1914) by Dudley Wright (1868–1949). *The Time Machine*: The 1895 science fiction novel by H. G. Wells (1866–1946).

p. 203: *Berenice*: A character in Poe's story of that title (1835).

p. 205: A literal transcription of two celebrated lines from stanza 7 of "Ode to a Nightingale" (1819) by John Keats (1795–1821): "…magic casements, opening on the foam / Of perilous seas, in faery lands forlorn."

p. 208: The chapter title is clearly adapted from Lovecraft's "The Whisperer in Darkness" (1930).

p. 211: Clavilux, the musical instrument described in this chapter evidently existed at one time, and made an impression on Wandrei. He mentions it in the introduction to his first collection of shorts stories (*The Eye and the Finger* [1944]), and has the hero of his futuristic story "Colossus" play a "light-piano" (*C* 123).

p. 213: The first sentence of Poe's "The Fall of the House of Usher" (1839).

p. 213: The first seven lines of the *Aeneid* of Vergil (P. Vergilius Maro, 70–19 BCE). In James Rhoades' translation: "…Of arms I sing, and of the man who first / From Trojan shores beneath the ban of fate / To Italy and coasts Lavinian came, / Much tossed about on land and ocean he / By violence of the gods above, to sate / Relentless Juno's ever-rankling ire, / In war, too, much enduring, till what time / A city he might found him, and bear safe / His gods to Latium, whence the Latin race, / And Alba's sires, and lofty-towering Rome."

p. 213: Three sentences purporting to be from the Bible: 1) John 1:1; 2) a misquotation; the closest version is Revelation 6:10: "How long, O Lord, holy and true, dost thou not judge…

"; 3) misquotation of Song of Solomon 7:2–3: "...thy belly is like a heap of wheat set about with lilies. Thy two breasts are like two young roes that are twins."

p. 213: An unidentified couplet from an ancient Greek poem.

p. 214: Random sentences from chapter 5 of *Hydrotaphia or Urne Buriall* (1658) by the English writer Sir Thomas Browne (1605–1682), best known for *Religio Medici*.

p. 214: Si ego componi...: Tibullus, III, ii, 26

p. 217: ROTC was in fact a compulsory and very unpopular class at the University of Minnesota during the period of Wandrei's attendance.

p. 219: See the Afterword for the real basis of the incident described in this chapter. Wandrei made fictional use of this experience in his stories "The Monster from Nowhere" (*DD*), "Something from Above" (*C*), and "If" (unpublished).

p. 220: Center City: A fictionalized version of St. Paul, which should not be confused with the actual town of that name 40 miles northwest of St. Paul. Wandrei would later use that name as a stand in for St. Paul in several other stories, most notably in his "Cyrus North" mystery adventures for *Clues* magazine. For a more detailed study of the geography of Center City, and how it compares to St. Paul, see "Introducing Cyrus North" by D. H. Olson in *Pulp Vault #14* (Tattered Pages Press, 2011).

p. 232: The reference is clearly to *Weird Tales*.

p. 233: *Ebony and Crystal: Poems in Prose and Verse* (1922) by Clark Ashton Smith (1893–1961). Wandrei had first come into contact with Smith in 1924.

p. 241: The utterance by the White Queen in chapter 5 of *Through the Looking-Glass* (1871) by Lewis Carroll (1832–1898) reads: "'The rule is, jam to-morrow and jam yesterday – but never jam to-day.'"

p. 244: Walter de la Mare (1873–1956), English poet, short story writer, and novelist. Claude Debussy (1862–1918), French composer. The spelling "De Bussy" was common in the early part of the century.

p. 246: "Ode to the West Wind" (1819) by Percy Bysshe Shelley (1792–1822). "The Garden of Proserpine" is a poem by Algernon Charles Swinburne.

p. 256: *Melachrino*: A type of cigarette.

p. 257: Marie Laurencin (1885–1956), French painter and engraver.

p. 257: A slightly different version of this prose-poem has been found among Wandrei's papers, entitled "Hymn of the Deathless Two."

p. 259: Lucian Taylor is the protagonist of *The Hill of Dreams* (1907) by Arthur Machen (1863–1947). See the Afterword for the relevance of this work to Wandrei; also chapter 49.

p. 267: Ryder's *The Race Track*: A painting (1895) by Albert Pinkham Ryder (1847–1917); now at the Cleveland Museum of Art. Odilon Redon was a French artist (1840–1916). Many have compared Clark Ashton Smith's artwork to that of Redon, although Smith claimed that he knew little of Redon's work when he began his paintings.

p. 280: Perhaps an echo of Poe's "To Helen" (1831):

> Helen, thy beauty is to me
>> Like those Nicéan barks of yore,
> That gently, o'er a perfumed sea,
>> The weary, way-worn wanderer bore
> To his own native shore.
>> On desperate seas long wont to roam,
> Thy hyacinth hair, thy classic face,

> Thy Naiad airs have brought me home
>
> To the glory that was Greece,
>
> And the grandeur that was Rome.

p. 282: *Bibelot*: A magazine (1895–1914) issued by the specialty publisher Thomas Bird Mosher. Tossella: almost certainly a misspelling of Enrico Toselli (1883-1926), whose "Seranade" ranks among his most popular works. *Hydrotaphia*: by Thomas Browne (see note for page 214).

p. 284: Trimalchio is the central figure in the lengthiest surviving section (the Cena Trimalchionis or "Trimalchio's dinner") of Petronius' *Satyricon* (see note on p. 202). It recounts a lavish feast given by a wealthy businessman.

p. 284: *Hybla*: In Greek myth, an Earth goddess, specifically the protectress of bees, hence of honey.

p. 286: *Old English,* a play by George Arliss (1868–1946), dates to 1924.

p. 298: A story told by Aristophanes in Plato's *Symposium* as a (possibly jocular) account of the origin of humanity: When human beings were first created, they consisted of two halves, a male and a female; but they challenged the Olympian gods, who cut them in two, so that from that time on each half has been searching for its mate. See Plato, *Symposium* 189C – 193E.

p. 299: *The Thief of Bagdad*: The celebrated 1924 silent film starring Douglas Fairbanks, Jr.; a landmark in the use of special effects. Some of the dialogue and scene descriptions were written by the poet George Sterling (1869–1926), mentor of Clark Ashton Smith.

p. 312: *Kubla Khan*: A weird poem written in 1797 by Samuel Taylor Coleridge (1772–1834), who claimed to have dreamed more than 200 lines of the poem but could only set down about 50 when he awoke.

p. 313: Algernon Charles Swinburne (1837–1909), a leading English poet and critic of the later nineteenth century.

p. 314: "La Belle Dame Sans Merci" (1819) by John Keats. "Full Fathom Five" is an untitled song sung by Ariel in Shakespeare's *The Tempest*.

p. 319: "Atmosphere of Houses" is also the title of a story by August Derleth (*Prairie Schooner*, Spring 1932). Wandrei was apparently concerned about copying Derleth's title, writing to him (February 1, 1933): "...no point in duplicating your own fine treatment of the theme. Don't want to be subject to charge of plagiarism. This seemed the only approach I therefore might utilize" (ms., State Historical Society of Wisconsin).

p. 320: At the time this novel takes place, the ninth planet, Pluto, had not been found; its discovery in 1930 was one of the triumphs of modern astronomy.

p. 322: Michel de Montaigne (1533–1592), French essayist and philosopher.

p. 323: A reference to three novels by Thomas Hardy (1840–1928): *Jude the Obscure* (1895); *Tess of the d'Urbervilles* (1891); *The Return of the Native* (1878).

p. 326: Walter Pater (1839–1894), English essayist and aesthetician; Kenneth Grahame (1859–1932), English children's writer best known for *The Wind in the Willows* (1908). For de la Mare see note on p. 141.

p. 327: *The Memoirs of Fanny Hill*: A celebrated work of pornography (first published in 1748–49 as *Memoirs of a Woman of Pleasure*) by the English writer John Cleland (1709–1789).

p. 327: Aubrey Beardsley (1872–1898), English artist and illustrator.

p. 327: The reference is to a variety of writers: the English poets Algernon Charles Swinburne (see note on p. 313), Rupert Brooke (1887–1915), William Blake (1757–1827), and John Masefield (1878–1967), at that time the poet laureate of England; the American poets Edna St. Vincent Millay (1892–1950), Elinor Wylie (1885–1928), Walt Whitman (1819–1892), and Edwin Arlington Robinson (1869–1935); the Norwegian dramatist Henrik Ibsen (1828–1906); and the German dramatist and novelist Hermann Sudermann (1857–1928).

p. 329: A reference to Clem Haupers, celebrated regional artist and lifelong friend of Wandrei's. For his portrait of Wandrei see the inside back flap of *DD*.

p. 330: "The Listeners" is a weird poem by Walter de la Mare. The poem tells how a "Traveller" comes to a house for some unspecified purpose and knocks on the door; no one replies, but "a host of phantom listeners" senses his presence. The poem is included in de la Mare's *Collected Poems* (London: Faber & Faber, 1952), pp. 284–85.

p. 347: Edna St. Vincent Millay. See note on p. 327.

p. 356: *Tristan und Isolde* (1860), an opera by Richard Wagner (1813–1883).

p. 356: The opening line of *The Hill of Dreams* by Arthur Machen. See note on p. 259.

p. 359: A reference to a limited edition (150 signed and numbered copies) of *The Hill of Dreams* (London: Martin Secker, [1922]). Wandrei owned this edition (see Donald Wandrei to H.P. Lovecraft, 5 January 1927; ms., John Hay Library).

p. 360: The phrase "lost generation" was first coined by Gertrude Stein in a letter to Ernest Hemingway. He quoted it in the preface to *The Sun Also Rises* (1926).

p. 361: The Lotus Eaters Club was an actual social club at the University of Minnesota.

p. 363: A reference to the British novelists James Joyce (1882–1941) and D. H. Lawrence (1885–1930) and the American writer Gertrude Stein (1874–1946).

p. 364: Oswald Spengler (1880–1936), *Der Untergang des Abendlandes* (1918–22); translated as *The Decline of the West* (1926–28), a landmark work in the philosophy of history. The title translates literally to "The Decline of the Land of Evening."

p. 365: "Abdul Abulbul Amir" (1927), a song arranged by Frank Crumit (1889–1943). 2) "The Devil Is Afraid of Music", a song by Willard Robison (1894–1968).

p. 366: Christopher Robin is a character created by A.A. Milne in *Winne-the-Pooh* (1926) and other volumes.

p. 366: Peter Pan is the central character in J. M. Barrie's play *Peter Pan* (1902); Anna Pavlovna is the central character in Leo Tolstoi's *Anna Karenina* (1875–77).

p. 368-369: "St. Louis Blues": A 1914 song by W.C. Handy. "Chloe": A 1927 song by Charles Neils Daniels and Gus Kahn. "Old Man River": Actually "Ol' Man River," composed by Oscar Hammerstein and Jerome Hart for the musical *Showboat* (1927). "St. James Infirmary": A 1930 song by Joe Primrose.

p. 375: *Pollyana* (1913), a popular novel by Eleanor H. Porter in which the central character resolutely puts the best light on all events, however unfortunate.

p. 377: *cacoethes scribendi* ("the itch for writing"), a celebrated phrase in *Satire* 7.52 by Juvenal (D. Junius Juvenalis, c. 60-c. 140).

p. 380: The reference, as will become clear later on, is to the fashionable magazine *Vanity Fair,* not the novel by William Makepeace Thackeray.

p. 382: A reference to several compositions for piano: "The Golliwog Cake Walk" is a solo by Debussy in *The Children's Corner* (1908); the "Hungarian Rhapsody" (actually 19 such pieces) is by Franz Lizst (1811–1886); "Le Cathédrale Engloutie" is by Debussy; it is No. 10 in Book 1 of the *Preludes* (1909–10).

p. 382: A reference to a variety of German dancers, Mary Wigman (1886–1973) and her pupils, Harold Kreutzberg (1902–1968) and Yvonne Georgi (1903–1975).

p. 383: "Inverts" was at that time the scientific term for homo-sexuals.

p. 385: "…and the rough male kiss / Of blankets…" "The Great Lover" by Rupert Brooke (1887–1915), ll. 36–37. In *The Collected Poems* of Rupert Brooke (New York: John Lane, 1915), p. 121.

p. 386: A reference to three popular magazines, the *Saturday Evening Post, Vanity Fair,* and *Harper's Magazine.*

p. 387: *Letters to Women*: A 1929 novel by Joseph Auslander (1897–1965).

p. 387: *Angels and Earthly Creatures*: A 1929 volume of poetry by Elinor Wylie (1885–1929).

p. 387: *Robes of Thespis*: A 1928 book on costume design by Rupert Mason.

p. 387: Leon Bakst (1866–1924), a Russian artist.

p. 387: *The Memoirs of Fanny Hill*: See note on p. 354.

p. 387: Beardsley's illustrations for Aristophanes' play *Lysistrata* were first published in an edition of the play in 1896.

p. 394: Paul Cézanne (1839–1906), French painter; Virginia Woolf (1882–1941), English novelist; Sergei Prokofiev (1891–1953), Russian composer. For Kreutzberg see note on p. 411; for *Vanity Fair* see notes on pp. 409 and 415.

p. 398: Wandrei is attempting to render the difference between *phileo* ("to regard with affection") and *erao* ("to love"), the latter of which usually carries a sexual connotation.

p. 405: *Ave atque Vale*: "Hail and Farewell." If Wandrei had wished to be exact, he would have rendered *Requiescat in Pace* ("May he [or she] rest in peace") in the plural, *Requiescant in Pace.*

p. 420: Laocoon, in Graeco-Roman mythology, was a Trojan seer who sensed that the "Trojan horse" presented by the Greeks as a gift was a ruse; but Apollo, supporting the Greeks, sent two immense sea-serpents to kill Laocoon and his two sons. The classic treatment of this scene is Vergil's *Aeneud* 2.199–233. Wandrei's use of the term here is evidently meant to suggest the fulfillment of Drew's predictions of his impending break-up with Helione.

p. 423: A reference to the Latin poet C. Valerius Catullus (c. 84– c. 54 BCE), who became infatuated with a woman he named Lesbia. The quoted line ("A thousand...") alludes to lines 7–9 in poem 5: "Give me a thousand kisses, then a hundred, / then another thousand, then a second hundred, / then still another thousand, then a hundred."

p. 423: Dante Alighieri (1265–1321) in the latter portions of *The Divine Comedy* (*La Divine Commedia*) speaks of his love for Beatrice. The quoted line ("Abandon hope...") is, however, a reference to the emblem supposed to be displayed on the gate of Hell (*Lasciate ogni speranza, voi ch' entrate*). See *Paradiso* 3.9.

p. 423: A reference to characters cited in the *Sonnets* (1609) of William Shakespeare (1564–1616). The quoted lines are from 97.1–2 and 64.11–14.

p. 423: "The House of Life" is a sonnet sequence by Dante Gabriel Rossetti (1828–1882). Wandrei has quoted Sonnet XLIV ("A Superscription') in its entirety. "Bridge of sighs" should be "breath of sighs."

p. 427: "Mood Indigo": A 1930 song by Duke Ellington (1899– 1974).

p. 427: "Chant of the Jungle": a song composed by Nacio Herb Brown for the film *Untamed* (1929).

p. 429: Johnny Weissmuller (1904–1984) won five gold medals at the Olympic games of 1924 and 1928, and set many other swimming records, before becoming cinema's "Tarzan."

p. 432: "Old Man River": See note on p. 368-369.

p. 432: Ted Shawn (1891–1972) and St. Denis (1877–1968) were a team of American dancers and choreographers.

p. 432: "St. James Infirmary": See note on p. 368-369.

p. 441: *ipsation*: Evidently Wandrei's coinage for the act of masturbation; from the Latin *ipse* (oneself).

p. 445: "the well of Democritus" is a phrase coined by Joseph Glanvill (1636–1680) in reference to the works of God ("which have a depth in them greater than the well of Democritus"), cited by Poe on several occasions (see, e.g., the epigraph to "A Descent into the Maelström"). The reference is to a popular conception of the Greek philosopher Democritus (c. 460-c. 370 BCE). The Witch of Endor is a character in the Old Testament who raises the spirit of the dead Samuel for Saul (I Samuel 28:7–25).

p. 468: The first two lines of de la Mare's "The Listeners" (see note on p. 330).

Afterword
S.T. Joshi

It is commonly said that everyone has one novel in them —
the novel of his or her own life. Donald Wandrei had two novels
in him, but the autobiographical novel proved to be the second,
and much the better, of the two. Within a span of less than
three and a half years, from the fall of 1929 to the beginning of
1933, Wandrei — then just beginning his career as a writer of
horror and science fiction tales — produced two novels, *Dead
Titans, Waken!* and *Invisible Sun*, the former of which
appeared in quite different form as *The Web of Easter Island*
(1948) and the latter of which remained unpublished until this
edition.

On September 9, 1929, Wandrei told his correspondent of
nearly three years, H. P. Lovecraft: "I...am now working on a
story of age-old horror." [1] He immediately asked Lovecraft for
the Latin versions of the phrases "Devil's Highway" and "God's
Highway," suggesting that he had already drafted the opening
chapter. The next surviving letter to Lovecraft does not occur
until June 26, 1930, at which time Wandrei gave more details
about his novel, which he now named *Dead Titans Waken: A
Mystery of Time and Spirit*:

> As the title probably suggests, it is a romance of terror
> and horror, commencing near the locale of Stonehenge
> and concluding on Easter Island. This is the novel which
> I began in New York last summer, and which I mentioned

to you at the time. The novel has great possibilities, if I can successfully achieve a rather stupendous feat in handling so long a work. I have many incentives to keep me at it — the sheer pleasure of creating, my father's failing health, necessity of improving my financial condition, and the interest of some three publishers who express their willingness to consider the novel when completed. With time, energy, and a little luck, I may be able to complete it by the early part of August. [2]

In October Wandrei announced that the novel was "completely halted" by his father's several operations and by his graduate work at the University of Minnesota, but that it was nevertheless "more than three-quarters done." [3] In this same letter, Wandrei noted that a chapter from it, "slightly changed," would be appearing in *Weird Tales* as "Something from Above." If so, then the novel underwent significant revision in the fourteen months before Wandrei deemed it complete, for nothing remotely like "Something from Above" appears in the finished version of *Dead Titans, Waken!* Indeed, it is difficult even to conceive how the plot of "Something from Above" — involving two groups of extraterrestrial entities, one from Saturn and one from even farther gulfs of space, battling for control over an anti-gravitational element called Seggglyn — could in any way have been a part of *Dead Titans, Waken!* as we now know it.

It is not clear exactly when in the interval between October 1930 and the very end of 1931 Wandrei completed the novel: he merely told Lovecraft on January 6, 1932, that the novel "was done a week ago." In any case, although he acknowledged "at least two major weak spots," he was nevertheless so anxious to get it off his hands that he had already sent one copy to publishers and one of the two carbons to Lovecraft, with instructions that he pass it on to August Derleth and Clark Ashton Smith. Wandrei never named the "three publishers" who had expressed interest in it some years before, but it appears to have been sent only to one publisher — Harper &

Brothers — where it was rejected. Wandrei regrettably ignored Clark Ashton Smith's sensible suggestion of submitting it to *Weird Tales* as a serial.[4]

Dead Titans, Waken! is clearly a first novel — perhaps as much of a "practice" novel as Lovecraft deemed his own first attempt at lengthy narrative, *The Dream-Quest of Unknown Kadath*. While Wandrei manages well enough to sustain interest from beginning to end, and more significantly to conceive of a plot sufficiently complex to require a novel for its exposition, the writing on the whole is somewhat clumsy and — in spite of the length of time during which it was being worked on — occasionally seems a little hasty. Nevertheless, it is scarcely a work of which any writer need be ashamed.

Perhaps the novel's greatest interest lies in its foreshadowing of Wandrei's later work. Clearly, it anticipates his later shift toward mingling horror and science fiction. It is noteworthy that the final chapters contain the core of what would become Wandrei's most celebrated science fiction tale, "Colossus" *(Astounding*, January 1934) — the notion that our own universe is merely an atom in some incalculably larger super-universe, and that it is possible to break through to this vaster realm.

The Web of Easter Island was dedicated to Lovecraft; the first version bears no dedication, but the influence of Lovecraft nevertheless hangs heavy over it. The incomprehensible gibberish uttered by various human characters — an echo of the speech of the titans — is clearly modelled upon the R'lyehian language introduced by Lovecraft in "The Call of Cthulhu" (1926). Indeed, if one removes the first three letters of the word "septhulchu," one sees a very elementary anagram of "Cthulhu." Wandrei's use of the documentary style — filled with letters, diaries, newspaper clippings, and the like — also reflects Lovecraft's similar usage in "The Call of Cthulhu" and "The Whisperer in Darkness." One wonders, in fact, whether Wandrei's omission of the story "Something from Above" (however it would have fit into the novel) reflects his sense that *Dead Titans, Waken!* already owed too much to Lovecraft; for that story, with its account of a strange meteorite falling on a plot of farmland, is clearly derivative of "The Colour out of Space."

Lovecraft's own reaction, when he first read *Dead Titans, Waken!*, was what might be termed reservedly enthusiastic. Although noting numerous points that might require revision, especially in terms of psychological motivation and adequate emotional preparation for the horrors depicted, Lovecraft nevertheless felt that "The novel as a whole is a great piece of work." Clark Ashton Smith's reaction was still more enthusiastic:

> Your novel came o.k., and I have read it with immense pleasure. The plot seems all right to me, and I do not see that it calls for any structural modifications. My only suggestion is, that the wording might be touched up in places, in the earlier chapters. The later chapters are superior in style, it seems to me — especially where they are written in the first person. The tale is full of imaginative ideas; and some of the descriptions of strange phenomena — the changeability of the pitted image, etc. — might stand considerable amplification.[5]

Writing to Derleth, Smith was somewhat more blunt: "I got a very favorable impression of the general plot, but found the style uneven, especially in the earlier chapters. The later ones, especially those written in the first person, seemed much more adequate."[6] Lovecraft, too, opened up somewhat more to Derleth:

> ...the chief criticism I give it is that the first & second halves are atmospherically incompatible. He began by surrendering to the popular "action" tradition, but grew cosmic & poetic after he got started into earth's bowels. In the first part bizarre horrors are introduced without adequate emotional preparation, but later on the cosmic vision gets really tremendous at times — so that I extracted a whale of a wallop from the performance as a whole, & wish I could have written it myself![7]

Lovecraft was right in remarking to Derleth that the novel would face difficulties in securing a book publisher; indeed, after his initial submission, Wandrei appears to have lost interest in *Dead Titans, Waken!* and shelved it. By this time he had already begun work on his second novel-length work, *Invisible Sun.*

The revision of *Dead Titans* did not occur until the mid-1940s. In February 1946 Wandrei — evidently responding to Derleth's wish for horror or science fiction novels for Arkham House — was suggesting some possible new titles for the novel, since he had come to dislike his original. He rattles off a whole list of them: *They Will Come Again; They Who Enter; The Web of Easter Island; They Shall Wake Again; In Their Power; To Haunt the Future.*[8] Incredibly, Wandrei's preference was for *To Haunt the Future*, but no doubt Derleth prevailed upon him to choose the one we know. It is not clear when actual revision commenced, but by February 1947 Wandrei stated that the *Web* "bubbles along," [9] noting that he had already written 15,000 new words of text. By the end of April, Wandrei was on the "last few pages" of the revision and claimed to have written 35,000 words of new text. He asserted that "The novel is a good 300 percent better than it was," but there is reason to question his judgment.

The major revisions in the novel — aside from mere rewriting of existing prose, which indeed is extensive throughout — are as follows:

Chapter III of *Titans* — a nearly unaltered interpolation of the story "A Fragment of a Dream" (1926) — has been placed as Chapter XII of *Web*. The context, therefore, is radically changed: whereas in *Titans* the "dream" occurs as a result of the train accident in which Carter Graham is involved, in *Web* it is the product of Graham's concluding battle with the titans on Easter Island.

Much of Chapter V of *Titans* has been dropped, and an entirely new chapter (now Chapter IV) inserted into *Web*. This is the chapter in which Dan Farrell pilfers the green statuette and takes it with him in an attempt to cross the Atlantic to

America (in a seaplane in *Titans*, on a ship in *Web*). In the newer version Wandrei has added a painfully coy and purportedly risqué love element on board the ship. Many readers have noted that this chapter simply does not fit in the narrative, and indeed much of it is occupied with a romance that has no bearing whatever on the plot. And yet, Wandrei actually thought this chapter much superior to its predecessor: "I particularly like the new chapter, which is rather sexy but completely motivated whereas the chapter I discarded rambled all over and had no real reason to be in the book."

The most significant change, perhaps, is that Graham's diary — which in *Titans* occupies the entirety of Chapters X, XI, and XIII — is now reduced to a single chapter (X) in *Web*. Even this chapter is narrated with far greater sobriety and more tempered emotionalism than its original (especially with the entire omission of the interpolated piece, "Myrna" — an adaptation of the then unpublished prose poem "The Delirium of the Dead" — in which Graham relates his youthful love of a woman who dies and whose grave he subsequently violates out of grief). To my mind the newer version fails to bring Graham to life, even though it may harmonize somewhat better with his persona as a sober scientist. Chapters XI, XII, and XIII of *Web* are not presented in diary form — again, in my view, to their detriment. Evidently Wandrei did not agree, in 1947, with Clark Ashton Smith's dictum that these first-person passages represented some of the most vivid writing in the novel.

In regard to stylistic changes, one can again make good arguments that the earlier version on the whole stands up better than the later one. By 1947 Wandrei had for some years ceased to be a practicing writer, and perhaps his rustiness shows. It is true that some stylistic infelicities — especially in the later portions — have been eliminated; but on the other hand, some quite vivid passages have been unwisely omitted. Consider the following passage from *Titans*, where Graham recounts his emotions when reading of the history of the world over the 500,000 years from his own time to the time in which he finds himself after battling the titans:

...I read most of all as a traveller marooned in time, desolate in the midst of plenty, and with gravely wise companions wherever I turned, lonely in the heart of the highest
civilization humanity had ever achieved, and aching with
the burden of old griefs and irrecoverable years, of vanished cycles and an oblivion that had plundered me of my
rightful life in the days when the world was young.

Whatever one's judgment about the relative merits of *Dead
Titans, Waken!* and *The Web of Easter Island*, we can all find an
interest in a novel begun by a twenty-one-year-old in the vigor
of budding authorship who, when he completed it some
months prior to his twenty-fourth birthday, was already a sea-
soned veteran of the pulps.

Invisible Sun is a different proposition altogether. The existence of this novel had been known for decades, but there
was doubt as to whether it was completed or, if it was,
whether the manuscript survived. As it happens, both the
original handwritten draft and the final typescript are intact,
and we are now in a position to assess both its strengths and
its defects.

Wandrei began the novel very shortly after he returned
to New York from Minneapolis in August 1932; in contrast to
his long and apparently sporadic work on *Titans*, Wandrei
finished *Invisible Sun* in a matter of months, from
September 1932 to January 1933. This time Wandrei sent
the completed work to Derleth first – presumably because,
as a mainstream writer, he might be more astute in judging
this mainstream novel than pure fantaisistes like Lovecraft
or Smith – and Derleth's adverse judgment of it was at least
partly responsible for Wandrei's permanent shelving of the
work. It was, however, like *Titans*, submitted to a publisher
(unspecified) immediately upon completion, but was evidently rejected.[10]

Wandrei supplied the motivation of the work a few months
before he began writing it:

For a long time I have been germinating a second novel,
semi-autobiographical, partly based on experiences I
have heard of, as an excursion into what might be called
the poetry of realism. I think I shall begin work on it
shortly. God knows it will be an arduous and exhausting
task, since I want it to be without question the best and
most mature work that I have yet done. I feel that the time
is about ready — far enough away from experience so that
the work will not be one-sided, and yet not so far that the
fire and the intensity will have burned low.[11]

Wandrei expressed the core of the novel in Chapter LI, when
Sven discusses the plot of the novel he himself is working on:

I start with a situation, the most important in the protagonist's life, that is, my purpose begins there though the
situation actually concludes the novel. No, I won't tell you
what the situation is. We'll assume that the hero is Mr. X.
The great crisis of his life is Y, a decision, we'll also
assume, to drop out of sight and go to some remote place
to live in oblivion the rest of his days. When X is making
this decision, all the influences of his past experiences
would be brought to bear. In the white heat of extremity,
the extraneous parts of his life would be shorn away, but
everything that contributed to his decision or that would
be affected by it would stand out clearly in his mind, or at
least they would form an undercurrent in his thoughts.
These past experiences would come as flashes of memory, pictures of old occurrences, but they would probably
be in a sort of confused flux....The novel would begin
with the first and earliest of these experiences bearing on
the crisis, but each scene or memory picture, for the sake
of unity and art again as well as life, would be presented
immediately, as it happened when it was in the process of
happening, and with no hint of the catastrophe which I, as
the artist, know already. An apparent irrelevance might
be presumed by the reader during the early pictures and

episodes, in that they might seem disconnected, but as he read on, he would begin to see the design above the threads.

This, in essence, is *Invisible Sun*.

Taking these two passages together, we can assume that the basic thrust of the novel is the attempt to explain how Drew Gordon came to fall in love with Helione Forrest and, when she jilted him, killed her. Within this simple scenario Wandrei adds a mass of detail about Drew's upbringing, so that the reader can understand what led him to his final act.

It would be an engaging exercise to trace all the autobiographical elements in *Invisible Sun*. We shall touch upon only the highlights here; many are perhaps lost in oblivion, given the relative absence of documentary evidence regarding Wandrei's early life. First and foremost, does Helione have a real counterpart? She appears to be based loosely upon Barbara Fawcett Craigie, whom Wandrei mentioned in 1927 as "one of the two friends I have made at the university." Wandrei does not elaborate on his relations with Craigie in any correspondence I have seen, but Richard L. Tierney states that at some point in his life he "came within an ace of marrying" [12] her, although this probably occurred years after the writing of *Invisible Sun*, perhaps around 1947. However, extensive correspondence from Craigie to Wandrei survives, and it becomes clear from this that the two of them were becoming very close; but then Craigie wrote Wandrei a poignant letter (postmarked September 25, 1929) in which the subtext is that Wandrei should seek someone else upon whom to bestow his "friendship," since the two of them share few interests in common. One is led to believe that Wandrei was already infatuated with Craigie, and that she was attempting to restrain him or keep her distance from him, because she felt at this time that a serious relationship between the two of them would lead to disappointment. However, Craigie and Wandrei continued meeting until at least 1931; a definitive break may have come about the next year. Several of Craigie's known characteristics correspond with those of Helione Forrest: she was habitually late, she tended to gossip, and she was obliged to take care of numerous siblings, often yearning for a place of her own.

The other friend mentioned by Wandrei is Hjalmar Björnson, an Icelander who "writes…in a rugged, saga-like fashion" and who is clearly the model for Sven. Björnson published a few pieces in the *Minnesota Quarterly* during Wandrei's involvement with that magazine (run by students of the University of Minnesota), but beyond this we do not know much about him. The character of Pudge is very likely based upon Ed Megroth. He and Wandrei were initially friendly around 1931, but they later became heated adversaries; Megroth actually married Barbara Craigie sometime before 1944, but the marriage did not go well and they separated in 1946. It was around this time that Barbara re-established contact with Wandrei, leading to their contemplated marriage. A photograph of Megroth, taken on Memorial Day 1931, depicts Megroth as decidedly pudgy. Wandrei and Barbara are also in the picture.[13]

Many other details in the novel — some significant, some trivial — echo Wandrei's own life. He himself had entered the University of Minnesota at the age of sixteen. He had had horrific problems with his teeth. His mother cooked "excellent meals" for him. He had witnessed a fall of red snow in January 1926 — an incident that he cited in a number of his tales. Wandrei had been profoundly influenced by Arthur Machen's *The Hill of Dreams*, of which he owned the rare "blue paper" edition of 1922; and it could well be said that that novel's sensitive portrayal of the struggling writer inspired *Invisible Sun*'s minute depictions of Drew's moods and sentiments.

Drew's discovery of Clark Ashton Smith's *Ebony and Crystal* from an ad in a pulp magazine (clearly modelled on *Weird Tales*) is a faithful echo of Wandrei's own discovery of Smith's work in 1924. In a letter to Lovecraft he noted:

In three months — the summer I read "Ebony and
Crystal" and "The Hill of Dreams" — my ideas underwent
a complete revolution, and I walked to the opposite side of
the fence, changing from a half-materialistic scientist to a
romanticist and idealist and aesthete.[14]

At the very time he wrote the above passage in April 1927,
Wandrei had already conceived of some unspecified novel and
stated: "I am going to devote a chapter of my novel to Smith..."

In responding to one of Derleth's criticisms of *Invisible Sun*,
Wandrei asserted that the episodes in Chapters VI and VII "are
exact and faithful reproductions of the most frightful experience I ever had." The allusion is to the callous reaction of two
women following the death of a little girl in a fire, leading to
Drew's violent misanthropy and misogyny. Wandrei went on to
remark:

I have never had any faith in people because, as a result
of that experience, all possibilities of respect for human
beings were destroyed in me before they ever had a
chance to develope [*sic*]. You yourself can realize what a
profound shock such a series of events would have had
for any sensitive mind, young or old.[15]

Richard L. Tierney reports Wandrei telling him "that at age
seven he had been devastated when a fire originating in a
chocolate shop had burned down the St. Paul Public Library."
Whether the incident related in Chapters XIII – XV — when
Drew as a teenager develops a crush on a librarian but is shattered when she marries another man — is real is not clear, but
one suspects that it might be. Wandrei reported working for a
year and a half (presumably during high school) at the St. Paul
Public Library and the Hill Reference Library.[16]

But the interest of *Invisible Sun* lies not in how many correspondences with Wandrei's own life there may be, but in its
lapidary prose, its vividness of incident, its emotive power, and
its cumulative effectiveness. Some passages may perhaps be

awkwardly written, some incidents clumsy and unintentionally comical, but as a whole *Invisible Sun* is a moving human document that fully sustains Wandrei's attempt to create a "poetry of realism." Certainly the most arresting passages — aside from the bold depictions of sexual activity — are the several instances where Wandrei uses the still new device of stream-of-consciousness to convey an interior monologue. Two passages in particular — Helione's lengthy reflections in Chapter LII, leading to a startling but subtly expressed masturbation fantasy, and Drew's concluding swirl of thoughts, as the varied incidents of his entire life pass through his mind in the course of his murder of Helione — rank, to my mind, among the finest passages in Wandrei's entire oeuvre.

It does not appear, however, as if the early responses to the novel were very enthusiastic. Derleth in particular expressed severe criticism of the novel, much of it evidently focusing on the amount and nature of the sexual episodes. Incredibly, the ordinarily prudish Lovecraft defended these episodes:

Regarding the repulsiveness of the latter scenes — to which, amusingly enough, the otherwise none too squeamish Comte d'Erlette is inclined to object — I do not think that they form any breach of artistry. It is the business of the artist to relate whatever is significant in reality; & if this rottenness truly typifies an important stratum of contemporary youth, it is certainly of grave significance as a social tendency. Nothing is gained by whitewashing or sentimentalising. What is essentially beastly & inartistic in life must be bestially and harshly shewn. Blame life, not the artist. The loathsome lives of the swine portrayed in this novel, if they are indeed a widespread & characteristic phenomenon, are logical results of the so-called "new morality" which proceeds from the abandonment of harmonic patterns & aesthetic values in the art of living. Our younger generation now glorify fornication, adultery, & sodomy. Next will come a worship of incest — with brothers & sisters, parents & children, glorying in a warmer tie now despised by "old-fashioned prejudice" — the frenzied maenad & the goat of the Sabbat. A beautiful world, with beautiful trends, is that world of anti-Puritanism which our young friend [Frank] Belknap [Long] exalts so passionately! You have shewn it as it deserves to be shewn! [17]

Wandrei's purpose in his depictions of sex may not exactly have been what Lovecraft states here, but no doubt he was gratified that at least one reader did not find them overdone or cheaply titillating.

Nevertheless, even though Wandrei disagreed with the bases of many of Derleth's criticisms, his negative reaction — along with that of a New York couple, the Overbys — persuaded Wandrei to abandon any plans to revise and market his novel. "Three critics of the four I chose have now seen the thing and unanimously disagree, but unanimously ripped the thing to pieces. I have already junked it." [18] Certainly, Wandrei would have had difficulty securing its publication in 1933, if only because of the sexual episodes; but *Invisible Sun* does not deserve its eighty-year oblivion.

A final note on Wandrei's use of the pseudonym, Carrol Amworth. He is a little vague on the subject, but explains some aspects of the matter to Derleth: "I have decided to publish under a pseudonym, and henceforth continue publishing part of my work under the nom-de-plume, part under my own name, for a variety of reasons too long to go into." [19] Possibly Wandrei was planning to use the pseudonym for "mainstream" work and his real name for his horror and science fiction writing, since he had already become widely known for that work. Wandrei's two novels are both flawed, but both powerful in their own ways. *Invisible Sun* reveals a marked improvement in technique and emotional maturity from *Dead Titans, Waken!*, and it is unfortunate that adverse reaction dissuaded Wandrei from continuing work on it and from completing any new work in the novel form. By the mid-1930s he had found his niche as a prolific writer of science fantasies for the pulps, and — although in the later 1930s he did write several plays, including one, *Love to*

Murder, which he described as a "mystery drama" [20] with elements of satire — he did not make any concerted effort to return to mainstream writing. By the early 1940s he had virtually given up writing altogether, producing in the remaining four and a half decades of his life only a handful of short stories and some poems. But the two novels in this volume both display, in their very different ways, a literary promise that for many and complex reasons was never fully realized. Both should be read as much for their insights into Donald Wandrei's life and mind as for their own intrinsic virtues.

1. Donald Wandrei to H. P. Lovecraft, September 9, 1929; *Mysteries of Time and Spirit: The Letters of H. P. Lovecraft and Donald Wandrei* (San Francisco: Night Shade, 2001), pp. 240–41.

2. Donald Wandrei to H. P. Lovecraft, June 26, 1930; *Mysteries of Time and Spirit,* p. 252.

3. Donald Wandrei to H. P. Lovecraft, October 27, 1930; *Mysteries of Time and Spirit.* p. 260.

4. See Clark Ashton Smith to Donald Wandrei, 6 April, 1932; ms., Minnesota Historical Society.

5. Clark Ashton Smith to Donald Wandrei, March 1, 1932; ms., Minnesota Historical Society.

6. Clark Ashton Smith to August Derleth, February 24, 1932; ms., State Historical Society of Wisconsin (hereafter abbreviated SHSW).

7. Clark Ashton Smith to August Derleth, January 21, 1932: *Essential Solitude the Letters of H. P. Lovecraft and August Derleth* (New York: Hippocampus Press, 2008), 2.443.

8. Donald Wandrei to August Derleth, February 22, 1946; ms., SHSW.

9. Donald Wandrei to August Derleth, February 11, 1947; ms., SHSW.

10. "...the original is now in the hands of the first prospective publisher..." Donald Wandrei to August Derleth, February 1, 1933: ms., SHSW.

11. Donald Wandrei to August Derleth, July 11, 1932; ms., SHSW.

12. Richard L. Tierney, "Introduction," *Colossus: The Collected Science Fiction of Donald Wandrei* (Minneapolis: Fedogan & Bremer, 1989) p. xix.

13. The photo is in the archives of the Minnesota Historical Society. I am grateful to Dwayne H. Olson for supplying me with a photocopy of it. (See page 458 of the revised and expanded second edition of COLOSSUS, Fedogan and Bremer, 1999.)

14. Donald Wandrei to H. P. Lovecraft, April 17, 1927; *Mysteries of Time and Spirit*, p. 81.

15. Donald Wandrei to August Derleth, February 1, 1933; ms., SHSW.

16. Donald Wandrei to H. P. Lovecraft, February 7, 1927; *Mysteries of Time and Spirit*, p. 29.

17. H. P. Lovecraft to Donald Wandrei, February 27, 1933; *Mysteries of Time and Space*, p. 321.

18. Donald Wandrei to August Derleth, February 18, 1933; ms., SHSW.

19. Donald Wandrei to August Derleth, January 24, 1933; ms., SHSW.

20. Donald Wandrei to H. P. Lovecraft, March 17, 1937; *Mysteries of Time and Spirit*, p. 390.

Dead Titans, Waken!
2017

This work was originally prepared for
Fedogan and Bremer in 2003,
but did not reach print at that time.
Instead, an initial Edition was published in a
Limited hardcover printing by
Centipede Press in 2011.

This First Trade Edition is, for practical purposes,
a restoration of our original conception of the work.
Published by Fedogan & Bremer Publishing LLC,
3918 Chicago Street, Nampa, Idaho 83686-8909